PALS

PALS

Three Guys from
Another Time and Place

Featuring
Nick Drizos, National Resource

Carl E. Ring Jr.

VANTAGE PRESS
New York

Cover design by Polly McQuillen

FIRST EDITION

Published by Vantage Press, Inc.
419 Park Ave. South, New York, NY 10016

Manufactured in the United States of America
ISBN: 978-0-533-16264-2

Library of Congress Catalog Card No.: 2009906068

0 9 8 7 6 5 4 3 2 1

To the many helping hands along the way

"After all the mortal yawpings, the only thing of timeless value is friendship, borne as it is on the five enduring pillars: kindness, generosity of spirit, respect, admiration, and love."

—A pal

PALS

1
Bang

October 10th—A very short day, as it occurred . . .

There may have been nicer days, but not in our part of Florida. April and November are usually our best months, but this October had been especially pleasant. By any measure, it was a gorgeous day—the bluest of skies, big puff clouds and subtle, gentle zephyrs. I've always liked that word, *zephyr*. Sounds like it feels, one of those words. I had been overcome and burdened with grief and sadness, but a lovely day is a great distraction. It was October tenth—a particularly easy day to remember, as in 10/10. Plus it was the birthday of a longtime pal. I was about to give him a buzz when I got really distracted.

2
Knowing Women and Manly Men

October 21st—Awakening and first recalls

I'm still distracted as I recall the day's events from a hospital bed. I'm told today is October twenty-first. I haven't had any visitors to console me yet. I imagine that will change in the next few days or so. At least the visitor part; consolation may be a different matter.

"Good morning, Mr. Drizos," comes the cheery but authoritative voice of Nurse One, as she is known. I'm being attended by three very lovely nurses, and more than attractive, which they are, they also have nice ways about them. I imagine them to be anywhere from their late thirties to early forties, which are fine ages for women. Maybe the best, because women cannot be lovely until they pass thirty, preferably forty, at a minimum—at a very minimum. They can be hot, striking, glamorous, voluptuous, and more, but loveliness needs some veneration. It's around that age that they get comfortable and at peace with themselves, getting free of the bitchiness of earlier years, confident, fun to be around, able to balance the lady thing with some guy stuff. Also becoming aware that they have a great deal to offer, in addition to the obvious. In a word or two, they have become sensuous, or is it sensual? Those kinds of things. I also find an extra pound or two along with some character wrinkles to be just about irresistible, but that's just one guy talking. Plus they're smart and sophisticated—and that's an ultimate turn-on. For some of us, anyway.

I'm told that all manners of relationships tend to develop with nurses and patients and that a few actually flourish, though most remain unrequited. I'm thinking it's kind of an extremely civilized dominatrix thing. These women have this obvious, uncontestable air of command about them, although even the dullest among us can dope out that they are here to get us back into the game. They are authoritative and obviously smart, and they've probably heard every story there is, which just adds to their stature and mystique. They know we are looking to them for responses, any responses. Any responses indeed. Like it's Stockholm syndrome or something, except they're hot and I'm on my back. And the whites they wear add to the mystique—mundane and starched but oozing sex in a way you wouldn't understand unless you've been there. These are special, very special, women.

Some women seem born just to be poured into these outfits, and I swear they are sexier by lengths more than most babes in bikinis. So you let your libido do as it wishes. Maybe it's all part of the process, that forbidden fruit thing, and the notions we conjure will get us there faster—wherever "there" is. We men are a funny lot, aren't we? Even though I've almost had my balls blown off, my autopilot steers me toward pretty women as though I were Tyrone Power and they were my leading ladies; they have a way of making us feel like the matinee idols we know we're not. And important, too. God bless them.

So here I am, in the softly lit whiteness of a hospital—a whiteness as aseptic and sterile by contrast as the hot whiteness of my attending nurses—where I am getting my first twitchings of what is commonly called recall. On the tenth I was headed to my garage and, in my best twenty-first-century, time-saving rush, I hit the auto-start button on my key chain. I may or may not have heard the explosion, but I'm pretty sure I recall the flash. I don't know whether it was the garage door or the old swing set that saved me. The former apparently shielded me from the shrapnel of jagged car parts, while the latter stopped my flight some six or eight feet from the garage. This was no small deal, as I am what most folks would graciously regard as portly. I gather it was a big-time, killer car bomb. As in someone was trying most earnestly to cash me out.

Me, Joe Average, a nobody in the grand scheme of stuff. What kind of a twisted son of a bitch would want to ice me, much less blow me up? When I do my my introspective self-diagnosis thing, I arrive at the same blind alleys. I've got no enemies of any consequence. I don't owe anybody any dough. I don't do drugs, and I'm not dillydallying with any jealousy-provoking women.

I'm feeling like the Edmond O'Brien character in *DOA* who gets poisoned for reasons unknown to him, or maybe one of the characters in a Ludlum novel who's walking around with some showstopping piece of information he's not supposed to have. Bombs always seemed to me to be a statement of exceptional anger, so I can only guess that someone was really interested in settling something with a most violent finality.

Maybe it was a mistake. Yeah, that's most likely. That blast was meant for somebody else. I wish. My name is shown clearly and boldly on my mailbox. There is no ambiguity as to who lives here. None. So, let's face it, I was the designated receiver. Someone wants me dead. I suppose all will be clear in due time. At least that's what the hospitable folks hereabouts continue to tell me.

I'm also told I have been in short periods of wakefulness for the last couple days after having been in a state of very deep sleep. I'm now accurately described as a semimobile and bruised mass, so I can only marvel at the body's recuperative powers. Even more so at the brain's efforts to shut down certain sectors during the aftermath of trauma. Maybe that's why I return to my fondness of soft, lovely women. I'm being directed, or directing myself, to more pleasant notions while the matter of reassembling me is being attended to in a deeper, more serious background. By the way, my name is Nick Drizos. I'm having some serious recollection problems, but I know I'm Nick Drizos.

I don't know jack about modern medical practice, but I do have a picture of sorts of the past few days. In one sense there has been a great swirling of activity as though a construction guy has been working and consulting with an architect—clipboards and charts in hand—clearing debris, untwisting things, and reconnecting circuits with the mission of restarting me. My perceptions are like muck battling clarity. At the same time, there is a peaceful overlay. It is much like being anesthetized during serious surgery, except that for brief instances I have been aware of both the surgery and of the inducements toward consciousness. I wouldn't refer to these goings-on as an out-of-body experience; more like an in-body experience where you're invited to watch. A competing notion is that I'm being manipulated by a bunch of folks in white smocks; but what the hell, I'm getting the big freebies—three hots and a cot, as we used to say in the Corps. And they treat me nicely with most agreeable potions. Sleep may be among the more underrated events in the modern world, so you won't hear me complaining. For now, anyway.

It seems very much as though different parties with different tasks have been proceeding along. The one group would be reconstructing and, from time to time, would request the other to reduce the sleep effect so as to measure progress. This, or something like it, may be what is occurring when people recovering from surgery are said to be going in and out. At some point it seems a decision is made that the subject is ready for something resembling consciousness. In any event, that's how it all feels to me. From total non-recall, to pleasant confusion, to a progressing and increasingly assertive consciousness.

It's not especially surprising that I fashion such amateurish visions of my highly complex inner workings, because, as it happens, I'm a bond trader—one of the very best—even though I'm not what you would call a marquee player, as in you've probably never heard of me. But I am very good at what I do.

Over the years I've had my own shop, but I've also bunked in at a number of household name firms from time to time. I call myself a bond trader, but I really manage people's wealth. The one constant is that my clients stay with me and move their accounts with me as I travel along. Most of them do, and the reason they stay with me is because I am very good.

'Good' is a term of art in our business. The reason I am good is that my clients come first. There is no doubt that it's *their* money I manage, that it was probably hard to accumulate, that they aren't getting any younger, and that the first mission is not to lose it. I was fortunate to have started in this business quite a while back when the best guys roamed the financial landscape—guys whose word was the real bankable deal, whose handshake was better than a three-inch contract from some big uptown white-shoe law firm. Manly guys, the old two-fisted sorts. Not like many of the impostors around today. The old-timers were the best. They're dying off now, but they were the best. They taught me the game from a whole bunch of first-hand experiences and great stories.

I remember when I was the wet-behind-the-ears kid, and the uncommonly generous men who helped me get started in this business. I can see them all very clearly right now. Probably because I want to see them. More likely, I need to see them. I especially remember the day the five of them interviewed me and then hired me at day's end. I had had two previous interviews, so I expected they would invite me to join the firm as a summer hire. We didn't have internships back then.

Scotty was born in Glasgow and emigrated with his folks to our little town of Wills Grove, Pennsylvania, in the 1930s. He served in the war in the Eighth Army Air Corps, which distinguished itself by its incredible heroism and its equally incredi-

I started my visit with them in the care of Les Horvath and Scotty Kinloch. Les was the boss, the clear boss, because the other guys wanted him to be. And it was a fine choice. He had stature and was a real presence. Plus he had been fortunate enough to have had two years of college.

More than anything else, he set the tone. Since he was straight up, so was the firm. Like the other four, he had braved the Great Depression and served in World War II. He had been an airborne ranger in the European Theater, or ETO, as he called it. And like the other four, he would deflect questions about that part of his life and make it clear, without being nasty, that he preferred other subjects.

Les chose to spend our time together discussing what he would expect of me on the one hand and how I might want to apply myself to make the most of the engagement. Unlike a lot of senior folks, he was most generous with his time. It was also clear that he wanted smart people around him—people who would add to, rather than diminish, the collective intellect. He was just totally secure.

Scotty was born in Glasgow and emigrated with his folks to our little town of Wills Grove, Pennsylvania, in the 1930s. He served in the war in the Eighth Army Air Corps, which distinguished itself by its incredible heroism and its equally incredible—more accurately, horrendous—casualty rates. A most likeably extroverted guy and a man's man if ever there were one, Scotty was the firm's entire sales and marketing team and had developed a thriving presence in the fifty-mile radius he referred to as the firm's principal market.

He also made regularly scheduled sales visits to Pittsburgh and, to a lesser degree, Philadelphia when our little firm landed a municipal bond offering. Every once in a while he would make the rounds of the larger firms in New York, as even those big guys liked to keep relationships with the small fry out in the boonies. It was a fairly cooperative world in those days, and Scotty represented his partners and colleagues very well. Like Les, he was generous to a fault to guys like me.

After spending almost half the day with Les and Scotty, they moved me on to visit with the other three senior guys.

I was then dropped off with "Stems" Hadley. He was called "Stems" because he lost one hand completely and part of the other in Tarawa by jumping on a Jap grenade and shielding his squad from most likely being wiped out. He happened to be rolling up a blanket when he saw the grenade come spiraling in. That afforded his torso some protection, but his hands were lacerated—one beyond recognition and repair. Riddled with shrapnel, he was sent home a bona fide hero and awarded the Congressional Medal of Honor, but never displayed it or cared to talk about it. I used to say he made the Marlboro Man look like a weenie.

I spoke with him about his experiences as a marine in the Pacific one time and only one time. He said that's the way it would be. He allowed me to ask anything I wished, but only if I promised not to revisit the subject again ever. I promised. With Stems, as with the other fellows, a promise is a promise. There was nothing the least bit ambiguous.

He only had one piece of advice, which he repeated twice that day: "Always do the right thing, but don't expect any reward or any thanks. You do right because it's right. If you don't know right by now, then your folks and the fellows have really let you down."

Stems was also known to be not just generous, but *incredibly* generous. He had a brother, Brian, who was characterized as "slow" when in fact, he was mildly retarded. Brian was a good fellow, though, who tried hard to be productive, and everyone liked him. Stems had established a trust fund for his brother and had built it to a respectable level. I asked him why he had done that, more as a matter of understanding his motivations.

I wasn't surprised when he said, "It was just the right thing to do. Brian wasn't nearly as lucky as I."

I was dumbfounded initially by the "not as lucky" remark, but it made more sense as I got to know Stems. He went on to say that he had gotten to see *Death of a Salesman* with Lee J. Cobb, who introduced the world to Willy Loman and who, to many of us, stands as the archetypal Willy.

Stems just didn't understand Arthur Miller's message when the wildly successful brother stood by and watched Willy decline and ultimately take his life. I can only guess that was added impetus for him to provide for Brian, because "you're supposed to. It's the right thing to do."

Stems also had a loving wife and two beautiful young daughters. For all I know, they didn't want for much of anything and Stems never thought of himself as anything but a fortunate guy.

And I felt fortunate to be taken into the confidence of these manliest of men. I have never stopped wondering if I could measure up to Stems's example of quiet heroism. And he was just part of this amazing group.

Like Les and Scotty, he was expansive and forthcoming in nature and said he would be available anytime I thought I needed some help or guidance.

Stems then escorted me over to PO'd Kemmons for his "final look" at me. PO'd, pronounced "Pea Owed," stood for "pissed off," his natural state; he just said, "Hiya, kid, whadda ya hear, whadda ya say?" It was Jimmy Cagney's line right out of that great classic *Angels with Dirty Faces*. That was his standard greeting for me. He liked me. I know he liked me, because he told me so.

PO'd, like Stems, was heavily decorated in WW II. When he returned he noted that his neighbor Paddy Breslin had gone off to fight the enemies of our country so that he could return to his bicycle shop. Small problem. The mass production needed to win the war meant that small companies would become obsolete. And they did. There were no small companies anymore, at least no small bicycle companies. Paddy went to work in a big factory, and Kemmons railed at the craziness of it all.

The other guys were happy to be home and alive, so they named old Kemmons PO'd. He was a great guy and one you would want in your foxhole. He loved this country like few others, but he did come to hate the government, all government. He'd walk around with a book of Carl Sandburg's verses and, given the slightest encouragement would spout his favorite . . . "the man in the street is fed with lies in peace, gas in war." Nonetheless he was a terrific guy and part of the moral and spiritual wall that always backed me up. Totally honest.

PO'd was rarely at a loss for words, and he regaled me with a few pieces of advice mostly about when to tell folks to shove it. After having proffered his best advice on me he walked me over to Studs Armine for the last word.

Studs was what most folks today would call "a piece of work." He was the iconoclast of the group, though back then none of us knew what such a polysyllabic word might really mean. Studs had a philosophy which, I would come to learn, was: Give the world a goosing at least three times a week.

I'm not sure anyone really knew what Studs had in mind, but he got my attention the first time I met him.

I was just an interviewee at the little firm in Wills Grove, and the guys were introducing me around. I had met just about everyone when we stopped in front of a door with the painted label S.A. Armine. Scotty knocked and was greeted with, "Come on in. I'm a Democrat, I like everybody."

Scotty half pushed me in and says, "Are you there, Studs?"

A voice, presumably belonging to one Steve "Studs" A. Armine reported, "Roger, come on in."

And Scotty finished his half push.

I was about two feet into the office of Steve "Studs" A. Armine when a guy with his back to me says, "How ya doin', kid?" I was about to answer when old Studs whirls around and presents himself and the biggest johnson I've ever seen. I'm about to

9

have a nervous disorder of some sort when I realize that the king-size johnson is a dildo, replete with a blinking red light on its business end.

Studs then says, "Hey, kid, I work like a horse, I might as well look like one."

Then he laughed. Once I got over the initial shock, I did, too. Studs would turn out to be one of the most honest guys I ever encountered. I prospered greatly from my acquaintance with him.

There are guys who are menacing, and there are guys who are wiseasses but mean no harm. Studs was the latter. As my time at our little firm unfolded, Studs would emerge as the storyteller and the guy who'd remind me to be professional, honest, courteous, and gracious, but also never to take any shit if I was sure I was in the right.

There it was, an all-star lineup if ever there was one. Any time I looked back would only affirm and reaffirm what a wonderful bunch of guys I had been privileged to work with and to be with.

These guys—fellows as they preferred to be called—were something. Not only upstanding folks of the absolute highest caliber, but very engaged in everything from local goings on to the most important worldwide geopolitics. I don't mean to get maudlin or mawkish, but one just won't see their likes again.

In later years some would write belatedly about this very special generation, but only a few actually captured the truly heroic aspects of their deeds and sacrifices. I was totally privileged to be in their presence. Like I said, these guys-fellows were characters of the first order and great storytellers, but first they were just the realest of real men.

That's maybe one of the biggest things I miss these days—good stories told by hot-stuff, great storytellers. Whether it's around the dinner table, in a locker room or at a party, this is being alive at its most flavorsome. It may even be why we learned to walk upright. Stories are the best. Besides, in the last analysis, everything is a story. Name something that isn't a story. And a good storyteller belongs at the top of the pile.

Don't get me wrong, I'm not pitching willy-nilly for the good old days. There's plenty of stuff that's much better now, but the losses of storytelling and the old apprenticeship ways sadden me. These days it's mentor this and role model that. Most of it is from guys in a hurry to guys in a bigger hurry. Or girls, but I can't bring myself to use today's repugnant politically correct unisex lingo. Just can't say chairperson or peoplekind. Guys means people. Could be men; could be women.

We had big advantages in times past, if only because things happened and evolved more slowly. Sometimes it occurs to me that present-day life is like proceeding ever outward on a spinning disk. You still make the same number of total orbits before you're done, but you're spinning faster and faster. The hamster on the ever-speeding up treadmill comes to mind. So does the question: Why? And do I really need the cheese that badly? Is it good to be perpetually fatigued? Aren't quality of life and relationships the really important things?

So what does all this have to do with my present state, and why would anyone want to blow away a no-name bond trader?

In a word, I don't know. I'm curious, but I don't know. I think my retreat to more pleasant remembrances is a necessary part of trying to reconstruct things. It seems to make sense in the present circumstances, but I've always had this tendency when trying to regain some equilibrium in confusing times. Go back; try to find the most recent point where things made some sense. Then regroup and go from there.

I must be in an important phase of healing, because I am becoming increasingly peaceful and less anxious as I move into and through this phase called recovery. I also believe in God, though I don't subscribe readily to any organized religion these days. The reasons for my belief and faith are many. First, there's the vast scope and sheer wonderment of it all. Is there such a word as "wonderment"? There should be.

Even the smallest part of the go-round world of which I am aware is just beyond my comprehension. I've been told by some that the whole deal was just atomic chemistry at work; no more, no less. That's a fine argument, except who was or is the chemist? Plus, there are such things as human kindness and generosity of spirit. I've yet to see the chemistry set which produces those, or similar, items. I put a bit of sodium (Na) and a little chlorine (Cl) together, and all I get is salt. It never speaks or walks or growls or sings or dances or contributes to charity or starts wars or anything. It just lies there being salt. And, in my own insignificant case, I have been in the depths of sadness and at the limits of personal endurance several times. In each and every instance, some force from somewhere has urged me to move along. Even if it were my own doing, something enabled it. I wouldn't attempt to lay these thoughts on anyone else, so just put me in the quiet believer group. Some might say fatalist. And, P.S., I'm alive at the moment. Thank you, somebody.

In the meanwhile, bond trading is an okay way to do stuff with others. Unless you totally absent yourself and do the solo thing, which has crossed my mind a time or two, you've got to do stuff with others—the interaction thing. It's even better when you are an accomplished pro, and better yet when you deal with nice people. Like a lot of endeavors, there are many possibilities. You can make a living, or you can even make a fortune. Mostly it gets back to what you're all about and what you think you want. Much of it depends on individual wants and sensibilities, and mine were pretty well formed in large part by the old-timers I was privileged to work for and later to work with. It was a different time back then and the whole world of finance was tiny compared to the present times. The prevailing thought in those days, among the guys with whom I was affiliated, was that if you put the clients first and did a good job for them, you'd always have enough money—or dough, as we used to call it. In some quarters today, that would qualify one for membership in the Boy Scouts. But that's my deal to this day. Being straight is a good thing; maybe the only thing. I just can't abide chiselers.

When I say old-timers, I'm not exaggerating. Some were in their seventies. It was a very different world back then. Folks didn't retire. Retirement benefits hadn't been invented and hadn't kicked in to the political backdrop; they just kept on working. A few had been to college and some had finished high school, but many, if not most, had gotten no further than eighth grade or so, having had to drop out during the Great Depression. Not to mention signing up for World War II. They were a smart group, but

12

then public education worked pretty well in those days; maybe because it was an acknowledged privilege and was received as such. I now believe that high school in those days was probably equivalent to today's college, as far as "smarts" are concerned. In general terms, the old-timers were quite well spoken and quite erudite—especially about national and international history. And, why I recall I can't say, they all had extremely handsome penmanship.

It was from these guys that I picked up much of the enduring jargon of the business: Sometimes the best way to make fast money is the slow way; sometimes the best way to double your money is to fold it and put it back in your pocket. Of course the great-granddaddy of all: "Buy low, sell high." And also: "Above all, your word is your bond." A personal favorite came from one of the more senior guys who advised that happiness is impossible if you're envious. "After all," he would say, "your candle won't glow any brighter if you blow the other fellow's out." They used language like that—"fellows," for example. And so it would go, day after day. It was like a postgraduate course with no tuition expense. It was good just being around these guys. Real men, just no-bullshit real men.

Like starting in most other businesses, bond trading seemed overwhelmingly daunting and difficult at the outset. Lots of moving parts, that kind of stuff. I recall telling one of the senior guys that it was awfully complicated, and that I wasn't smart enough to get it. (Bear in mind we had no computers, so all the financial calculations had to be done by hand.) He responded with a riff that has had major impact on me since its utterance. He observed that smart was okay, and that I was probably smart enough to do well. He added, however, that curiosity is the best of all traits so far as intelligence is concerned. If you are curious—about the world you live in, about the way things work, about the reasons for events, about the whys and hows—you will always overcome any lack of smarts. With curiosity on your side, you'll almost always be able to dope things out. And if you can throw in some ingenuity and industriousness, you'll be okay. In any event, I agree with those observations and sentiments and have tried to live by them. As much to honor the memory of the old-timers as anything else.

I don't think I'm trying to recall anything specifically right now, and I'm not particularly engaged or focused. I know I'm in the latter stages of middle age, closer to the end of the trail than the beginning, but, at the moment, I'm reasonably relaxed. More or less generally random notions seem to be gliding about me.

*   *   *

I've always liked October. No matter where I happened to be in October, it was ever a wistful time. Irrespective of geography, the same patterns emerged. The sun was starting to move lower in the sky, and days were perceptibly shorter. And there were always sentimentally evocative aromas associated with autumn. We burned leaves when I was a kid; it seemed natural. . . .

A shadowy, low-resolution picture of three adolescents and the word "pals" has been one of those recurring images for the past couple days. And movies, particularly old movies. I'm not capable of much effort, so I'll assume I had a couple of pals and we liked old movies. Why this would come to the fore is odd. "Yes it is," an inner voice seemed to confirm, "it is a puzzlement." There followed a fleeting picture of Yul Brynner himself in his 1950s' king of Siam outfit. This is a curiosity, a most profound curiosity.

Curiosity. That's one that's way up there on my personal altar of admirable things. Right now the mere thought of the word gives me twinges of a low, somewhat subtle, gut-level pain, not unlike the small electric shocks used to motivate lab animals. Definitely a message to leave it alone, at least for now. Leave what alone? I feel like DeNiro doing Travis B. . . . . "You talking to me? Well, I'm the only one here."

I get the feeling I'm going to be talking with some folks, and that'll be a problem. A big problem, because I write like I speak, but I don't do either as I think. Like most of us I have towering thoughts, but they rarely emerge as memorable speech or prose. While I have the most brilliant of ideas, I have an incredibly difficult time articulating them. Maybe that's just the way it is. Maybe we're all disadvantaged or impaired in some major way. I

14

have come to regard this inability to articulate my inner brilliance as a minor social curse. And worse, not able to execute the great concepts I conjure up. It fatigues me just to acknowledge that. All those world-changing big-time notions imprisoned forever within my being. I can imagine spectacular things, and there they remain—just so many imaginings. Talk about world-class frustration.

And it gets worse. At times it seems I am the involuntary recipient of multiple thoughts and, occasionally, an especially brilliant gem. To some this gives the impression of my being inattentive, which is not the case. It may be as one thought just triggers another, I lack the ability to place them in orderly sequence. For folks like us, staying "on point" is particularly challenging.

Still worse, my critics—I have a few—pick on my black/white sensibilities and deem me a linear thinker, incapable of nuance. For my part I can tolerate "nuance," and I'll admit readily that many things are coated with shades of gray. At the same time, "nuance" is also a vehicle for bullshit, isn't it? Your choice. . . .

Sleep seems to be a good idea now. The arms of Morpheus—speaking of pals—beckon. Sleep is always a good way to duck out if you can, and I'm good at that. I like all kinds of things, but sleep has to be at, or at least near, the top of the pile. There's nothing quite like going unconscious, especially when things are all bitched-up. For me it's like putting up the "off-duty" sign and waving a middle finger at all my troubles. And, in this joint, wherever and whatever it may be, they have a way of making sleep into some form of recreational therapy.

I've been on the inside of the in-and-out routine long enough in my stay here at the Happy Times Motel to pick up on the stealth aspects as a featured part of the daily regimen. As the guy once said to me: "You ain't as dumb as you look," so I'm ready to go unconscious and to play the game anyway it has to be played.

The local folks have been administering a poke here and a shove there, presumably to get me to say or do something of interest to my gracious but somewhat remote and sterile hosts.

15

There are only so many possibilities, but the greatest seems to be that I know something these folks hold in some regard. Of course, it's always possible that I've fallen in with the last of the surviving goodie-two-shoes Samaritans. That, however, would be right up there with the odds of me sitting on the throne with the queen of England, so chances are they are looking for a Chatty Cathy. It could be worse. Even with the pinholes in my limbs, I'm not sure I've ever been more relaxed. Being relaxed is as close as one can get to a Zen state, and I wouldn't mind staying there for a while. Neither, apparently, would my benefactors (or captors). But each most likely for very different reasons. Going back over the path I've hewn isn't all that bad.

*   *   *

Lately I've been revisiting the picture and pals deal. The something in the background was, and is, a movie theater marquee. The two pals were, and remain, Jackie Slater and Richie McAlister. We hung out together back then. Christ almighty, we still hang out. We've been pals for almost forty years. Pals is not a careless rubric. The very notion of pals is serious stuff to guys like us. Being, and/or having, a pal is a big deal, a very big deal. Pal is a serious word, at least with us. It's somewhere beyond blood brotherhood and is based on the unspoken word. It's when you just know what the deal is, how it should be, and how it's going to be. You just know. It's friendship, respect, duty, and honor all rolled up into an adolescent pact that has survived beyond anything resembling reason, but it *has* survived.

More than anything, you probably need a misplaced sense of romanticism to be a pal and to remain a pal. In our lexicon, pals is somewhere north of the "All for one and one for all" thing. That would have been a starting point, a minimum expectation. So, what's a Nick Drizos? He's one of those guys who is hopelessly hung in his own imagination. Maybe he is his imagination. His greatest stuff never quite makes it past what it might have been. Just like in the movies . . . the old movies. Great ideas, but . . .

As near as I can reconstruct, it all began with the movies. The imprint of good guy versus bad guy must have been just about indelible on me. And my pals. Likewise the heroic woman,

16

the one who would routinely turn down riches and who would acclaim for Joe Right who, often as not, was broke but honest. It all began with Roy Rogers and Gene Autry and Hopalong. Later it was Shane. But most prominently and forever it was Bogie. *Casablanca* probably became my metaphor for life. Bogie/Rick says so long to Ilsa—clearly the most beautiful, most sensitive woman on Earth—at the airport. Well I guess so. I guess that's the way it had to be. My balls ached for a month. Incredible. I'd have killed Paul Hendreid, made off with Ilsa, and laid the rap on Claude Raines.

Of course I wouldn't. It just wouldn't have been right. Bogie was the man that the rest of us wanted to be and still want to be. And so it has been. Me versus me. One of me is hopelessly tied up in fantasy, while the other—knowing better—presses for a reentry to reality. There are probably a number of twelve step programs for us folks, but so far we persist. We're nuts and we walk among you, but we're high-grade nuts, so show proper respect. Or something like that.

As a palliative of sorts I dialogue with myself. I have designated my colleague in these dialogues the Nick 101. He is, in fact, my inner being—a constant travel mate and dialogue companion. Freud would have framed it as a splice between the ego and the id, or something like that. To me it's much simpler. Just talk to yourself, except that you know that you're just talking to yourself. And get answers in return. For me it's a dialogue with the Nick 101.

But it's nowhere as complicated as one might imagine. Folks like me just see things in black and white. Hence we are doomed to remain in the keeping, and at the mercy of, our more adolescent notions. Our detractors will continue to refer to us as linear. To me, that's just another contemporary cliché from people who can't think. At the end of the journey, adulthood, urbanity, and sophistication are just so much bullshit, aren't they? Is hypocrisy really the principal lubricant of polite society?

If you get nothing else from hanging with me, get this. The only two things that really count are truth and romance. Everything that is good can be found and stored in either or both of truth and romance. That's it—no rebuttal. You'll find that on page 126 of the as-yet-unpublished but eagerly awaited *Nick Drizos: On Life*. Use it in good health.

My other most significant guardrail has been, is, and will remain fair play. It's not just something to admire, it is the ideal to which one must aspire. To some this makes Nick a simpleton in our oh-so-sophisticated world. To which I would respond: bullshit.

We play make-believe in the grown-up thing, but, as we go along—each of us in our own unique great drama—the Peter Pan syndrome is more powerful than most might care to acknowledge. It was especially painful for me when the white hat good guy gave way to the antihero—the guy who was and is essentially an ambiguous slob. Or something like that. Fitzgerald referred to being borne back ceaselessly into the past. Maybe it's the same thing or a variation on that theme, as many of us continue to be drawn back to other times for reasons often beyond our most lucid imaginings. But, just in time, here comes my pal Morpheus. On this occasion he's in a hypodermic in the hands of one of the lovely ladies. Want to see a willing subject. . . .

It says October twenty-first on my handy little bedside calendar. I've just had a wonderful sleep of which I am thankfully aware. I'm beginning to feel like an actual person as I respond increasingly to the natural stimuli here in my little special-purpose condo.

I'd like very much to know what the weather is like outside, but my room has no windows. Another thing about which to be curious. The Garden of Fatima quandary comes to mind—that place where all things are known, but few are revealed. All in time, one supposes. Besides, I'm feeling better, much better.

If you haven't gathered, I'm Greek. In fact a lot of my pals refer to me as "Greek." Not "the Greek," just "Greek." As in, "Hey, Greek." I like being Greek for a plethora—I love that word too, plethora—of reasons, starting with the many notions of Athens and all that originated there. The great thought, the great institutions, and some big names: Socrates, Plato, Sophocles, and my personal favorite, Pericles. The pride thing. In many ways, most of just about everything—barring technology—started there.

Not to mention the heroes of Thermopylae. And do we have the best mythology, or what? Makes me feel good.

The food is fine, too. Give a real Greek like me some lamb, grapes, figs, olives, and feta cheese, and other naturally abounding items, not to exclude seafood, and I'll do well by you. You'll have a swell time. That's another word—swell—from the old-timers.

The surviving Greek culture has many distinctions as well. That relatively recent movie about the big fat wedding was not only funny, it was surprisingly accurate. There was one serious flaw, however. The magic substance was not Windex; it was and is vinegar. From administering to minor cuts, burns, and bruises to emergency topical treatment for heart attacks, it's vinegar. So use that in good health, too.

But back to my celebration of being Greek. Food is another pleasant area to dwell upon when diverting focus from pain. Not just the many ways it can dazzle the senses of sight, smell, and taste, but also for its lyrical aspects. So, always add some music.

Music is, after all, the most obvious requisite for a truly fine meal. I take care, however, to distinguish eating from dining. The former can be a solitary event, but dining is the essential centerpiece for gatherings, hearty lustiness and, above all, a forum for gifted conversationalists and storytellers. Dante had his layers of Hell, but I have my levels of Heaven. I place storytellers in the penthouse—presuming they have been decent with respect to most other admission criteria. While on earth, they belong at tables with good companions and fine food. Add the cocktail of your choice and, who knows, maybe you get lucky if you get my drift. Lovely women, dining, music, and lively conversation may well be truer basics of life than earth, wind, fire, and water. And what's better than the things that boys and girls can do together. As we used to say in the 1960s, "Get Zorba up here."

Zorba remains our most Greek over-the-top metaphor for self-indulgence and an occasional excess or two, but food was a large part of his festive nature. It's difficult to imagine anything festive without food. Maybe that's where the notion of festival came from. In any event, from selection to preparation to presentation to consumption, food is a marvel. And thoughts of it make for a decent proxy for companionship while I try to make sense of my new reality. Even Oliver Twist, being served cold gruel at the wretched orphanage, sang, "Food, Glorious Food." He was really with the program. At least in the play and the movie.

The food given me in my present quarters has been sustaining, for which I am grateful, but I find myself yearning for some personal favorites to offset the sterility of my surroundings. For the past few years, Indian cuisine has been a special attraction.

Not only the food itself, because food—just like music—transports. I think about India as well. More at an instinctive level than anything else, I have long been fascinated with India. If I were in my twenties or maybe even my early thirties, I might well head straight away for the subcontinent. I've never been there, but I have a sense of it, a notion or two. I guess it to be a compelling and milling confusion personified by its almost rhapsodic spirituality and mysticism. All this derived from a brutally bloody past and immersed in a disorderly present. It is a country with the largest middle class, as presently defined by global sociologists. Its Bollywood produces more movies than we do in the states. Here again a confusing and bewildering array, ranging from silliness that makes the Three Stooges look like high art to the most thoughtful and movingly evocative epics, and, of course, everything imaginable between these extremes. At the same time it has an educated class of enviable intellect, which coexists with widespread poverty. Its renowned Institute of Technology has become world class in every respect. I personally think India will emerge as a first-rate manufacturing and trading nation. Just one guy's opinion. To me, it is just an amazing tableau.

My recovery must be accelerating. In recent moments my foreground thoughts have moved away from the tender graces of women and the ever safe harbor of my Greek heritage to India. So far as I know I am not trying to recall specifics, but I feel as though murk and clarity are busy resolving themselves. India. That same visceral electro-nausea is palpable again, but the leave-it-alone impulse seems to be offset by a larger sense of let-it happen. India, but why India? What's the thing with India? Thought patterns emerge: why India? I seem to be searching for connections of low resolution dots. All of which makes for fuzzy pictures.

Among other things that now cross my mind, I wangled a ticket back in the 1960s when the great, especially in his opinion, Charles de Gaulle addressed the National Press Club in Washington, D.C., I got the ticket through Jackie Slater, a high school pal who would later win highest acclaims for journalism, and about whom I'll be saying more later. De Gaulle was an imposing figure, as well he should be with that name. Charles of Gaul or, more simply, Charles of France.

Later, he would go to Canada and agitate for Quebec Libre. But, on that day in the 1960s, he had come to pay homage to himself, and the swooning press seemed happy to oblige. After taking credit for repulsing the Nazis from Europe (while he was a distant elsewhere), he proceeded to expound on his favorite topic: Le Grand Charles Shares His Prescient Thoughts on Geopolitics. His scholarship was exceeded only by his self-adoration. Nonetheless, he ventured many predictions and projections, all of which were dutifully reported by our fawning press corps. We had a President from Texas, but this guy was from France. The elegance thing, even faux elegance, sold well in those days. We were really quite young, and apparently a quite impressionable, country just those few years ago.

At that time, the Soviet Union was expansive and less than subtle in expressing its longer-term objectives. China was imagined to be harnessing its great reservoir of humanity, and would no doubt become an important international player, but the Soviets were of greatest interest. Containment of the Russian Bear was thus uppermost in the vast majority of actively aware and engaged minds.

Following his prepared remarks, the Great One acceded to receiving a few questions. My pal Slater, a recent high school graduate who represented The Young Journalists of America, was recognized, and he inquired if India could be part of a global containment of the Soviets.

De Gaulle listened imperiously. His posings and posture couldn't have been more predictable if he had been parachuted in by Hollywood central casting as the translator conveyed Jackie's question. It must have hit what you might call a hot button, because de Gaulle's face flushed visibly. He glared at Slater and said, in French subsequently translated—and I would swear to the words—"India is a dust bowl of memories, capable of nothing."

The adoring press noted his comments, but a few of us felt a sickening impact from the answer, like an unexpected punch to the gut, or lower. It was gratuitous, dismissive and totally unnecessary, especially from one who regards his nation as the unquestioned father and master of global diplomacy. He could have made his point in decidedly more gracious manners, especially to an earnest teenager. And without implying stupidity to both the question and to the questioner. I took it as a form of bullyism. Then again, it is strange how we choose to file things and events away. This guy was a dick, a real dick. Maybe it isn't so strange, and maybe that was the beginning of my attraction to India. If the obnoxious Frenchie de Gaulle says no, maybe I say yes. Maybe it's as simple as that, and so maybe that was the beginning of my attraction to India. But what do I know?

I'm back to the murk and clarity conflict. Sounds like a cheap law firm—Murk & Clarity. I go from subject to subject. I wonder if I'm cuing up the subjects or my drug-dealing hosts and hostesses are producing the show.

Thoughts of women, Greece, and food are receding. I'm being pushed to the wheres and whys, and India is part of it. Happily, as my old friend Hal Sandstrom would advise: "There's no problem so big that sleep can't suppress." Courage seems to be asserting itself and suffusing through my very being. I am being encouraged to continue to reconstruct, and to go down the road named "India." I choose to dream of India.

Things have been kind of slick here lately, maybe even cool. I know I'm being managed through whatever process I'm in, and I know I'm being fed a bunch of chemicals which aren't all that objectionable. In fact I think I like them, as they seem to just slide me into dreamland ever so pleasantly.

They probably all begin with the word "psycho" and have the phrase "tropic" somewhere in their long names, but they're kind of enjoyable. I tend to wonder to myself as they move me along just what longer term effect they might have.

One of my many wonderings is: What's a Nick Drizos, anyway? I'm sure I have some opinions, but if someone rolls me over and looks at the active ingredients label, I hope they'll find such items as good guy, straight (meaning honest) and usually found in the company of beautiful women with his clothes elsewhere. I've been having the greatest dreams lately, especially about women, so I'll just concede to the chemicals again. I do love women and I really love being with them. And I really mean with them. What's better than the things men and women can do together?

So, what am I? And who am I? I know I'm Greek, that I have two pals, one of whom is Jackie Slater. I know I love food and gifted conversationalists and story tellers. I'm a bond trader and among the best of that bunch. I have attractions to Greece and India, and I'm generally very curious.

What else do I know? It seems like my head has been filling up with random pieces of the humanoid mosaic called Nick Drizos. A name here, an incident there. All very random. Maybe it's just the way things reassemble. So it's not so much what else do I know. It's more just what do I know?

Mostly I know that I love women. I also know that life is just shit bag backwards as a pal of mine from Canada used to say. By the time you finally dope some things out, your better days are behind you. Maybe it's not that bad, but youth—for guys anyway seems to be a battle between testosterone and sensibilities with the latter usually finishing out of the money. I should also add that girls are usually dipshits till they get past whatever deal they do in their teens and well into their twenties. Maybe they—boys and girls or men and women—should be withheld from each other till the grander epiphanies occur. Like when they can really appreciate each other.

Don't get me wrong. I am convinced beyond all ambiguity that tits and pussy are among the best inventions ever. Right up there with fire, the wheel, the printing press, and even beer and pizza. It's just that if you're a guy, and you don't adore the woman they belong to, it's all bullshit. And so are you. The modern-day flat-bellied, indiscriminate bed-jumping plastiques just don't do it for me. There has to be a connection, a deep connection or it's just . . . so much jive.

When we're young and full of whatever it is that we're full of, we get thrown into this horse race of doing weird stuff for unknown tribal or ritual compulsions. Just observe the natural ease among and between elderly men and women as compared to the classical teenage tension. As Whittier noted, the saddest words are indeed "It might have been!" One can only imagine the middle ground. Once sincere love and feelings are in place, it has a chance of working out.

And so it is with me and, I'm here to tell you, a lot of other guys. And so it is with the three lovely women who have been attending to me. It's just that they don't know what an emotional and sentimental love bucket they're dealing with. Or, if you must, love bucket with whom they are dealing. So I'll just hope they are conjuring all manners of unspeakable things to do with me . . . or to me. I hope I haven't been talking in my sleep, because it will be awfully difficult to explain the many differences between dirty old lust and the loftier notion of adoration—and there are differences; very profound differences.

Moreover (I learned that neatly upscale word "moreover" from the lame-o investment bankers and lawyers in our business—I use it because I used to say "and not only that") there are certain women who simply command adoration. I call them "knowing women" because, among other things, they just know. They know that an arched eyebrow from a well-turned-out lady is more provocative than bumps and grinds from the amateur hour in some meat-market saloon. They know that understatement is far sexier than today's in-your-face deal. They know they can reassure you in a situation which might be edgy or dicey, and, with a touch of their hand on your arm, they can tell you when it's time to go. Mostly they are comfortable with themselves because, in a short phrase, they know how to get the best out of a guy. For them—for you both. They tend to see us for what we might be and they generally succeed in getting us to be the man we'd be proud to be. And they know, among all things, that

24

most guys in truth want to be brought to heel in some respects. And these ladies can do all this without reducing a guy's sense of himself. It's almost like leadership where you get people to do what's really best for them anyway. And, if you don't sign up for the program, they're gone. They are also very rare. If you find one, if you can feel it, hang on.

The deuce of it is, the bitch of it is that most guys aren't smart enough to dope this out. And that's a shame; maybe a tragedy in the grander scheme of what "might have been." Some of us will never know. I know, but I haven't quite gotten there. Haven't really had the chance.

Reminds me of the old and very bad joke about the Indian—American Indian—standing on a corner well traveled by pedestrians and chanting, "Chance, chance, chance." A well-meaning observer suggested that maybe the fellow meant to say, "How." "Me know 'how,' " came the answer. "Me just want a chance."

Like I said earlier, I have these towering thoughts but they don't compute well with my linguistic limitations. So you either get it or you don't and you either agree or you don't.

In the meanwhile, like the death and taxes deal, one has to sleep. . . . Sleep is right up there with lovely women, food, and stories . . . old friend Morpheus didn't disappoint and wrapped me in the warmest pleasantness of happy times. One of my lovely attending nurses just administered a little needle-borne nudge into dreamland. A nice way to call it a day.

I had no other priority than to enjoy my ride into peaceful ness. I dialed up the 101 and advised that he was in charge, and to give me a shout if anything interesting arose. Otherwise, I'd see him later. Use your discretion on the wake-up call. *Buenos noches, amigo.*

A propos of not very much, I smoked for a few years and I like my Killian's Red and a few assorted cocktails, but I've never done drugs. Just never held any attraction for me. I could get used to this versed stuff, however.

Anyway, I'm just floating around doing the weightless thing, and when you're a bit portly, the weightless thing is a real treat.

No aches, no pains, no worldly cares. I'm in a state of complete receptivity. I'm alert, but I'm out. I'm out, but I'm alert.

I had no sense of time before the folks hereabouts lent a helping needle. Now I don't know what century I'm in. But it is the Garden of Fatima, and I'm about to hear some stories. I love stories. Have I mentioned that stories are the best?

The 101, at his loyal best, probably fought off the seductive narcotic and opted to play code breaker and guardian of the surrounding body. That's a good 101; I'm in your care.

Time was not a dimension. It had no relevance or meaning. Maybe it is as a French philosopher said: "There is no such thing as time, only events. Some events are bigger than others."

Me, I'm just drifting. I have no volition. I'm a sleeping blank page. Back to autopilot: what dreams may come. And come they did.

I was about eight, and there were three of us. My face was prominent, while the other two were blurry and indistinct. We were in a shallow wading pool playing a game with scale model warships. One of the other two feigned injury and dropped to one knee. We rushed to his aid, propped up our fallen comrade and called for the nurse. Almost immediately, the young Susan Hayward appeared and ministered to the make-believe wound. We had just seen a rerun of the Gary Cooper classic *Beau Geste*. We were Vikings and had just taken a pledge never to shrink from duty and never to cry. I was Gary Cooper. The Robert Preston and Ray Milland characters turned to face me. And each one of us loved our Susan Hayward.

As we strode from the pool, one of the faces clarified itself and became prominent. It was Jackie Slater. We were standing next to each other shoulder to shoulder and smiling at our naval victory, when our comrade slipped between us, put an arm over each of our shoulders and proclaimed, "We're pals." There we three great warriors stood: Jackie Slater, Richie McAlister, and me.

It was a big moment and a bigger pronouncement. "Pals" had gravity. It wasn't blood brothers or did it carry any heavy-duty ritualistic sense to it. It was stronger than friends, and at that age, meant that we'd stand up for each other. Nickie, Jackie, and Richie.

Over the years we did. We weren't inseparable, but we were pals. It was a happy time. It was a fun time, and an innocent time. We had not much sense of the world outside of Will's Grove, Pennsylvania, and why should we? We were too busy making our own entertainment and growing up pretty much as most kids did in those years.

It was a simple time, and while one was and is compelled to press forward, I am nonetheless drawn continually and wistfully to those days. The world hadn't become disconnected and the critical mass of evil had yet to recreate itself. It was, especially for us adolescents, a very simple time. Except for radio programs and movies, much, if not most, of our entertainment was produced locally by the three of us. We were big on imagination and its many by-products.

Our parents had been through the depression, WW II, postwar recovery, and the McCarthy era. It was time for a breather and a little fun.

Jackie and I would later talk about our preceding generation, about their quiet heroics and about how much they wanted us to attain plateaus which had been foreclosed to them. The six-day work week had just been reduced to five-and-a-half thanks to a half-day reduction on Saturday. This was a big deal, a true watershed event. Dads, who used to collapse on Sunday, were now much more in evidence. Many had returned from the horrors of the war, and most had managed to resume their lives. We thought of these men as the truest of heroes and imagined they would have great stories to tell. We would understand later, but we were generally mystified at their avoidances of their wartime behavior. The subject was almost always changed, deflected or ignored. They just didn't want to talk about it. In not so great a length of time, we understood. Parties were a big thing for our parents. Grown-ups would get together on some sort of rotating basis at one person's house or another. The moms all dressed up, and I especially liked the hair styles from those days. They'd all have a couple of drinks and then one of several sorts of dinner would follow. It might be a sit-down with the good silverware, a group collaboration with people assigned different courses, or a so-called potluck where they made do with what was available. More times than not they'd sing a song or two, and they'd often dance. The fox trot was the big item.

Most of the dads had stories to tell. When it was our turn to host one of these parties, I'd camp out on the stairs, well out of sight, but well within hearing range. At some point someone would say something like: "Hey Fred, tell that story about the moose in Cincinnati." Laughter would always follow. Whether it was the booze, the companionship, or just the chance to have a little relief, I don't know. They laughed. God bless them.

What I did know was that I loved stories, and I loved good storytellers even more. In the course of a few years, our house must have been the party site a dozen or so times. Though the same stories would be repeated invariably, I never tired of them. Nor did my admiration for good story tellers ever wane. I think it was around that time when I concluded that, in the last analysis, everything is a story. A movie, a book, a play, the day's events, yesterday's lunch, everything. And the folks who can tell those stories . . . well, they are just the best.

For my pals and me, we were probably middle class, but we didn't know what that meant. We each had what are now regarded as the standard items: sneakers, blue jeans, a Roadmaster bike, a Flexible Flyer sled, and assorted sports gear. There were also some board games, but sophisticated toys were not to invade for years to come.

Boxes were a big item, and big boxes were very valuable. They facilitated a variety of things—making forts, facades of western towns, and group toboggans in the winter. Prosperity and money had not yet arrived, so imagination was king.

Admission to the movies cost fifteen cents. Our parents could thus buy several hours of relative peace once a week for a quarter. On reflection, this would be one of my first lessons in dealmaking and different viewpoints. I thought my parents were being generous. They were, but they had their own agendas as well.

Richie, Jackie, and I rarely missed the Saturday matinee. That fifteen cents bought admission to a newsreel, a cartoon, a serial adventure, a western, previews of coming attractions, and sometimes a double feature. The remaining change would buy popcorn or the confection of your choosing. Mostly the quarter bought a lot of peace for a lot of parents.

These epics would start at noon and end around five-thirty. As we exited, we'd be greeted by a setting but still brilliant sunset. On many occasions, headaches were the norm, because we sat so close to the screen during the Western shoot-'em-ups that we practically ended up covered with powder burns and horse shit. Why some things remain lodged with you, I don't know. But find a better bargain, or a better way to be with one's pals. The movies were a big part of these years. The three of us tended to like and dislike pictures pretty much in accord. Hollywood had not yet become the megacenter of entertainment, so our fare was a mix of new movies and re-releases.

Action movies were our favorites at the beginning of our cinematic odyssey, but in time we began to tolerate romantic comedies and love stories. We even began to show glimmerings of picking up on the more sophisticated pictures.

We had favorites. We would discuss, debate, and defend our views. My favorite actor was, and still is, Burt Lancaster. He was always into some heavy action and he had the singular greatest laugh of any motion picture actor before or since. Bogie was in a class by himself; among the others I opted for Burt.

Jackie was drawn to James Cagney. While not short, Jackie bore resemblance to the actor and liked Cagney's toughness and resolve. Over time Jackie manifested a bit of a swagger. Whether that was mostly Jackie or whether Cagney had insinuated himself into Jackie's being doesn't much matter. It fit him and Jackie has worn that jaunty swagger, more of self-confidence than anything else, for all the time I have known him. He's gritty.

His personal film favorites were *The Story of G.I. Joe* and *Guadalcanal Diary*. Not because of the war drama, but because of the two featured wartime correspondents, Ernie Pyle and Richard Tregaskis, respectively.

Richie had matured a bit quicker than Jackie and I, and acquired a taste for romance well before us. His favorite actor was usually the guy who got the girl. At the movies, he'd often peel off

29

and relocate for a while to enjoy Maureen Williams or some of the girls who were similarly inclined. We'd invariably regroup and start the walk home, but more times than not we'd have to clear Richie and his shirt of some lipstick. It was fortunate that our first stop was always Jackie's house and that the bottle of Carbon Tet, the wonder cleaner of those days was ever-present and available. We'd get the last trace off, and Richie would giggle. It was harmless stuff in an innocent time.

By our midteens, I had become Nick, but Jackie and Richie were still Jackie and Richie. We were good students and we all participated in a variety of activities. We were all pretty good in sports, but Richie was especially good in baseball. Jackie was the smartest, Richie was the most popular, and I got the best grades, but only because I was a "digger," working really hard. I was the best dancer, because I had to be. Jackie had a maturity that appealed to some girls, and Richie appealed to all the others. Dancing kept me in the game. In third place, but in the game. In all, we were a pretty social and likeable trio.

We stayed close friends without any major blowups. Some say that kid groups of three cause problems, because things always end up two on one. The standard wisdom just didn't apply to us, though.

By the time we were high school seniors, we could pretty much read one another's thoughts. One time, for instance, Miss Fletcher announced that we would be presenting our book reports in chronological order. Almost instantly, Jackie and I rose and strode to the door. When Miss Fletcher inquired as to our behavior we announced in unison that we had read *1984* and our reports wouldn't be due for years. The class got a big yuk, and Jackie and I got to take a visit to the principal for some remedial work on manners. Richie had a handful of Maureen Williams during the hilarity, so he probably didn't care too much.

Richie was smart enough. But sometimes when the three of us would observe something together, Jackie and I would have a similar take. Richie, as many times as not, would have a different angle. He hit a high-water mark in that respect during one of our chemistry teacher JJ's lectures. JJ, a devout foe of the demon rum, deemed it his responsibility to serve up object moral lessons to us seniors, who were soon to be in the "outside world." On one occasion, he spread a few dozen worms on the counter and bid us all to crowd around. He then poured pure alcohol on the annelids, which died in relatively short order. Pleased with himself and the obvious power of his sermon for temperance, he called on Richie and asked him for his conclusion. Richie responded, in all sincerity, "If you drink a lot, you'll never have worms." I'm told that's an old-time story, but it really happened. I was there. Another big yuk from the class, and another trip for Richie to see our principal.

These were quite innocent times in small-town USA, without the frantic mobility of today's world. Everybody pretty much knew everybody else, and most of society's rules were enforced through personal restraint. And, despite some of the kid stuff along the way, most of us absorbed the moral guidance better than the adults probably supposed.

We didn't drink much, and if we did, we usually walked. One time just before graduation, the three of us drove to a nearby lake and got pretty well lit up. Jackie had driven his father's car, and declared himself impaired after a few cans of beer. He concluded that we would walk the few miles home. I concurred without protest, but Richie insisted he was as sober as JJ and suggested that he would drive us home. Jackie reached a conclusion in seconds and quickly locked the car and hurled the keys fifty yards into a field. So we walked home. The better part of the story was the tale we concocted to explain the loss of the key, and the location of the car, but no one got killed or maimed. It was rather tame in those days, and I don't think we were unrepresentative of our age group, especially in smaller towns.

Soon enough we were college-bound, each of us to a different school, but we stayed pals. Jackie wrote. Richie, having a bit more money and more side interests than we, used the phone. I did some of each. We all came home each of the three intervening summers and our three-way "palship" continued in place as we matured.

While nothing diminished our connection, we were each developing our own unique personas. Jackie became devoted to

31

writing, and his skills of observation and talents for portrayal and illumination grew steadily with time. Richie was a steady B student and, given his warm extroversion, was headed for stardom in the business world. I kept on at being a digger.

The summer between our sophomore and junior years was one of the more memorable. I think the three of us were grasping, each in our own ways, that things do in fact change and evolve. With a mix of joy and melancholia, we each seemed to be steering pretty good courses. While we had all met and made new friends, the earlier bonds endured. We continued to seek each other's opinions about our most personal concerns.

I enjoyed Jackie's letters, which were much more than just news from a close friend. His ability to narrate and describe were beyond me. While my letters to him were reasonably informative, his were evocative. He consistently made the routine interesting and could easily illuminate the not-so-obvious. He mixed irony and humor and almost always had a fresh view on something. More than anything else, with pen in hand, he was possessed of a maturity well beyond his years, with an attitude toward writing that bordered on duty. He had little tolerance for mediocrity. Reportage had to be clear and complete. Business had to be crisp, concise, and logical. The personal had to be informative and amusing. Any less, he maintained, was insulting. He was a professional long before he became a journalist.

He would go headlong into journalism, and it would be no surprise when he would win plaudits and acclaim from audiences as well as from his peers. I have long regarded E. B. White as the finest pure writer of essays and other short subjects, and Edward R. Murrow as clearly the nonpareil journalist. Jackie came as close as any to those two titans. He was that good.

I also spent considerable time with Richie that summer. A solid B student and as affable as a young man can be, he had a natural instinct for business opportunities. He was particularly adept at adding smart features to mundane products on which customers would spend more money. He constantly tinkered with notions of how to make something better or more convenient. He loved the ladies and, more importantly, the ladies loved Richie. A born entrepreneur, he reaffirmed his calling almost daily.

We weren't changing as much as just growing. Our basic instincts and attitudes were all pretty much in place. It seemed that we were each like time-release capsules, manifesting new facets as we progressed. Each had our own distinct timelines, but there were changes.

Richie was becoming a fatalist. Not with a dark side mentality, but rather of having little control over what was to be; perhaps it was more like wanting no control. He seemed to radiate a very gracious air. If it worked, it worked. If it didn't, he'd do something else.

I was still the digger, the least changed, or evolved, of the three of us. While Jackie and Richie were pretty well on course, I was relatively directionless. I wasn't lost or despairing or anything of that sort—I just hadn't found anything resembling a calling. Nor did I have any particular aptitude. I remained the digger.

In that same summer, I fell into my job with the local brokerage firm as an assistant to the four resident bond traders, gregarious and friendly guys who were generous with their time. At first I was hesitant to disturb or interrupt them, but they made it clear for me to pipe up so long as they weren't in the middle of a trade or something of obvious importance. An enjoyable summer would unfold as the beginning of my life's work.

By our senior year, Jackie had already distinguished himself as a talent. The editor in chief of his college paper since his sophomore year, he also wrote occasional pieces for *College Town,* a prominent supplement in the local paper.

When the Pope visited the United States that year, he addressed the United Nations, speaking in both English and French. Toward the end of his address, when he informed the audience that he would conclude with his message of peace in Latin, this essentially shut the UN down; if there are languages for which that body has no translation capability, one of them is Latin.

This widely reported event was one of the major events of the year. It had been audiotaped, and a prestigious New York paper carried the pope's Latin peace message translated into English and discussed it on its editorial pages.

That translation would propel my friend Jackie Slater into the public arena. A journalism major, Jackie minored in history and Latin and had studied Latin every year from eighth grade through college. He was a true Latin scholar. I thought it was cool enough, but Richie would rag on him, usually saying things like, "That'll help you expand your circle of friends," or "Where are you going to find the dead people to talk to?" Jackie would just shove him, and retort, "You mean 'with whom to talk.' "

With his usual interest and tenacity, he translated the pope's message and found the New York paper's translation to be not only wrong, but substantially wrong. In a most gracious move, he sent a short note to the editor of that great paper and directed his attention to the error. A week passed with no response; he would have settled for a form letter thanking him for his interest and would have let the matter go. But, Jackie is nothing if not earnest, so he telephoned the editor. He was ultimately connected to an assistant who dismissed him brusquely.

Jackie then sent a note of similar content to that paper's arch rival and, in a very thoughtful memo, pointed out that "It was reported that the Pope said thus and so. This, however, was a faulty translation; what he in fact said was . . ." The rival paper appreciated this nice opportunity to irritate its major competitor, and it published Jackie's well-written note prominently alongside its editorials. He may not have been quite accorded carte blanche at that point, but Jackie had become a part of the fourth estate's landscape.

Time seemed to move more quickly as we approached graduation. The three of us were together during spring break of our senior years when Jackie voiced a similar sentiment about time and its apparent acceleration.

I said, "It does, Jackie, or at least it should seem to. When we were five, one year was one-fifth or twenty percent of our lives. Now it's one-twentieth, five percent. Each year is getting smaller and smaller when measured against the increasing passage of time, so it has every appearance of moving faster."

He regarded me with an *I never thought of it that way* look

34

and simultaneously hijacked the expression I had stolen from my trader friends: "You ain't as dumb as you look." That homely expression would air itself at one time or another just about every time two or three of us got together.

We all graduated on time and regrouped again to talk about the directions we would take. As usual, Jackie was the most focused. He knew what he wanted to do and where. He was headed for New York City to be with the big boys and to see just how good he was.

Richie wasn't sure, but neither was he worried. He had a general picture of the things to do and be and more than enough confidence and self-assurance to get there. By acclamation of his pals, Richie would do okay.

I had gotten over my initial fears of the financial world and was coming along fairly well. While I didn't have the focus and passion of Jackie, or Richie's brio and joie de vivre, I was competent and likeable.

I hadn't given much thought to either geography or a career, and I had every intention of staying with the small firm. Shortly after graduation, the five senior guys—that is, fellows—took me out for a dinner, a nice and touching gesture.

They were the realest of the real folks I ever met in business, before or since.

They had brought one investment banker with them, a big hitter from one of the top New York City firms. Normally traders and bankers didn't hang out together, but he and they liked one another and had become pretty good friends.

It was a fun time as usual. They told stories, one after another, some I'd heard and some new. After dinner, they toasted me a time or two and wished me well. I was now the only college graduate in the trading group.

Les, ever the senior trader, asked me, "Well, Nick, what are you going to do with your new sheepskin?"

"I expect to report here on Monday morning and continue to be a trader. What else would I do?" I responded.

"No, laddie," said Scotty with a deeper than usual brogue as he laid that considerable paw of his on my shoulder. "The lads and I have discussed it. It's time for you to take your shot in the big leagues. You'll be off to New York."

"You're kidding."

"We're not either kidding," said Scotty firmly.

I was met by the other four faces confirming the content and intent of Scotty's directive. Despite the flattering reference to the big leagues, my first reaction was that I was good enough to be a junior guy, but I wouldn't make the cut as a long-term player in the big leagues.

Scotty spoke up again: "You're a good lad, Nick, and we'll miss you but it's off to the Apple with you."

I was touched again by the generosity. I guess it was a help that I was a "good lad," but they were a fine bunch indeed.

"Before you ask," said Les Horvath—whose catchphrases "You ain't as dumb as you look" and "You're smarter than you look" we'd all adapted—"we've got a bunch of friends up there, and you'll have no shortage of interviews when you jump on the train."

It was one of those eminently logical decisions that still didn't feel right. Losing friends is never a good part of any alternative.

The fellows picked up on my readily observable feelings and offered several comforting comments, noting that all the firms were connected by telephone. We'd be trading with each other for years to come, and we were only seven or eight hours away by train or car.

"And only an hour and a half by plane, Nick, when you hit the really big time." And I'm thinking, me on a DC-3 someday. Two engines, the whole deal; that'll be the day.

That brought a good-natured laugh from the fellows, and I was lifting my third or fourth Killian's Red.

Les turned to the banker, Pete Bennett, and said, "What advice would you have for our young friend, Pete?"

Pete paused momentarily and said, "I have a few items that have served all of us pretty well for a long time. The first piece of advice is never stop trying to improve. The second is always remember that people want to do business with people they know, like, and trust. In the end, people do business with their friends.

36

Third and last, try to have twenty outgoing phone calls a day. Stay in touch, because you're in the business of making friends. The first piece can be acquired, the second piece must be earned, and there's no reason not to do the third. Also, try mightily to keep envy out of your thoughts; it's toxic and unproductive. Lastly, don't ever get discouraged. When one door closes, another invariably opens. That's my best advice and good luck to you."

Scotty placed his other considerable paw on Pete's shoulder and said, "Well put. Pete. You speak for all of us." Five heads nodded and those old well-worn, but decorous, beer steins were clunked and clanked again.

It was hard, and I do know the right words were difficult. It was very hard to suppress my tears, but I did. And they were pleased that I did. I think they knew that I'd be doing things they had only dreamed of. And I'm pretty sure they wanted me to have the shot that they never had. Like I said, a selfless bunch of fellows. It was time to go. I stood and hoisted the old beaten and thoroughly weathered leather case I'd used for college and work.

Scotty regarded my briefcase and said, as he had many many times before, "You still going around with that old bag?" Everyone laughed. It was a good end to a memorable evening with genuine friends.

I shook hands all around and started to leave, not the least sure of where I would be in the days and weeks ahead.

"Not so fast, laddie," said Scotty. "We've got our pride, you know. We can't have you off to the big time with that case." He gave our waiter the high sign, and a neatly wrapped box was placed before me.

"Open it, Nick," said Les.

I was stunned. It was a very fine leather attaché case with "ND" beautifully embossed by the handle.

I was agape. "What can I say?"

"It's not what you can say, laddie, it's what you can do. Make us proud."

They walked me to my car, and I drove off as a grateful recipient of heartfelt affection. I would visit with them many times in the years ahead, but this memory of good fellowship became a prized possession.

So off I went. Full of jeunesse and all that goes with it but, make no mistake, scared stiff. I don't know whether I was more scared of failure or facing the fellows after finding out I couldn't cut it.

But a strange and fortuitous thing happened. It became clear to me that when one or more of such folks stand up for you, there is no way you will fall short of their expectations. It's like getting a boost of confidence and a ten-point bonus on your IQ all in a confused-but-happy package. Their good wishes were invaluable.

In later years I visited with the fellows and asked how I could repay my many debts to them. Scottie said, "That's our good lad. You do owe, but not necessarily to us. Just use your best judgment and be to others what we may have been to you. And, if you keep that attitude, you'll be repaying us many times over."

Like I said, an incredible bunch, and thanks to them, I did pretty well. Certainly better than had they never been so generous to me.

So there we were, the three of us. Each launched in pretty good fashion.

3
In the Real World and Off
to a Fine Start

October 22nd-

As per my conversation with Jackie on the relative speed of time, the next few years really accelerated. Jackie, Richie, and I made time to get together a few times each year. We would do whatever it took to accommodate whichever of us had least control of his schedule. Everything still began and ended with "pal" but, with no particular effort, we had grown up and were continuing to mature. Our conversations were decidedly more urbane. Our vocabularies had grown considerably due to the cosmopolitan settings in which we found ourselves. Happily for me, we still identified as three guys from a small town.

Richie had done particularly well in the areas of sales, marketing, and advertising. His novel way of looking at things underpinned more than a few sales and promotion campaigns. He wasn't a heavy-duty number cruncher, and he couldn't tell you much about demographics. He'd just absorb a situation and ask, "How come you're doing it that way?" I suppose that that particular aspect was not unique to Richie. What was unique was that he had an answer to his question at the ready. And many more times than not, it was a good answer.

I asked him about his special talent a few times, and he'd usually just dismiss it and prefer to talk about women. Richie still loved the ladies and vice versa. Richie was not very philosophical, and except for his fatalism, which would surface from time to time, he was not given to being impressed with himself. He was confident, likeable, and humble—a nice way to be.

I suspected he might have had a genius gene or two, because

39

like most such people, he could refine a lengthy explanation down to something very bite-sized and very understandable. The way really smart people can.

On another occasion, he had just had some more success, the details of which are unimportant. I asked him about it, and he was uncharacteristically forthcoming. He said, "I looked at this thing and thought it would be easier for customers and users if I changed x to y. Then I talked with the engineers and manufacturing guys and asked if it would cost any more to do y instead of x. They said no, and it might even be cheaper. Then I went back to the product manager and asked him, "How come you're doing it this way?" I'm told Richie was referred to, from time to time, as "How come Richie." I can't confirm it, but it fits. He could simply most often see a better way.

Jackie was doing very well. He was recognized and respected, which is just as he wanted things. He could have become a celebrity quite easily, but saw that as total betrayal to his profession and to his own specific calling. Jackie regarded himself as independent and above the battle. Way above.

He was regarded as an investigative reporter of the highest caliber, and his writing was magnificent. It was elegant and it flowed. His articles followed Jackie's Rule: a beginning, a middle, and an end with a punch line logically developed and supported. And Jackie's corollary: if it doesn't have a punch line, don't write it. Don't waste the reader's time.

He had many memorable moments. On one occasion he was asked to attend an important presidential announcement, which was to be given by the then secretary of commerce in Washington, D.C. Jackie was already among the more savvy reporters and knew the announcement was a low-level deal. He was well prepared by the time he rolled into the pressroom.

The secretary greeted everyone and, after the ritual pomp, got down to his announcement. It was, in fact, very low level. Jackie knew that every president had his own way of putting out "leaks" or trial balloons. The secretary was this president's leaker. There was some hot news flying around and a couple of the old hands had traced it to the good secretary. While doing

40

some Q&A, one of the old- timers pieced it together and made it clear that the secretary had had a hand in this item.

The old hand then said, "Mr. Secretary, it looks like you can't keep a secret." There followed a polite and gentle wave of laughter, which assured that everyone in attendance was an "insider." The habit in those days was to rise. If recognized, you could then ask your question. Jackie rose, and being both quite well known and an infrequent visitor to these sessions, was recognized.

"I think," said my friend Jackie, "what my colleague meant to say is that you can keep a secret just fine. It's all those people you tell it to that can't keep a secret."

The session was televised, and while the participants were mostly silent, the TV audience roared. Jackie took another giant step in public recognition. He hadn't meant to call attention to himself, he was just spearing the lapdog press.

Jackie was also well known at all the watering holes where members of the press hung out. He'd been to all or most of them, but figured quickly that not only was there no news at those places, these guys had become hacks and waited for some tipster to drop a hot one on them. To me or close friends, he'd invoke Fred Allen's old line and say, "Those guys couldn't originate a fart after a Hungarian meal."

Jackie got along all right with his colleagues in the press, but he opted to seek the news out rather than hang in a saloon. He was mostly always on the move.

One day, it was a Good Friday, and he was in D.C. It was about 2:00 p.m. on a very nice day. He'd be heading back to New York later that evening, but had some time to put to productive use.

He found himself in a front of a courthouse and went in. The judge had a number of drunk and disorderly and vagrancy cases in front of him. These guys had obviously never taken JJ's course.

The judge, a white-haired Irishman, looked totally harried. He'd obviously heard just about every story that one can imagine, and he looked a bit weary. He wanted to be elsewhere on this particular Good Friday. Somewhat abruptly, he stood up and asked in a booming voice, "And how many of you might be Catholic?"

A few hands went up, so he asked again in a rising voice, "I said, 'How many of you might be Catholic?' " Enlightened owners of sharp elbows poked their neighbors. Heads nodded and an occasional amen was heard. This from a sea of bloodshot eyes and alcohol-saturated pores awaiting a heavy-duty deodorant-dispensing man.

He nodded approvingly. "All Catholics, are ya? That's good, that's very good. If I dismiss all charges against you gentlemen, how many will proceed directly to mass and say prayers for your redemption?"

This group was nothing if not street-wise and pretty quick on the uptake. Those hands that didn't rise immediately were quickly forthcoming following a jab to the ribs from one or more neighbors.

The judge then said, with a hearty bang of his gavel, "All charges dismissed. You are all free to go."

Almost predictably one of the bigger and more slovenly booze offenders proclaimed with great difficulty, "It's a wonderful thing you're doing, your worship. May the . . ." Equally predictably an object of some weight found its way to our speaker's head.

The judge, having regained the floor, repeated, "I said, you're free to go."

They did. Jackie approached the bench as the new repenters fled, and thought he heard a muttering from the judge to the effect of "And sin no more." My friend the journalist, as I used to call him, thought this a great story and handed it in to the AP on the human interest side. It was a typical Jackie Slater story and was received well. My friend could always tell a story, and the judge became known as a guy with a heart in D.C. As I now note again, it was a different time.

The event could have been a one-off, except that Jackie and the judge got to know each other, enjoyed each other, and become close friends. Jackie was to tell me a story of this friendship, but only after the judge had passed away.

It seemed the judge had graduated from law school and returned to his home state to start a practice in his beloved rural setting. Unfortunately, his plans were derailed, as he failed the state bar exam three times. Somewhat dejected, he returned to D.C., where he'd attended law school. There, during the prohibition era, and only because of the connections of a very close friend, he landed a job as an Assistant D.A.

In those crazed days, a Mr. Big bootlegger would be apprehended routinely. Following the front-page headlines, our Mr. Big would, even more routinely, cut a deal and offer up a couple of his "lieutenants" who would actually serve some time.

Enter Jackie's friend the judge. He liked to chew on a cigar and emulate the projected toughness of Edward G. Robinson. He was short on physical stature, but very long on personal courage. He had what we called moxie.

The judge, then an assistant D.A., would grab one of these big-time bootleggers and ignore their offers to cough up some small-timers. "Nothin' doin', you're doin' time," he would say in more than a few memorable headlines with matching photos of our tough-guy assistant D.A. He apparently didn't know, or didn't care, that judges who didn't "play ball" with the mob routinely disappeared in those days.

He wasn't playing to the gallery, but he acquired a bit of celebrity. So much so that the feisty guy from Missouri who followed FDR put him on the District Court in D.C. In not all that many years later, he found himself on the Circuit Court.

Years later, the famous botched Watergate break-in occurred, and a president became unemployed. Years after that, Jackie confided to me that his friend the judge told him the story from his point of vantage.

"It's a funny thing how things work, Jackie," the judge said. I was on the schedule to hear that case. And, mind you, I'm a lifelong Democrat, but I'd been around D.C. long enough to know that both of those parties are always pulling those stunts. I'd have dismissed the case with a smack or two, and that would have been the end of it. I was tired, and wanted to do some fishing with my nephew, so I removed my name from the rotation.

"Sonofabitch, but Long John, who has a hard-on for RMN you can't believe, takes my slot. He gets the case, and, well, you know the rest. By the way, speaking as one, I never believed there was a Deep Throat and still don't. Sometimes, it's like old J. P. Morgan used to say, 'There's always two reasons, the one we come to know and the real one.' In any case, Jackie, when you hear people going on about how the system worked, just give some pause. There were other factors at work."

I stare at Jackie and say, "So when are you going to make this into a book. This has Pulitzer written all over it."

Jackie puts his arm around me and says, "Pal, you never, that is to say never ever, betray or violate a confidence. What was told to me by a friend will never see the light of day." He gave me a look that said, "And you'll never violate that confidence either." I nodded. There was no ambiguity.

And so it went with Jackie. I did take the opportunity to tell him again how much I enjoyed and admired his writing. He was pleased with the sentiment and said so. I went on to tell him that I was aware that I was conscientiously trying to emulate his many writing and speaking skills and I hoped that he wouldn't be offended. He just replied that I was a pal and that was fine with him.

And so it remained, I was a poor man's Jackie Slater. I still wrote and sounded like a guy from Will's Grove trying to be Joe Cosmopolitan.

I also visited with Richie often, sometimes when I was on one of our many "road shows." Those were the debilitating two-week efforts in those days to sell a particular bond issue, but we were both becoming quite mobile in our new and active business settings. One time we were both in Kansas City, Missouri, and grabbed a steak dinner together. The food was good, but it was just great to rally with a pal.

He was still very much on the ascendancy and his small-town USA star, as he called it, was shining as brightly as ever. Like Jackie, he remained well within himself; his business-world celebrity status hadn't changed him a bit.

We'd had a couple of drinks—shooters in our parlance—and we were having a fine time. I told him how pleased I was to hear that he was known as "How Come Richie."

He laughed and said, "That's some PR guy's idea, and it's all right with me. If they'd just look a little deeper, they'd bare all my secrets. Nick, it's just not a big deal. All I do is look at stuff and imagine there must be a better way. That's it. Maybe a little more. I mean customers are paying a lot of money for this stuff, so why not give them the most value we can?

"Maybe I think, gee whiz, life's tough enough," he said. "What can I do, or what change can I make, that might make life a little easier for folks. It's convenience. In this nutso world, it's always convenience." That was at the heart of his collapsible luggage and the plastic dishware ideas—both big commercial successes. "It wasn't a big deal. All I did was to get off my ass and ask some folks if we could change this or change that. Maybe I should be known as 'Richie, life's tough enough, how can I help you?' "

I stared at my pal and just admired the hell out of him. Like Jackie, he was a pal, and he was the guy who had accorded us Pals with a capital *P* status to begin with. He hadn't changed a bit.

I had taken the old envy story to heart years ago and was thoroughly delighted for my two pals. Each in his own way was banging the ball out of the park.

Me, I was still the digger, but I was doing okay. I was running Jackie's and Richie's accounts and doing a good job for them. I was also bringing in a fair amount of new business as well. I wasn't a star like my two pals, but I was doing very well.

What was even better was that the three of us got to go home a few times. We had made some dough and were anxious to compensate for some of the many hardships our parents had endured. They, the parents, remained gracious. They always resisted our efforts, and were most pleased that the three of us had met the expectations borne of their many sacrifices. Nonetheless, we managed to drop off new TVs or refrigerators or the dresses we knew our moms liked before we beat it back to our jobs. We were the happiest of guys in the happiest of times.

On one of our last visits home, the three of us were saying our good-byes at the airport. We noted that our early trips home were by car, bus, and train and we got a little whimsical at the thought.

Richie's plane was first. We did our three-way hug which came more than naturally, and Richie was off.

After watching Richie's plane go wheels up, I spontaneously blurted out to Jackie: "Do you know how proud I am to be your friend?"

"No more than from me to you, Nick."

"It's more than that, Jackie. If it hadn't been for movies, classic comics and Cliff Notes, I wouldn't have known much about history, literature, or the world. I wouldn't even have had any inklings about motivating myself to personal growth. I've probably learned more things about more things from being around you and reading your writings. When I ask myself to name my most important teacher, it's always Professor Slater.

"The truth is I have tried to emulate you, but the bigger truth is that it comes out as a funny mix of elegant Jackie and old-time Nick Drizos."

"That's a nice sentiment and I'm flattered, but hold off on the elegance thing, Nick. Sometimes it flows, but as many times as not, I get all jammed up. As much as not, it's work. Sometimes I want to heave the typewriter out the window." *Yes, he said typewriter.*

"And while we're about it, let me say that I think you're as good as they come, and I regard myself as blessed to have such a good friend. You're out there and you're being the best Nick Drizos you can be and," he added, with a slight laugh, "you're the best Nick Drizos I'll ever know."

Jackie wrote, as I called it, evocatively. He could manipulate the English language as few others. Impressions, pictures, thoughts, it made little difference. And he could set and hold tones. He never had to say, "You know what I mean?" He could match words and phrases to his thoughts effortlessly, or so it appeared. I had great thoughts and the clearest of pictures to relate, but I wasn't Jackie Slater. I would never be Jackie Slater, but he didn't mind that I was trying. I'm sure he was flattered.

I got it, and it felt good. I flushed a bit and then walked him to his gate. In our usual style, I waited till his two-engined prop plane was airborne and then checked the ETD of my flight.

In my quiet moments I reflected on our unique little trinity.

Since age eight, we had indeed been pals. We'd done all the usual things. Sticking up, comforting, sympathizing, doing the sounding-board thing, visiting in hospitals, going to funerals. But there was more. There were uncommon and unspoken ties. I was a lucky guy, especially because Jackie and Richie held similar feelings. It was pretty good progress, I thought.

As I waited for my plane to board, my thoughts went back to Les Horvath and my early days beside him on the trading desk. Every once in a while, he'd give me an upward nod with his chin, which meant, "I want to grab a smoke outside; c'mon with me."

We were sitting on the little patio where we'd sometimes grab a quick sandwich for lunch. "Did you ever notice how the guys on Desk B operate?" he asked.

"Like how?"

"Well for starters, they seem to be in a continuing contest, and they seem to be occupied with their relative standings. And they're not a very happy bunch."

I said I hadn't noticed, but I thought about it, and it made some sense.

I knew he was doing his best to give me one of his lifetime messages, and I cleared my mind of every distraction. "Nick," he said, "you're good at arithmetic. You know if you have some amount of something and you give part of it away, you'll then have less."

I nodded and guessed he had something of impact to say, because he always started with a totally simple notion.

He nodded as well, and continued, "That's true for most things, but not for kindness and generosity of spirit. With those two, the more you give, the more you get back. I'm not talking about willy-nilly donating your way to the poorhouse, don't get me wrong. What I'm saying is that if you're lucky enough to be around good friends, you can't give too much. And if you're a real friend, they'll do the same. Plus you'll be peaceful and happy."

He rose, ground out his Chesterfield in the ashtray, and said, "Does that make sense to you?"

I nodded again. He put an arm around my shoulder, and we returned to our little island of controlled bedlam.

Some thoughts get assigned to special places in one's being, kind of a storage area to hold and safeguard one's personal axioms of life. This one was to stay with me and was to remain prominent.

As was the case, these aphorisms, anecdotes, and stories accumulated and played on each other. During my return flight, I thought about how Les's comments had made such an important impact on me. I think they reinforced my parent's efforts. That's most likely why, each for our own particular reasons, we returned home at fairly frequent intervals. We had some great friends, our parents being the best among them. We had worked diligently and applied ourselves; we were also benefiting from an expansive and opportunity-laden world denied to our parents. We were doing what would become known some years later as "giving back," but it seemed only right and proper. It was a good world, and I was elated that I had these many opportunities to do for myself and for a great circle of friends. One could only look forward to more.

Then dark times came in a place called Vietnam. It turned into being a time when handshakes no longer meant anything, when governments would sell you out and when things, the things I treasured and loved the most, would basically come apart.

I was aware that I was shaking, spasming might be more accurate. I rolled to one side and stared at the green fuzzy light. My focus improved, and I saw that a bedside clock read 5:45 A.M. What next? I could only wonder.

My shakes weren't subsiding. I hit the call button. When I rolled over again, I was greeted by a guy who looked like a doctor and said his name was Jack. *Must be Doctor Jack,* I surmised.

"Hello, Nick. How's it going?"

I was sweating a damp and uncomfortable sweat, but I was feeling pretty alert. "I don't know, Jack. I've had a series of mostly pleasant remembrances, but I'm more confused than anything."

"This is all about you, Nick, so just tell me what you'd like to do now. Would you like to talk or would you prefer some more solitude."

48

I was taken by Jack's literal and sincere bedside manner. I said, "I think I'd like to talk."

"That would have been my choice, Nick. If you become too uncomfortable or tired, just say so and we'll knock off."

I nodded and related my best, and fairly brief, summary of my recollections. While my dreams, or thoughts, seemed to have taken a long time, it only took several minutes to recap them.

"That's good, Nick, you're pretty much right on course. Often times, one has to get back pretty far to regroup before confronting the missing pieces. I've been here a while, and just from observation it was clear that you weren't having any particularly troubling thoughts. You're now back to Vietnam, but you've dealt with that, so I don't expect any significant difficulties as you continue to fast forward.

"As I have tried to summarize for you, you've had two big and genuinely traumatic events; physical damage from the blast and the understandable anguish and torments of the many blank spaces. The first mission for us was to get you strong enough to physically get your mind going again. You're well through the blast, with some loose ends here and there, but you're ready to fill in the last holes.

"I can say this because I know what you'll encounter and you'll manage your way through it on your own terms. That's about the extent of the contributions I can make now. You should go back to sleep. Would you like some assistance, or do you just want to nod off by yourself?"

I glanced at my government-issue clock and noted the time at 6:15 A.M. I'd had only the briefest talk with this guy—this Dr. Jack—but I had the clear notion that returning to REM land would be comforting and rewarding. I opted for another nap.

I had come to like the happy fluid, so I nodded and pointed toward my arm. I'm sure I was once again in what had become a familiar state of peace very quickly.

I've noticed some odd things over the years. One is that I've often awoken from a very happy dream, so happy that I tried to get back to sleep and rejoin myself as unstoppable hero, irresistible lover, adored athlete, or whatever my starring role. I don't recall even one success in these efforts.

This time was different. It was as though the freeze-frame was waiting for me and the conductor was bidding me "All aboard for Dreamland." Richie, Jackie, and I were busy addressing Vietnam. We were all going, there was no question in any of our minds. I'm sure the prevailing thoughts were that our parents had done it. It was something you were called on to do, and we'd do it.

Jackie was borderline 4-F, because his ever-thickening glasses had rendered his sight twenty-two hundred. He was going, however, and wouldn't accept the word no. He had zero doubt that he would be a frontline war correspondent. In his usual style, he prevailed and was awarded a special commission.

Richie remained on his own unique autopilot, and just knew he was going. He went through OCS, emerged as a second john, and was assigned to an infantry unit at Fort Benning, Georgia. He and Jackie overlapped there for a few weeks, because the irresistible Mr. Slater insisted on going through jump school with an airborne unit. He was refused, and for one of a very few times, his demands and pleadings were rejected unconditionally.

He was able to make a deal, however. He was allowed to attend the school as an official observer, was allowed to take the training, and was allowed to make one jump with this class. The unit took him into their outfit as an honorary member, and was pleased when he received his jump medal. Jackie was not going near combat as a leg reporter. A macho thing, but part of the well-earned esprit and, in Jackie's mind, an absolute rite of passage to gain and maintain the respect of these guys. A macho thing indeed, but a rite of passage. No one was going to call him "leg"—a grunt, a non-jumper.

I was an ROTC guy and had been assigned to Fort Gordon, Georgia, as a second looie in the MPs. It was the happiest of coincidences that we were all in Georgia for a few weeks, as we managed to get together on a couple occasions.

We also talked with our folks often, and got to visit home, though, unhappily for the three of us, not together as had been our chosen style over those many years. Our folks, each in their own way, had ominous feelings. They did their best to suppress them, but we each picked up on them. The cherished wisdom of our parents seemed to endure; they had sensed that this conflict would end badly. The thought of Canada or other evasions never surfaced, but they didn't like what they foresaw.

I may have been in dreamland, but I was very aware of fast forward being in effect again. The war was over, at least for the three of us. I spent the entire time in Fort Gordon and was honorably discharged as a company commander. My unit had been scheduled on two occasions to deploy to 'Nam, but each time the orders were rescinded.

As I expected, Jackie was no less than a true frontline war correspondent. If anything, he gathered yet more respect from the honesty of his reports. He drove a course right down the middle and stood in clear contrast to the war shills on the one side and the equally dishonest doves on the other.

Richie spent about half his time out of harm's way in Saigon and the other half in some nasty campaigns. He was highly regarded by both superiors and subordinates. In the last few months of his eighteen-month tour, he sustained a minor wound when his company was ambushed. He received a handful of medals for gallantry during that particular operation and a purple heart for his wound. He was dismissive of the awards, but not out of contempt; he was just never comfortable being cited for heroics.

Richie was home first and, next to his family, I was the official greeter. A few months later, Jackie returned for good. Ironically, I, who had not been sent to 'Nam, was the last to muster out.

We were three happy guys when we got to New York and sat down for a few beers. Well, kind of. We each knew that we weren't going back to work as usual, because we now appreciated there probably was no "usual" anymore. I guess we were, more accurately, three somewhat dour guys who were happy to be together. We had been jolted from what had been a peaceful progression of many years. We were different. We each came to wonder whether the intermittently peaceful post-WW II period was normal or aberrant. We were the same guys, but had acquired what some clinical folks referred to as "baggage." It would

51

remain our continuing query as to whether war or peace was the natural state of mankind.

Richie and I had the easier time of making our latest transition. I, because at bottom, I hadn't seen the horrors firsthand. Richie, because his fatalism effectively diverted him from worrying about much of anything. In his own way he had always been at peace and was always resigned and reconciled to whatever he encountered.

Jackie was a quite different person. While Richie and I managed to come to terms and acquire some equilibrium, Jackie grew despondent. While he never faltered or wavered in his affection and devotion to the troopers and to his country, he manifested a deep sense of betrayal by the government. His post-'Nam writings were almost totally devoted to this theme. The country, however, very much wanted to bury that episode and was not much interested in being reminded. Jackie found himself writing to smaller and smaller audiences.

And he had a far bigger issue. He became incensed at the treatment of the returning Vietnam vets and of the sophistry displayed by the many commentators. He took up the cudgel for the vets, as I imagined he would.

A constant theme he would pound was to the effect that "No matter the cause, no matter the public sentiment, no matter the betrayals, no nation can treat these fine young men as they have been treated. They were called and they served. Now they are owed. The only acceptable attitudes are thanks and gratitude." He gradually proceeded from a "how can you?" to a "how dare you?"

Jackie's audience had shrunk and had become primarily those who already agreed with him. He was, in effect, preaching to a diminishing and tired choir. His personal tone remained gentlemanly, but he gave furious vent to his anger and frustrations via his writing. He also began drinking heavily. Within one year of being home, he had just about isolated himself. The Jackie Slater I had known all my life was gone.

Richie, for his part, retuned himself into what I call a pragmatic fatalist. He returned to his past practices and scarcely missed a beat, a seamless reentry. It was as though he'd taken a

52

leave of sorts, for he was once again putting his deft focus on things that could be done better.

I had grown not to be surprised by Richie's actions. I had learned that my friend whom I had thought to be Mr. Random, was in fact a thoroughly focused individual. But when he stopped by my trading desk to announce that he was headed for the orient for a year or so, my jaw literally dropped.

At first I was speechless, but then I said, "Now let me get this straight. You did a tour over there where people had a specific mission to kill you. Now you're going back?"

Richie is Richie. "Listen, pal," he began, "I don't think those folks over there wanted to kill us anymore than we wanted to kill them. Sure, there are some psychos everywhere, but most folks are pretty docile and just want to live in peace with a few pleasantries. Black, white, yellow, brown. It don't matter; there are more similarities than not."

Well, that was hard to argue on any rational basis, (Richie's genius gene at work again I surmised), so I said, "Okay, pal. What's the game plan this time?"

"We've got two hundred seventy million souls hereabouts. Plus or minus. There's six billion on the planet. Almost a third of them are in Asia; that's two billion folks. Suppose I could find something that each one of those two billion folks would like, and suppose whatever it was cost one buck. That's a couple billion dollars, pal."

"Listen, Einstein, you're the best that ever did what you do, whatever it is that you do, but you're not going to get to two billion people."

"Okay, make it one billion at two bucks a pop."

"Richie, Richie . . ."

"I'm going, pal, it's a done deal. I'll make like Marco Polo, except I'll bring back more than silk, jade, and some recipes for pasta."

In truth, I didn't doubt him for a moment, but I guess I still felt dazed.

"Listen, Nick, you don't have to be brilliant to make out in this world. A bit of smarts with some ingenuity and energy is a good program. I'm off next week. I'll even buy you my good-bye dinner."

We did have that good-bye dinner, and a fine dinner it was. No expense was spared, and he picked up the tab. He wasn't leaving for a few days, and I asked him about his pre-departure plans.

"I do have some other friends you know, pal." Indeed he did, the ladies still loved Richie.

It was getting close to one of our good-bye times, and we began to act accordingly.

"I'll miss you, pal," he said, "but keep doing a good job with my dough, okay?"

"Like the sun will come up tomorrow, Richie, you know I will. You also know that Jackie is in a bad way, don't you?"

"I do, Nick, and I wouldn't peel off if it weren't for the destiny thing. I've gotta do it, it's no less than a calling. I've spent hours, days and weeks with Jackie, just as you have, and I'd never desert either of you. You know that. You also know that we've paired off and tag teamed our way through every problem we've ever had. Whoever was the best for what was at hand took the lead. I'm good, but you're better, Nick, so try to bring Jackie back. I expect no less. I'm not deserting you, I'm just heeding my calling. Besides, you're each owners of RAM, Inc."

"And what might RAM, Inc., be?" I inquired, biting once again on the dangling straight line.

"Well, it's Richie A. McAlister, Inc. 'Today a thought, tomorrow the big time.' "

And Richie took off.

Our once indomitable trio was, for the moment, in disarray. Richie, as usual was on that same fatalistic, maybe deterministic, autopilot and would play out the hand he was dealt. For reasons I could scarcely understand, I believed an invisible spirit would move him along nicely. In the meanwhile, I felt a void as never before.

Jackie was becoming increasingly detached and was going downhill with no abatement. He and I were both single and living in New York, so I was with him every other day. Probably due to faith from the great beyond, I had no doubt that Jackie would get through this tunnel; that's what we had come to call problems—tunnels. Life to us was either blue skies or tunnels. Friends were there to share your blue skies and to help you through the tunnels. And pals would preempt any asking for help. Pals remained the highest human accolade.

What was interesting, if not unique, was that Jackie never got cross with me. He always appreciated my presence. I had expected him to get abusive, but that never happened. So I stayed with my friend as he just became more withdrawn. I marveled at how strongly the bonds of our friendship must have been secured those many years ago. And I was very grateful.

He got to a point where I was worried about his being able to just perform the basic everyday living and survival chores. Not so much that he couldn't; rather, that he'd just lose interest. Without much effort, I got Jackie to move in with me. He was no bother and continued to appreciate my every effort. It was becoming increasingly difficult to get him to talk, however, and that was alarming.

The problem had gotten extreme; I couldn't allow Jackie to make the final slide into total shutdown, so as a last-ditch effort to connect, I started drinking with him. One night we were quite elevated or depressed, and what's the difference anyway, and I asked him what it would take to get my friend back the way he used to be.

Maybe it was because we were both pretty well lit up again that he felt no inhibitions. "Nick," he said, "your friend will always be here. We decided that when we were seven or eight years old. It's just that somebody or something has ripped my heart out. I don't like it, but that's where I am. There's just less of me than there used to be, but your part is in no danger. It's like I have a 'Nick' button which lights up when you start yapping and causes me to be attentive. Anyone else, except you, Richie and some of the old-timers, and, I just don't give a rat's ass."

Then, as we're walking down saloon row on Second Avenue, where there is truly something for every sexual, political, gender, cosmic, or musical persuasion and preference, and most likely without meaning to pile on my severely ragged emotions, he says, "Buy me a drink, pardner."

What the hell, I'm unraveling pretty badly myself so I put on my enabler hat and we duck into Del Bravo's. Talk about eclectic, this was some joint. Mostly guys, and mostly straights. A bunch of sweaty Rugby players, some downtown swells, bankers and lawyers, assorted great pretenders, some neighborhood fixtures, several professional ladies, some college kids, a couple "industrial hostesses," and a few vets seemed to be the cast of folks for this evening's yet-to- unfold human drama. The folks rally in and wait for something to transpire. If the drama isn't forthcoming, you can count on a provocateur or two to stir the pot. It's basically the amateur hour, but maybe life is just so shitbag dull that folks have to provoke something to enhance their otherwise dull dipshit lives. Like I'm so squared away. Anyway . . .

Apparently the Bad Blue rugby team had played and beaten the Chelsea Irregulars pretty good at the Randall's Island facility. Judging from the big-time swagger, a few of the ruggers were mean and looking for a fight. A few guys obviously 'Nam vets, were hanging quietly in a dimly lit corner, just having a few beers and being otherwise almost invisible.

Apparently one of the Bad Blue ruggers had decided his successful day would not be complete without some social commentary, so he, Moose something-or-other, ambles toward the vets. At just a few feet from the vets' table the Moose guy lets fly a string of infantile but truly disgusting epithets for the vets including the timeworn baby killers and the like. He went on to suggest they take their loose-fitting fatigues and foul-smelling selves elsewhere.

One of the vets started to rise, but was restrained by the other three at the table.

The brief silence was then pierced by a clearly audible, "Hey, asshole, you talking to me?"

I didn't have to turn and look to see Jackie shuffling toward the rugger. Nor was I surprised when the Moose guy launched a half swing, half shove, which sent Jackie sprawling to the floor.

Reflexively I stood and, as it was my turn to play Musketeer Two, said, "Hey, dickhead, over here." The Moose guy dawned a look that spoke eloquently, if silently, to this sudden embarrassment of riches—two patsies to bounce around. How good can it get?

I'm not a particularly good duker, but I am pretty savvy. Among other things Les Horvath had taught me was that if I got into it with a bigger guy, I should move toward him, assume a crouching position, and offer the top of my head as a target. The thought was I might get lucky and cause the belligerent to break his hand.

It was a swell idea, but didn't quite work out as intended. The Moose guy blasted me with a good shot on the top of my head such that my next stop was the juke box. I was surprisingly unhurt, so I thought I'd give the master plan another shot.

I was almost on my feet when a guy approached my rugger friend on an oblique to the line joining Moosie and me. He was about five eleven and moving quickly in a somewhat gliding motion. In very short order, he laid three or four bone-crunching blows on the once intimidating leviathan. The Moose quickly sank to his knees, holding his newly crimsoned face.

Just about as suddenly our Kid Galahad wheeled and offered himself to the quieted ruggers, but there were no takers. A couple of his seconds did step forward and drag their dazed and bloodied comrade to relative safety.

The intruder then grabbed me by the arm and pulled me over to help Jackie to his feet. It wasn't clear whether the booze or the Moose's action had put Jackie to sleep.

Our new friend helped me get Jackie into a chair and offered me his card. It said "Danny Ryan" and had a phone number. On the back was some handwriting. He turned to me and said, "Get Jackie to this place"—indicating the handwritten address on the back of his card—"quickly and I mean, quickly. If he gives you any grief, call me and I'll help you. He's just about at rock bottom, you know."

With one more contemptuous look at the rugby goons, we strode to the door and Galahad disappeared.

I woke up the next day with a banging headache and wondered if it had just been two drunks talking to each other. I had no choice; I played my remaining cards. "Jackie, I said, you wouldn't break my heart, would you."

He cocked his head and said in measured tones, "Nick, I'd never do anything to hurt you."

I grabbed him and said, "Jackie, you're killing me. You've got to come back."

"What would you like me to do, Nick?"

"Come with me to a dry-out clinic. I've got an address. I'll even check myself in with you."

I expected an argument, which was not forthcoming. I still don't know if it was because of his fatigue, my stirring oration, divine intervention, or a shot of luck, but he said, "Okay." His body struck a pose of "What the Hell, why not?"

We checked in at the detox center. When asked who the patient might be, two hands were raised. Jackie thought this was funny and snickered.

The program there was simple in the extreme; separation from the offending substances and talk with professionals. Jackie had little, if any, problem from booze withdrawal, but he didn't take to the professionals.

To this day, I don't know how or why it came about, but we were just lounging around between counseling sessions in the outdoor courtyard decked out in our chenille bathrobes. The ones which hollered "escapee."

It was a nice day, maybe an eight plus on a scale of ten, and we were just mumbling about one thing or another. As Crazy Guggenheim used to say on the *Jackie Gleason Show,* "We weren't doing nuttin'. Just hanging around on a nice day."

We're sitting on a couple of Adirondack chairs just taking a break from our dreary schedules when a guy in a wheelchair rolls up.

He nods at us and says, "You're Slater, aren't you, Jackie Slater?" Jackie was more than surprised and says, "I am, and you?"

The fellow says, "Lieutenant Eddie Blanton." He wheels over and extends a well-muscled arm to Jackie. They shake hands and regard each other.

Blanton then pushes himself into a sitting position of attention. This guy has something to say.

"I know you from 'Nam, Jackie. We all knew you. You were

the best. Anyway, my pal Danny Ryan called me and said you'd be dropping in."

Jackie, looking a little puzzled, says "Danny Ryan? Where do I know that name?"

Eddie sits up again, takes a breath to compensate for his obvious discomfort, and says, "Danny Ryan was an officer in 'Nam in the First Cav. He served with distinction and was much admired, loved, and followed by the grunts. He kept many of them alive in some terrifyingly nasty campaigns.

"When he returned he was thoroughly disgusted by the way the nation treated the troopers. He has a big, full-time job in sales, but devotes the rest of his time to one vet cause or another. He also cruises bars where vets are known to congregate to make sure the feather merchants—you know, civilians—don't mistreat the troops. I'm told that nobody messes with him. Anyway, he told me to look Jackie up when he got here, so here I am."

Jackie, as I had come to expect with his sense of manners and decency, says, "Eddie, shall I call you Eddie? Say hello to Nick. He's a pal of mine." And we shake hands.

Eddie says, "I'm Eddie."

After a short silence, Jackie says, "You say you know me, but have we met, Eddie?"

"Oh yeah, several times. I was with the First Cav in 'Nam. We were within an easy grenade toss several times. I'm not long on words, so just let me tell you in person that you were the best there was as far as I'm concerned. I'm a fan."

My longstanding and hard-assed friend was visibly touched and started to speak, but Eddie continued: "Not just for the straight reporting, and not just for your work when you got back. I appreciated that; we all appreciated that. You're one guy who stayed with us. I just like your style. As we say in my hometown, I like the cut of your jib. You're the real deal, Mr. Slater." Then he popped a highball, a salute to Jackie Slater.

I think it was at about the same time that our moist eyes drifted, and we saw that our new acquaintance was an amputee.

He defused the emotion, which was about to be loosed. "Tet offensive," he said, "we blasted them good and proper. They were just about done, but the vote counters saw it otherwise and sold us out but good. What else is new?" He shrugged his shoulders.

I've always known that Jackie would one day write the one book that remains to be written. It would be titled *What to Say When Nobody Knows What to Say*. It would cover all of life's overcoming moments. Deaths, moments of total despair, illnesses, disappointments, discomfort, the events of overpowering sadness when silence rules. I've no doubt that if anyone could do the undoable it would be my friend Jackie. But on this particular day, he was silent.

I don't recall who spoke first, but a lively conversation ensued. Somewhere during this chance meeting, Eddie asked, "So what are you doing here, Jackie?" Jackie was drawn to the ingenuousness of Eddie, and he said, "Well, Eddie, I just got so tired and pissed off at how they all treated you guys when you came home that I jumped into the bottle. That's the short version, and I don't want to be rude, but what are you doing here?"

"You mean, missing a leg and all, shouldn't I be in a VA hospital?"

"Hey, Eddie, I'm not looking for trouble and I don't mean any offense . . ."

"No sweat, Jackie, if that's okay with you, but I did the VA thing. I also jumped into the bottle as you would say, but I came to see things differently. I work here now. I'm not a plant, but I'll confess that I was elated when I got the heads-up from Danny. There's not that many people I want to meet, but you're one of them. Please take that as a compliment."

"I do, Eddie, I do."

"You might be interested to know, Nick and Jackie, I have a couple of prostheses and I can get around quite well. The casual observer wouldn't see me as any different from anyone else in the crowd. But that affords me two opportunities to help with the rehab. First, you have surprisingly good mobility and range in a wheelchair; the technology has come a long way, and it makes me more approachable to the new admittees.

"The first thing is to get them used to all the things they can get done in the chair. Then I can show up walking around. It's not a con, but we try to be sensitive to where they are physically—and usually more importantly—emotionally. Anyway, that's why you'll see me tooting around in my wheels."

He took a breath and regarded us. "So, Jackie, what's your mission, as we used to say."

"I'm here with my lifetime pal, Nick, and I guess I'm trying to shake my demons."

"I hope you do, Jackie. I sincerely hope you do. I also hope that you're not letting that particular demon 'bitterness' get a hold of you. I've been there, and it's the worst. Do you mind if I say a word about this outfit?"

We both nodded for him to go ahead.

"We're pretty basic and straight up. No eight balls in the corner pocket or any jive talk. You've heard that deal about 'Nobody can make you feel bad without your permission,' right?"

We nodded again.

"Well, maybe that's so if little Mary didn't get invited to Sally's tea party, but it doesn't provide much utility around here. Try laying that line on one of our guys, and he'll either try to get away from you ASAP or heave something at you, probably with a few very choice words.

"Hereabouts, we start at the other end. We believe that—unless you're some kind of macho loner—nobody ever makes it without a boost. The best of it is, if you can stay upbeat and stay in motion, you'll find no shortage of boosters around here.

"It's that old thing about kindness. Unlike most other things, the more you give away, the more you have, and like I said, we have no shortage of boosters here."

I almost went down for the count. That was something right out of Les Horvath's Playbook for Life. Eddie must have been around old-timers as well.

"I'm not here to tell you," he went on, "that we get a hundred percent sign- on rate, because we don't. Some of these guys are just about lost souls, but we still do pretty damn good. It really comes down to look forward and go or stay mired and die. There's not much in between. And there's nothing like a good example. Remember Leadership Principle number seven—set the example. Many, if not most us, regard that as number one. So, anyway . . ."

61

I looked at Eddie and we seemed to understand what had to happen next.

"Nick," Eddie said, "would you excuse Jackie and me?"

"Sure, Eddie," and I was gone.

Later that evening at dinner, Jackie said to me, "Nick, why don't you get back to your routine? I want to spend some time here with Eddie and these guys. I think it would be a good thing to do."

"If you wish, it's as good as done," I said, hoping that my beaming pride was not embarrassingly obvious. "How long will you be here?"

"If anything was ever 'I'll play it by ear,' this is one. Nick, I'm happy to be here. Turns out it was a good piece of luck to get smacked by that rugger dipshit. I'll know when it's time. I'll know."

Jackie stayed on at the facility for several weeks. He returned to New York, and we got together for dinner. I was surprised and relieved by his happier demeanor in so short a period, and also by the return of color to his swarthy, nicely complected face. He told me he would be moving back to his own apartment and would be getting back to his life's work. I didn't ask about the particulars of his stay, knowing he'd recount it all at a time of his choosing. I didn't have any fear of a recurring battle with booze, because that was a symptom if ever there was one. In all, it was one of those things that reaffirmed my own personal sense of faith. I could only wonder as to circumstance, serendipity, or something else. What I did know was that we were trying to do something. And even if my friend Paul Craig's admonition not to confuse motion with progress endured, motion helped.

I also recalled a day with Les at lunchtime on the old trading desk. One of his bunch had been working like fury and getting nowhere. He sat down to join us and lamented that maybe he was the old rolling stone that gathers no moss. Les, always one to lend an uplifting hand, said, "So you gather no moss, but you gather momentum, and sometimes that's better." The message was, progress or no, you have to stay in motion to have a chance for something good to happen. Years later Jackie would summarize his apotheosis, as he called it, at Fair Elms. He talked extensively with Eddie. During one conversation, Jackie was going on about the carnage, the horrors and, worst of all, the sense of betrayal he bore. He said he was becoming increasingly incoherent until he was shaking, sobbing, and pounding his legs with his fists.

Eddie just grabbed him, hugged him, patted him, and repeated, "It's okay, it's okay." Maybe that's part of the unwritable book. Maybe it just reduces to being there and to murmurings, which transcend. For Jackie, it was weird, cathartic, magical and mystical, the comfort given him by a man who had endured barbarism but refused the easy and understandable paths to self-pity and bitterness. Eddie and Jackie later made a few trips to visit with other vets. Eddie reminded him that they remained divided into two basic groups. Some would look forward, while others were mired in the past. Eddie regarded this as the fundamental choice to be made every day of his life, and he reaffirmed that in his brief but daily prayers. The major mission was today.

Jackie has come to terms with several problems. First, he had been cursing himself and second-guessing himself for not foreseeing the stateside sellout of Vietnam, but the vets got him off that surprisingly quickly. The implicit message was that if these seriously wounded guys could pull themselves together then Jackie would be a small man indeed not to follow their leads. In short order, he threw in with the forward-looking group and apply himself to two areas. First, to support a number of veteran organizations and, second to be a sentinel against such future debacles. He would often repeat Eddie's homely, but apt, cliché that "You can't make much headway with both eyes on the rearview mirror, but you'd better take a backward glance now and again to remind yourself of where you've been."

In not very long, he was welcomed back to a Jackie Slater-starved world and was soon again a syndicated columnist. He published his always superbly directed and masterfully composed comments in his column *In Other Words*. It was so well received that he was accorded the rarest of tributes in his world. The only acknowledgement of the author was the initials "J.S." at the bottom of the column.

One of the new Jackie columns attracted almost global interest, leaving no doubt that once a master, always a master. While he continued to heed Eddie's advice, and also Satchel Paige's, about not looking back, he had made one exception, if there were an important object lesson to point up. He focused on the 1961 inaugural address and specifically upon the "Ask not what your country can do for you; ask what you can do for your country" segment. Applying his own unique sensibilities and powers of observation, he urged his readership not to choose between these two, but contemplate both questions continually. He then posed a third.

It began: "Ask what you can do to become the person of greatest wisdom and kindness." He then developed the notion that as the citizens of a United States, but, more importantly a united people, that fulfilling one's highest calling would be a better choice than the "ask (and ask nots)" implied.

He also wrote columns that exalted the triumphs of the underprivileged, probably as much to encourage the vets as anything else.

During this period, Richie was making major headway. We talked from time to time; he still preferred the spoken word. He was a busy guy, and his calls came from one place or another half way around the world. That was Richie, the ever- moving ball of energy and imagination.

Richie called me after about ten months of absence and advised that he would be in New York for a few days. He had a lot of business to attend to, but his first priority was to reunite. I called Jackie, who was now operating out of North Carolina. He claimed that it was a peaceful place, conducive to thoughtful writing and that when he had to chase a story, air travel was pretty easy. I always thought, but never mentioned, that it was also close to the airborne guys at Fort Bragg.

The date was set, and we rallied at eight A.M. at Richie's hotel. We were served an elegant breakfast in his room overlooking Central Park. Jackie and I had stayed very current with each other, so our get-together was dominated by Richie wanting to hear the latest from us and vice versa.

Richie had missed most of Jackie's collapse and all of his recovery, but he insisted on hearing it all from Jackie. And Jackie obliged.

Richie squared up to Jackie and said, "My reaction to 'Nam couldn't have been more different from yours, and I've thought about it no small amount of time. In the end, I think I just have lower expectations from my fellow man than you do, Jackie. Does that make any sense?"

Jackie said, "So far as it goes, Richie, but I think I've moderated my views and my general outlook. I used to think of mankind as an orderly mosaic in which most people are interested in contributing to an inherent greater good. I've since been disabused of that general notion, and now try to let the daily goings-on fit as they will."

Richie nodded, then stood and said, "I want to ask you two something, and I want a totally honest answer. Deal?"

"Deal," we responded like the chorus of frogs we had become years ago.

"Okay, you know that you are my two dearest friends in the world."

We nodded.

"Jackie, do you think I ran out on you when you . . ."

Jackie said, "Not once, not ever did I have any such thought. I'd have been beyond disappointed if you hadn't set out as you did. I am even somewhat disappointed that I had to chew up so much of Nick's time." He looked fully at me.

"We've had a pretty good way of handling our problems over the years, and mine resolved about as well as it could. I know to a certainty that had it been one of you, we would have done things just about the same way. Just so you know, I was never into the 'woe is me' thing. My deal was that I had been focused sharply on my writing for so many years that when I found myself in the postwar days, I was just overwhelmed with issues to address. I was lost and had no bearings.

"Nick did exactly the right thing; he kept me moving, and he tried to keep me engaged. In the end, we had some good luck. Two of you wouldn't have been any better, so don't give it another thought."

"Straight deal?" asked Richie.

"Straight deal," said Jackie.

Letters and phone calls aside, we had much to talk about and we got to it. I noticed once again that we had our own style of conversation. I've been in all manners of gatherings, business and social, where it seems everybody is taking a deep breath and waiting excitedly to talk. We were always just about the opposite, totally engaged toward which of us was being the storyteller of the moment. We had our own unique style, or group norm, as high-priced management consultants call it.

Jackie and I were current with each other, so we gave short recaps for Richie's benefit. He was pleased that we were both doing well and settling into a world far removed and far different from that of only a short while ago.

"Not bad for three guys from a small no-name town," Richie concluded.

"Not bad at all," said Jackie looking at Richie, "but how about fleshing out the real news behind those post cards and notes you've been lobbing in?"

"Well, it's a bit of a story. Are you up for one?"

A needless question, Jackie and I both thought. If there was one thing the three of us loved, it was stories—especially from one of us. We laughed, and Richie got the nonverbal answer.

"As you two know, better than anyone, I was never much of a detail guy, but I was always pretty big on picking up on emerging trends and on ways to move them along."

Had Richie been applying for a position somewhere, that terse remark would have been a compelling resume.

"Well, war brings its well-known horrors, but it also, in its own perverse ways, brings opportunities. One of them this time around was the jet plane and the industry that has sprung up around it. It doesn't make the world smaller, as the ad guys like to say, it just makes it more accessible.

"People and things will begin to move as never before. I see this as a long term and irresistible trend. We'll still have all manners of land and sea transport, but jets and other aircraft will cause changes as never before. I think that's hard to argue, so that became great thought Number One.

"I also tend to do better in places or situations where my

ideas have a shot at making some impact. I was lucky in the states, but I really didn't do much that some others won't do better. I could probably get senior in some big company and play marketing mastermind for a while, but I prefer being closer to the actual business. Plus, I tend to like and relate to working guys more than to execs and other functionaries. It's not that I dislike some folks, I just like others more.

"Those primitive thoughts made me focus on the Far East, or as it's now called—the Pacific Rim. It's densely populated and has no shortage of resources, natural and otherwise. Basically, it's an undeveloped land of vast opportunity characterized by only the most primitive logistics. Plus certain lands over there are as breathtakingly beautiful as anywhere on the globe.

"I didn't distinguish myself in Economics, but I did glom onto the notion of comparative advantage, that every nation or country does some things very well—maybe better than anyone else. Lastly, except for some Brits and foreign nationals who have become good international traders, there just aren't many non-Asians—especially Americans—over there.

"I began to convince myself that there could be some swell opportunities for a young guy with some new ideas and a bit of energy. I often wondered if I was just hyping myself, but finally it got to be time to fish or to do something else.

"I spent the first several months headquartered in Bangkok and got to know the local business guys there. Nixon had opened China a bit, and I established relationships there as well. In not too long a time I was getting to know, and more importantly, getting to be known by a number of folks.

"The comparative advantage thesis was being borne out constantly. What was also being borne out was Bennett's words to Nick way back when."

"You mean people do business with people they know, like and trust?" I said, half-amazed.

"Yeah, Nick. Remember, 'People do business with their friends.' And I mentioned that just so you know I was paying attention to you."

The warmth rising in me could only give rise to a smile.

Richie stopped to have a sip of coffee, and Jackie said, "As

Scotty Kinloch used to say, 'Richie lad, what a hot shit you turned out to be.' "

God, but I enjoyed these times.

"You want to do something else now?" asked Richie.

"Absolutely not," said Jackie.

"Okay, but tell me when you get weary of this." And he continued: "While I was getting to know the locals, I was also talking with a variety of transportation companies. I began to do no more than coordinate things and I became known as a helpful problem solver. Sometimes the problem was as simple as a guy who couldn't physically move something, so I'd get more people. Later it was about getting some machinery. In these endeavors the medium of exchange was trade. My first sales came about from swapping ideas for goods and then trading them elsewhere. RAM, Inc., started doing its first business.

"Most of these engagements, as we used to say in NYC, were local things for local use. In time I began to meet some folks who made things. They were manufacturers, but didn't know it, and they had market opportunities of which they were unaware.

"In pretty quick time I forged some alliances with some of these guys who made very basic but very serviceable products. I then got around to getting to know other traders and agents for foreign companies. Packaging was identified as an early issue, and I helped start a few little companies who could get these products ready for shipment.

"By the end of the first year, RAM employed about twenty-five people and had associations and relationships with several companies. We were just about in the black, and opportunities were surfacing faster than my abilities to address them."

Richie also discovered something in Asia that he had probably harbored for many years. He just doesn't think it's very difficult to excel, especially in service-oriented businesses. And it's made easier by the pitifully low motivation of so many, those whose work efforts and ethics are guided by the question "What's the very least I have to do?"

I know Richie probably as well as anyone. My take on his success is something like this. Since so many of the unmotivated were his competitors, it didn't seem that difficult to excel. And he did. Moreover, and here's the happy part, a good boss can motivate his employees to excel more easily than you might think. In the process, the given employee usually ends up on a fast track to promotions, more money, higher self-esteem, and generally becomes a much more attractive person. And Richie was just a natural, no-bullshit stem-winder. Folks liked doing stuff with him and for him. And he did his best to always treat everyone respectfully. One could go on and on, but there are simply people who are natural leaders, and Richie McAlister was one, and a damned good one at that.

"To keep things simple, I had a big world map on my modest office wall. There were a number of trade patterns, which were obvious. Some north-south and some east-west. A few months back, I started reading travel statistics and saw what I imagined could only be a long-term pattern of growth.

"I had already become a freight forwarder and import-exporter, but I would have some important guesses and decisions to make. The big worldwide companies would be here and would quickly capture any and all large-scale business, so the industrial side would not be viable for me.

"My relationships with local manufacturers and my skills in packaging and presentation stood to be a handsome little business. The local side was also where I was best directed because I was fortunate to be assimilated into most business locations. Part was because I have come to like and appreciate both Buddhism and Hindu. While they have their whack-a-doodle aspects, just like ours, there is a core of peace about them, which I find attractive.

"And a funny sidebar. The name 'RAM,' which was just about accidental, played very well there. It was the ending of many Hindi names and is easy to pronounce. And, the way they pronounced it, it just happened to rhyme with the Buddhist chant 'ommm.' In fact, I am known as RAM. Like 'Rommmm.' I haven't heard 'Richie' in a long time now."

"I also got to know the way the folks operate over there. The business practices range from straight up one hundred percent honest to totally deceitful and not just a few variations in between. I've managed to cope with them as well as with the corruption.

"They and I agreed to honor each other's practices. Their practices end at the entrance to my facilities, and my practices end at the entrances to theirs. In between we take care to respect each other's priorities and idiosyncracies. It seems to satisfy the important mutual respect issues and it seems to work pretty well. In addition, all the RAM personnel, excepting RAM himself, are locals. I also attend all ceremonies and rituals when invited. Mostly we try to focus more on our many similarities as people than on our differences.

"I've also gotten to learn a bit about their banking and financing systems. They are primitive, but I can't imagine it will be too long before all the U.S. and European big boys increase their presences dramatically."

"So, is that the heading for RAM for the future?" I asked.

"Well," said Richie, "I don't think so. I think it will be a nicely growing and prospering business for quite a while, but I've had to make a decision.

"The personal touch which I've been lucky enough to establish will serve me well on a nice, but limited basis. Sooner or later, and probably sooner, the big boys will organize things, and little guys like me will be the exceptions.

"As Groucho would have said, it's time to play 'You Bet Your Company.' It is, and I've decided to roll the dice on personal travel and some select services for small businesses. It came down to carving out some areas where the big boys won't trample me and where I can add something of value. And the word convenience will be in there—front and center.

"It's just starting now. I've had some encouraging, but not conclusive, results. We've opened six offices primarily in vacation travel destinations and in a couple business cities, Hong Kong most prominently.

"The long-term pattern is going to be driven by currency and the irresistible bargains offered in the rim. Purchases by travelers are becoming increasingly important to the local areas, but getting them home ranges from a nuisance to very difficult.

"Anyway, that's where we are, and that's my story."

70

"All hail RAM," said Jackie, with his coffee cup raised.

Before long it had gotten past noon.

Richie said, "I haven't been here in a while. Are you guys up for some air and a little stroll?" We were, and down to street level we went.

We decided to head south and take a trip to the observation tower on the Empire State Building. We walked and chatted about all manners of things from the profound to the trivial.

Richie was anxious to hear about this guy or that girl and we obliged to the best of our knowledge. We talked a bit about politics, sports, and other low-level things. While we were all doing pretty well, we were somewhat restrained and just didn't feel like spending much time on darker events. And that made some sense. This was our time.

So there we were. Richie the well traveled, Jackie the well spoken, and Nick the digger. An odd trio, but a happy trio.

For all of our collective savoir-faire, we would have been taken as first-time visitors when we got to the observation deck; it was exhilarating. Jackie would have framed it more eloquently, but exhilarating will suffice.

We strolled up to and through Central Park, noting the wonderful weather. At about two o'clock, we were attracted to an outside bar set next to a little waterfall.

"Who's up for a beer?" I inquired.

We entered this little parklike setting, found a small table, and ordered some beers. I think we all found it a bit transformational. The well-known noise and push-and-shove of the big city seemed to abate somewhat. Thoughts, which were inhibited by the ambient goings-on, seemed to rush forward. We could read each other pretty well, and I think we felt a bit sentimental.

"We're different," I started.

"We are indeed, Nick, we are indeed," said Jackie. "We came along at what history will record as a very special time, some say an inflection point."

"As you say, Jackie," added Richie, "and we were wrenched into another time altogether. There was no way we could ever been prepared for it, so my take is that we made it through, and I'm thankful to be with my pals."

Pavlov couldn't have been more evident. The glasses clinked and we had a moment's relief.

"I don't mean to be like a dog with a bone who won't let go," I piped up, "but we are different. We'd be different anyway if only because of the passage of time. And we are well different in some ways because of 'Nam. Those aren't the differences I'm talking about.

"I think I'm talking about the weight of wisdom, the stuff we've learned and acquired by just moving along and doing our best. And, Jackie, I know you subscribe to the 'no preoccupation on the rearview mirror thing,' but what I really wonder about is whether we'll be as good as our parents were."

"First of all," said Richie, "it's as good as they are. While we're counting what's right, all six are alive and well."

I nodded and said, "Absolutely, and I don't mean to speak for you guys either."

Jackie said, "You do, Nick. I'm sure Richie feels the same. Right, Richie?"

"No question," said Richie, "of all the things we could argue about, that's not one of them. Case closed."

"What I'm talking about, and I need some help because it gets jumbled, is the weight of the wisdom we've acquired. I think constantly about the way they guided us along, probably more than they'll ever know. I worry that I'll not find the words . . ."

Jackie sensed that the sentimental one was losing his grip and put an arm around my shoulder. "That's not the rearview mirror you're looking into. You're looking into yourself, and that's not only okay, it's admirable. And what's wrong about trying to drive yourself toward admirable qualities?"

"Thanks, Jackie, but you want to know what passage recurs and recurs to me?"

"You know I do, Nick."

Well, it's Fitzgerald's last line from Gatsby: 'So we beat on, boats against the current, borne back ceaselessly into the past.' What's that all about."

"First, Nick, that happens to be writing at its apex. Second,

72

and I'm not being a wise-guy critic, it means whatever you want it to mean. There are good reasons to evoke memories, and yours are okay with me."

"Me too, pal," said Richie.

"Okay, I'll let it go, but how come all the current literature and plays is about guys whose parents were miserable frauds and who scarred their kids unspeakably?"

"Nick, I've spent a lifetime on those themes, and my only honest answer is that I don't know. What I do know is that I choose to find people of kindness and to tell their stories. I am in the business of telling people's stories through them, but not speaking for them and I won't start now. If you asked me my opinion, however, I'd advise you to turn your worries elsewhere. We have done well by our folks and vice versa. Do you really wish to ask for more?"

I just nodded and put my head on Jackie's shoulder. I was still confused, but I felt better as I recalled Bette Davis's last line in *Now Voyager* about not asking for the moon while we have the stars. I think that's what Jackie meant.

We've always been pretty good about getting back to equilibrium. This time Richie was the agent of remediation.

"Hey, pals, we've been gassing away pretty good. It's getting late and this is my last night ashore with you guys. Dinner is at seven-thirty at Chez Something-or-Other. I've got the address somewhere here, so why don't we rally there at seven for cocktails. After that, I'm gone for a while."

So we adjourned. Richie grabbed a cab, and Jackie and I walked to my apartment to change into "grown-up" clothes and revitalize ourselves.

Dinner was all that I had anticipated. We were all over the place and caught up on stuff we thought we had long forgotten. I managed to stay away from my creeping nostalgia, probably due in no small measure from the pre-dinner cocktails and the swell burgundy ordered by Richie the bon vivant.

Richie was still confidence and relaxation personified. He really liked working people and they liked him. The service was great, and it couldn't have been a nicer setting. Nor could I have been happier to see my two pals on top of their games. Nonetheless my wistful side was grabbing me again, and I sensed a tunnel ahead. No tangible reason, just one of those feelings, but I stayed with the program.

We were just a little bit sprawled in our comfortable seats, and each of us probably thinking about releasing our belts a notch. My after-dinner Drambuie was spreading its familiar warmth through me when Richie lightly slapped the table and declared, "Well, pals, it's time to get back to our respective deals."

We were in the grand entrance of the restaurant when Richie said, "Wait here a moment. I'll be right back." He went out the front door at a brisk pace while Jackie and I could only wonder: What next?

"He's a pistol, isn't he, Nick?"

"As we say up here, Jackie, he's a hot apple."

Our jaunty friend strode back and smiled his best Richie smile. He was holding a disposable camera, beckoning the maitre d', who almost sprang on him. I think they had become financial partners during the course of our stay.

"Henri, mon ami, would you be so kind as to take a few snaps of my pals and me? We need a remembrance of your beautiful surroundings."

"Bien entendu," came the snappy response.

We assumed our familiar pose, the tall Richie standing between us with his long arms on our shoulders. I think the man took about a dozen shots. Richie's aura must have been in effect, because no one seemed the least bit annoyed or distracted by the uninvited light show.

We said our farewells and recited our many good-luck wishes. We embraced one more time and then Richie stepped into his awaiting limo. We all waved till he turned a corner.

Jackie and I kind of gawked at one another, but then went back to my place.

We talked a while, but quickly noticed that it had been a very full day.

I took Jackie to the airport the next morning, reminding myself that life goes on.

Roger, life goes on. Even in this, what would Richie call it, whack-a-doodle hospital. Nonetheless I really enjoyed seeing Jackie and Richie again. For real or virtually, it didn't matter. I had gotten pretty good at reentering my dreamscape, so the 101 and I downshifted to all engines stop. What do I do for a living anyway?

I'm well rested, I'm ambulatory, and I'm feeling okay. Unless someone has another plan, I'll be getting back to my trading desk pretty soon.

4
The Raj, Ben, Invictus, and the Spooks

October 23rd

As I have noted, bond trading is a good way to make a living. And it's fun. It's good for people like me who are curious and who like puzzles. Whereas common stock is something you buy with a view toward selling at a higher price, there is no guarantee of a favorable outcome. A bond, by contrast, is a financial instrument, which includes, most notably, a promise to repay the amount of the bond and which pays interest while you await repayment. Part of the fun is assessing the worthiness of the underlying promise, or "the credit" as we call it. They come in all qualities, or grades, and for the most part they are less risky securities, being "senior" than common stock, sometime called "junior securities," of the same company. The standard bond has a face amount, an interest rate, and a stated maturity, or maturities, setting out when the bond's face amount will be repaid. But strange things can happen between here and there, and it can get a bit complicated.

The key word is "trading." The bonds I deal with, for the most part, are issued publicly, and are traded on various exchanges. Generally, prevailing interest rates are the most important external factor and are most indicative of whether bonds will gain value or lose value. As it occurs most usually, when interest rates go up, bond prices/values go down. And vice versa. More importantly, small interest rate movements can cause relatively big price movements in some bonds. And if you own several hundred million dollars worth of a particular bond issue, the smallest changes in value can be big stuff in dollar terms. So when you hear some folks haggling over a fraction of one percent in interest, it's usually a big money deal.

Without getting overly arcane, different people can own bonds for very different reasons. A guy with five million bucks, for example, can be very happy to hold some six percent muni bonds for the long term. This guy is very pleased with the three hundred thousand dollars of tax-free annual income. He isn't very concerned with the up-and-down changes in value of the bond itself; he's a long- term holder for income. I deal frequently in high-grade, tax-free bonds, so that guy would have a very handsome stream of tax-free income. Not bad. A happy fellow.

There are also people and institutions who, for various reasons and objectives, are vitally concerned with the underlying value of the bond. These guys, as opposed to long-term holders, are interested in how the bond "trades" from time to time and how to realize gains from the changes in the value of the bond itself. This kind of investor is a trader. He cares more about the value of the bond from time to time than the interest income the bond produces. As that Russian comic said: "What a country!" There's a market for more tastes than not. These days you can make a bet on almost anything.

I do both of these basic alternatives. I have several clients who are interested almost solely in income. These folks usually have several million dollars of principal and are looking for a steady income. I also represent those who wish to basically make bets on which way interest rates are going. They tend to trade fairly frequently.

Either way, it's a challenging deal. Even though the basics are fairly straightforward, there are enough "moving parts" to produce a pretty intricate business. Plus computers have entered the fray and further broadened the sometimes almost bewildering array of financial products called bonds. Then, throw in people. Whether you're buying for the longer term or intending to trade at fairly frequent intervals, you're going to be dealing with someone on "the other side of the trade." If you're buying, you have to find a seller, and vice versa. That's why there are many folks like me in this business.

Like any other business, there is a hierarchy, which is well known to the pros. Moreover (remember?), like any other business, one must pay his dues—the nicer way of saying "getting screwed a few times" before you become a pro. After a while, pretty much everyone knows who wears what color hats, who are the good guys, who are the dummies, who should be avoided. It's like most other businesses. Everyone knows who's "good."

I'm probably recognized as being near the top of the pile. I know what I'm doing, most of the time, my word is solid, and I don't go for too many hip fakes. I also recognize some outstanding peers. One such is Raj Maphal. Raj is in fact the Indian equivalent of a nickname, short for a hopelessly longer handle. And one does not pronounce the "ph" as an "f". To us, it would sound like Raj Mapal. It would rhyme with Taj Mahal, except for pronouncing the "p."

Raj is an excellent trader whom I came to know through the ordinary course of business as well as from serving with him on some industry association boards and committees. Our mutual appreciation of Indian cuisine only strengthened what became a very natural friendship.

A native Indian who emigrated here several years ago, he finds Florida very much to his liking and is now a U.S. citizen. I'm pretty smart, but in most instances, I'm intuitively smart. That is, I usually get to the right answer quickly and then reassure myself over a longer period of deliberation. Over the few years of our acquaintance, I correctly assessed Raj as being at least one level up from me; he is smartly intuitive. He can give the impression of being intuitive, of flying somewhat blind, but he has usually divined the correct answer, or answers, well before he speaks or acts. Unlike others in this star-system business, he would never be taken for haughty, imperious, or condescending. He's the real schmazz.

Our friendship was based initially on our profession. More times than not when one of us was trying to execute an assignment, we would usually call the other looking for "the other side" of the trade. It later became routine for us to refer new clients to each other, especially when it was apparent that personal chemistry or the given investor's objectives would be better served elsewhere. In my case, if a client doesn't have total trust and confidence in me, he's gone. And so am I.

After not very long, we settled into having dinner together a couple times a month. This became a pattern, which was rarely interrupted over the past few years. We seemed to move effortlessly into conversations, which, while social, would tend toward uncommon subjects.

I recall one in particular a few years ago concerning a celebrity who had severely damaged his spinal chord and had become paralyzed. We were enjoying one of the many curry dinners he had proposed.

"Why can't the spine be reconnected electrically, or electronically?" I said, more than asked.

"How so," he inquired with his usual politesse and curiosity.

"I don't know, but it seems that the spinal chord carries impulses from the brain to particular body parts and that these impulses govern motion," I went on.

"That is my understanding as well, my friend."

"Well, in the same way that a severed wire, or wires, can be spliced or reconnected from source to terminus, why not with the spine."

"And you would propose?"

"I don't know that I propose anything, but available technology does include computers, microsurgery, and fiber-optic filaments, many of which can be bundled into a space much smaller than a human hair's diameter. Why then couldn't connections be made from one side of the break to the other? Even if there were thousands of such connections, why couldn't they be reconnected with high-speed computers and high-resolution optics? Much like using a light to figure out which two ends of a wire complete a circuit."

"An interesting thought. I have had similar thoughts, but I've gone down the road of genetic medicine. That maybe one day, vital organs and body parts will be replicated genetically. That there would be a branch of medicine, maybe sooner than we think, called organ replacement, or some such, but your remedy could be more immediate as it would use existing capabilities. How would you propose to bring this idea to the fore?"

"I don't know. It's one thing to have a potentially exciting thought; it's quite another to sustain it to transformation into something useful. I just get these notions from time to time. I can observe a problem and I can imagine a solution, but connecting the many dots—my particular personal cliché—in between is clearly beyond me. Maybe that's why I trade bonds."

The conversation turned to other matters, and we retired after another pleasant get-together. We hadn't accomplished anything, but I felt a sense of renewal from talking again with my friend.

One other dining occasion with Raj was memorable. It was informative as usual, but I gained a bit of inner peace as well. We had been discussing mankind's greatest historical innovations over a period of several weeks. After many discussions we were virtually agreed on our top-ten list of the greatest accomplishments. Not in the same order, but that might come later. Like most such lists, the printing press and radio ended up near the top. The printing press, although ancient in present context, still remains a wonder.

Prior to old Gutenberg, A could tell B or the monks might get together and make ten copies. Thus intelligence spread at the pace of that slow-moving shelled animal. Then came the press and the first knowledge explosion. Incredible. Brilliant.

In like manner, once radio came, all manners of harnessing the electro-magnetic spectrum were just functions of time. Who were these guys?

We were each in our own states of admiration of these many inventions. For my part, I was less interested in the particular invention itself than in the state of mind, or the motivation, of the inventor. What force drove them? Did Newton wake up one day and declare he was going to invent calculus? I posed this to Raj.

Shifting a bit in his chair, with his trademark calm over his face, he said, "A marvelous question, my friend, why or what indeed. I agree that the motivation is at least as inspiring as the subject matter. I too have thought of this very point."

"And you have an opinion?"

"Not in so many words, but I am drawn to the body of

thought that there is no such thing as invention. There is only discovery. All the knowledge there ever was will always be. There is no invention, only discovery."

I was pretty sure that this was his considered opinion, masked very cleverly by his genuinely authentic humility. Appreciative of his efforts to avoid pedantry and lecturing, I took his point.

"How do you imagine this discovery works in practical terms?" I asked. "Do you suppose that most of us actually use only four or five percent of our brains and that, therefore, these great steps are taken by those who can employ six or seven percent?"

"That might be the case, but I am more persuaded that it is state of the particular brain, maybe the state of the particular person, than the size of a given brain."

"And this aspect of the theory you find attractive, how does it play out?" I inquired.

"I am persuaded, my friend, by the notion that some brains, or perhaps souls, are very much at inner peace and thus very receptive to knowledge. It's hardly a new theory and no more than many established religious philosophies have espoused for centuries. We speak of the brain, and that may be apropos, but some souls are simply more receptive to external phenomena than others. We are all instruments. Some more attuned to that which surrounds us. It may be that part of what we call knowledge is simply mapped into us. Perhaps it is mapped into all of us, but few of us can actually discover our very selves. It could be that we are all receivers and each one tuned differently. I am sure I do not know the workings, but I do believe there is truly very little invention. Discovery is, to me, the far stronger argument. And I am further persuaded that each of us can increase our potential for such discovery by clearing our minds and hearts to allow such knowledge to invade us."

"You seem to like the word 'persuade,'" I noted. "It would seem as though you have spent more than a little time on this matter."

"Probably no more than you, Nick. While I am about it, where did you get that notion about spinal chord repair? I could suggest that you merely posed the questions to yourself and let your mind work unfettered. Or let me ask you this: how many times have you struggled with a problem only to yield to sleep. And of these many times, unless you are very different from most of us, how many times did you awake refreshed with a workable solution. Or, conversely, how many times have you tortured yourself with a problem and retired with your solution carefully written down on paper. And, of these times, how often were these great solutions indecipherable scribblings?"

"More than a few in both cases," I responded.

"You are no more than human, Nick," my friend said.

The idea of discovery over invention stayed with me—most profoundly. I imagined Beethoven in a totally relaxed state letting what would later become his revered "Moonlight Sonata" just drift over him. Or Gutenberg, or Marconi, or Cole Porter or Michelangelo. It didn't matter; I began to think in Raj's terms. It wasn't brilliance; it was being at peace and in tune with oneself that really permitted the unimaginable and the unthinkable.

As a fun kind of thing, following my many dinners with Raj, I began to read some of Einstein's work and found it was more like poetry and prose than astrophysics.

He—Einstein—would propose something, some astral notion, and then add "as you would expect." Right! As you would imagine, as you would expect. As who would expect? Your regular genius, that's who! At the same time I came to believe that Raj wasn't referring to this theory or that proposition. These were his own original thoughts. Once again, he was too thoughtful and too humble to assert his own genius. My regard for this very unusual man continued to grow.

During one of our more whimsical dinners we got into the notion of the hereafter. Predictably Raj was attracted to the Nirvana thesis, and, per usual, his comments were edifying and soothing.

"Do you believe in spirits?" I asked of my friend.

"I hadn't thought of that, Nick. What are your thoughts?"

I gave him the mercifully short version of Drizos's lectures on the Great Beyond.

"Basically," I said, "life does end with the white flash, which many near-death folks have observed. It's like turning off the TV when the white dot rushes to the center of the screen. Sometimes the final jolt is strong enough to launch the soul. These people become celestial. In other cases, the final force is insufficient and these folks remain in our proximity. Some are by nature helpful and beneficent, so they become good spirits. Others have a nasty bent, maybe being pissed at not reaching escape velocity, so they cause problems for us folks. The others just loll around and giggle. Something like that."

Raj chuckled politely. I was a bit embarrassed. I asked for the check.

But I grow weary again. The dots I am being directed to connect clearly include curiosity, India, and my friend Raj. I choose to follow Hal's advice again. Enough of the thing called recovery for a while. Sleep looks good.

I had been introduced to Gail whom I had come to know as "Nurse 1". She advised that I've been "in and out" for the past couple days. She is, in fact, as lovely as I had imagined, and is probably correct. My sense is that I've been in a dream state for a while as my old friends Murk and Clarity have been beating me about. The swirl has been ongoing and, while I'm making some progress, confusion has had the upper hand.

"You have a visitor," announced Gail, in her cheery but professional manner.

"Hello, Nick," said the intruder in an impressive but friendly voice. My recognition patterns quickly identified the speaker as Adams. I think he called himself "Ben." It was an easy recall, because the voice was Alan Ladd from the climax of *Shane*—the best Western ever, not that *High Noon* was second rate. Or *Red River* third-rate.

It was an impact voice. It was Alan Ladd, no question. He should have been saying: "So you're Jack Wilson, I've heard of you." This, of course, being the prelude to the best gunning down of a bad guy in celluloid history. Jack Palance asks: "What have you heard, Shane?" Shane replies: "I've heard you're a low-down Yankee liar." The rest was, is, and remains cinematic greatness.

Alan Ladd died young, too young, but that voice had worked itself into my longer term memory and was speaking to me right now. Alan Ladd had become the symbol of fair play to me as well as to my two pals. The notion of fair play was whiffy to a lot of guys, but to us three it was the bedrock on which all would stand or fall. And it has stayed that way for almost forty years.

"How are you, Nick, we've been worried about you," said my neo-Alan Ladd.

"I know who you are, Adams, so spare me the happy talk and the soft con."

"Listen, Nick, it wasn't supposed to go this way. Happily, the docs and staff will have you together quickly and life will go on. And, besides, my name is Blake."

Gail intervened and informed my visitor to cease and desist and that it was time for my sleep-inducing medication.

I thought that a good idea and bid my visitor a peaceful good night. My last thought was of Raj and to be at peace, to let it go wherever it is going.

I woke on October 23rd feeling more bruised than I had been a few days ago. Apparently this is the price of acknowledging the conscious state and letting go of the supporting drugs and pain killers. JoAnn, Nurse 2 and a total looker, was on duty. I'm pretty sure she's Italian. And what a shape. Like Gail, she looked like she was poured into that simple but totally elegant outfit. I was reminded of W. C. Fields who once described the object of his very intense affection as "having a figure like a roped-in mattress." We Greeks have a thing for our Italian cousins. They may have overrun us, but there were certain offsetting pluses. And she couldn't have been more attendant or charming.

"Did I have a visitor, or was I just talking to the happy medicine?"

She replied, "Yes, you did have a visitor, but the visit seemed to overtax you, so sedation seemed to be the best course. He said he'll come when you are amenable. And, good news, you'll be ambulatory tomorrow."

Adams? Blake? The voice was Alan Ladd, and I should know. I've seen Shane so many times I can lip-sync the entire movie. The more correct statement is that I do lip-sync it. It's definitely the same guy.

I tried to relax and succeeded only in causing my head to

pound and my heart to thump. After several minutes of this effort, it became apparent that one does not try to relax. The words "try" and "relax" do not cohabit or compute readily. Instead I imagined a blank sheet of paper. Soon I was floating in a void. It was effortless and very pleasurable. I found myself generally disengaging from my surroundings and even from myself. I may have been awake or asleep, but the difference was inconsequential. If I felt anything, it was lightness and an inner warmth. One part of me asked another part to tell a story. I was floating in a trancelike state, weightless and carefree. I liked it and wondered only why I hadn't come here years earlier.

I heard Alan Ladd again. I was in a car driven by Raj. He had driven by while I was taking one of my long early evening walks on Schooner Pier and suggested we have a nightcap. I folded my portliness into the passenger seat and became quickly aware of another presence.

Raj said, "Nick, say hello to Ben. He's a friend of mine."

I turned to meet this fellow but saw more of a shadowy form than of a person. He leaned forward and said, "Hello, Nick, I feel as though I know you a bit. Raj has spoken of you often. He's quite an admirer of yours." It reminded me of the scene where Michael Corleone is taken for a ride with the murderous Salazzo in the backseat. Except Adams, with the Alan Ladd voice, had to be a good guy.

I turned to shake hands, and he moved toward the front seat. As his face emerged from the dim light, he extended his hand and said, "It's a pleasure to meet you." He had a pleasant face, and I took him to be in his late fifties or so. He was also Alan Ladd with that very distinctive voice. No question.

I turned and glanced at Raj, but he had chosen silence for the moment. My thoughts sped quickly to Robert Service's *The Shooting of Dan McGrew,* and the line that goes something like: "There's men that somehow grip your eyes, and hold them hard like a spell . . ." That spell or something like it came over me at the sound of my new acquaintance's voice. It wasn't just the tone or timber. There was a clear authority to it, a very persuasive authority, but a benevolent authority. I felt little hesitancy that I'd do just about whatever Alan Ladd asked me . . . or told me, cheerfully and obediently. And now he was in the backseat.

It couldn't have been more than a few seconds before I attempted to pick up the conversation, but in that briefest of intervals, I wondered if I had seen *The Secret Life of Walter Mitty* a few times too often. I am nothing if not possessed of a rich and fertile imagination. There must be many folks like me in those regards, and old James Thurber probably giggles from his resting place.

Why would Raj happen by and introduce me to someone in such a weird circumstance? My good manners lurched me from my brief disengagement, and I turned again to look at Adams.

"I know you may find this a bit unsettling, Nick, but please indulge me for a few moments. I'd like you to spend a few hours with Raj and me, if you can spare the time."

Reaching to my book of business clichés, I said, "That would be fine. What can I do for you?" Emulating Richie, I added, "How can I be helpful?"

"To get to the subject, I'm involved in high technology, very high technology, and I'd like your opinions on some related matters. I'd very much like your opinions and your impressions."

I glanced once more at Raj, but he had reaffirmed his choice of silence.

"I'd be glad to be of help, but I think you may have the wrong Drizos. I think you're looking for Drizos the systems guy. I'm Drizos the bond trader.

"I know that, Nick. I am looking to you for help and advice from some of your other skills."

"I'm not sure I have other skills, but I'm pretty sure I have none that relate to technology."

"That may be the case, but I would be very grateful and appreciative if you could spare us some time."

My third glance at Raj elicited a nod. A switch had been activated. With absolutely no intervening thought, I said, "I'd be pleased to do so. When would be a good time?"

He leaned forward and touched my arm in a firm but gentle fashion and said, "It's now Friday evening. Raj tells me your schedule is clear for the weekend. If you could join us now for a

86

brief trip, we will have you back well before the opening bell for Monday's market opening."

I stammered something of no consequence and looked again at Raj who finally joined the conversation. "It would be a good and helpful thing, my friend."

We all like to think we are pretty hip and alert, and I'd like to remember my reaction differently. The truth is I said, "Okay."

I had been in the car for only a few minutes and had been transfixed on this strangest of meetings. As I turned to take a more normal posture, I realized we were on the Interstate.

Once again the Alan Ladd voice spoke. "I must ask you a favor, Nick. Our work is both ultra-secret and extremely sensitive. We cannot put you in the position of possessing certain information and of compromising yourself."

Am I going mad by stages? Alan Ladd, Dan McGrew, and now going down the hole to Wonderland. Maybe I don't know Raj very well after all. Maybe I'm in a car with psychopaths. I'm a bond trader, for Christ's sake.

"Raj, enough. This isn't funny. How about just dropping me back at the pier, and I'll call you from the trading desk. Then you and Mr. Mystery can go play 'I've Got a Secret.' I'm what's wrong with this picture."

Raj, being mindful of his driving, said, "Adams, is it all right if I speak with Nick?

"Please," intoned Alan Ladd.

"Nick, two important things for you to know. First, you are the dearest of my friends. I would never let harm come to you. Second, the matter for which we are asking your time is truly of great importance. And I need not say, were the situation reversed I would assent and comply without question or hesitation."

Some people can lay guilt trips, but that was a beauty. Succinct and penetrating.

"Okay, let me get this right," I started, doing my best Groucho Marx shtick. "I'm going to take a trip, talk about something for which I have no talent and be back here for business as usual on Monday. Is that the deal?"

In his most reassuring tone, Raj said, "You will actually be home before six on Sunday evening."

My thoughts continued to flash. It's a good thing they—my thoughts—are essentially weightless, or the top of my curly-headed pate would have blown off. How many times have I yielded to a "trust me" and how many times have I ended up in the penalty box? This is nuts. The only right answer is no way, no how, no, no, and no. But Raj is a friend, and if I know anyone with real integrity—otherwise the biggest bullshit word in the dictionary—it is he.

"Suppose I say yes, which I very much doubt, who is going to know about this?"

Alan Ladd responded quickly, "Just Raj, me, and a couple technicians who are vital to the dialogue with you."

Dialogue? The closest I've ever come to *dialogue* has been presenting some new wrinkle in bond trading to a bunch of my peers over a rubber-chicken lunch in some second-rate hotel.

"That does it, Raj, just drop me at the first gas station. I think you've clearly got the wrong guy. You two better sharpen your crayons, and redo your playbook."

"Nick, I can appreciate your sense of my presuming on your friendship like this. I will ask you one more time to help us with an urgent problem and, at the same time, to do something for the nation. Please take a moment to consider my request. In the case you do not wish to proceed, we will return you to the pier, and you may take total comfort that this conversation never took place."

Conversation never took place? Talk about a delayed reaction for the light bulb finally going on. These guys are spooks, for Christ's sake. It made no sense whatsoever. Now I felt like Michael before he dispatched the chief and the mob guy. My eyes were like a video game, which was accelerating to the frenzied socko boffo conclusion. Nothing made sense, and less came to mind.

I'd been in this happy company for less than fifteen minutes. I hadn't done anything strenuous, but I was enervated. There was no answer, except that I had gone quickly insane or was in a truly fruitcake dream sequence, which would soon deposit me back at the trading desk.

I read a speed-limit sign and counted a few telephone poles just for a sanity check. So maybe I really am in a car, and maybe this stuff is really happening.

While my outreach for constructive thoughts went to naught, one seemed to stick. It had to do with the endless wrangling and petty negotiations, which, it seems every financial deal must endure before a final closing. I've endured many of these exercises in teenage ego fits. The ones in which the overly high priced advisors—lawyers and bankers—insist on testifying to their brilliance.

At one of these closings, one of the principals—the seller—did everything but answer the final and deal-closing question. And he took about three hours to not do so. At length, one of the gifted old-timers approached Mr. Reluctant and said something to the effect that "I can appreciate your many reservations and concerns, but in business we ultimately come down to two words. One is yes, the other is no. It is time that you revealed your preference. It is of no consequence to me as it will not change my life style, so please make known your preference and we will all abide by it." As it occurred, the guy said yes and a speedy closing followed.

The object point is that it doesn't have to be business. One can only ruminate for so long. Plus I have mentioned that I believe in God. So here I was with a true and valued friend and still comfortable that a grace was shining on me. Alan Ladd didn't matter much in this lightning round of thought. And there were no maybes; it came down to yes or no.

With a tightness in my chest and with a voice not readily recognizable, I stared directly at Raj and said, "Okay, I'll do it."

Raj touched me on the shoulder and nodded his appreciation. He then added, "Thank you, but there is one small detail, effendi." I don't know the origin, the correct spelling, or the proper definition of "effendi" but Raj would refer to me as such from time to time. According to him it meant something like esteemed friend, or brilliantly shining majesty, filler of my life's most tormenting emptiness or whatever compliment the recipient might wish to accord to himself. Nonetheless, this time "effendi" meant there was more to come.

I was already feeling like the long-pursued client of a whole-life insurance salesman. I was beaten and could no longer resist his relentless hounding as he pushed policy and pen into my hands for signature.

"A detail you say." I was in. The deal was done, so there would be no quibbling. "And that detail might be?"

Adams spoke, "Nick, this is serious business, the most serious. We're going to take you on a plane ride of some duration. This will be followed by a short land trip with certain evasive actions. It is critical for all of us that you have no idea or the slightest conception of where you are going or where you will have been."

I had said yes, I was resigned, and by this time my curiosity—my goddamned curiosity, my most highly valued curiosity—had overcome any sense of fear which, had I been in my right mind, would have put me back on the pier less than a half hour ago.

"Okay, okay, okay. I said I'd do it."

"That's not the detail, effendi," said Raj. "We'll have to sedate you," he said in a somewhat hushed and almost embarrassed tone.

"Sedate me? I'm nuts enough to go along with a make-believe bond trader and a guy I've never met, and you say sedation is a detail?" But it was hopeless. What next I wondered. Maybe Alan Funt would show up and tell me to smile into the candid camera. Or maybe this was an addition to one of those real-life TV deals where dessert would be some detestable concoction. I'm a bond trader, for Christ's sake.

But I can't undo a handshake, certainly not with Raj. So, it was hopeless.

"All right, sedate me, but at least tell me what you're using. I've taken enough of a beating to deserve to know that."

"It's much like versed," said Adams. I was beginning to believe that he wasn't like Alan Ladd, he was Alan Ladd. "You'll have a fairly short nap and wake up in total control of yourself with no aftereffects."

It's like versed, the man says. I almost wanted to yell that the joke was on him. I love versed. I had it administered twice in

90

a hospital for minor procedures. The first time my girlfriend accompanied me to the prep room. The attendant explained versed and told me, I'd be in dream land directly. I asked if I should start counting.

I woke up feeling as good, if not better, than ever. There were several people around, and I sounded like a commercial going on about the great night's sleep I'd just had. The attending doctor informed me I'd been out for fifty minutes. It was so good, I think I went back for a second procedure just to get the versed. Later I asked if I might have a six-pack of the stuff. That of course drew no laughter from those serious folk.

It was time to roll up a sleeve. If I had to travel with a couple of certifiables, I could do worse than cozy up to Mr. Versed.

Adams leaned forward. The sharp prick of the needle was welcome.

I wasn't disappointed. So far as I know, I slept restfully. When I awoke I was seated in a very pleasant room, despite its lack of windows. My first thought was to ask once again for a six-pack of the nighty-night juice, but it was time to pretend to be a grown-up. In attendance were Adams, Raj, and two others whom I took to be the technicians.

"I suppose it wouldn't be received well to ask where I am?" I inquired of Adams.

"You suppose correctly, Nick, and I apologize for the abruptness of the past several hours. Permit me to introduce you to what we call Invictus. Permit me also to introduce you to two of my most senior colleagues—Victor Berkeley and Tom Hunter."

I was surprisingly calm given my whirling tour down this fanciful, latter-day yellow brick road. But here I was with the wizard and his fellows. One of the old traders from my past used to tell me I wasn't as dumb as I looked, that being a compliment when I did something especially good. Right, and your real names are what? But I'm a guest, so I'll make nice with the other kids.

I shook hands with Berkeley. He appeared to be in his early fifties. He was quite overweight and had a balding head. He didn't exactly make me look slim by comparison, but he was quite large. Had I met him randomly, I would not have associated him with technology. To call a spade a shovel, he looked like a jerk, a fat jerk with a nondescript face. His face looked like he was blowing a bubble of sorts through his shirt collar. My initial visceral impression was one of disquiet, but he disarmed me quickly with a pleasant smile and extended his hand. "Call me Vic," he said. Upon reflection, he seemed a pleasant fellow.

"Nice to meet you, Vic."

Tom was, by contrast, totally different. He was just about six feet and quite trim. I guessed sports figured prominently in his background. He had a natural warmth about him, but I wouldn't have associated him with technology either. "I'm Tom; some call me Tombstone," he offered with a firm but not obnoxious handshake.

"My pleasure, Tom." God, but I'm sharp, a regular gifted conversationalist, I thought to myself. This was a guy who'd be hard not to like, I thought.

Still sounding like Alan Ladd, Adams excused his two colleagues leaving the three of us in my new weekend retreat. For his part, Adams was around five eleven, maybe six feet, slender and trim and had an attractive everyman look about him. In my movie lexicon, he probably would have been cast more times than not as Jimmy Stewart's best friend—as the old line goes. Not much about him drew attention his way, but given our meeting and the strange place in which I found myself, it was clear the man carried a lot of hot cargo.

For a moment the three of us just regarded each other. He motioned us to sit and rubbed his chin vigorously. Most times I would be taking this as a where-do-I-begin gesture. I had no such illusions, this man was very much in focus.

"Nick, I thank you again for placing your trust with us. It was more than a leap of faith, and it is appreciated. Let me now tend to my end of the bargain. You are in a place we call Invictus. We are a virtually anonymous intelligence agency with a small staff and a large budget. I am the chairman, as I have been for almost five years. I report directly to the president and only to the president. Aside from the president, our existence is known only to three senators, no one of which is a committee chairman, and I meet with them separately. They are unknown to each other in this regard. Only the president and I know their identities.

Our mission is national security. We were established to provide the best possible technologically assisted intelligence. We have first priority on intelligence spending, and we have one-way access into all the other intelligence agencies—military as well as governmental. There were many reasons for our founding. One of the paramount objectives was to create an intelligence agency, which could withstand, or better yet, avoid politicization and publicity. This in turn dictated small size and absolute secrecy.

In our time, we have unearthed and averted some nasty goings-on. We've also missed a few. I'm sure you've heard the old spook line that our triumphs go unheralded, but our misses are front page news. That's only half true for us. For good or ill, we've never been heard of, so we get neither credit nor blame.

We have several missions, but I want to talk with you about only one of them. I should add that at the end of your meeting, you will be returned to your home, and nothing will ever be said about today's goings-on. For example, as you have pointed out, you're a bond trader. Even if you insisted on going public with your adventure, it wouldn't attract much attention. The story line would be bond trader visits a place he can't identify to talk about super-secret stuff. It would be just another alien sighting story. Wouldn't have legs as they say in the news business. In fact, the couple of issues we discuss will be a bit obtuse so far as you are concerned and not readily connected to our underlying purpose."

No joke, I thought to myself. I was paying attention, at least I was trying to pay attention, but I was all over the place as is my habit. Up popped an image of those late-night radio talk shows from the fifties, which featured suitably weird people for its equally weird late-night audience. These soirees routinely presented souls with distressingly fantastic tales. One of the more memorable broadcasts involved a guy who had just teleported in from Venus. He was only able to stay on the air for a few minutes, as he was obliged to meet his counterpart from Saturn at a pre-determined rendezvous in Central Park and to then proceed on with his interplanetary mission. Bond trader with strange tale would no doubt remain my little secret.

When I reconnected myself to my present circumstances, I realized Ben had been continuing on. I'm not sure how long I was elsewhere, but I did my best to snap myself back to attentiveness.

"More importantly, we know you very well, Nick. You are of good character. We know you deal a hundred percent straight up in business. We know you've been euchred by some slickies, but you've never sought revenge. We know that while you don't excel in golf, you don't cheat either. We know you from your preteen years in Pennsylvania and more. Generally speaking, you are not a risk. And we don't get involved in the rough stuff, so you have no worries."

"Not to interrupt you, but as you said, I'm a bond trader. What could I possibly say, do, or know that might interest you? And by the way, where do you get off snooping on me? But, since you've been through my most personal stuff, what should I call you?"

"You can call me Ben, but that's just to be civilized during your visit. I have a new name daily. It's just part of the game, part silly, part deadly. As to our subject, we'll get to that shortly."

"Let me fill you in as to the schedule. We got on the road about ten p.m. last night. It's now Saturday afternoon. You slept restfully for almost fifteen hours, courtesy of some high octane versed. You'll be here for about a half day, and you will be returned to your home by early evening on Sunday."

"For now you, Raj, and I are going to enjoy a peaceful lunch and talk about a number of things that have little direct bearing on your visit."

"And this will all make sense at some point?" I inquired.

"Most likely it will," said my new acquaintance, Ben. "In the meanwhile, let's adjourn next door and enjoy some lunch and some conversation."

We left our meeting room and walked down a narrow hallway into a small and tastefully appointed dining room. Ben motioned for us to be seated. I think he hit a hidden buzzer, and a young man entered to offer us a pre-lunch drink. I had a particular brand of beer in mind, and of course it was available. Ben and Raj had both ordered diet sodas.

"As I said before, Nick, we are very grateful for your accession to our invitation. I can imagine how strange it still must seem. Before we go into free-form mode, let me tell you a few things, which might be of interest. First, a bit of why you're here.

"There are in this nation a number of people with important talents and skills—important in terms of security issues. Over the years they have come to be designated as National Resources. Many have been well known to the point of celebrity and as national heroes. Einstein, Fermi, Teller are among the well-known group. There are, however, a few hundred of whom you have never heard. Other national resources. Each in his or her own uniquely talented way has been similarly designated and each has been of important service to the nation. A few on more than one occasion, but the overwhelming majority now lead regular lives and anonymity, so far as their connection with us has been and is concerned.

"That's the basic deal here, Nick. We'll probably see you only this one time, but we will retain you on record as a national resource. It may not be much comfort, but we will provide two opportunities for you to withdraw. One is right now. The second will be shortly after our lunch. Is that clear?"

"It's very clear," I answered. "I don't get the implications, but your statement is very clear."

Ben continued, "There is one other point. Upon returning to your chosen trade, your business volume will increase noticeably. You won't become rich, but it will add to your comfort. This is by no means a payoff, but it is recognition of your contributions to date and to those which might follow. This business will be from your standard type of clients and will be totally straight up legal. We direct a fair amount of business through strategically important banks and financial institutions and, for our part, having an honest trader such as yourself in the mix is a good deal in its own right. And as I mentioned, you may withdraw from any further conversation with us and be returned home with our gratitude and no hard feelings."

"Since I have another chance to withdraw, I'll play for now.

Meanwhile would you care to expand on my contributions to date?"

"More about that later, but for now let's just relax a bit."

I took my appointed seat at the spare but handsome table. There was no menu; nor was I asked what I might like to have. In quick order I was served a tossed salad of lettuce, arugula, grape tomatoes, and fresh blue cheese on the side. This was the salad which, given a choice, I would have requested. I was also presented with a second Killian's. I thought back to my days at Fort Gordon and Officer's Training School. Attention to detail, attention to detail, always attention to detail. Does this guy miss anything?

Had Bond, James Bond, strolled in, his martini would have been waiting and served up directly, stirred not shaken. Or is it shaken not stirred? Whichever. Well, why do things halfway. You've got my attention, I thought.

But why be surprised, and why be anxious? These guys could have dispatched me at any time of their choosing. Be at peace, I suggested to myself. This is so unworldly that you might as well enjoy it. Suppose it is the end of the trail. It could have been worse. Put your helmet on and get back in the game. Easy for you, I noted to myself via the Nick 101, but what's the game?

I hadn't been making many decisions to this point, so I decided to take charge of my own volition, and ordered myself back into the surroundings. I was advising myself to banish surprise as a consideration and instead to enjoy my new-found surrealism. Nonetheless, having confronted the word "surprise," I was taken back to a story. More things than not take me back to a story. This particular one was about Noah Webster being caught in the closet by his wife while fondling a young maid. Supposedly Madam Webster said, "Noah, I'm surprised." The dictionary guy, as the story goes, replied, "No, my dear, I'm surprised, you're astonished."

I do this all the time. If there is a constant about me, its multiple thoughts racing around for reasons I just don't understand. And, that I can't control. Maybe I don't wish to control. In any event, I soon became given to a series of sounds somewhere in the range of giggles and chuckles.

Ben and Raj remained quite composed. Ben asked, "Are you having some discomfort, Nick?"

"I am, Ben, or rather I was. I'm afraid I may have missed some of your last remarks. I apologize, but I think I have spent the last few moments in trying to come to terms with this, for want of a more descriptive word, event."

"Not at all," said Ben. "How is your introspection coming along?"

"It is, all things considered, all things of which I am able to consider, all right. I've decided to do what you request of me to the best of the abilities you may think I might possess. I apologize for my self-absorbed reverie."

"No offense taken, Nick. You didn't miss anything of import, and I'd encourage you to be forthcoming with any observations or comments you might have."

"Fair enough, Ben. I don't know what you expect of me and I don't want to presume to do your work for you, Ben, but don't make me out to be Snow White. I've got plenty of faults and more than a few warts."

"That's probably so," said Ben, nodding in general agreement, "but in our business, it isn't a question of the person being flawed, it's how badly flawed."

"Did you have anything in particular in mind?" I inquired of Ben.

"I do. I mentioned your getting euchred by some slickies."

"Roger. It happened because I put trust where it wasn't warranted. The recriminations I felt on my bad judgment were as rough to take as the money hit which was, for me, quite large. So I cocked up a few ingenious get-even schemes, which would have been both illegal and entirely immoral."

"But you didn't act on them," said Ben.

"No, I didn't, but I'll tell you what went through my mind, because you should know. I'll give you the same option you gave me. You might not want to talk any further when you know something of my darker side."

"An even trade, Nick, as you wish," he stated, as he motioned me to continue.

"I work in an industry with a bunch of good guys and some

real sleazebags who prey on the trusting and unsuspecting. There are many scams, a couple of which run all the time and cost countless millions. Both are usually on the short- term trading side where people trade, or roll over, a large amount of capital several times a day. And both occur where guys aren't satisfied with their good fortune and their relatively privileged life styles.

"The first is where a trader simply misprices a security, just a bit below fair value. He sells the security to his accomplice somewhere on the outside at that bargain price. The accomplice then immediately sells the security at a gain and puts the difference in the pot. If you're working with fifty million bucks, not a very large amount for trading, say, T-Bills, one-hundredth of one percent is five thousand dollars per year. Five Gs. Do this a couple times a week and at the end of the year, there is a lot of money in that pot. You can let your imagination run, and it isn't difficult to work several variations on this theme. Mostly they're done amid a ton of trades by the same people, so they get lost in the sheer volume. The employer gets screwed, along with the customers, and some sleazes walk with the stolen, and often, tax-free dough.

"Some folks say, yeah but now there are computers, so the system should be more secure. Right, that's why the Frenchie trader lost several billion bucks and how many more he may have squirreled away before getting caught.

"The correct answer is that there are more variations on the theme and that computers actually make the scams easier. But, no matter, the only question is when will today's scams come to light. Or to make it easy for you, think of it this way . . . if you put a big pot of money out there, it's just a question of how many guys will try to grab a bit. Or, more pertinently, how many scams are ongoing right now? And when will they be illuminated with shocked headlines? Just wait.

"The second is used mostly to launder money, or frequently to finance politicians quietly and illegally. Here, commodities is the game of choice, but it can be done with other instruments. This one is really simple. A guy with a lot of dough simply executes a buy or a sell of some commodity. A few hours later, or maybe a few days later, reverses the transaction and closes it out. He's got a gain, or he's got a loss. With some fancy bookkeeping, he merely puts his name on the losing side of the trade, and his beneficiary's name of the winning side. The guy with the dough gets a favor; the guy with a favor to give loses a few bucks but owns a politician. And life goes on.

"I mentioned that I had cocked-up a variation on these basic scams. It would have been a precedent-setting beauty."

"And?" inquired my host.

"It was no-go. It was never a possibility. I just couldn't do it. In the end, revenge is a poor currency and tends to bankrupt those who seek such score-settling."

"We know," said Ben. "Or more correctly, Raj knows, because you told him and I know because he told me."

"Moreover," he continued, "we are quite current on such scams, as you put it. One of our major missions is to detect and interdict the flows of funds from those who would do us harm through their agents. We mostly target international banks, but sometimes we come upon incidental activity and, when practical, we refer it to the feds or local guys."

These guys are on top of their game, but is there any privacy left for the Greek bond trader? "Jesus, Raj, is there any confidence you won't violate." A poor choice of expletives I thought to myself and an even poorer outburst. I knew instantly that if Raj had told my host anything, it was most likely only for some very high purpose.

"Be at ease, effendi, all will be revealed to your satisfaction," said my friend.

And, as usual, I took his advice, and assumed a yet more comfortable position in my very comfortable chair. "Okay, how can I be most helpful, Ben?"

Ben was the most engaging of conversationalists and probably a master interrogator as well. He directed me easily from one subject to another, and I obliged by being even more chatty than is my nature. It was like ratting on myself, and I enjoyed it. It was like turning myself in. It was like confession, except that there would be only the relief of unburdening myself. There would be no punishment. Maybe this is a side effect of my dream-land potion.

Somewhat abruptly, Ben said, "You like movies, don't you, Nick?"

Before I could respond, he added, "I especially mean old movies."

"I do, yes," I said, trying to mix assertion with apology.

"Don't get sore at me, Nick," he resumed, "I'm now talking only in the most personal of opinions. This is totally off the re-cord, and probably off the reservation as well, but my opinion is that you're a bit of a romantic. I'd bet a little bit of dough, as you would say, that *Casablanca* is one of your all-time favorites. I'd even bet a little more dough that you see yourself as Bogie in the final big scene from time to time."

I said Ben was good; he was also very clever. Yes, I like old movies. Yes, I like Bogie. Yes, I adore *Casablanca*. And yes I do go off to funnyland imagining myself to be a bigger-than-life hero from time to time. I'd pay big dough just to have a cup of coffee with Ingrid Bergman and gape at her. He not only picked up on that, he also dropped in words like "dough" and an expression like "Don't get sore"—both right from the thirties and for-ties—just to leave no doubt. Had he added, "Gee, Nick, you're a swell guy," I might have expired.

I wasn't pleased with this last bit of labeling, but I wasn't an-gry, either. I had already come, in this briefest of time spans, to regard Ben as a man of goodwill and of good faith. I was puzzled.

"Why would you go off on such an unrelated tangent?" I asked, regretting that choice of words as quickly as they were spoken. I should have asked why he would make such a point of my frivolities. Plus, what's a related tangent? I slumped notice-ably in my chair.

"I assure you, Nick, I mean no offense," he said softly and re-assuringly. "In fact," he went on, "I share many of your thoughts and feelings. Furthermore, I think many of those yearnings for the make-believe, bigger-than-life folks keep me going. Ours is not a pleasant business by its nature, and without an anchor to windward, given things such as we have been discussing, it

100

would be very difficult not to lose one's way. Please take this as an explanation and as an apology."

I nodded, but sat mostly frozen, not feeling especially conversation-worthy.

A fair part of my weekend in this distant place had gone by, and I was most anxious to ask when we would get on with the business of this meeting, but I was also embarrassed and afraid of saying something awkward.

I am positive without reservation that Ben picked up on my state. He half- waved at me and said, "What would you like to know about us, Nick? I'll tell you whatever I can."

He did this, got me back in the conversation, like the accomplished host who moves people around, especially those having a difficult time, so seamlessly that they don't recognize the work of an expert social catalyst. The next day, the guests would recall only what a fine time they had, how conversations flourished, how the time rushed by, and how they would look forward to the next time out. He's versed with a sense of social grace.

He sensed that I was groping for a starting point and said, "How about what we do and why for starters, Nick?" I nodded again.

"In the broadest sense," he began, "we have several missions, but two are especially important. The first is to continue the development of leading-edge surveillance technology. The second is to be engaged by the president for very specific and highly defined projects.

Regarding the first, we focus very intensely on three things; movement of certain people, movement of certain materials, and movement of money. We use every available means to advance our knowledge of these three factors. A great deal of it from twenty miles up and above, but another large part at ground level."

I took a page from Ben's well-written book and stood up slowly.

He looked at me with a bemused smile, which only broadened. "I sense you would like to move the conversation in a different direction, Nick."

"I do, Ben. What you do is essential and fascinating. I still treasure my time in the army, and I think I'm a pretty good and loyal patriot, but . . ."

"You've heard enough. I could sense that. I'm not here to motivate you, Nick. I thought it only fair to give you a sense of what we are all about. As I said, in a short while, we're going to offer you a return home with no hard feelings."

"I get that, Ben, and I appreciate the sincerity. What you do really matters less to me than how and why you got into this business. I wouldn't mind hearing about that, unless it's off-limits."

Raj rose as if to protest, but Ben raised a quieting hand and Raj again seated himself. "I'd be pleased to do so, Nick," he said while riveting his eyes directly upon mine.

"This may rise to the sentimental, Nick, but, as honestly as I know how to tell you, here's the short version. I've always loved history and I especially love ours, so I have been long disposed to some kind of service. At the same time, I couldn't sell ten dollar bills for fifty cents each, so anything resembling politics was and is out. I can't, and won't, run around kissing babies' cheeks and their parents' asses and shaking hands indiscriminately. Politics, even if you call it government or public service was, and is, a nonstarter for me.

"I go back to the Founding Fathers and have never had reason to regard them as anything but the most amazing aggregation of individuals since the beginning. I try not to throw superlatives around thoughtlessly; but I mean to say the most amazing ever. The fact, and it is fact, that this group of men, coming together more than two hundred years ago, would have such an incredible grasp of human nature and geopolitics remains overpowering to me. They may have been the first and last group of true statesmen. I say this with full knowledge of how the many historians have illuminated their many quirks and human frailties. All this considered, they were, and remain, amazing."

I found myself nodding and rocking a bit in my chair. Soon I might be saying, "Amen, brother." For a guy who wasn't a self-proclaimed salesman, he had already grabbed me with his opening remarks. But that was an easy sale, because he had only

102

articulated thoughts I have carried around for years and years. Plus there is no easier sale than to another salesman.

"The U.S. Senate, which is largely a collection of walking, preening lard tubs, proclaims itself as the greatest deliberative body in the world. These guys are at best—*at best*—dwarfs in comparison to the founders. If Churchill were to address this self-adoring, self-promoting collection, he'd probably paraphrase himself along the lines of: 'Never before in the annals of human endeavor have so few done so little with so much.' Very over-rated, and they don't get much done."

With the singular exception of Raj, conversations with my peers in the business have rarely risen beyond the arid. Local politics might surface for a while, but only if someone's meta-phoric ox was getting gored. Otherwise fast cars and women, or, usually more frequently, cars and fast women, seemed to domi-nate. Drugs would probably be front and center as well, but my crowd is on average only a few years from AARP time. Laxatives and anti-acids are the chemicals of choice. I eased myself further into my chair; I was enjoying this man even though I had a clear and atavistic sense of incipient melancholy.

Ben paid me a not incidental compliment. He cocked his head toward me and employed body language clearly asking whether he should continue. Whatever my outward gesture, he surmised quickly and then, as an added courtesy asked, "Would you like me to go on?"

"I would," I replied smartly, "and while I don't have an espe-cially bright view of our national leaders, isn't 'preening lard tubs' a bit strong? I don't expect a lot from them, and I find many of them generally smarmy, but . . ."

"I take your point, Nick, but here's the way it has gotten. Many principled, well-intentioned men and women work their ways to these high offices. Some used up their Faustian deal in-ventory to get there, so they're basically adornments. The major-ity of the remainder is usually done in by the system. Everything is seniority, so the newer folks give way to the seniors. If I could change just one thing at the federal government level, it would be tossing the seniority system, unless I could get term limits. Even those that keep their inner lights learn that nothing happens if you can't get the votes. The punch line is that an otherwise good bill goes through the well-known sausage machine and emerges with favors for all its supporters. In the end these guys do with ten bucks what an average guy could do with five. Lard tubs may be offensive, but regrettably, it's accurate. It's become show biz, Nick. In a word, we're fucked."

Now this was a funny turn. We all drop the "f-bomb" from time to time and mostly it's crass and vulgar and employed for emphasis, rage, or some other effect. From Ben, it was more like a one-word omnibus requiem for something gone awry and dying. It was arresting, but not shocking. I took it as an unquestionably heartfelt measure of his being one step from discouragement. And I had already come to know, that for Ben, being discouraged would be tantamount to dead. It was as eloquent as it was simple. For reasons I may never understand, however, I knew to a certainty that Ben would never so yield.

"As for preening, just dial into a senate or house hearing on cable TV and observe. When they're not posturing, they're talking with their aides to assure they have their next articulate lines ready. I may be a bit rough on them, Nick, but it's so mediocre it's painful.

"I won't bore you with the sadness that overcomes me when I contemplate the continuing dumbing down and the mass ignorance of the today's electorate. The reason I won't bore you is that the founders wrote wistfully and ominously of the probable short duration of the new republic. Not one of the founders—Franklin, Jefferson, Washington, Adams, Madison, Hamilton—not one had much confidence in the survival of total democracy. Some of them foresaw a distant time in which those who contributed little or nothing would outnumber their opposites. Some saw a time when this new majority would vote themselves largesse, and that would be a time of collapse. They had taken the lessons of the Greeks and the Romans well.

"For my part, and in my opinion, we are not yet in decline, but the ascendancy is over. We have done a good job of exporting manufacturing and are now doing a good job of exporting the service side. And our energy policy is, forgive me, fucking imbecilic.

"For the several decades of our ascendancy, we followed a

104

pattern of dropping off low-skill jobs and supplanting them with employment borne of new technologies. But the internet, the global markets, and our own complacency have combined to create a nasty brew. I know you use regression in your business, and I know you are familiar with 'regressing to the norm' as it's applied to large systems. That's where we are, and our norm is now mediocrity."

He stopped and turned to find his water glass, clearly gathering himself.

I started to speak, but he said, "One more second, Nick, and you can have the rebuttal. What makes things worse is that we are on a bad path with respect to our historically enabling technology lead. Today, well over half of the students in our graduate technology school curricula are foreign. Worse, a larger percentage of the professorial staffs are also foreign. We have done a fine job of globally marginalizing ourselves."

Taking note of Raj and his generally upbeat demeanor, I thought, but did not say, *"Jesus, Ben, what the hell are you doing here? You could be the poster boy for despair and hopelessness. You make me want to stick my head in the oven."*

He was relaxed and very peaceful. I was getting the sense he was taunting me for some as yet not-illuminated purpose. Not bullying me, but acting very much the irritant, dropping some raw meat in front of me and wiggling it about.

He settled back, and left less doubt it was my turn than if he had told me in so many words to pipe up. I was beginning to get comfortable with the style here; it was very much like that of the old-time probing, cajoling Jesuit teachers. Fair enough, indeed. I tried to put on my good behavior and careful wording filters, and said, "That's neither a very upbeat picture or outlook you seem to have. So . . ." Then I retreated into another awkward silence.

"So," he continued for me, "you want to know why I do what I do?"

"That would be a good starting place for my purposes," I responded, getting a bit more familiar with the prevailing style of discourse here in hoo-hoo land.

"Because I love this country, Nick. That's the alpha and

omega of it. The fact that it prefers to ignore the multiple lessons of history and the fact that it seems to insist on driving the metaphoric national bus over the cliff repeatedly before exercising prudence doesn't deter me. There is nothing like the USA. The major problem, I should say one of the major problems, is that technology has grown staggeringly in the last 100 years, but human nature hasn't shown much progress in the thousands of years we've been around. Like so many great nations before us—as history repeatedly demonstrates—we've become smug and complacent."

"I'm just a guest here in this strangest of places, Ben, but you go too far with your fed bashing. I've formed an opinion, or overview, that they tend to resemble show biz. The common traits I've found are the needs for public personae and public exposure. I imagine most of these folks worked continuously for that kind of validation along the way. The lead in the school play, class officers, big jocks, activists, big deals. If anything were to be in common, I have come to reckon it as a compulsion; the salmon has got to get upstream, and these guys have to get into office. In the process they become more like celebrities and our media aids and abets. My biggest problem is that, to put it gently, they badly confuse stewardship with ownership. But with all my beefs, from taxes to strangling regulations to the pandering, I just won't cross the line into labeling them as fundamentally bad. As other perceptive commentators have noted, including Pogo, Walt Kelly's comic strip alligator and sometime social observer, we largely have the government we deserve. Besides, you can't have panderers without panderees, and the entitlements continually sought are only more logs on the legislative fire. Like I said, I'm a guest, but I don't swallow what you said, and I don't believe you do either."

And then a compulsion, mine or the 101's—it doesn't matter—burst out of my now madly pulsing pores, "You're a vigilante, a totally nutso vigilante."

"Well, Nick, I guess it's so about you not being all that dumb after all. Vigilante it is. But tell me, how else does it ever work? What was Shane? What was Bogie in countless movies after he's been falsely accused or imprisoned? It's just about always one

106

guy, or at least a very small group that gets anything done. For Christ's sake, Nick, no more than twenty-five or thirty percent of the folks wanted revolution back in 1776. Most wanted to play nice with our British landlords. Do you really want to hand everything—meaning our many and unique freedoms—back to them?

"Freedom is the thing, Nick. It doesn't come easy, and it isn't taught in school anymore. As to the Congress, it used to be representative. The blacksmith, the farmer, an occasional lawyer. They'd serve a couple terms and then go home. Now we have permanent politicians. That wasn't the deal. Fifty years ago, almost ninety percent of the congressmen and senators were vets. Today it's around five percent. Get it? Things have diverged from the way they were supposed to be."

Without so much as a breath or a collecting pause, Ben continued, "But in fact you're right, Nick. I did exaggerate a bit more to provoke and engage you than anything else. Sometimes there is no substitute for a little bombast when time is precious, as it is today. I do hold to the ascendancy being over and that mediocrity is our present bearing, but I will apologize for the personal assaults.

"I should also tell you that our organization is carefully maintained in total apolitical terms from me, as director, throughout the staff. We have our missions and execute them to the limits of our capabilities. Over the years Raj and two other individuals have been my frustration managers. Aside from Raj, and now you, I am deemed one hundred percent apolitical. Raj thinks I am a little overdone and overwrought from time to time, however."

"So, Ben, do you see yourself as the head vigilante?"

"I wouldn't put it that way, Nick. But someone better be looking out for what the guys in the congress used to be doing. It's a damn good thing for us that there were cold warriors back in the 'fifties and 'sixties. Like it or not, some of us better be on duty. Get it?"

In between the verbal pyrotechnics of my "visit," I'd been enjoying my simple but distinctive salad. It was especially crisp and tasty, very unlike the brown beauties I make featuring the tired lettuce from my museum-piece home refrigerator. I must have been getting on to the style as well, because I had hardly touched my second Killian's. Instead of a third, a glass of chilled water would be requested. My salad plate was completely clean and looked ready for a return to the pantry for reuse. Before I could wonder, my entrée arrived. Stone crabs, no less, with a choice of mustard sauce or drawn butter and a side of broccolini.

I no longer found these mini-happenings to be of much surprise. These guys knew me to my last debit and credit. Nor would they have to worry about old Nickie hitting the media with his magic carpet ride story. With not a great deal of incremental effort, they could publish the unauthorized biography of *Nick Drizos, Bond Trader* in short order. I'd read it with great interest and probably gain more insights into Nick Drizos and how he got this way than from my couple of rounds with the "how do you feel about that" folks.

This time I kept pretty good eye contact with Ben and Raj and did my best to keep my roaming thoughts to a manageable few. I wore a look, to the extent I can strike a look, that was supposed to pass for an "I'm thinking" interval.

"I love the country too, Ben," I said. And not only for what it has offered and what it has allowed me to do. I very much understand the fragility of freedom and liberty. I'm very grateful for both, but I don't do what you do."

"Who knows why we do what we do, Nick. You left the army as a company commander in the MPs and you thought seriously about re-upping. There is no telling what you might be doing today, had you done another tour."

Now it's my military record. Maybe there will be a chapter on Nick Drizos, national hero. "I suppose that's right," I said, as I took the first bite of my lunchtime treat. Maybe the exact same food tastes differently in different settings, but these stone crabs would have been outstanding anywhere, anytime. The sauce was, of course, exquisite.

"Plus," said the long silent voice belonging to Raj, "you got into your present line by sheer happenstance. And you stayed with it despite opportunities for many midcareer shifts."

"And you," I said, while rising and feigning a handshake, "must be my old friend and counselor Raj."

"I am indeed and will remain so at your sufferance, effendi. As it occurs, you are both a better man and a better friend to me than you might know."

I am by nature inclined to the sentimental, perhaps overly so, but I was very touched by this comment. My mind went right to Clement Moore and his protagonist contemplating old Santa. Soon I knew I had nothing to fear.

Raj and I abated our brief reunion and turned to Ben as though scripted to do so.

"Is our simple lunch to your satisfaction?" Ben inquired.

"In every respect."

"Good, then just a postscript or two on our government. Simply put, it's way too large and, to me, it teeters between irrelevant and harmful. It's difficult to find many institutions that don't betray themselves and their constituents after they become what most would call large. It's the same in businesses. The best management teams are in small and medium-sized companies. They have the ability to stay in touch with their important constituencies—their customers, their own people, their suppliers, and even their shareholders. When companies get to large and mega-large size, the execs become politicians and begin to resemble senators. There are some fundamental benefits to size. One such is inertia; it would be even worse, however, if these guys could change course quickly. It's much better that they just lumber along—but at a price measured in mediocrity units.

"In the end, they are indispensable in the servicing of the largest economy in the world. They don't innovate as well as they used to or create many jobs, but they are essential. Notwithstanding these castigations, some outstanding mega companies exist, but the vast majority is bound for mediocrity. Regression to the norm is very much at work."

"I still don't get the connection with your comments and why you seem so at ease with your chosen mission."

"You mean because I seem to heap gratuitous and semi slanderous comments on our great country?"

"That would do for starters," I responded.

"Well, time is beginning to be a factor, Nick, but it comes down to not being able to walk away from something you love even if it's all bitched-up. Plus I like old movies maybe as much as you. One of my favorites is *Hospital* with the late and very great George C. Scott. He's the head doc at an inner-city community hospital where the word 'community' is very much misapplied. The care is poor and the clientele is worse, but he keeps coming back for his daily beating. At the film's climax, he tears off his whites, resigns, and stands in the middle of a big city street howling his joy at being free at last. Moments later he is joined by a comrade of many years who asks if he'll be going back to his post. Old George says, 'Oh sure,' and the film fades out. Like I said, you can't walk away from something or someone you love, or from something you know you have to do, just because it's all bitched up."

"So are you the un-bitcher-upper, like the uncola," I said, somewhat brazenly.

Ben chuckled. "You might say that. One of them, anyway. I'm not alone; there are other vigilantes out there."

"Like I said," he went on, "we are virtually anonymous, so we don't have to put up with the needless chicken shit and that, worst of all, just about totally useless of poxes, the media. Plus we have narrowly defined missions which makes life tolerable."

"Isn't that a 'how's your wife'; compared to what deal?" I asked.

"If you mean, relativity counts here, I'd say that's fair comment."

"The last piece of how I got here is that I cycled through Vietnam. I was there during Tet, and it was all you have heard. I also met two of your pals while I was there—Slater and McAlister."

I felt like Quasimodo had clanged my clapper at the mention of my two dearest friends in the entire be-damned world. Is there any more personal data to drop on me? Do these guys ever stop? What next?

Slater was a journalist and was extremely well liked and popular. I met him while I was at Fort Benning going through a phase of Airborne Ranger School. He insisted on going through jump school, even though he knew he would never see a parachute. He wanted to wear the wings, as he refused to be referred to as a "leg," meaning not airborne, not a jumper, and thus a doosh bag. McAlister was decisive, heroic, and daring by inclination. He was also fatalistic and very at peace with himself. Not a day passed that he failed to assure me that it would be his last. I liked both of them, each in a very different way."

I was now agape again. This was beyond coincidence. Again the wise one seemed to pick up on my consternation. Not to mention my two "pals."

"It was exactly coincidence, Nick, nothing more. Simply random events and passings. To give you some comfort, Nick, I can tell you that neither I nor any member of our organization has ever contacted Slater or McAlister concerning you. We have investigated them, as well as many others of your acquaintance, but we have never had contact with them.

"I met them both in Vietnam, which was a disaster for me. I have a bunch of medals that proclaim me as valiant and all that you are supposed to be, but it was a disaster to its core. The human carnage was brutal beyond telling, as was the ruination of otherwise breathtakingly beautiful land. Worse, however, was the unthoughtful involvement in the first instance. Still worse was the tactical idiocy of being at the mercy of motivated and politically off-limits guerillas. Worst was the treatment by our own countrymen of those of us returning from one or more tours of unspeakable horror."

I sensed my generally functional, but not exceptional, senses coming to the fore. "So," I started, "since you would never be in a position to send troops into danger, since you would never run a war and since you couldn't correct a nation's betrayal, you set yourself to uncovering trouble at its earliest possible point."

"As Les Horvath said to you on the trading desk at Marlowe & Finch, 'You ain't as dumb as you look, Nick.' That's a reasonable summary, but I'd add to provide the best intelligence so that avoidable casualties would remain just that."

I had gotten fairly attuned to the thoroughness and detailed aspects that Ben found so natural that I merely shrugged. The Les Horvath quote occurred almost thirty years ago. I guess I must have mentioned it to Raj. I returned to my crab treat, which remained delicious.

"As I mentioned before, Nick, we have a pretty light agenda hereabouts. It's deep, but it's limited in scope. We don't have many meetings. In fact, one of my indices of measuring the worth of a company is the hours actually worked versus hours in meetings. As you would imagine, I give highest marks for high work-hours to meeting-hours ratios.

"When we do have meetings, however, we tend to make them contentious. There seems to be little sense to have a meeting if there is unanimity, but more importantly, we fear becoming inbred and therefore encourage the point and counterpoint process. When time is a factor, we adjust, but that is our chosen style. At meeting's end, without fail, we reach consensus and move onto the next phase of the engagement or problem."

"I think you are absorbing our style, effendi. At bottom, as it must be, is substance. But then comes style. It is a language of its own dimension, and around here there is a definite style. We don't have a policy and procedures manual. One gets the style, or one goes elsewhere. More accurately, those lacking or eschewing our style are not asked aboard.

"And, in the limited time we will have together, Ben thought it important to give you a sense of the mission and of himself as a person. As for my motivations and my favorite movie, those must be left for another time."

Ben then reassumed his directing role. "By the way you have cleaned your plates, I gather you were very hungry or you found our limited menu to your liking."

"Since you know most of my clichéd snappy patter, maybe this Groucho Marx special will suffice. 'The food was good, the company was enjoyable and the price was right.' In truth, the food was excellent."

I began to note that my ever-wandering mind had been more focused than not in the last hour or so. I had a dot or two to connect. It seemed important. "A minute if you will, Ben." This time I didn't wait for approval. I was getting into a state somewhere between emboldened and comfortable with my present environment.

112

"Yes."

"Back to your picture, *Hospital*. In addition to all his travail, didn't the Doc tend to be an early boozer with some frequency? I seem to recall that cocktail time for him sometimes began around ten A.M."

"He did indeed, and to respond to where you are going, I had a very heavy- duty problem with booze, which began in the final stages of my last tour in 'Nam and continued for several years. Being sober had little appeal. My marriage disintegrated, and I became a lost soul. We don't have the time to tell the whole story, but I travelled to India. The reasons and the circumstances are not particularly important. I did find peace, or what for me has been a lasting sobriety. I also met Raj there. That was well over twenty-five years ago. How I got here is well beyond what you need to know and what you should ever want to know, but you are correct in recalling the doc's affliction. I think we all want to think of ourselves as capable of something heroic or of some larger import. Mostly I carry his image, the image of a guy who confronted his demons. I'd like to think that after the film faded to a close, the doc took the pledge. And I think most of us believe in redemption as well. I'll say again, that's about all you need to know."

It was crisp and concise, strictly matter of fact. I asked, he answered. With only the faintest of changes in his bearing, he seemed ready to continue.

"I can see why Raj numbers you as a close friend, Nick. I'd enjoy your company in a more normal setting, and I'm pleased that we could get to know you a bit as a person. I know I was a bit lengthy and tedious, but, within practical limits, I wanted you to have a sense of what we're about and that for the most part, we're fairly normal. Right or wrong, we're trying to keep the country safe," Ben stated.

"I'm on board, Ben. Like we say at my trading desk, how can I be helpful?"

"I guess you've anticipated and preempted me, Nick. Should I take that as rejection of our offer to cease and desist now and for you to return to your everyday life?"

"It is, Ben." I extended my arm and we shook hands.

"I'm happy to hear that, Nick. Follow me. We're going to a room we call The Point for a shorter, and perhaps more confusing, discussion. Coffee and Greek tea will be available."

"One request, Ben."

He nodded and motioned me to continue.

"A couple of things. First, I presume that we'll finish our business in fairly short order, following which you'll return me to my chosen reality."

Ben nodded again. "That's the deal, Nick."

"Okay, and I also presume I'll be given a fairly concise debriefing including the rules of the road and the ways things will be. I presume also that I won't be seeing Raj again."

"That's very economical and very accurate, Nick."

"Would it be possible for me to have a few minutes, then, alone with Raj before I'm prepped, packed, and shipped?"

Raj turned to Ben, indicating wordlessly that he would very much like to be accorded such a brief session.

Ben paused uncharacteristically and said, "It's agreeable in principle. We're like the airlines in that we put some slop time into our schedules. Right now, we're running a little ahead. I estimate that we'll be able to grant your request. The session comes first, however, Nick. We'll use our best efforts to accommodate you, but no promises. You have my word. Is that sufficient?"

"It is," I said, and we instinctively shook hands again. I'd gone for the quick nod before, but I felt just fine with Ben's promise.

"You said a couple of things, Nick," he said, partly by way of showing that he was paying as much attention to me as I was to him. "What might be the other?"

"Early on you said you had had some successes and some failures. I know this is probably improper, but what can you tell me?"

"As to the successes, Nick, I can't say anything except that we have defused more than a few large-scale problems. They have each been classified and may or may not ever make it into the public domain. You'll have to take that as the full extent of the answer to Part A.

"As to failures, you must know that number one—there is no

114

number two by comparison—was nine/eleven. It was a total breakdown. In largest context, there are three major pieces required for effective intelligence. First, you must have good, meaning accurate, comprehensive and timely data. Second, you must have only the best integrative capabilities, as both the good data and the noise invariably issue from multiple sites and multiple sources. Third, you need the highest levels of interpretive skills, because even when assembled, the best data often paints highly ambiguous pictures. Items two and three are highly iterative.

"The short version is that we had much good data, but the system broke down. The right data did not get to the right places. You can fill in a lot of the blanks.

"Another factor was the sheer barbarity of using innocent people as flying bombs. To many, even hardened field agents, this was beyond contemplation. The worst of it was that nine/eleven was the second attempt on the same target. There is no way for history to understate the magnitude of this blunder.

"It has been noted that our human assets, the agency name for spies and informants, had been curtailed by well-meaning, to be kind, but ill-informed and unengaged politicians. That was a factor, but there was no excuse."

"None of our missions bore specifically on what became nine/eleven, but we did send along significant amounts of intercepts for several months' preceding.

"I imagined there should and would be a thorough house-cleaning of our several key agencies. In due course, and in that spirit, I offered my resignation. It was refused, and we now play in a highly notched-up game.

"I think often of old George C., and as you can probably guess, I have been close to having that most inviting first shooter on several occasions. But whether it's Bogie or the doc or your momma's reading of stories and fables, these things sustain us. At least they sustain some of us. So, I wasn't jerking you around, Nick. I expect you've had similar interludes. Maybe not as dramatic, but serious enough in their own contexts."

He knew I had. I was deflated, but I had asked and I had been answered. Gathering myself and my wits, I rose and followed along with Ben and Raj to see what was behind door number two.

As we walked along, Ben at the lead with Raj and I abreast, my tendencies toward disjointed thought asserted themselves. So, what is this guy all about? Funny he should mention the Founders heeding the lessons of the Greeks and the Romans.

Having spent my life trying to be the best pseudo-intellectual I could be, I had my own opinions about those two primal civilizations. For me, the lessons, or punch lines as we say in my business, were two. The Greeks determined you could have democracy or a republic, but not both. The Romans showed you could have democracy or an empire but not both. If I had the skills to write on the subject, that would have been my continuing heavy-duty thesis.

So where does that leave the USA? And why is Ben behaving like its savior?

In a moment it became clear. There are such things as patriots, and I'm in the presence of one—a broodingly melancholy one, but a patriot nonetheless. As I recovered from my latest flight of Nick Think, Raj nudged me.

The Point was a quite large room, probably about sixty feet square. Like the rest of Invictus, at least the portion I had visited, there were no windows. The floor was an unimposing light gray tile, most likely selected for ease of maintenance, and the walls were painted in soft beige. The lighting was indirect, sufficiently bright and very pleasant. It looked like a no-nonsense, but accommodating, layout. There were a number of consoles of considerable size arrayed around the room's periphery. They were not of the blinky-light variety, and there wasn't any whirring, so I gathered they were not in use.

Raj and Ben motioned me to a mid-sized conference table, and we sat more or less in unison. I was accorded the head-of-table seat with Ben and Raj on my immediate flanks. Presently we were joined by Berkeley and Hunter. This setting, and the past few hours at Invictus, had taken me back to Fort Gordon and beyond, so I rose smartly to meet them for the second time. We shook hands and took our seats, Hunter next to Ben, Berkeley next to Raj. The table was essentially bare except for some ice water, note pads, and a few pencils. I wondered if the seating arrangement had anything to do with seniority or importance. At a gut level, I liked Tom. My initial ill feelings toward Berkeley returned. But, it was time to pay attention again. Ben asked, "Would you care for some coffee or tea, Nick?"

"The water is fine for now, maybe something stronger later, thanks."

I was awaiting a cue from Ben for the resumption of activities, when the door to my right opened. A slender and stylish woman in white slacks and a black turtleneck paused and looked at Ben. He looked at her and asked, "Status?"

She replied, "Clear and operational."

Ben said, "Thank you, Anita," and she left.

"Security," said Ben. "We sweep the entire facility several times per day and immediately before any meetings. We're clear, so let's begin."

"Let's begin," I repeated. *Begin God knows what?* I wondered.

"Nick," said Ben, "we'd like you to recall a dinner you had with Raj about four weeks ago. I'm confident you can, and Raj may be able to fill in a point here or there that evades your recollection."

Right, I thought, he just might be able. The 101 chimed in with a laugh.

"It was on the continuing subject of discovery vis-à-vis invention and you had posed that genius and madness were probably closely related," said Raj.

"I remember it well. That was not my intended major theme, but I remember it well," I responded. I was beginning to get a sense of the style to which Raj had alluded earlier. My take on the Invictus style was let's get to the discussion points quickly, and that was my immediate aim.

"I can summarize it reasonably briefly if you wish," I went on.

Ben nodded as I expected.

"Okay, the background was that the daughter of a close personal friend of mine has had several episodes of epilepsy. I was looking forward to that particular dinner with Raj to talk about epilepsy in particular and to the exclusion of all else.

"While driving to dinner that evening, I concluded that—correctly or otherwise—epilepsy is a battle between order and chaos in which chaos prevails. Whether the underlying cause is electric circuitry or chemical flows didn't matter. I have no competency—I should say I don't know squat—about such matters and, as I've noted before, I am more productive in describing end points than in arranging and connecting the many intervening dots.

"In the course of that same drive, which took about a half hour, I noted that my own thought processes bordered on the chaotic. For no apparent conscious reason, I had cocked up a heavy-duty experiment some time ago consisting of playing an old tune repeatedly on my car's CD player.

"As it happens, the tune is 'Come a Little Bit Closer'—also known as 'Bad Man José'—by Jay and the Americans. Its playing time is two minutes and forty-seven seconds, not exactly a lifetime.

"I would attempt to listen to every word without having my thoughts drift elsewhere. This is quite different from singing along. In that mode you are connected. My challenge was to drive along with the CD playing and to be able to recall the lyrics in toto. After several repetitions of this exercise, my ability to stay so connected dropped off after about twenty to thirty seconds on average. To this day, I am yet to listen to this CD in its entirety without yielding to other thoughts.

"Maybe once, but I was aware of other notions contending for what I now refer to as my foreground processing time.

"It might be the death of a friend, a baseball statistic, a wish to be someplace else, unfinished tasks, a nude woman, a wide variety of things. My inability to stay focused on the most simple of tasks was alarming.

"It seemed that an analogy of some sort might be helpful, and I thought of my personal computer. It has clear partitions, I thought, so I'll assume my most personal computer, my brain, is likewise configured. The computer has its systems side and its applications side, which are designed to be separate from each

118

other or not, depending on some specific set of rules. They interface and inter-react only when they are supposed to. Being software driven, but otherwise mechanical, or electromechanical, the design seems to foster relatively endless repetitions of constancy, but they do crash from time to time.

"Maybe what we call a crash occurs when the systems, for want of a better term, gets out of sync. And maybe this is the inanimate equivalent of epilepsy. If a couple of applications get tangled, that might be petit mal. If the systems side contends with an application or applications, that would be grand mal in my analogy.

"As you can see, I'm not very capable of trailblazing innovating thought. Mostly I have to rely on observable stuff for analogies."

I began to be more than a little self-aware and noted to myself that I had stayed very focused, maybe uncharacteristically focused. I was also aware, however, that my mind was trying to entertain other thoughts. The main contending message seemed to be a flag from some internal control indicating it was now time to regroup. I paused and, almost like a guy with Tourette's syndrome, out came, "But then as Clint Eastwood said, a man has to know his limitations."

I glanced around fully expecting to see rolling eyes and shaking heads. My audience, however, was either actually engaged or just extremely professional and polite. Maybe they take courses in implacability.

I shook my head apologetically and pushed myself away from the table. Looking squarely at Ben, I said, "I'm sorry. I've got two problems. First, my normal working environment does not accommodate monologues. Trading consists of short clippy lingo that barely qualifies as English. We do this all day, hundreds of times. The cliché is that it's mind-numbing, and maybe it is. Maybe that's why my attention span is so limited. But second, and more importantly, I must be wasting your time with my amateur-hour science show . . ."

Ben laid a fatherly hand on my forearm and said, "First, Nick, unclench your fists and relax. You are proceeding very logically and we are very interested in your continuing. Even if the session fails to intersect our particular objectives, it will have been a good use of our time. Please continue."

Where do these kinds of guys come from, guys like Ben, I wondered.

"Okay, thanks," I said, with my embarrassment receding. And I went on.

"Taking my crude analogy to the next step, I thought of the many human involuntary functions as the systems piece and conscious actions as the applications piece. There was also the subconscious to deal with, but I set that aside. I started with the notion of a basic overload, as when many thoughts contend for execution but result in mental paralysis.

"For my purposes, this was ADDS, the attention deficiency phenomenon. It's really not inattention, it's more like not being able to select an action and get to it. The physical manifestation can be the well-known blank stare.

"This made further sense, because I know a kid whose mom exhausted every available remedy in treating what had been diagnosed as ADDS. The kid seemed to be able to do most things all right, so long as it was one at a time. But if asked to do a second while the first was in progress, there was trouble. And, if given a list or a number of things to do, the kid would freak.

"She, the mom, finally assumed the role as chief therapist and with great patience would prevail on the kid to do one thing, just one thing. Later on, two things in succession and so on. After several months, the kid became what we would call increasingly normal. Was this a reconstruction or an overlay of some sort of a work-around? I don't know, but it seemed to be a triumph of order over chaos, or at least action over inaction.

"To the extent that this made any sense, I imagined that several conscious thoughts might converge for address or execution, but something didn't work. In a more violent attempt to resolution, as compared to the ADDS symptom of inaction and/or apparent inattentiveness, this might be petit mal.

"The same might manifest from some sort of crossed circuitry among or between involuntary functions. Or there might be a literal short circuit between involuntary and voluntary actions. Depending upon the strength or violence of the contention,

120

a greater conflict might be what we regard as grand mal seizures.

"In any event, I have come to regard the human body, at some mysterious level, as being by nature, totally compliant with its best interests. It certainly tries to recoil from danger, it certainly tries to heal itself. So, I thought, and this is my exact thought, for which I apologize: it's as Father Duffy might have said, there's no such thing as a bad body. Honest to God, that's what I thought." It's my movie syndrome at work, about which Vic and Tom knew nothing. Maybe Tom because he is likeable, but . . .

The four of them actually chuckled, but then quickly put their good manners back on.

"Just as a side bar," I continued, "I've been going on for several minutes now recounting the day and time of your particular interest. I'm almost finished with my recollections of the drive to meet Raj. Shall I continue, or speed up, or what?"

Ben said, "We're doing fine for time, Nick. Just proceed as you wish."

"On the one hand I found myself feeling pleased with my new discovery, as Raj would say, about these matters. At the same time, for all I knew, all these many great insights were on page one of a first-year med school book. I didn't know whether to feel great insight or total discouragement.

"As has been my continuing experience of involuntary thoughts coming to the fore, I also recalled a comment made by the professor of a speech course I took in college. He noted that we think at several hundred words per minute, and sometimes much, much faster, but we can only speak coherently at much slower rates. This by way of saying it is not easy to speak publicly in an organized fashion for any appreciable length of time. Crashes can, and do, occur frequently just in this simple exercise. Perhaps it's a lack of synchronization.

"That may have been the thought at that time, but on this particular night I had a different conclusion. Perhaps we are, for simpleminded purposes, just a system. A living, breathing system, but just a system.

"I had gotten to the conclusion of this self-torment, which

was that any system must be in sync. Just as computers have clocks and registers, so too must the human body. Or at least a timing belt as in a car engine to assure that all the various physical, chemical, electrical, and electronic events take place when they are supposed to.

"For example, it would be a real mess if the body started trying to digest something before it had been fed. In any case, we know intuitively that many discomforts and maybe even pathologies occur simply because the sequencing went awry.

"All of these and other profound intrabody events will be discovered in due course, and will be another important triumph of order over chaos. Whether ADDS, petit mal, or grand mal, it will all be ultimately knowable and thus ultimately remedial.

"In my case, I don't think I have ADDS, but rather a variant. For me, thoughts just keep coming, but they do tend to get addressed in some order. It comes down to synchronization. Car engines get tuned and retuned continually, as do computers and all manners of other equipment.

"Today we have CAT scans, MRIs, and a wide array of diagnostic gear. While they are truly impressive, they mostly detect and then indicate bad physical stuff. Even with the host of other instrumentation, we must be very fairly primitive in the matter of grappling with what the human body is all about."

I thought to myself, then said audibly, "If I were smart enough, I'd run people into my lab and hook them up to the synchromometer, totally assess the brain and find out for certain what was working and what needed attention."

Ben nearly did a "backover flip," as Jackie Wilson sang those many years ago, while guffawing in a most unexecutive fashion. Guffawing, there is no other word, he guffawed and repeated with moist eyes: "The synchromometer." His colleagues were restrained, and Raj was bemused.

"Yeah, the synchromometer." That's what I said. More importantly was how I said it. I was getting into my infrequent but unpleasant bare-the-fangs state, and I felt myself getting into a familiar hostile attitude. I have tended to get this way over the years when I sense condescension or a putdown coming.

I continued, "You take your high-priced car into a service

center, and they hook it up to a computer and measure everything from fuel flow to ignition timing. So why not hook up a guy's brain to measure all those functions? Gland secretions, neuron firings, electrical levels. Why not? Just because I don't know how to do it doesn't mean that the existing diagnostic stuff isn't trivial compared to where it will be one day." I really had an edge. I must have been pleased with my outburst, because I felt an enormous pressure drop in my chest. Ben put up his hands, palms outward, in the classic no-offense style and said, "I'm not laughing at you, Nick. It was just funny and totally unexpected."

Strangely, I wasn't the least offended and required no assurance. They asked, I'm answering.

I continued, "Someone will find the keys to returning a body to a well-functioning state of sync. Once again I had posed a problem and had gotten to a resolution of sorts. Per always, however, the dots would remain unconnected. Nonetheless, if it can be thought, it can be done. That was probably more of a hope than an expectation, but that was my working conclusion from my session with myself.

"The last thought I had before parking and joining Raj on that particular night, which seems to be causing such gaiety here at Invictus, was a bit of a corollary on the chaos versus order battle. I pictured the aurora borealis and a rainbow. The first item of interest to me is that we say 'the' aurora borealis, but we say 'a' rainbow. While this is the accepted pattern of usage and description, I don't think it means to say that there is one omnipresent aurora borealis and that rainbows appear and melt away.

"The observation was that most of us regard rainbows as especially orderly while the word chaos, or chaotic, would not be misapplied to the aurora borealis. Each, however, is quite beautiful." My head began to hurt, because I was now mixing chaos and order with beauty. I was annoyed and had a bit of my well-known edge on when I joined Raj, who had arrived a few minutes earlier and was already seated.

"I was disheveled mentally and, while walking to our table, I had a quick thought about an old-timer with whom I'd travel on business. He was a very senior guy and, to this day, if I were to picture a true gentleman financier, he would still come to mind.

At the end of a traveling day, we'd bunk in at some modest hotel and head for the saloon. He'd always ask, 'Need a drink, Nick?'

"I'd invariably reply, 'I don't need one, but I'd like one.' On this particular evening, I needed one.

"I galumphed across the floor feeling, probably looking a bit like Ralph Kramden in one of his more frustrating moments. While Raj would never be taken for Ed Norton, he was about to be my foil for the next several minutes. Blissfully unaware of the coming tempest, he was sedate, and the contrast was more apt than you might imagine.

"For the moment I was Ralph Kramden. Big thoughts, always big thoughts, but I remained Nick the bond trader. Raj rose, and we shook hands.

" 'Hello, my friend, and how are you this evening?'

" 'How am I? How am I? I'll tell you how I am,' I almost bellowed. *Jesus, I am Ralph.* All I needed was Alice to come by as the waitress. Instead a young man materialized and I grabbed him by the arm. 'Get me a Killian's Red,' I directed. No 'please,' no nothing, just 'get me a Killian's'.

"I'd had my Ralph moment and attempted to retreat into myself, which occurs more frequently than I would wish, more than a little embarrassed. Raj was initially taken aback, but quickly changed his look to one of concern.

"I waved at Raj and started an apology for my behavior, which one of the old-timers would have referred to as bumptious.

"Raj smiled in his calming manner and asked, 'What is the matter, my friend? You seem in a state.

"I gave him the short version and felt a bit better having offloaded my many cosmic concerns.

" 'You have a fertile mind, Nick. Whence do you suppose these many ideas and notions spring?'

" 'Where do they come from, where do they come from? You want to know where they come from? I'll tell you where they come from!'

"On full autopilot, I spewed out, 'Number one, they come from outer space because there's more of that than anything else. Number two, they come from prisons, hospitals, and insane asylum inmates, because those poor souls have the most disposable

124

time. Number three, they come from other lunatics to whom I am connected electronically. Or number four, and most likely, I'm going nuts by stages.'

" 'No such, effendi, I think it is that you are simply a bit overloaded. It is time for you to refresh yourself. You should think seriously about a visit to a more tranquil setting.'

" 'Not your worst idea ever,' I responded.

"Seeing me in a decidedly calmer demeanor and in a receptive disposition, he asked, 'Where would you most like to be?'

"I have a habit of staring off somewhere when I try to think through a question. As we were essentially out of doors in a roof less atrium, I stared skyward. To my very great surprise, I found myself staring at the fullest of full moons, which seemed unusually bright.

"I looked back at Raj and quickly said, 'Up there, out there.'

" 'Up where, out where?' he inquired.

" 'The moon, or somewhere in space. It just seems there would be an incredible sense of peace. Not to mention beauty. I could be like Kingfish from *Amos and Andy*. Doing nothing and doing it slowly.'

"We started dinner, and I had a second drink. I had gotten calmer by measures, and we had settled into a more typical Raj-Nick conversation.

"As in most of our free-form chats, it took a life of its own and the subject became space, space travel, and what we might live to see in those regards. When Raj asked, as he was prone, what would I request if given one wish, I answered quickly, 'To see Earth from the moon.'

"He said, 'You can essentially do that now with pictures from the many satellites.

" 'I suppose,' I said, and thought, *Maybe it's time to drop the Peter Pan routine and become an adult,* a somewhat repulsive thought.

"We diverted our attention to dinner and there followed a silence of several moments.

"Then it happened again, random thought central came on the air and began broadcasting to station NICK. I sat up abruptly, startling Raj.

125

"Before he could inquire as to my latest flight, I said, 'You know what would be really cool?' The words were no more in midflight when I realized the idiocy of the question, so I spoke before Raj would have to invoke his propriety.

" 'What if you hooked together all the satellites around the Earth. You could have a real-time picture of the entire globe.'

" 'Hasn't that been done many times, effendi?'

" 'I'm talking about super-high resolution, so you could make out individual people.'

" 'Nick, I know little of what you suggest, but even one such picture would involve trillions upon trillions of pixels. Where would you store them?'

" 'No sweat, Raj, in outer space. There's more of that than anything else, remember?'

" 'There is indeed more of that than anything else, but where in particular would you put it?'

" 'That's easy. I'd use either a rainbow or an organized aurora borealis for my carrier. Better yet I'd use a combination of AM and FM. Back in my old army days, we'd use FM for line of sight and AM for earth hugging.

" 'In any case I'd take the pictures and put them on a carrier beam which would travel in, or on, a predetermined path. I'd have all the bandwidth I wanted and since the speeds are known and calculable, I'd always know where each data parcel would be. I could access highly specific historical data using any number of algorithms.

" 'If I thought I'd need x amount of storage I'd have a loop of a few miles or so. I can do the math on this myself, so it couldn't be too complicated. There's almost no limit to the number of sizes and shapes one could create for storing all this data, or more correctly, pictures. The whole deal would be the ability to bend or deflect and reflect a beam of given bandwidth.' "

I was coming to a pause to take a sip of water when I noticed Berkeley and Hunter looking at each other. I thought I saw Berkeley looking at Hunter and mouthing the words "Deflect and reflect" to himself.

"I went on at some length explaining to Raj the myriad ways one could form all manners of data beams, which I believed to be my own coined phrase—data beams. Certain energy sources could be originated on Earth or from satellites. The modes were many. And while I'm coining terms, you might find my nomenclature for extraterrestrial ray deployment of note. I call it beamology, beamometrics, and beam memory management."

The Drizos edge came over me again, and I glanced around. I saw four totally professional, attentive faces awaiting further word from the head of the table. I didn't know whether they were in fact interested, being sensitive to my obvious delicate pride, or whether they had simply concluded I was a loony. For a second, I really didn't care, as my inner peace regained control.

"I think Raj found the many subjects of some interest, but he did ask me if that wasn't a great deal of work for a motion picture of the Earth. He went on to suggest that he found my harangue—per his gentlemanly ways, he called it a discussion—on the generalized area of brain and/or spinal pathologies much more compelling and timely.

"I'm coming to the end of my recollection, Ben. How are we for time?"

"We are in very good shape, Nick. We'll have ample time for you to conclude and for your debriefings."

Ben added, "Nick, that was a fine recap." He looked at Vic and Tom and asked if they had any questions or comments. I gathered that was a fairly pro forma ritualistic gesture and was not surprised when they replied no. Ben then excused his two colleagues, and we three sat back.

"As you say," I continued, "Raj had grown weary of my Buck Rogers and Flash Gordon rant and we went back to a quieter, less stressful discussion of my treatise on epilepsy and, in his words, related business. The basic theme of our dinner stayed on point for the next hour or so as we went back and forth on the human condition. I got to the synchromometer again, and by his reaction, there was little doubt we had finished another of our pleasant dinners together.

"I had gotten quite peaceful by this time. Maybe just being with my friend and his ever graceful consideration was the cause, but I was getting peaceful. We were enjoying an after dinner drink and Raj asked if I would be following up on my thoughts of epilepsy and related disorders. He said related, because he thought the logic was well based, if more poetic than empiric.

"It was my old case of dots and voids, so I said, 'I'd think about it.'

He said, "I would encourage you, and I know a few people in the field. If you would be interested, I would be glad to make some introductions."

"As we waited for our cars, Raj told me that he would be traveling for the better part of the next month. It would be part business, part relaxation.

For reasons, as usual unknown, I didn't ask him where he would be. That seems to be a bit clarified now. That, and a memorable drive home, because of the especially brilliant moon, is my recollection of that dinner to the best of my honest and thorough ability."

Other words failing I just said, "thank you."

Ben then regarded me as though inviting comment. Or so I thought.

"Ben, I said, I'm back to where I was during our car ride. I have no idea what you want with a pedestrian bond trader like me, but, if I may say, I think I'd enjoy your company in another setting. I will say, however, that while I haven't done any heavy lifting, I am quite tired. I feel drained."

"As well you might be, Nick. No matter how you cut it, I understand this to be a fairly strange and imposing place."

"I sense I'm near the end of this novel experience."

"You sense correctly, Nick, it is now time for me to read you the rules of the road, as you put it earlier. You and I are going to spend a few minutes together in that regard. Then you and Raj will have a similar amount of time for what must be some very personal matters following which you, Raj and I will reconvene briefly. I will say again before we formally part, you will leave with our thanks."

For a guy who was in freak central, in a car with a couple of loonies, a few hours ago, I was beginning to anticipate the male equivalent of postpartum depression. Maybe it was the Stockholm Syndrome again, except that I felt no sense of personal danger. Only personal ignorance.

Ben excused Raj who rose and left smartly. Ben then said "Anita" to no one in particular. That same stylish woman appeared through a sliding door.

"Status," inquired Ben.

"Secure," said the woman called Anita.

"Last sweep?" asked Ben.

"Eight minutes ago," she replied.

"Thank you," said Ben and she disappeared silently.

"Well Nick, I hope you enjoyed your visit to spook central as you might call it, and I hope we have been decent hosts."

"You have, Ben. You have indeed. If I may say, most of my acquaintances and business colleagues regard themselves as good judges of people. I don't; I've been screwed over more times than not, and, even given these many lessons, I'm no better than fifty-fifty at discerning real people from the other group. Or as one of my sergeants used to say, being able to tell chicken salad from chicken shit.

"That's another colorful simile, or is it metaphor, Nick, but I don't get your point."

"The point is, Ben, that I think you are in the for-real group. What I would like is for you to tell me I'm right or that you screwed me over big time. I wouldn't even be offended if I were wrong again."

He then grabbed my forearm and fixed me with a steely glare from his tired but soft blue eyes and said, "Nick, I've been nothing but the real deal and you'll leave here with more of the same. I would add that my record on people is not much better than the one you present, but I'm not going to ask you, Nick. I've already concluded that you're okay. Okay from me is a rave. But like I said, you needn't answer."

We just stared at each other. He was probably focused, while I had a number of different thoughts and notions.

He broke the silence by saying, "Okay, Nick, to paraphrase your earlier comment, here's the way it's gonna be. Not going to be, but gonna be. Are you with me?"

"Roger," I said impulsively.

129

"As to the debriefing, it won't surprise you, that should anything remotely resembling a contact between you and Invictus ever emerge, it would be met with one hundred percent denial and obfuscation. And would probably include personal attacks on your sanity. You know that right?"

"I know that."

"We both know that you were cleared in the army for Secret and would have been cleared for Top Secret had you stayed in the service. Plus I've made some considered judgments about you, so I'll give you a straight short message."

He paused again and I obliged by saying, "Okay."

"You recalled during your dinner with Raj his advice to pursue the potential causes of epilepsy?"

"I did, and I related same to you during my soliloquy."

"It was good advice. Am I registering with you?"

"You are. You're saying stay away from the satellite stuff."

"You read me five by five, Nick, said my host as he trotted out some old army jargon meaning loud and clear. "You ain't as dumb as you look". He didn't miss much and he saw me giggle at the IQ reference.

"Here's the deal, Nick. We're doing some fancy stuff with deflecting and reflecting, but not in the ways you imagine. We think it may advance our technology to a major advantage level, so again I would urge you to focus on your more humanitarian objectives."

"As in epilepsy and related?"

"Just so," replied Ben, as Raj would have said. "I won't ask if you have a problem with that. That would be trivial and bordering on the offensive. Instead I ask you, man to man, if you will respect and comply with my request."

"I will, Ben, but you give me too much credit. I'm not your basic gifted technologist. I had responded giving my answer the weight, spirit and emphasis it deserved. I hardly knew this guy, but I gave my word and that was that.

"I appreciate that, Nick," he said in a low but forceful tone.

I'll do as I say Ben, but in the spirit of man-to-man honesty I think I am absorbing here, you should know something". Before seeking an inquiry from Ben, I added, "I have discussed my beam bending thesis with a couple high tech companies. In particular, Atlas Microwave out of Chicago and Plasma Technologies in Atlanta. The CEO's of these two companies are friends of mine."

For the first time in my less than two days of acquaintance with the man, Ben flushed visibly.

In what I can only describe as a professional deflection of his own, he nodded and mumbled something like "interesting."

"This is a problem, isn't it Ben?"

"It could be, Nick. How involved or detailed did these talks get?"

"I talk to these two guys at regular intervals. My beam stuff was incidental to other subjects, but I have to say, it was deemed interesting by both of them."

"I don't know much about your business, Ben, but it looks like some damage control will be forthcoming. Am I wrong?"

"No, you're dead right, Nick. We can talk about this at another time, but I would ask you to avoid this subject in the future. If you talk with these guys, please do not attempt to advance the beam discussions. Can you do that?"

"I can and I will, Ben," I said with conviction and resolution though I wondered if my sense of full disclosure and honesty had been misjudged and misplaced. Had I started a potential chain of adverse actions and reactions. I was very unsettled and my stomach churned some nasty acid.

"That would be good. It should not be a problem if you don't advance it. As I said, it would be good for all if you stuck to the epilepsy and healthcare set of topics. In all, everything should be manageable. With your assent, I would like to proceed with the debriefing. You'll understand if we don't make any further mention of beam deflection, won't you?

"I will and debriefing sounds like a good thing to do now."

Like the gifted professional he is, Ben returned to his role of gracious host. I could almost feel the bumps being removed and dissolved from the air between us.

"Tell me Nick, out of curiosity, do you have any take-aways, as they say in the biz world?"

"I do, Ben. I think you guys are straight. I'm glad you're here and I wish you the best. I think you're a little tough on the elected guys, but I don't disagree violently. I am particularly pleased you agree that there can't be panderers without panderees. That was especially economical in words and had a powerful impact. And last, I get the message that you're in serious stuff so, count on it, I'll keep my word.

"And this may be totally not appropriate—I hate that word, appropriate, maybe more than just about all others in our language. It usually conjures up an image to me of some thoroughly detestable nerdy dweeb or dweebette bitching about one thing or another. I hate it, but might we get together some time down the road?"

"It's more likely than you might think, Nick. I'm getting close to the end of the trail here myself. Self assessment has to fight off self delusion and there are very bad consequences for confusing irreplaceable importance with going stale. Plus, believe it or not, mine is a fairly high energy level slot. In short, I spend a major portion of my time trying to identify and select my successor, so we might have stone crabs in a much more leisurely setting some time."

I just nodded. "I'd like that."

"We'll be parting company soon. I already told you that some high grade business will be running through your trading operation. I know you'll give it first rate attention. You'll also be getting three phone numbers; alpha, beta and gamma. I thought, being Greek, you'd like that. Alpha is a line to me. I expect you'll never use it as it's only for dire emergencies. Beta will be a number for Raj. Needless to say, we'll have to move him on. Both alpha and beta are totally secure and continuously swept, so you can contact Raj from time to time, and I'm sure you will use your best discretion. If we think, or have cause to think otherwise, this number will be discontinued. You won't be having your weekly chats, but things may change as Raj will be calling it a day in the near term. Last, gamma is for local emergencies such as healthcare, accidents, and suchlike. Got it?

"I got it. Where are the numbers?"

"They'll be sent to you in fairly inconspicuous modes. Maybe on a utility bill. Maybe on a bank statement. You'll figure it out. Any questions?"

"Alpha and beta seem clear, but why the generosity with gamma. I have health insurance and I'm well attended by some good doctors.

"It's the old two-way street, Nick. While we are as straight up as we can be and while we will continue to endeavor to stay that way, the national mission comes first. Moreover, while we don't regard you as a priority risk, it makes sense to avoid situations which could have exposure for us. For example, if you were to have a medical procedure involving sedation, we would want you in a secure facility. You follow me?"

"I do, but how would you know?"

"Nick, we're human and we're fallible, but to use your expression, we're not the amateur hour. Got it?" he inquired again.

"I got it."

"Let me double back to Raj, because somewhere inside you may feel betrayed. As I'm sure you can appreciate, Raj has to move on. He would have been scheduled for reassignment soon in any case. I'll say the following only because Raj is a true and devoted friend to you. I met him many years ago when I was one step removed from being a lost soul. The details aren't important, and I mention this to you only because we share a similar affection for the man.

"Raj is largely responsible for my being in my present position. He is and will remain my most valued counselor. He was originally sent to Florida to direct a number of intelligence activities. His meeting you and your ultimate friendship were coincidences. Had it not been for your curious mind and your animated soul, he might have spent his years here and moved on without notice. Nick, that's the short version and all you really need know.

"We have some time remaining for Raj and you to rally one last time as he would put it. We'll then send you on your way as promised."

Ben ushered me into a small anteroom where Raj was seated. My weird mind began to race again. This time the contending senses were sadness and confusion. From somewhere within the cavern of my being a sentimental bomb detonated. I was at one of those unexpected and unimagined points in life

133

where feelings are overpowering and words are inadequate and useless.

Raj rose and, has happened on many occasions, his presence radiated serenity. He smiled. I was reassured and felt very much at peace.

I said, "I suppose this should be brief."

"That would be best, effendi."

There were many things which had been unsaid during our many times together, but it was clear that most, if not all, didn't require the spoken word. I said something to that effect, and Raj nodded.

"So how do you think this will all play out," I asked.

"The only true and honest answer, my friend, is that I do not know. I do know that I am nearing the end of my involvement in this business and, sooner rather than later, I would like to turn my attention to a number of the more pleasant endeavors which have eluded me these many years. While I am unable to project a timetable of events and geography, I would be most pleased and desirous of continuing our friendship. It would be my greatest pleasure if that could be within arms reach. At this point, effendi, I can only express my desires, but I promise I will act on them.

"You should know, my most esteemed friend, I have had several bouts with sadness since I determined you should speak with Ben. I have had an advantage over you in that regard as I have had time to become peaceful. My several thoughts these past weeks were of impending loss, but that is wrongful thinking. The more important thought is of the good fortune we have enjoyed through each other's company. I hope in time you will come to a similar state."

I nodded, and that was probably the most eloquent thing to do. It was time. More time together would neither change the near term course of that which must be done nor sever a friendship borne of sincerity and kindness. It was time.

I mumbled a similar thought which he may or may not have heard, but he knew very well what I meant to say.

"Raj, I will miss you terribly, but the only important thing for me right now is to wish you the best life may present you and, above all, peace."

"And to you, effendi, as well. I will carry you in my heart forever."

Prolonging our farewell made no sense, and Raj opened the door for Ben.

Abruptly, but without provoking offense, Ben said, "Nick, we've covered everything. It is time for you to return to normalcy. I speak for my colleagues and myself when I thank you again. We wish you well."

I took a seat and began to roll up the sleeve on my other arm. "I presume we'll be doing it here," I said.

"We will," said Ben as he produced a syringe from a pocket vest sized case.

Down in the direction associated with sleep, and down I went quickly but gently. I think I recall Ben saying to Raj, "he's a good fellow."

Or maybe that's just what I wanted him to say.

The cab driver said, "here we are, fella. Schooner Pier in Hale's Point."

As before I sat up feeling alert and refreshed. I looked about and found myself once again in happy rhythm with my surroundings. The sun was low on the horizon and people of all ages were flocking to the pier to see another of our spectacular sunsets.

I checked my watch, which read 5:45 P.M. I asked the driver, "may I have the time please."

He replied, "about quarter to."

"Thanks."

"You must have had a long weekend. At least that's what your pals said when they called me from the train station. They said to bring you here, but to let you sleep till you felt like getting up."

They must have fed me smart pills back at my weekend retreat, because it seemed second nature to just meld myself into my new conversations in polite but bland fashion.

"Yes, indeed, it was a long weekend, but it's always nice to be home." That part was easy, because I really am a home body. I like traveling and I like the places I've been able to visit. But, in the end, I like being home.

"How much do I owe you, pal?" borrowing from the friendly dialect of one of our traders from Jersey.

"It's all taken care of. Your pals picked up the tab. You must have been really sleepy; you barely made a sound all the way from the Hightown Station."

I dug into my pocket and found some loose bills. I reached over the seat and handed him a twenty.

"Not necessary, sir," he said. "Your friends were very generous."

I insisted by squeezing his hand around the Jackson and said, "Well then, have one on me at cocktail time."

It occurred to me that the last time I had gotten into a car, things got a bit surreal, so I eased out somewhat gingerly and took in the familiar sights. I don't know with any accuracy how long I had been out, but I had awoken with that same feeling of restfulness and well-being. I reflected briefly on my recent journey, but was quickly overcome with the natural beauty of my hometown. Life goes on, I thought. Life goes on.

I closed the door and waved good-bye to the driver. I probably said, "See ya next time," because I just about always do that, some kind of closure thing.

So here I was back in Hale's Point.

5
Doctor Jack

October 24th

Except I'm not in Hale's Point. I'm in a softy lit, obviously functional room. It's probably a hospital. And my low-tech calendar says it's the twenty-fourth.

It is a hospital, I concluded, but *it's a movie,* I thought to myself. It's definitely a movie and I've seen it, or parts of it before. *You're damn right it's a movie, numb nuts, and you're damn right you've seen parts of it. You're in it.* My companion, the 101, provides constancy but not necessarily fellowship. I have come to regard some as preferable to none, so we endure each other's company.

Then the swirling started again, but the call to order things was quickly answered, and events seemed to be arranging themselves into some sense of rational patterns. The question was not *Where am I?* The main question is *When am I?*

Then the twin notions of muck and clarity reintroduced themselves. I had a very strong sense that we had met and chatted in similar surroundings at various times.

I was sure I hadn't been drinking to any extent, but I had a case of the old whirlies. This time it wasn't the bed or the room that was spinning, but a rush of ideas and impressions. Things that would happen in the future were colliding with unclear recollections of my past.

The answer was really quite simple. I'm in an asylum, and I'm nuts.

That wasn't difficult. Immediately following that bit of self-diagnosis, a very familiar inner peace engulfed me. And why

137

not, most of my friends and acquaintances are similarly disposed.

That wasn't difficult at all. Get rid of the self-denial, admit to your reality, and the euphoria of freedom settles in. Then relaxation, then sleep.

I think I slept for a while, because my last conscious thought was of the simple flowers not far from my bedside. Now I'm facing a small nightstand adorned only with a simple container of water and some paper cups. Sure enough, I roll over, and there are the flowers. Brilliant.

I also seem to recall that I had some serious pain and knife-like stabs when I rolled around, but they have receded quite noticeably.

"Good morning, Mr. Drizos," says a pleasant voice.

I look at this equally pleasant face a bit quizzically.

"It's only me, Mr. Drizos, Jeanette."

"Oh sure, Jeanette," I responded in my best I-knew-that fashion.

It's not a question of who am I. I know I'm Mr. Drizos, Nick Drizos, and the proud owner of the Nick 101, a limited but loyal and ably functioning semiconscious alter ego—one that speaks back to me.

"Good morning to you, Jeanette. I must have been daydreaming a bit."

"Well, you're making swell progress, Mr. Drizos, and you'll be walking around again today."

Swell, is it? The 'thirties and 'forties again. Oh well, she probably meant nothing by that. Maybe everything really does go around and come around.

"How long have I been here now?" I asked, trying not to sound totally ignorant.

"Well, let's see, you were admitted on the tenth. It's now the twenty-fourth. And, better yet, you're scheduled for discharge in two or three days. But, I don't want to forget my main mission here. What can I do for you?"

"Oh, nothing right now, Jeanette. I think I might just want to nap a bit. And, please call me Nick." I think I had been getting to know and like this woman.

"I'd be happy to do that, Nick. If you want anything, just buzz. I'm only a few steps away."

"Thanks again for everything, Jeanette," I said, as she turned and left.

I must have slept for a while, because the whirling confusion seemed to have slowed greatly. The 101 was at work: *Let's start with what we know and then patch together whatever we can.* Great idea I thought. Deep thinker that I am, as old Hal would have observed sarcastically. Who is Hal, I asked silently of the 101? *In due time,* came the muted response.

So I'm Nick Drizos. What's a Nick Drizos? Let's just start with nouns and adjectives and see if we make any progress. *Fine, but as Paul Craig would say, "Nick, you often mistake motion for progress."* Who is Paul Craig? *Never mind,* came the 101's echo. *We're stuck. Let's just try to move; motion is good.*

So, I'm Nick Drizos. What else? Pudgy, or as I prefer, portly. (*Were I a woman, I'd be "full-figured,"* I mused whimsically.) Bond trader. I know all that.

How about some verbs and adverbs. Likes? Likes women. What kinds of women? Many kinds. Mostly mature. Mostly relaxed. Mostly good-humored. What else?

Food. Greek food. Other food? Indian food.

And then the swirl slowed, becoming first translucent and then almost crystalline. At least portions of this frenetic mosaic called recall. It was happening. The first olive out of the bottle deal. Get that first one out and then . . . "Jesus, Nick, if it weren't for clichés, you couldn't speak at all," I could hear Hal Sandstrom, the would-be Viking and investment banker pal of mine, say. Oh, that Hal.

"Oh really, Hal, well clichés may be the bane of elegant conversation, but they're economical and they're descriptive and they're largely true. And you're making me feel like a pinhead."

People. Names. Old and strange comments. What else is in there? Places. Hale's Point. The trading floor. Schooner Pier.

I was making some progress or I was making no progress. I didn't know, so I sat more or less upright in my comfortable but boring bed and stared effortlessly at a blank wall. It was a nice feeling. The 101 was off duty and I felt totally untaxed. It was a most pleasant interlude.

Jeanette appeared and asked in gracious tones if I would like some dinner.

I was about to say no thank you, but she continued, "Gail told me that you had requested some curried chicken and rice. That was off-limits during your early days here, as it would have been a little rough on your system, but we have some for you if you wish."

That did it. Curry, which I could almost smell. India. And Raj.

"Yes, thank you very much. I would love some curry."

"Be back in a few," she said, and sped off in her professionally efficient manner.

From there it all flowed together. *Recall is a funny thing,* I thought. *The stuff is in there, it's just that it can't be accessed. Or it's being suppressed. But it's in there. Somewhere.* Whatever the cause of not being able to get to it, a simple and pleasant association with a certain food had opened a path. I could only wonder, absent my fondness for curry, if I would get to the same state of awareness. As has happened repeatedly, I started thinking of various therapies for epilepsy, ADDS, and other pathologies. *I'm Nick Drizos, all right,* I thought, as the 101 issued a back-to-the-business-at-hand order.

The proverbial weight of fear and insecurity had been removed, and I was aware of my own circulation tingling in my fingers and toes. Recall was becoming a nonissue; the same was not true, however, for time and timing. I had no trouble recounting a series of events, I just wasn't sure of when they occurred.

I went over the events as I was now recalling them several times, and was satisfied that each rendition was identical to its predecessor. That is a habit of mine in general. When I have successfully mastered something for the first time, I do it over a few times, often several times, to assure myself that the first success wasn't random luck. I think I do that, because I am pretty much a classic digger, a nicer way of saying I'm not very smart. Plus sometimes I fear forgetting how I achieved the particular goal, and maybe repetition will reinforce my memory. Or maybe I'm

140

just insecure. I still recite the U.S. presidents in order at least once a day, or name the eight states that begin with the letter "M." I'm hopeful they're just quirks, but that's part of what makes a Nick Drizos.

I was now at a point where I was feeling good about my life's activities up to the tenth of October. A little more R-and-R, and I would be back on the trading desk. Life is good; I'd like to be part of it.

Then it struck me almost savagely. I departed from that place, Invictus, on September eighteenth. It's now October. I have no memory of the intervening time.

I prepared myself for another crash. Prepare may be a stronger word than my actual capabilities in the face of what I imagined was coming. Resigned myself might be more accurate. What would it be? Pounding headaches? Maddening screaming voices? Calls from lost souls?

Where were my internal safeguards? The 101 had also assumed the worst, and I could imagine the little microchips lighting up the off-duty sign. *Do your worst,* I thought, and then went limp.

No sooner did I lie down to enjoy the inevitable, as the old homely phrase goes, when there appeared in my minds eye a clear picture of Raj with, there is no other word, that beatific smile. Once again, I was at peace. I would fear nothing.

"Relax, effendi, I am with you," the animated phantasm seemed to say. "No harm will befall you. I swear."

And relax I did. All would be revealed in its own time. For now drowsiness and the pleasure of dreams would conspire once again to light the return to my former reality.

"Good morning, Nick, it's Jeanette. And how are you feeling this morning?"

"Quite good," I said, "due in no small part to you and Gail, JoAnn, and whoever else has been caring for me. Yes, I'm feeling quite good."

"I would imagine you must be hungry by now. I brought your dinner, but you were sleeping most restfully." She decided a good night's sleep was the best therapy. She asked me if she made the right call.

"It was a very good call. And yes, I would love some breakfast."

After a brief discussion, we settled on a couple of poached eggs and bacon, some orange juice and coffee, and she disappeared once again.

The breakfast was wonderful. I think it was especially good, because I was at peace as well as very hungry. My insides were no longer in turmoil, and I was probably producing zero stomach acid or whatever it is that turns an otherwise fine meal into an unpleasant experience with all manners of impolite aftershocks.

A short while later I was walking about unaided and feeling fairly secure. My daily route had been up and down several halls and then into an exercise room where I would be assisted on several machines and finish on a treadmill. I was walking without discernible pain and was feeling just about normal. Normal for a portly guy.

Because my balance was also deemed normal, I was allowed to shower by myself. This was a treat of the highest order, and I luxuriated under the spray. Like many others of my acquaintance, much of my greatest thinking is done in the shower, so I took the opportunity to commune with myself. *Nick, my boy, your mind is on the mend and your body is approaching its former status. So you can't recall a multiple-month period. Most likely you will, but if you don't, you don't. It is what it is and it will be what it will be. Let it go.* I'm sure that Raj was in there somewhere, but whether or not, I was surely taking the advice he would have proffered.

I must have stayed in that wonderful shower every bit as long as I had imagined, for when I returned to my room, the physical therapists were awaiting me. "I'm sorry to have kept you waiting, fellas, but I got captivated by the shower. It had been a while."

They just waved it off, and the one they call Herc (I gathered, short for Hercules) said, "No sweat, you're our only mission for today."

Being somewhat portly, as I prefer to describe myself, I'm

given to numerous aches and pains. As a result, I've sought relief on many occasions from local physical therapists and sports medicine guys. I've had ultrasound, several types of electrotherapy, and thought I was generally au courant on this art form. These guys, however, had a bewildering array of gadgetry and proceeded to employ them in a carefully orchestrated sequence. They would hit what they called an occasional hot spot, but their efforts were being accepted gratefully. I was moving further and further into progressively greater relaxation and was sure I'd be asleep in a short while.

"Hey fellas," I asked, "will you be needing me, or can I drift off?"

Someone answered, "We'll need you to supply some resistance for a few exercises, so we'll do them first and then you can drop off as you wish. How would that be?"

"Sounds fine to me, just tell me what to do."

They then led me through a series of stretching, compressing, and torsion activities in which I was asked to resist. As I'm sure they've been told many times, they were very accomplished and their efforts were much appreciated; these guys were exceptional. In fairly quick time they advised me they no longer needed my active participation and that I could nod off. Among other things, I felt as though my circulation was working at a new level and bringing relief and comfort to virtually every part of my being.

Whether I was in deep sleep or, for me, in a new state of carefree rest, I am not sure. And whether I was dreaming or imagining, I can't say either. In either case, it remains that I am a bond trader with a set of senses, developed over many years. It is not surprising that I would take them with me when I leave the land of wakefulness.

I often lay my head down with the Bard's words, "What dreams may come." I like to dream, probably as much as I like old movies, and I've had some beauties. Such it was, as I gave myself over to my two therapists.

I found myself sitting on a favored bench in Schooner Park, gazing at the Gulf. In short order I was explaining the world, or my small part of it, to myself in bond trader lingo. I always start with the greater context that the world is cyclical. There are short cycles and longer cycles, but the sun comes up and goes down, the tides ebb and flow, and this is our lot. Those are the longer cycles.

Me, I'm mostly a short-cycle guy in practice. At my level, bonds trade up and down with gains and losses as the consequence. There is upside and downside. For me, at the very present, there is great upside as I'm now recovering. But there's always downside.

That must have been a trigger of sorts, because I awoke in semi-panic. The therapists were gone, so I must have been out for a while. And disquiet and unease began to reinvade. Who'd want to blow away a bond trader? I had asked that of myself many times in recent days. And why can I recall all of my existence as well as ever, except for the most recent several weeks?

Why? Because someone doesn't want me to. Those images, memories, and impressions are being suppressed. Then the worst happened, and I bolted forward, almost convulsing.

It became more than clear; it was shatteringly obvious. The Invictus folks. Whether Ben was for real or just another of the many guys who had played me was a question. But irrespective of that, he had made it clear beyond doubt that his mission came first. That's the only line of reasoning that makes any sense.

I either blabbed something damaging, or they had serious second thoughts about me. They probably concluded that a dead squirrelly bond trader was the best sort for their purposes.

Back comes the 101 playing point-counterpoint. So why would they bring you here and nurse you back to health, cumquat—a term of deprecation I am wont to use.

The immediate response was one of acquiescence, but then my downside self posed the rejoinder. Yes, it went on, a dead Nick solves all their problems, but since you escaped the blast, there is no body. And with no body, there is a great deal of explaining to do. And situations in which there is great explaining are not situations agreeable to the Invictus folks. Yes, they are the assassins, but they have to resurface the old Nick and in fairly short order. The disappearing Judge Crater deal is probably a nonstarter for them.

And then, more clarity. What I thought was a gap in my memory is exactly backwards. I am not being nursed back to health. I am not being assisted in recovering my memory; it's being erased. The most recent few weeks or so are unknown to me. In short order, I will have no knowledge of the past couple of years, and then I'll be a total void. Then it's just the matter of reprogramming me as selectively as they wish, and the old Nickie D will be back among his old pals. Harmless and good to go, as they say in the Corps. A McMurphy lobotomy—a Cuckoo's Nest special. No clue, no harm to anyone.

That's the way it was.

You're nuts, screamed the 101, more as a parting shot than anything else.

Some explanations are just too fantastic, and that was one of them.

I was sitting up holding my head in both hands and sweating most disagreeably when I heard footsteps coming toward my bed.

"Hello, Nick," said a new voice. "I'm what you call your attending physician. Please call me Jack."

I managed a very weak "Hello, Jack."

"I've been the head of the team putting you back together, Nick, but I've avoided you in your waking hours because you had, and continue to have, some nasty problems. You have improved enough to begin some serious dialogue with me, but as recently as a few days ago careless words here or there could have triggered bad outcomes, including a relapse."

He stopped for a moment and regarded me cautiously. "Nick," he continued, "you appear distraught. Can I help you with something?"

"I'd hope so, Jack. That's what one usually visits a hospital for, and I'm not being sarcastic or a wise guy. I've had a full gamut of post-trauma reactions as you folks call them. I've pronounced myself paranoid, delusional, and well on my way to total dementia. I could use some honest words right about now."

He pulled up a tall stool and leaned back so that he's just about eye to eye with me, then paused rather dramatically and said, "You mean, 'Give it to me straight, doc'?"

Another line right out of the 'thirties and 'forties. It was de rigueur for countless pictures when the good guy, or a bad guy turned good, has waved off encouragement and just wants to square things as best he can. It's alongside the line where the doc comes out of surgery and confronts the distraught spouse or parents and says something like . . . "We've done all we can. Now it's up to . . ." as he raises his eyes skyward.

Are these guys born of one nasty brood, or what?

He chuckled warmly and said, "I'm just jerking you around a bit, Nick. For your edification and comfort, I'm the chief physician for Invictus. I'm cleared well beyond Top Secret and I know your entire story including the episode of the past several months. I have no other job but to get you back to being Nick Drizos in every respect. I'll stay with you now or leave as you wish, but I think it would be most helpful if we began talking now. Your call."

He could have been related to Ben. He had much the same manner and engendered the same type of trust as Ben. The HR guy in that joint must be something. Likewise the selection process. They seem to have a collection of unusually nice people for such a miserable, a better word failing, profession. Confusion rose, subsided and was replaced by another relative calm. I initiated a search within myself. The 101 was stuck in neutral and managed only an on-the- one-hand, on-the-other-hand response. Hung in an indecisive loop. Will this be homicide, suicide, or some other cide? Or are they really gonna put old Nick back together?

So, it was like being back at Fort Gordon in a leadership class. Make a decision, Captain, make a decision, for Christ's sake! Wait a minute, this guy looked in on me a couple night's back. He introduced himself. I'm lost. Help!

It came back to the business thing: yes or no. A conclusion was not forthcoming, so I pushed the desiderata down to the bare minimum. If these guys, with all their high-tech paraphernalia and toys, wanted to eliminate me, I'd be gone. My memory-erase thesis was apparently right alongside the synchromometer and beamology creations. No, I concluded, they don't mean me any

146

harm. I've probably managed to become a total pain in the ass, but I'm not a termination candidate. Not now, anyway.

I said, "Yes, let's do talk."

Before I could continue, Jack replied, "Good call. Let's get to it. You can have first shot."

"What's fair game in this exercise?" I inquired.

"It will be as you wish, Nick. If you get into a high-risk area, I'll divert you. That's a major part of my responsibility right now. I did look in on you a while ago. We spoke briefly, but you were still a physical mess."

"Okay, then why don't you tell me what you can, what you want to accomplish, what we're going to do and how we're going to do it."

"Not bad for a simple bond trader, Nick. We've become accustomed to the soft con, as you would put it, that you use so I'll not be using any baby talk with you. If I get away from you with the medical jargon, just pipe up and we'll regroup."

And we started. He began with the blast and retraced the intervening time frame very much as I had reconstructed it. He touched on a number of details, some of the larger dots in the chain, probably to assure me of his knowledge base. In less than fifteen minutes, he had gotten to my present state of essentially total recall excepting the most recent few weeks.

He had consulted some notes, but only infrequently. And on those occasions it was usually to confirm a date or time. I had been nodding during his remarks, so there was little need to regroup along the way.

Although it was superfluous and functionally gratuitous, I added, "That's just about my recollection."

"Good." He nodded. "We'll be using that as our base from which to complete your restoration. Right now," he continued, "would be a good time to apprise you of your condition on the tenth and what has transpired since then."

"Please," I said.

"Setting aside your being the target of a car bomb, you were quite lucky. You were shielded fore and aft by the garage door and the swing set. You were tangled in the rope net when we got to you, and—"

I sat up vigorously. "When you got to me. How did you happen to get to me?"

Up came a Ben move. Hands extended, palms outward. "Not yet, Nick, we'll get to that. Very good, but not yet."

He continued, "The rope net acted as a cushion, or fairly rigid trampoline, and made for a relatively soft landing. You had several cuts, some quite large, but you had not lost any appreciable blood. Your pulse was low, but not dangerously so. You had three broken bones and a broken nose. There were also several deep bruises, which we call subdural hemotomae. Later, they would surface to the epidermis in their yellow-purplish sheen before we managed them away. The greatest concern was that your spleen had ruptured and your appendix was inflamed. The latter probably has no cause-and-effect relationship with the explosion."

I felt about myself and did not discern any evidence of this assessment.

Jack sensed my puzzlement and went on. "The bone breaks were, very fortunately, totally clean. We were able to fuse them using technology and procedures not yet introduced to generalized practice, but which we have employed for some time now. You also had several cuts and minor lacerations that would ordinarily have resulted in some very observable scars. Those were addressed and remediated further with plastic surgery. At certain times, especially in cold weather, you will be aware of the scars because keloid, that is to say scar tissue, cannot stretch and contract like normal epidermis. The spleen and appendix were removed without complication, and physically, you are just about as before."

I was dumbfounded and just stared at this guy.

"As to your recall, we made no efforts to assist you for the first several days. The first mission was to get your physical side as functional as possible. A body in pain must devote its first energies to stabilizing itself. If anything, we attempted to retard conscious thought during this first critical phase."

He paused again, clearly inviting me to pipe up. I accommodated him. "Makes sense, I suppose, but I'm very aware of things that initially just swirled and would alternatively get clearer and then more confused." I added some comments about the murk and clarity duo.

"All very natural, Nick. Depending upon the degree of impairment and the age of the owner, the body will set about reassembling itself. Some of the case studies we have approach the supernatural, but then what we know is trivial compared to what we will discover eventually."

"You may be familiar with one of the old classic experiments where people were given glasses to wear for an extended time period. These glasses turned everything upside down. After a while, and without fail, each person's brain could reinvert the images, and they performed a given number of tasks as before with the glasses on. Later the glasses would be removed, and everything remained upside- down. Shortly thereafter, the body adjusted again and went back to pre-experiment normalcy. We have also witnessed instances in which major portions of a brain had been destroyed by a particular pathology, yet the brain managed to transfer a number of functions to other portions of itself. These situations are many and vary greatly in degree. All this, Nick, by way of saying that your body would have done no less than you would expect."

Another one. As you would expect.

The lately lazing Nick 101 awoke and prompted me. "Correct me if I'm mistaken, but in the short while we've been together, you seem to have dropped more than a few of my colloquialisms and mannerisms."

"You are exactly right, Nick. We are very familiar with some of your key speech patterns and, as you noted, we employ them for low-level stimulation. My diagnosis, which was supported by your early progress, was that you would ultimately attain complete recall. And, as I mentioned earlier, you are nearly as physically fit as before. No issues there. We had, and continue to have, a problem, however. That problem is time, and I'll get to that."

"So I have repaired myself?"

"Largely, but not exactly. We employed a number of external stimuli. Some to this point, as it turned out, have been more effective that others."

I was paying attention, but I felt another incoming Nick

walkabout moment. "I want very much to stay with this, Jack, but these windowless surroundings are depressing me. I'm feeling suffocated in a very real sense. Plus the lack of real world sounds is very disorienting. Would it be possible to see something real and to breathe some real air?"

"It would, Nick. I'm very glad you asked. Get your robe and slippers and follow me."

I had expected a "Sorry, but no can do" response. I was elated, so I followed my new counselor out the door and down the familiar nondescript hallway. Instead of heading toward the rehab center, we made a couple of left turns and confronted an elevator. Jack placed a palm on a pad of sorts and looked into an eyepiece.

Presently the door opened into a basically standard elevator car. There were two columns of unnumbered buttons and little else observable. Jack pressed a number of the keys in a sequence, and the car started moving upward quite slowly. After what seemed to be about ten seconds, the elevator stopped and the door opened.

"After you, Nick."

I stepped out onto a small, walled patio about twenty feet square. I guessed it to be late afternoon. I had been a bit anxious, not at all sure that there was an external reality. The dream sequence notion had persisted despite all the assurances to the contrary. I was very pleased that leaving my nicely appointed cave seemed a very natural thing to do, although my eyes burned much like they did when we adolescents would exit a Saturday movie matinee.

We were about six feet above ground level and totally surrounded by trees of lesser height. From my old sailing days I remembered that one can see about ten to twelve miles or so from sea level to the horizon. Being about six feet up, that might extend to maybe fourteen miles. Fourteen miles of trees, almost two hundred square miles. This was no corporate campus. I had to be in the midst of a national park. No surprise really; government stuff.

Jack smiled and said, "Does this look familiar? Not the particular location, just the general ambience."

"It does," I said, feeling no small measure of relief. "I've asked this question before, Jack, and I most likely know the answer, but I don't suppose you'll tell me where I am, will you?"

"As you say, Nick, you know I can't do that."

He was gathering himself to advise me it was time to get back to work, but I preempted him. "Thank you very much anyway, Jack. You don't know how reassuring this has been. Shall we go back to your lab now?"

And we did.

In my suite, a couple of comfortable looking chairs now sat next to a coffee table where some equipment had been. Jack motioned me to have a seat, which I did. It was as comfortable as it looked.

"How about some coffee or tea or something?" Jack asked.

"Tea would be fine."

He rose and pressed my call button. JoAnn arrived almost instantly.

"Could we please have a pot of tea, JoAnn?"

She nodded and was gone again.

"We were talking about external stimuli just before my nature visit. Is that where we should continue?"

"It is, Nick, your notion about going in and out during recovery is a good way to put it. Some recoveries are basically one directional and straight ahead. Many others, like yours, are quite mixed. Thanks to Raj, we had a good sense of your likes, dislikes, speech patterns, your own particular way of addressing situations and a fair amount of your very unique thought processes. All this was helpful."

That about convinced me of a couple things. First, Raj is all he says he is about our friendship. Second, there is no reason to go to these lengths just to liquidate me.

Then a searing blast of horror from the 101: *Think stupid, you must have seen something in that six-week period that is awfully important to these guys. You said something to someone or you know something.*

So why don't they just ice me then?

God, you're stupid. Because they have to know what you said to whom, so they can take appropriate action.

Appropriate again. The word is so annoying, I missed my own thought parcel.

What?

And back and forth it went. The same thought: *Nick is dead. Just a matter of time.* How many times did this thought blast in and out? Maybe a few hundred in a second or so.

"You seem to be distracted, Nick, you're wearing a blank stare."

"It's not a blank stare, Jack, it's how I look when I'm terrified." I'm Al Pacino again; eyes going all over the place, mind racing to nowhere.

The 101 and I decided we'd continue on and set the dark thoughts aside.

"No, I'm okay, let's move along."

"External stimuli was the subject. We wired you and had been studying your brain-wave patterns. By the fourth day they began to come alive, but were jumbled. We knew how you regard women, so Gail, Jeanette, and JoAnn were carefully selected. We did a number of things running to the pleasure sectors of your mind. Mostly to make you receptive.

"We determined early on that the best course would be to stimulate thoughts about Raj. The thought was that your many conversations with him would help you connect many of the larger events. If we could initiate thoughts thusly directed, we were bound to make some progress.

"For a couple days, you wore earphones and listened to Ravi Shankar and other Indian music as well as *The Prophet* on tape. Fairly strong curry was present at your bedside for several days running. We'll never know conclusively, but we think it accelerated things a bit, a significant bit.

"Let me stop for a moment and dust off my resume. In technical terms, I am one of the best specialists in my field. I am as good as any and better than most. That's just objective fact as well as it can be proven.

"I am one of the best in overall terms because, in addition to technical knowledge and proficiency, I complete the loop as, regrettably, few others do. I'm the best you can get for what you need, but no one knows Nick Drizos better than you—especially

152

how you feel and sense things. It is my mere knowledge of this simplest of facts that puts me on top of the pile. That is, the real holder of the keys to your recovery is you. I will make my mark one day in public, but if you and I are going to get you all the way back, we'll have to be fully trusting partners. Not somewhat or mostly, but fully trusting partners."

Yeah, like going into the door-to-door knife sharpening business with Jack the Ripper. I thought I'd come a long way in suppressing, repressing, and otherwise pressing the discouraging language used daily in my pedestrian trade, but just what in hell am I doing here?

I almost did the Ralph Kramden: "You wanna know how I feel, you wanna know how I feel? I'll tell ya how I feel." But I didn't.

"Are you getting fatigued, Nick?"

I tried my response out first on the 101. It went like this. *No, Jack, I'm getting ground down. I've been gamed by you folks from day one. So maybe you'll kill me, but I'll die with your precious secrets first.*

Attaboy, rumbled the 101. *You really gave him a piece of your underdeveloped, if not overactive, mind.*

So why not answer the question. I did. "No, Jack, I'm not fatigued. I've just had enough of your degenerate games. It's obvious to even a pea-brained bond trader like me what you guys are selling. I've seen enough cons to recognize one when it smacks me around enough."

I fully expected that the good cop, or in this case, good doc/shrink, would now attempt to calm, soothe, and otherwise comfort me.

Imagine our surprise—me and the 101—when I got, "Who the hell do you think you are, you stupid Greek bastard?! I'm spending my valuable—very valuable—time with you and you're being a near-perfect asshole.

"I've made a career of putting guys back together who had been torn apart by enemy fire or land mines or you name the barbaric instrument, and you're gonna start your sissy-boy whiny routine. If it weren't for Ben, for whom I'd walk through hell with

153

a can of gasoline, I'd drop-kick your sorry ass out of here. And wish you ill in the process, you meathead."

It didn't make any never-no-mind, as an army pal from Kentucky used to say. It didn't make any difference if they were going to kill me or make me poster boy of the month for Patriots International. It just didn't matter.

The silence was painful. I had known this guy for a few hours, and I was ready to apologize. And I did, but not before flashing to the ending of *Body and Soul,* circa 1947, where John Garfield, the champ who wins the big fight he was supposed to throw, says to the mob boss, "What are you gonna do, kill me? Everybody dies." And apropos of very little, how gorgeous was Lilli Palmer?

"Okay, Jack, I'm just a simple-assed bond trader in with the big boys, so let's level. Here's my deal. I can remember everything pretty well except for the weeks between leaving Invictus HQ and nearly getting blown away. How come? How come everything else seems in place?

"What went on in that time window? It doesn't take one of your heavy-duty technology guys to figure that I either said or saw something adverse to your interests." *Adverse to your interests; pretty good lingo,* I thought. "Anyway, you guys have concluded that a world without a particular bond trader is a better place. So I'm a dead man. Except first you have to determine the dimensions of my indiscretions. Then I'm a dead man. Right?"

"Nick, as we used to say in Jersey, you are a total hoople. If anything remotely resembling your lunatic rant were the case, your brain would have been empty of its burden some time ago. The tell-all, drain-all technology has been around since Christ was a corporal. I'll tell you one more time. The only thing of interest is getting you back to normal, whatever that might be for a total dipstick like you. And the only reason I'll put up with you is because the man you call Ben asked me to. And that's the whole deal."

I looked and felt like a guy on the wrong side of an argument and wondered only how to square things. Even if I'm getting played, these guys are the best. I just shrugged and looked hopeless.

"Nick, what I've told you is the God's honest truth. Would you like to hear it from Ben himself."

"I would."

"Well then, you will. He'll be here tomorrow in the A.M. Now, your choice. Would you like to continue, or would you like to wait till you see Ben?"

This was one of those beauties where I'll be wrong irrespective of my actions, so I just shrugged and murmured, "Let's keep going."

"Okay, Nick, here's the short and simple version. You can remember most of your past, because you are generally comfortable with it. It fits you and it makes sense to you. It's part of a Nick Drizos, and you're used to it. You recall things because, whether pleasant or somewhat painful, they seem an accurate reflection. You've learned to cope. At the same time, you are avoiding and frustrating certain recalls because they are painful, or at least too painful to address. Or maybe just too big and confusing. Or just not believable. For you specifically, some recall is just too intense. It's an overload, and your circuit breakers have popped for the moment. "Over time you will confront and surface these recollections as your unique psyche permits. And you will resolve all important issues. That's the way it usually works, and that's my best educated outlook for you."

"Okay, so if I'm going to recover in due course, why is time an issue? Why are you putting the big hustle on me?"

"That's easy, Nick, take a deep breath and relax, and I'll give you the straight stuff. Right now, you're in a well-known clinic where you have been since the tenth. At some point, you will be returned to St. Mark's Hospital in Hale's Point for release, and life will go on. The most sensible thing is thus, very clearly, to have you in total control of yourself so that you can resume your life as before."

"This joint is hardly a well-known clinic—" I started.

"I know Nick, but that's our story. There is a totally isolated, totally secure section of that clinic staffed around the clock with our people, and only our people. That's where you are as far as anyone knows. All that is known is that your status has been moved from critical to improving. The news coverage has been

155

sparse, and luckily for us, there have been several high-profile scandals and other sordid events to occupy the press and the public, neither of whom is especially known for tenacity."

"We arrived at your house moments after the blast and helicoptered you here. Many decisions had to be made immediately. If we've learned anything over the years, it's that it's not the events that trip people up and topple institutions. It's the cover-up. There was no plausible cover story available, so staying as close as possible to the truth was the only course.

"Planting a body or any of a hundred obfuscations just made no sense, so the reported news was locally known bond trader, Nick Drizos, was critically injured today when an explosion erupted from his garage. Authorities have converged and an investigation is underway. Mr. Drizos has been evacuated to a secure facility for obvious precautionary reasons, et cetera.

"It was, as you would imagine, the biggest story to ever hit Hale's Point. And it was quite intense for the first week. But, as the old saw goes, life goes on, and things have calmed down measurably.

"The plan is to try to accelerate your recall, so that you can be transferred to St. Mark's for some routine observation and a release shortly thereafter. The greatest probability is that you'll be received as a sort of local celebrity more than anything else. There may be some investigative reporting that suggests a botched mob hit. Wrong address or something like that. As further background, there will have been an FBI investigation of all your business dealing for the past ten years. There will be a hearing and you will emerge with a spotless record. As much for photo-ops as anything else, some dignitaries will formalize the occasion with warm praise.

"There will be a few that remain suspicious, but, in the end, the question will be: 'Who'd want to kill a bond trader?' "

The 101 roused itself again and screamed, *These guys do, that's who.*

I suppose I'm like most folks, but, if anything, a little toward the simple side. I guess I have most of the emotions that most do, but I mostly use only four switches. For me they are engaged, enthused, confused, and dumfounded. I was clearly on switch four.

156

Maybe that's owing to the four classical Greek humors—phlegmatic, dogmatic, choleric, and sanguine.

Dumbfounded.

So there we were . . . staring. Staring with a difference, however. Jack was staring intently at me. I was just staring.

"Nick," said my most recent friend, "we started out making some progress, but we've given most of that back. Just tell me what you want to do. Or better yet, why not tell me in your own strange words what a Nick Drizos is."

"What do you mean, what's a Nick Drizos? You guys haven't left a shred of me to myself, I've got absolute voids in my recent past, and you're being major-league ball breakers."

"Well, Nick, there's a good example. As far as oral or written communications, and especially oral, you are one confusing guy."

My thoughts were clearly aligned and clearly combative, and I was about to regress to juvenile invective, but he continued.

"You go from extremely lucid to totally disorganized. You go from the King's English to jargon and lingo. To be as honest as I can, you're a schizo in some areas."

I'd never thought about it, but he was right. He was exactly right.

The internal humming started up again. The 101 reminded me of Edmond O'Brien in the film noir classic 1950 *DOA,* where the picture opens with O'Brien reporting a murder. When the SFPD cop asks whose, he replies, "Mine," explaining that he'd been poisoned by a total stranger.

That's me. I stumbled into some big secret, or blabbed or did something bad. These guys will jolly me along until they know what they need. Then it's over, just like it was for O'Brien. Except he got an Oscar for his troubles. Not for that picture, but a few years later for *The Barefoot Contessa. DOA* gave him a big IOU. And that's how Hollywood works. If only I knew how this deal works. Naturally, as a postscript, the 101 had to comment on my alphabetic construct: '*Getting an* IOU *for* DOA.' *Cute.*

Christ, almighty, this guy's got me pegged. I can't even think consistently, much less speak coherently.

"You're probably right. Ben noticed the same thing, and I

157

gave him a partial explanation. I work around a trading desk, which is no more than eight hours of constant short, rapid barkings. I think I referred to it as mind-numbing during my time with Ben. Away from the pit, as it is called by some, I enjoy the writings of the masters. And the appreciable time I've spent with Raj and with Slater . . ."

I had just taken another big one to the gut. With the word "Slater," pain shot through me. It was a body blow, and I doubled over. I thought, What's the deal with Slater? and took a second blow right in the gut. I was literally doubled over and in the process of falling out of my chair when Jack restrained me.

"Are you okay, Nick?" he asked in a very concerned tone while trying to reseat me in something resembling comfort.

I just stared at him.

"I think I've set you off, Nick. I didn't mean to, but maybe we should let things go for a while."

I wasn't paying much attention to Jack, so I decided to entertain myself for a bit. The game would be that I would call up Slater to my prime thoughts five times and see if I registered the same severe pain. It may have taken a few seconds, and the result was predictable. Five shots of decreasing intensity.

Jack was perplexed, and I was enjoying it as much as anyone can enjoy something of which they have no understanding.

He was speechless, so it was time for some old Fort Gordon leadership. "Here's the way it's gonna be," I said.

"I'm weary, and I've gotten to the point where I don't really care about much of anything. If I live a while, I'll work through this horror show. If you guys ice me, then it's over. I just don't care. But you can go stuff yourself with the schizo jive. I'm several people just like everybody else. I'm Nick the bond trader, I'm Nick the good friend, and I'm a bunch of other Nicks depending on what I'm supposed to be doing, but I'm no more schizo than you, Dr. Smart Guy."

We just glared at each other like two twelve-year-olds in a schoolyard showdown. Something very bad was going to happen. I don't know which one of us smiled and then laughed first. Maybe the difference wasn't measurable, but the two of us roared uncontrollably. Sometimes you just have to get it all out.

Jeanette came racing in and stopped a few feet from us and looked at Jack with a "what do you want me to do?" look. Jack motioned her away, making assurances that everything was okay.

She said, "He's not to be overexcited or aggravated, doctor."

"I know that, Jeanette, and thanks for your concern. Everything is all right. Really."

She removed her look of worry and asked, "Can I get either of you anything?"

We both shook our heads no, and she departed.

Jack said, "That was quite an interval, Nick. Now I'm as bitched up as you. Would you like to change seats?"

"No, Jack, I just want to leave this earth without a mystery hour. I just want to know the way it is. I'm tired of being gamed and played, so I'll make you a deal that you have to take. I may like old movies, but some lines are part of the national registry, and the phrase 'a deal you can't refuse' is off-limits."

"So . . ."

"So, two things. First I'll finish my answer to the schizo comment, and then I'll get to the deal."

"You're on."

"As I have told you folks repeatedly, my daily work takes place in bedlam. Transactions involving some heavy bread are initiated and closed in minutes and sometimes seconds. This goes on unremittingly for the livelong trading day. We speak to each other in a jargon form-fitted to this lunacy over a period of many years. It's a shorthand, probably not unlike that which you employ when leaning over some bleeding body for hours at a time. One doesn't have time for elegance and politesse, does one?" I stated with a bit of a sneer in my tone.

Jack nodded.

I continued: "Nor is it an environment particularly conducive to gentility. It's about money and it's pretty crass, not to mention stressful and enervating. I like a large part of it, and I contend with the rest of it. I have two missions. First, to do well by my customers and second to make a living. In that order.

"Away from the livelihood piece, in my peaceful time, I enjoy the elegance of language, and I've been this way since my early

159

school years. Aside from the great authors, humorists, conversationalists, and commentators, I have benefited greatly from associations with two men. One, Raj Maphal, is well known to you. The other you may not know, but you should have heard of him: Jackie Slater." I paused and awaited a shock that, at best, was heavily damped and muted. *We're onto something,* grumbled the 101.

"And . . ."

"And you folks have had more than a few laughs about my disarrayed thought patterns. Well, that's just the way it is. Maybe I try to grapple with more things than I can handle. Or maybe I just get tired and confused. It isn't the easiest thing to go from slam-bang trading to Marcel Proust in a nod. Maybe the two Nicks just get a little tangled or maybe a little fatigued. And, by the same token, it wouldn't be effective to be on the trading floor to approach another trader thusly: 'Excuse me, my good man, but could you reiterate the substance of your last quotation on the six point two-five percent Pittsburgh Sewer Refunding bonds of 2014 with the sinking fund commencing in 2008 at par?' The trade would have been done and confirmed by word three. Elsewhere. And I'd be standing there holding Mr. Happy in my hand."

"Hold on, Nick, nobody is laughing at you. All, repeat all, questions and comments have been for one sole purpose; how do we best understand how this guy works so that we can get him back to his pre-blast days. Nobody has made any value judgments, so put that one away."

"All right, Jack, you're making your points."

"Sounds like you've taken care to say 'making' rather than 'have made.' "

"Okay, Doc, here's where I am. After all my years as a would-be adult, I'm still not that good at judging and measuring people, and I don't know whether you aim to rehab me or to dispose of me. At bottom, it doesn't matter much, because there's no way I'm getting out of here voluntarily. And even if I did, maybe I get a Wiley Coyote special, like one of those Acme safes drops on me downtown.

"So I'll go with the program. All I want is for you to tell me what happens to Nick Drizos, fully and honestly—no bullshit.

Dead or alive, imprisoned for life, I just don't care. In return for that, I'll do whatever you ask."

"Square you want, square you'll get. One last time. If you had been carrying anything of critical interest to us, we could have drained your brain long ago. And if a dead Nick was the only solution, that could have been accommodated as well.

"Not by us, but it could have been done. As Ben will no doubt reaffirm, you did all that was asked of you. He gave his word on his end, and to Ben, a promise is a promise. As your pal Robert Service would have said, 'A promise made is a debt unpaid.' Our only mission is to get you back together with total recall so the world can get back to enjoying the fruitcake whom we all know and love named Nick Drizos. I'm looking you square in the eyes and swearing that's the truth."

The 101 and I caucused. I got a lot of *maybe this* and *maybe that* from the inner caverns, so it was time for the chief bill payer to show some leadership.

"Okay, Jack, if that is your real name . . ."

"Peter Sellers as Mandrake talking to Colonel Bat Guano played by Keenan Wynn in *Dr. Strangelove*. I think the line was something like, 'Well, Mr. Guano, or Colonel Guano, if that is your real name, you're going to have to answer to the Coca-Cola Company.' Funny, Nick, funny. Just kidding, okay?"

It was okay. Who ever heard of a jolly hit man? *I do like these guys,* I thought to myself as the inner echo of *You'll be sorry, you'll be sorry.*

By now I was doing my famous shoulder-shaking laugh where I bounce around but no sound emits.

"That's a new one, Nick. Are you okay?"

"Jack, to paraphrase Descartes, 'I'm okay because I say I'm okay.'"

"Good to hear, Nick, now let me tell you some things that might elevate you a bit. I wasn't gaming you or playing you over the last couple of hours. I was doing no more than trying to get some of your blockages cleared, so that your clarity guy can emerge. If that takes a little heavy breathing or some ire, well that's as it has to be. You're in good enough shape to fill in the open items of the past few months. I wasn't trying to antagonize you."

I started to speak, but got the Ben special with the palms soothingly down.

"Even better, Nick, I could fill in those spaces for you right now."

"So please do . . ."

"I said I could. The far better mode is for you to piece things together in your own unique manner on your own terms and on your own time schedule. I wasn't patronizing you when I said no one knows Nick Drizos better than Nick Drizos. With some rest and a little prompting, you should be fully aware of all that has gone on. You refer to muck and clarity, I call it flux. Same notion. There will be some swirling and some confusion, but not as before. First you are far stronger physically, and second you largely have your bearings. Third, you've already recalled well over ninety percent of your recallable past. As is usually the case, the last increments are the most difficult, but you are well positioned and poised to get there."

"So let's do the chase scene, Jack. You said I'm strong enough and . . ."

"Not a good idea, Nick. You still have your unique thought process and that won't change. Your deal is that you try continually to put more data, or stuff, through the main pipe. If I started filling you in, I don't think, given your status now, that you would implode or relapse. But you're on a good track now, and it's best to follow success with what got you there. Please take my best advice, and just let it happen at your own pace. You're on a good tempo. We can always meddle later.

"It's about dinner time. You can even have a Killian's Red if you wish. JoAnn will be by in a minute. I suggest that I leave you alone to enjoy some food—I know it's not dining—and to collect yourself a bit. What I'd like to do is then come back for a few minutes and pick up again tomorrow." He paused and awaited a reaction, which was not forthcoming. "By the way, hot pants," he added, "Jeanette is married."

I was once again in a fairly peaceful state and said, "That would be fine. And thanks for the Dear Abby advice."

162

Jack smiled and left me alone, decidedly more comfortable in just about every respect.

My mind restarted and commenced operations again, but without the former hovering sense of panic and alarm. I imagined a log jam of contending thoughts, but, for whatever reasons, I anticipated an orderly process.

Presently JoAnn reappeared, rolling a cart covered with linen. It looked more like something from an upscale hotel room service than what one would expect in a hospital. And JoAnn looked just fine. Maybe it's like kids who fall in love with their teachers—especially fourth-grade teachers. Maybe nurses are fourth-grade teachers for older guys. I couldn't tell you, with any precision, but they are incredible.

She conjured with that apparatus masterfully—how torturous would it be to say mistressfully?—and turned it into a small dining table for one. She turned sideways and executed a slight bow/curtsy while her sweeping left arm graciously bidding me to be seated.

While my behavior with the spooks and their immediate affiliates may have been a bit rough, I had been the best of good boys around the lovely ladies. I took my offered seat and came to ease in my hospital-robed grandeur. There before me was a nicely colored, simple salad and what appeared to filleted grouper or something akin with a wonderfully smelling sauce alongside, and a few of those tiny red potatoes. I was a little surprised to see I had also been provided with metallic dinnerware. A signal of sorts for which I felt a sense of gratitude. Nice to be off the suicide watch. Maybe they'll let me have a belt and a real razor.

I am by nature what you might call chatty, and I thought to engage JoAnn. A second and better thought emerged quickly, which was to leave things alone and to get all As on my deportment card.

It was as though she sensed my restraint, the bond trader's equivalent of professional courtesy if you will. She smiled and informed me once again that she would be just a few steps away if I needed anything. I'll say only that I find her very, very attractive. Maybe another time.

Before departing, she pointed toward a newly positioned armoire and said, "We've put together a wardrobe for you. I hope you find it suitable. Jeanette and I put it together, so you can yell at us if it's a horror."

The front doors were open and I noticed a couple of belts. *I guess I am off the suicide watch,* I suggested to the 101, just to give my dark side some equal time.

"I'm told you'll be spending more time walking about, Mr. Drizos. As the famous woman says, 'That's a good thing.' Anyway, we're all very pleased with your progress." The she left in her usual gliding professional manner.

Holy mackerel, a kind word. It felt good. God, but it felt good.

The dinner was good, as good as it could be without human company. I resolved to ask for some company for at least one meal a day for the remainder of my stay here at Hotel Incommunicado. I guess I'd rather be alive and tormented, so long as I could enjoy some conversation, than dead and at peace. It's just not my time, yet, I mused. *I must be getting better when I muse rather than just think,* I noted to my inner companion.

I was starting to fall away. I'm not big on loneliness, and I was getting lonely. If you're Greek, you are nothing if not sentimental and emotional. I began to feel the old mantle enveloping me. I need some companionship.

As though on the other end of a wireless connection, JoAnn reappeared and started clearing my dinner accoutrement away. Once again, my plates and dishes looked totally ready for reuse. That's a big rave from me, because food and me are very well known to each other, and I am among the best in knowing the best.

I was startled a bit when JoAnn inquired when I would like my rubdown and massage.

Cosmopolitan high flyer that I am, I managed a grunting, "Huh?"

"Oh, I thought you had been awake for the last few. It's all about helping you keep a semblance of muscle tone and avoiding decubitus ulcers, better known as bed sores. They can get particularly nasty if allowed to develop unattended."

It seemed like now would be a good time, so I said, "How about now?"

"Can do," she said, "I'll be back in a minute. Meanwhile just slip out of your Calvin Klein designer sleepwear, lie on your stomach, and cover your fanny with this towel."

I complied and she was back as stated.

"I'll be using some witch hazel and then some light skin lotion."

Like a lady Santa, she went right to her work. The witch hazel had a pleasant smell and feel. In five minutes or so she had worked my shoulders, arms, back, and legs, and managed to cover a significant portion of my "fanny" without creating any embarrassment. Then she applied the skin lotion with a light but firm kneading action. This lasted for about fifteen minutes and created a noticeable increase in my circulation.

"All done," she said. "Get yourself reoutfitted in your jammies, and I'll be right back."

I again complied and in a couple moments, she reappeared.

Once again at my Emily Post best, I managed a drowsy but earnest thank-you.

"You're entirely welcome. We started these rubs on day three when you were less sensitive to your breaks and bruises. We alternate one- and two-a-day sessions. I hope they offset your discomfort to some extent."

"They do indeed. Thanks again."

As I've noted a time or two, some women just look incredibly attractive in their nurse clothing, and JoAnn was one such great-looking nurse. She could have sold War Bonds by the millions during WW II just by showing up. I really like lovely women.

At the same time, I hate rejection even more. That's probably why McAlister . . .

"Oh my God," I moaned, as another painful rip went through me. Jesus . . .

I was doubled up in pain. I mean as in P-A-I-N. It was like the heavyweight of your choosing belted me with his best solar plexus shot. I groaned.

"Are you all right, Mr. Drizos?"

165

"Oh yeah," I said lamely, "I must have moved into a funny position and hit a nerve or something."

"Are you sure? Don't go playing the big brave guy on me. You're not here to impress anyone with your toughness and courage. Let me know whatever might be causing you any pain."

"I'm okay, JoAnn. I appreciate your concern, but I'm okay."

She laid her predictably warm hand on my forehead and regarded me with her cool and impassive professional gaze.

"You're a bit warm, Mr. Drizos, I'm going to take your temperature."

She turned and produced an electronic thermometer fitted with a fresh tip to ensure that it was germfree.

"I know," I said, " 'Say ah.' "

She nodded, and I said, "Ah."

A moment later she said. "Ninety-nine, I guess that's okay, but just hit the buzzer if you feel any disquiet. You're getting close to leaving us, so I say again, we don't want any macho heroics."

Say again. Miltary stuff. Yeah, that makes sense. These women have seen it all, probably near the front lines. They are really good. That's another rave from me. When some one is good, they are the best.

"Doctor will be coming in to join you shortly," she said with a hint of arched eyebrows, "so don't do anything silly. Call me if you have the slightest discomfort, okay?"

First, I noticed the nomenclature, "Doctor," not "the doctor." She was definitely military. Second, does romance count? Probably not, McAlister would. "Holy Jesus," I mumbled as another shock went through me.

This time she just said, "Don't move, Mr. Drizos," and she sped into the hallway. In a trice, or less, she reappeared with Doctor.

Jack laid a quick glance on me and said, "It's okay, Jo Ann, you can leave us now."

"Are you sure, doctor?" she asked in a manner, which was clearly standard procedure.

"I am," he responded crisply, which only confirmed they'd done this repartee before.

"We call them association bumps," he said.

"Call what?"

"Association bumps. You had one earlier while you and I were duking it out. Apparently you just had another. You've got some heavy-duty stuff to deal with and your brain has iced them away pending your ability to manage them along. You stumbled onto something, which created an image. An unpleasant, or at least difficult, image. A command, most likely glandular, was issued to resist. That usually means a shot of acid to the stomach muscles saying, "Contract." The fetal position is usually the most logical place to turn, the place of maximum innocence and maximum protection. But, as you no longer weigh six or seven pounds, getting there requires a great abdominal effort. Hence, it should have seemed to you like a very powerful body blow. Our experience indicates that successive recalls of the same image tend to decrease in ferocity. Ultimately they become manageable."

I caught myself gaping again, and said, "That was just about how it seemed."

He smiled again and said, "Nick, you're going to be all right. You've got a couple or three major matters to bring to the fore. You'll do it, and life will go on.

"Like I said," he continued, "we know much of what evades you. My best prognosis is that you'll be au courant and functioning in a very short while. The best remedy is relaxation, and the best course is sleep. We should give this a rest for a while. But, I wasn't kidding, the best diagnostician for Nick is Nick. What do you think?"

"I think we've had enough of each other for a while. But, if you're not going to tell me my story, do you have any suggestions or guidance."

"I do, Nick, and it will sound simpleminded, but allow yourself to relax and think only of the prominent people in your life, past and present. You will manage to connect the dots."

"I don't know that that's particularly illuminating, but it's filed away. Meanwhile, I haven't done any heavy lifting, Jack, but I'm beat. Sleep sounds good. Would you happen to have a shot of that versed stuff around?"

"Funny you should ask," he said.

167

6
Richie the Philanthropist, a Small-Town Reunion, and Mary Lancer Blaine

October 25th

I was awake again and was surprised to find myself in something resembling a fetal position. I began to stretch myself and noticed Gail, Gail the beautiful, as I had come to regard her, who was being her usual attentive self.

"Good morning, Mr. Drizos. It's about eight-thirty. Would you like some breakfast?"

The many thoughts about my family prompted me to do a couple things. Put on my best manners and square some things with La Belle Gail.

"Yes, that would be very nice. But please, my name is Nick. Mr. Drizos is—"

"Your father," she said. "Normally that's not allowed, but I've been told that you may be addressed as you wish, so Nick it is. And what might you enjoy this morning?"

I thought some cereal and fruit with some coffee and juice would be pretty good, and she was off.

I sat up and, all things considered, felt pretty good. Before I could even think of doing much else, she had returned.

"Nick, we have some options for you. You may have your breakfast on the patio or here. And you may wear your PJs and a robe, or you may try on your new wardrobe."

Ask me a tough question, I thought. "The patio would be a real treat, and I'd love to try on some of those clothes."

"As you wish. Would you like to shower first?"

"That would be nice."

"Okay, Nick, you know where everything is. Just hit my call button when you are ready for breakfast." And she was gone again.

I guess we're on the DNK (Do Not Kill) list after all, I said to the 101. *Look at this, friend, a real razor and other sharp instruments. Okay, the bottles are plastic, but that's probably for my own safety.* I thought I heard the word "dunce" from somewhere within, but I was enjoying this most mundane of activities. I was in no hurry, but I attended to myself in fairly quick order.

Unlike some guys, it takes me about twelve seconds to brush my curly hair, so I'm usually pretty speedy with my morning routine.

In a short while I had pressed the call button and was following Gail down the hallway in my new and very pleasant regalia. We followed the same path as I had with Jack. She performed a similar routine as we entered the elevator, which, in turn proceeded as deliberately as before.

"Here we are, Nick," she said.

The door opened, and another beautiful day welcomed me to a sunlit vista.

Across the patio a man was standing, his back to me and bent a bit at the waist with his outstretched arms on the patio wall.

"Hello, Nick," said Alan Ladd.

I was neither surprised nor astonished. "Hello, Ben," I replied. We walked the few steps between us and shook hands firmly, very much like old friends do.

"I stopped by to look in on you a few days ago, but you were still struggling. It seemed best to defer any serious engagement. I'd like to spend some time with you, but only if you'd wish to."

I was on autopilot and responded that would be fine. I added, "I'd like that."

I have this thing about words that don't go together. Not oxymorons, just words that don't fit each other. In that regard, I'd already registered Ben as a warm professional meaning, I guess, a real and basically very nice person who happens to be in a nasty and thankless business.

I was getting onto his style. Personal, personable, but businesslike. I liked that, especially the absence of time-wasting jive and saccharine bullshit.

"Would there happen to be an agenda," I asked.

"There is, Nick. It's basically whatever you want to know, excluding only what I can't tell you."

"Does that leave much, Ben?"

"It does, and in short order the mystery hour will be over. I'd like to know where you are in your recall and reconstruction of events."

I started into my trip of self-discovery, but Ben raised his hand to its well- understood position.

"I'm current on a large part of that, Nick. Jack brought me up to date as of yesterday evening."

"Oh, Jack," I half-moaned. "He must think I'm the biggest horse's ass ever."

"Not so, Nick, and I'll tell you why as soon as you bring me up to your most current memories. Besides, he's the best there is, and his only job is you. He even likes you. According to Jack, you were coming up on the Vietnam era and the events immediately following. Just trust me, Nick, we're all on the same ragged page."

And I did trust him.

I complied. Once again, what had seemed a very lengthy dream, or sequence of dreams, lent itself to a fairly concise story.

He kind of grimaced and nodded. "You're just about right on course, Nick, you'll be out of here in a few days."

I started to respond, but he said, "I promise."

"Jack says you guys know the full story," I said, sounding more like a question.

"We do, Nick, and we've been here before. The only thing that makes any sense is for you to get to everything through self-discovery and in your own way. We can facilitate here and there, but as Jack says, this is all about you.

"I can tell you that you've got some nasty stuff to confront, but I can also tell you that you'll get through it just fine."

"So Jack doesn't think I'm a fruitcake?"

"No, Nick, he doesn't, a little off-center, but definitely not a fruitcake," Ben said with a hint of a grin. "Plus, anyone who's been targeted for a hit twice deserves some elbow room."

It was clear than Ben had intended to shock me, and he did.

I was back to dumbfounded with more than a generous helping of terror.

Several sentences got lodged and mangled in my throat. After a gagging struggle, I managed, "What twice?"

"Your car accident three days before the car bomb; that was a hit."

"What car accident?"

"I can and will help you with this one, Nick. Three days before the car bomb, at eleven P.M., you crashed your car on the winding hill road at Bayside Bluffs. Except that it wasn't a crash, it was a hit. It was an insidious and ingenious hit."

"Ben, you're going to send me over the edge again. Why are you doing this to me?"

"Because it's time for you to know; you're strong enough now. So just enjoy your breakfast, and I'll tell you the story. Then we, especially you, can pull a number of things together."

Enjoy breakfast and murder attempt, another mismatched pair. I had an observable case of the shakes and was about to throw up. Ben took this in, but proceeded.

"You went to dinner at the Bayside Bluffs with some business associates. You were having an after-dinner drink, which had been juiced with just a trace amount of a sleep-inducing narcotic. It was meticulously dosed for amount and for timing of effect. You were in the process of getting into your car when a stranger asked you for directions. It seems you were running a tad ahead of zero impact time, and he had to slow the schedule a bit. This guy was the 'fine tuner.'"

My chest was heaving, and my insides were a mess. I was the openmouthed, gaping Nick, but as he was talking, I saw a familiar face at the bar at Bayside Bluffs. A familiar face . . .

"These guys were good, craftsmen as we call them. They had plotted your course down the winding hill and calculated the impact area. The deal was they had removed the brake fluid. Not cut a line, just removed the fluid. They also knew that you rarely used your seat belt, so it looked like a slick and easy operation to

171

them. Unfortunately for them, and fortunately for you, we gather you were not quite impaired and you were reaching for a CD to play. It may even have been *Come a Little Bit Closer.* Anyway, you got dizzy and jerked the wheel while slumping over. You hit the carved rock wall before getting to the cliff line over which you were supposed to go. So you bounced off the windshield at about twenty miles per hour. The result: one live Nick Drizos and one irritated assassin. Some of your dinner companions arrived on the scene and hit 911. You spent an anonymous night in St. Mark's as a John Doe and were released the next day. Your blood levels were okay, and everything was chalked up to 'pilot error.' "

My whimsical side kicked in. Yeah, that's what I'd do if I wanted to ice a bond trader. For a guy who's seen a lot of nasty stuff, you'd think I'd be a bit hipper. Talk about not connecting dots. I just thought I'd been overserved and was lucky to walk away from an accident. What else was I missing?

Ben paused and looked at me. "Look, Nick, I told you we're in a nasty, table-stakes game. I'm sorry we got you into this, and I'll do everything I can to set things straight, but that's the way it is. So take my best advice, the advice of a friend, and just face up to what I'm telling you."

Neither the word "friend" nor the tone in which it was delivered were wasted on me. "Okay, Ben, I'll try. I'm not the Quincy of car wrecks, but wouldn't no brake fluid be a bit of a tip-off. Like the amateur hour?"

"That's good, Nick, but so are these guys. They didn't plant any explosives, because they wanted a natural-looking case of negligence. It was possible that the gas tank could blow, and that would solve everything very neatly. They also had one of their guys standing by with a flatbed wrecker, and he would merely refill the brake fluid at his leisure after towing away your remains. In fact, the wrecker guy got to the scene and towed the car, after receiving a cocked-up prearranged call. Your friends got there first, but no matter, he was able to refill the brake fluid before dropping off the car and disappearing."

"So I'm alive because of . . ."

172

"Luck, Nick, it goes both ways, and you had the good side this time."

"I thought I was under heavy surveillance."

"You were, Nick. Class five, top of the pile. Everything. Your house, your car, your office, your two greyhounds. Vendors, mailmen, FedEx, UPS, plumbers, electricians, anyone who might approach you anywhere, everything."

"So . . ."

"So to be a hundred percent honest, I don't know. I just don't know, but I will find out and then we'll both know. That I can guarantee."

"Okay, Ben, this is getting to be New Year's Eve in a nuthouse. I was at Invictus once."

"No, Nick, it was twice, and that's the God's honest truth."

I had another of life's great calls to make. I could just go over the edge and become a potted plant, as in catatonic, or I could try to work through this insanity. I searched for Richie, Jackie, Raj, my family, Les, Scotty, my friends. Nobody showed.

Then, in one of my Nick-hits-fantasy-road-again flights, I just looked at Shane. What am I worried about; what the hell else could possibly happen? Murk and clarity began another faceoff, but cleared much more quickly than has been the case recently.

As the swirling stopped, I saw very clear pictures of the Bayside Bluffs and in particular the nicely appointed saloon . . . and a familiar face peering at me. There followed something like a riffling through my mental Rolodex trying to hang the right name on that face. I do that a lot, but had no success this time around.

It crossed my mind to expand my basic Rolodex and add even the more casual of acquaintances in the last year or so. My constant companion, the 101, began to scream, *The guy from Invictus, the guy from Invictus. . . .*

My only data point for the location of Invictus was the vast wooded area, the closest of which I reckoned to be several hundred miles away. Why would someone from Invictus be at the Bayside Bluffs?

In an odd flash I saw him clearly. It was Tom Hunter.

173

Clearly, it was Tom Hunter. Now doesn't that compound the muddle?

Predictably the 101 screeched, *Well, dummo, how much data do you need? You're a walking dead man. They've tried twice. Sooner or later . . .*

Not now, I advised my friend. *For now I'm going to file this one away and just jolly along with Ben. We'll see who's gaming whom.*

"So when was my second visit?"

"Not for now, Nick, I'm just giving you a couple more dots. Even Jack has picked up your lingo. I think he may write a book on Mental Health Through Dot Connection."

I think he was being totally earnest, so my renowned shoulder-shaking laugh took over. I even got to give Ben the palms-out, no-offense deal.

Moods are funny things. Some settle in and become part of oneself. Maybe they are more properly called personality, or personal disorders. Still others seem to invade and be gone in a flash. I was beginning to wonder if I had any permanent moods. I'm just all over the place.

At that instant, I found myself coming out of one of my swirls, but headed decidedly toward the peaceful and reflective side of things.

It was a happy choice that I had ordered a cold breakfast and a happier turn of events that I had regained my appetite. I said to Ben, "It's breakfast time," and I set about enjoying my food.

Ben said, "I've got a few things to attend to, so I'll be moving on. We've expanded your run of the place a bit, so just let Jack and the staff know what you need or want. I expect to be back in a couple days or less."

He handed me a small paging device and said, "You can stay up here as long as you wish. Just hit the button when you want to return inside."

"Okay, do you have any advice for me?"

"No, other than to keep on as you have been doing. You're on a good course and, as I should have mentioned earlier, Raj sends his best." We shook hands and he departed.

The first thing to get past was Bayside Bluffs, an irony of ironies for me. Except for some stretches around Ocala and what might be called hills in the panhandle, Florida is flat. So flat that locals say that pancakes do their best to be as flat as Florida.

Florida is now the fourth most populous state and will, little doubt, soon displace New York as third. While many regard Florida as retirement central, is has a relatively young population and is a net receiver of people from our ever-moving population.

There has been much impact over the past several years on the infrastructure for highways, schools, hospitals, law enforcement, and all the essential services. With all the tearing down of the old and construction of the new, it had gotten messy. And Florida has a fragile ecosystem, not to mention the ravages of the occasional hurricane.

In short, the state was running out of space to which to move unwanted and otherwise indisposable stuff. The for-real environmentalists had a legitimate beef and made very strong cases for injunctions or substantial remedies. Throw in the shrill folks, the ones with no semblance of a life, and you're only a nine iron away from collective hysteria.

But a good thing happened. A few of the remaining statesmen fashioned a plan to remove the excess dirt and old construction material to an uninhabited site toward the northern end of the Gulf. The plan was to mix good ecology with some practical ends. In short a state agency was formed and financed, and an attractive setting came to life. It ended up as a three mile stretch or so which was a poor man's Big Sur. It obscured no views and would not obscure any planned or foreseen views. It became a habitat for several species of wildlife and served further as a retardant to erosion at the shoreline. It had a free observation point, and the only tip of the hat to free enterprise was a moderately sized, world-class restaurant with the best such view of any point in Florida.

The designer opted for the winding road to create a bit of a vista and to assure low car speeds. It had some critics, but in the main it was one of those instances where the typical warring parties could have a drink together and congratulate each other before returning to mutual disdain.

I was one of the early proponents and had contributed some of the initial capital for feasibility studies. I was also one of the managing underwriters of the initial and subsequent bond issues. It was always a treat to visit the place, as I had many times. I recall the night very clearly because I was in my old, rusting-out but loveable 280Z. I had just put on one those goofy bumper stickers saying something like: MY REALLY GOOD CAR IS BEING SERVICED.

So one particular October night I did the thirty-mile jaunt, looking forward to no more than a pleasant evening. Instead of pleasant, I get memorable. But it's time to clear myself of the extraneous and to get back to my ongoing mission of reconstruction.

The clutter is intruding again. Two thoughts are asserting themselves. One is the six degrees of separation thesis and the other is wondering who the rat is in *Reservoir Dogs*. Another time, I think I'll just lay back and stare for a while. It's a beautiful day.

So, alone with my somewhat impaired wits, I leaned back in my chair and thought, *What now, what else?* Without effort or conscious movement in that direction, I began to drowse again.

It was a beautiful day, and I thought of the poet. "What is so a rare as a day in June? Then, if ever come perfect days." Unless it's October, I mused. I was musing again. The first order of things was to order things and then to resume my maddeningly tedious game of Nick's Dots. I'm rested, and I think I'm awake. I'm so taken by the beauty of the day, I'm almost unaware of it.

I was enjoying the afterglow of our day in the city with my usual mix of joy and nostalgia, my usual mix of happiness for my pals and sadness at their being elsewhere. I felt myself getting into a five-year run. The 101 mumbled, *Roll 'em,* and we were off.

Jackie had found his stride, which was becoming the stride of a giant. He stayed with his down-the-middle approach and became increasingly sought as an unbiased and informative source. He was almost singular in avoiding what he called "the amateurish and sometimes hateful adverbial approach."

He refrained from lame expressions such as "too much." Instead he would present facts, "always good facts," he would say and array them against pertinent criteria. The reader would decide. He was much sought, but made only rare appearances on TV.

He made a bit of a stir on one of the more popular Sunday morning news shows. Shortly after the moderator posed the first question of the day to Jackie and his three colleagues, the show degenerated into a "let's all yell and scream at the same time" melee.

After a couple of minutes of this, the screamers took a collective deep breath. Jackie rose and said to the moderator, "I don't imagine I'll be adding much to this discussion." He removed his mike, took the host's hand in his, tipped his index figure to his brow, and left.

Many in the media slammed Jackie for his arrogance, and he received a few how-dare-you's, but his audience only grew. Letters to various editors had similar themes. An old trooper paraphrased an Artillery slogan about its regal sense of self, "Slater always lends dignity to what would otherwise be vulgar brawls. Sometimes it's best to leave the brawlers to themselves." Like Stella, Jackie had gotten his groove back. He was master of his groove.

And as the second star of our small town trio, Richie was really rolling. He built his travel convenience boutiques in airports and other centers of travel, and personal travel increased at rates well beyond Richie's initial estimates. He catered to individuals and small businesses. His whole approach was, by Jackie's testimony two words: convenience, convenience, convenience and service, service, service.

A traveler might have bought a stereo set in Hong Kong. Richie's people would be all over the guy in every manageable way. Where would you like it shipped? When would you like it to arrive? Please specify date and hour of the day? Would you like it shipped to a neighbor? What are the particulars?

The variations and opportunities to please just fed on themselves. Are you traveling elsewhere before returning home? Would you like us to send some of your belongings on to your next destination or destinations?

Richie was the best I have ever seen at working with a customer; probably because it wasn't work. He figured that a customer was a walking package of opportunities. All you had to do was ask. Do you have any important birthdays coming up? Would you like us to assure timely arrival of a gift. Oh, you have children. We have lovely this and lovely that at one store or another.

His stores were personal valets. In addition to the convenience, the price was right, and it was always a pleasant experience for the customer. Every day produced a new addition to this highly polished art form. Richie had simply taken the Golden Rule and transformed it to: "Do unto customers that which would make them happier."

The same with small businesses whose trade was bothersome to the big guys. He'd get the best rates for his business customers by coordinating their incoming and outgoing business to container-sized loads. Sometimes the best opportunities are the things others don't want to do, he would often observe.

I heard from him over the phone from time to time. I knew he was doing very well, as his investment account had gotten into seven figures.

Richie believed things always compounded on themselves. His trick was to get in the way of good things. On this venture, he had had his sails out and was riding the wind beautifully and making friends in the process.

He was talented as no other at making friends. He continually found business opportunities in which he could benefit someone else, and he was very good at turning potential competitors into collaborators.

He used to say, "I know that old deal about there's no free lunch, but I see it differently. I think you can get a free lunch, so long as the other guys get a free dinner, or vice versa." And, by those standards, there were a lot of free meals exchanged.

Sometimes I'd look at Richie's success in admiration but wonder: Could anyone do this? It wasn't brilliant, except that it

178

was. It was Richie brilliant. He started the business with his own unique personal touch, and he breathed that same touch into every last employee of RAM, Inc. Not surprisingly, the RAM folks tended a little toward cultists in their admiration of him, but Richie even managed that down.

In less than two years, we had well over one hundred of his stores up and doing well. They all traded under the RAM logo but used local dialect on their store signage, which always translated to At Your Total Service.

The big hotels welcomed him and provided space at bargain rates. He was like the concierge they would never have, and they all hoped that the incredible levels of service shown would translate to their own staffs. Airports were another natural commercially attractive venue for him.

He also had freestanding stores in the important business districts. Here again, he was brilliant. While most such entrepreneurs had difficulty supporting the large outlays for real estate and facilities, he always partnered with the prominent local banks and gave them part of the action. He called it the cheapest money of all. Brilliant. Capital became a nonissue, interest rates were favorable, and all prospered. He regarded sharing as just another opportunity, and he remained in the business of making friends.

He also underpinned his organization with a computer-based system from which he extracted a maximum of benefit. In addition, he became an important account for the computer companies, and never wanted for service or maintenance. He had also implemented the then little-known bar-coding technology and was about as well organized and controlled as can be.

Even though we talked frequently on the telephone, I knew he was continuing to excel, because the incoming wires for his investment account continued apace and in larger amounts.

About three years after our happy/sad get-together, Richie stumbled and stumbled beautifully into, as Bogie says at the end of *The Maltese Falcon,* "the stuff that dreams are made of."

Personal travel to and from the rim had grown at increasingly impressive rates. Infrastructures were being developed, and the folks over there had figured it was time to try to attract foreign investment. The big companies had established presences in most of the places they wished to be, but the real business guys, the small and medium-sized U.S. companies, were effectively shut out.

The natives didn't know them and, since the USA had become functionally xenophobic, or at least xeno-ignorant, there were still many of the well-known dots to connect. Richie had his own dot set.

As usual, what appears obvious in hindsight, was no such thing at the time, but Richie was to become a major connector of dots for fun and fortune.

He had become well known in that part of the world and, more importantly, he had become well liked. He had made a lot of money for a lot of folks and had always taken care to observe their highest senses of dignity and pride.

He was interviewed many times and would usually be Richie the downplayer. When asked what he did, he would answer politely and responsively. He would say, "We do *this* and *that*," and such and such—all according to local custom and mores.

When a friend would ask him what he did, he's issue a similar answer but usually add, "At the end of it all, I'm really in the business of making friends." That always made me feel good, as it was one of my acquired sayings and gave me a sense of indirect authorship. It's like stories. What else is there besides friends?

He continued to wear subdued western clothing there and resisted the temptations to "go native." Rangy as he is, in a world of generally much shorter people, that would have created quite a stir. Plus, given the prevailing mentalities, he was accorded near godlike status anyway, which he did his best to discourage.

He had become a very popular fellow and was more than a good and civic-minded citizen. Along the way he had picked up numerous things of great import, he would tell me, such as always ask a local his advice even when you are absolutely sure of something. He had painted himself into the culture.

His big stumble came when he was visiting some business associates in Thailand. They were very agitated and requested his help. As always, he invoked the native expressions and assured them he would wish to be of help. How may I be helpful, how may I be worthy of our friendship? And he meant it.

These guys believed they had stumbled onto some oil rich land. Richie toasted their good fortune, but they were despairing. After a lengthy conversation he understood their dilemma. They were little guys with no capital and no prospects of acquiring any. The local providers of capital—the banks and politicos—would find a way to take their land. That brought them to one dimension of grief. On the other hand they feared, with a fair amount of correctness, that big international oil companies would grind them under their rightly feared corporate heels.

"How may I be helpful? How may I be worthy of our friendship?" Richie would inquire.

"We seek you to tell us what to do, RAM."

Richie had friends, and Richie knew both sides of a good deal when he saw it. He knew several medium-sized oil guys, so, with the confidence of his Thai friends, he set himself to work.

After a number of carefully structured phone conversations with oilmen in Texas and Oklahoma, he settled on a couple of straight shooters named Mitch MacGregor and Bill Lear. He then devoted himself to the details of a plan for his friends.

He consulted in the greatest detail with his Thai friends, always taking great care to observe the many details in the order of importance to them. In many instances, they would ignore the most basic aspects of financial success for reasons accruing from centuries of agrarian life. Sometimes they would seek outrageous ends and, at other times they seemed to be doing their best to assure failure. It remained for Richie to explain, develop, and sell the basic ideas of a fair deal. How to share took the longest time. Richie thus served as friend, counselor, and teacher, probably showing more patience than that for which these Buddhists were renowned. Through patience and adherence to the locals' preferences, he concocted a deal that Richie believed would accommodate very different viewpoints.

After a number of reviews, Richie headed to Hawaii to meet MacGregor and Lear more or less halfway. They got on well, and the oil patch guys liked what they heard, and of course they liked Richie.

Richie returned to Thailand and reported to his friends. They were pleased. In less than two weeks, some of Ardmore, Oklahoma's finest "roughnecks" were practicing their craft on Richie's friends' land, or more properly in their water.

In the process of documenting things, Richie had acquired fishing, mining, and other "rights" from the local government functionaries. This had taken a great deal of explaining to his local friends, but at length they grasped the basic ideas.

As they were working in shallow water, the "seismo" work was brief and conclusive. They used words like "occlusion," meaning they were on top of a major field. These first-wave guys sent their findings back to MacGregor and Lear, and soon Richie's Telex was a full-time dispenser of coded messages.

It couldn't have worked out better, because they had found "easy oil," and it was "sweet," meaning low sulphur. Richie had also persuaded his friends to cut the local bank guys in on whatever good luck they might have. In that particular village, the owner of the bank was in effect the village tribunal.

It was determined quickly that this field required only the most simple of rigs and the lightest-duty drilling equipment. The oil was near the surface, and they didn't have to go through any really tough overburden. I'm not sure that the oil guys would call it overburden, but that's what we called it in coal country, where I grew up in old hard-rock, anthracite Pennsylvania.

Richie was no oil guy, but he limited the scope of the first deal to several hundred acres. Big enough to make sure everyone could get a fair shake, but small enough so his friends kept a maximum of control.

Within months, the first area had gone from "probable" to "proven," and Richie's friends had a commercial success on their hands.

Mitch McGregor was an especially happy guy, because he'd been awhile without a decent hit. In fact, he was being called "dry hole Mitchie," and he had an annual shareholders' meeting coming up at which event he imagined a "Texas necktie" party. As soon as the area went "proven," though, he put out a release and his previously swooning stock jumped 60 percent. Happily for him, he regained his local hero status back in Ardmore. He later said to Richie, "You saved my life, pardner. What can I do for you? I'll kiss your ass on the governor's lawn if you want. Just name it." That was never Richie's game, however, and he just put another friend into his personal passbook savings account. Later it dawned on old MacGregor and Lear that Richie's insistence on cutting them in for two percent was a fine thing to do. Lear, being a Yalie, was far more genteel and just said thank you . . . repeatedly.

Things change everywhere, but they change more slowly in Asia, unless something big happens. This was something big, and Richie's friends were ecstatic. They were basically farmers and fishermen, who would have been looked down upon by the tellers in the bank, had they ever been inside it. Now the boss of the bank wanted their friendship. Richie was happy for them. He had made friends into better friends, and he wished now to get back to growing his not-so-little company again, but his newly rich working-class friends had other thoughts.

The newly rich Thais invited Richie to a ceremonial dinner in their village to celebrate their good fortune. Richie had learned that these people love to drink only more than they love to gamble. He also knew that their greatest matters of self-concern were "face" and "luck."

They were a fairly lit up bunch when Richie arrived. Pangporn, or Pang as he preferred, the boss of the group, welcomed Richie and they enjoyed drinks together followed by a typical, but lavish, native dinner.

There were many toasts and many references about their new "happy chappy" status. Richie had toasted their good luck, and as it drew near time to depart, he noticed that Pang was receiving looks and prods from his partners. The headman appeared a bit flushed, but rose and told Richie how much he meant to their lives. Richie thanked them and started to bid them a good night.

Pang then informed Richie that he must share in their good fortune, and he must be their partner in the existing field and in the remaining areas to be developed. Richie demurred and said they didn't need him anymore, that they were now "big time." The entire bunch recoiled and urged Pang on with more looks, prods, and shouts. At length the headman told Richie, he must be their partner and he must own ten percent of everything they receive. Otherwise, it would be calamitous and ruinous bad luck.

They pleaded and they insisted. Richie asked if he might think about their most generous offer, because he felt like a thief. They stood as one and said, "Only deal yes."

Richie said they were his friends and he would do whatever they wished. With that statement Richie moved from being a rich man to being a very rich man. The adjacent fields were set out in lots per Richie's I-don't-know-anything-about-the-oil-business master plan, and an important national industry had begun. Mitchie and Bill Lear became honorary tribesmen, but Richie was Pang's right hand.

Certain fields were kept for development, while others were farmed out under a series of joint ventures. Between the upfront payments and cash flow, Richie became worth tens of millions of dollars with yet far greater prospects. As in hundreds of millions.

As had become his "kismet," Richie's activities compounded on each other. He had become a trusted friend to many, and his counsel was sought continuously. Back in the states, my business continued to grow, fueled very significantly by Richie's personal investable capital as well as from a new and growing entity, the RAM, Inc., pension trust.

Jackie and I were elated for Richie. It was time for another reunion, and we began agitating for one. Richie was happily disposed toward our request, but he was swamped.

He had become an agent for numerous Thai and Vietnamese business guys. It centered mostly on natural resources and some manufacturing. Richie had good "magic," and these guys would not take no as an acceptable reply.

It came from both sides, as small and middle-sized foreign investors wanted someone they could trust between them and the natives. Richie was their man, and each side wanted him compensated so that he would be available to set things straight when they went off the tracks—which was a common event. Richie, in trying to reduce his time requirements for these ventures, tried to reduce his percentage from ten to five. It was to no avail, and Richie became Mr. RAM and Mr. Ten Percent. He was becoming a wealthier man at an increasing rate.

I spoke with Jackie about this, and he told me of a Mr. Gulbenkian (or something sounding like that), who was a Lebanese or a Syrian, even though the name sounded Armenian to me, who became the "gatekeeper" of the oil interests in the mideast back in the twenties. Like Richie, Mr. Gulbenkian was wanted by both sides to keep the peace. And like Richie, he was accorded a big percentage of all the business that transpired. Or so the story went. Richie the Irishman, meet Mr. Gulbenkian.

In his spare time, as he called it, Richie's little business now comprised over three hundred stores, and it was booming. In one of the firsts of its kind, he was offered the chance to do an IPO at a stratospheric valuation simultaneously on the Hong Kong and in the USA.

Jackie and I were all for it, mostly because it meant Richie would be coming back to the states. Plus there was an important reunion of our little high school coming up. And, while our parents were still with us, they were starting to fail.

Richie was very much up for a trip home. From the tone of his voice, I had been gathering that he was tired. As we'd been told by successful guys along the way, it doesn't come for free. Stand ready to pay the price, or don't sign on.

Richie worked things out so that he would be in New York for the first day of trading of RAM International, Inc., on the NASDAQ system. The ticker symbol was RAMX, and Jackie and I were already significant owners of RAMX shares, courtesy of Richie.

From the way Jackie and I were behaving, one would have thought Lindbergh was returning home, and to us, it might as well have been. It was a big deal for three guys, who started their traveling careers on buses and trains, to greet Richie as he deplaned from the 747 at JFK.

We had all gotten in the habit, over many years of flying here and there, of taking our time getting off planes. On this particular flight, however, we expected to see Richie as the first guy through the door to the waiting area. And he was.

185

He walked briskly over to us, put down his attaché, and grabbed the two of us by our shoulders.

"God, but it's good to see you two pals."

He was still the same Richie, just as tall, maybe a bit fuller and with a touch of gray here and there.

We said, almost in unison, "Man, I've really missed you."

He smiled and said, "Well, get used to me. We'll be spending more time together."

"No shit," I blurted, and then ducked a bit to avoid the eyes that had turned on me. "No joke?" I asked, in a decidedly more modulated tone. "For true?"

He nodded dramatically up and down a few times as though to emphasize his comment. "I got some good sleep on the plane, and I've got a limo waiting. How about a couple of drinks and a little dinner at my hotel?"

And off we went.

We jabbered all the way back to midtown. Every time we asked about Richie's plans, he said, "Let's get back to the city with some drinks in hand first. For now, you guys give me the latest." Richie was already pretty current on our activities, so we filled the time with local and national goings-on.

Richie checked in quickly and said, "Order me a drink, and I'll meet you in the saloon in a couple minutes."

Jackie and I found a table away from the crowded bar and ordered up. The drinks and Richie arrived at just about the same time.

"Did I mention that I've missed you guys?" Richie said.

"We'll drink to that," said Jackie and me in virtual unison.

"So what's the deal, Richie, are you back for good?" Jackie asked.

"I am, guys, I am." Then, before we could ask why, he added, "It's time. It's funny. Funny peculiar, not funny ha ha, but it feels like most of what I have done in my life was run by a clock somewhere. I would just get the sense that it was time to do something, and for me, it's now time to come home."

"What's your clock tell you now?" I asked.

"Mostly that it's time. The truest of the truth is that I was lucky. I caught an incredible wave and was fortunate enough to let it take me on a fantastic trip. Plus, it was timing. I got there when things were starting up from just about a zero basis. Enthusiasm and goodwill were everywhere, because everybody saw they could do better. It was total growth; there was something for every one, but soon things will moderate and the pushing and shoving will begin. It's just time.

"RAM, Inc., is in good shape. There are almost five hundred stores now, and we've been granted an exclusive on a number of popular duty-free items.

"The staff and employees now own almost thirty percent of the company, and they run it beautifully. I'll be selling a big part of my holdings in the IPO, so I'll be down to about thirty percent as well. I have agreed to stay on as ceremonial chairman of the board, and I will chair the annual meeting until asked to step down. Otherwise I'm out."

"Makes sense," I said, "but it's kind of sudden, isn't it?"

"Maybe so, Nick, but it's been building for a while. In addition I have known for some time that my "magic" would run out one day, and, in that part of the world, that would be a very bad day."

"Your magic, you say?" questioned Jackie.

"Oh yes, Jackie, magic. In some places, it's 'joss', in others it's charisma, but they are similar notions. The Asians are very into ascribing great power to their fellows when they accomplish something heroic or admirable. Trouble is, the downside is worse. A failed magician is a man without friends or prospect of friends. He quickly becomes outcast, and worse, redemption is nigh impossible.

"The stores were one thing. They can go on just about indefinitely so long as they continue to observe local customs and continue to provide the highest and most innovative service. My middleman function was and is a clear short-term deal. I was lucky to get some good advice from locals who understood my many relationships. They taught me well to combine friendship and goodwill with distance. One doing such as I must be called from a distance and must appear from a distance. Had I become drinking buddies, as was my first instinct, my relationship would have become trivialized. It was very important that I be sent for when problems arose. It was very important that I dispensed great knowledge. But it was most important for these people to be able to dismiss me after I had served their ends."

"But their generosity with their wealth. What was that all about?" I asked.

"Differences, Nick, differences. I'll never understand all of it, or even most of it. I have thought about it till I wearied myself. The best I can conclude is that somewhere in their make-up, it is essential to give thanks. The best thanks are to the supernatural. And not to give thanks would ultimately cause unspeakable consequences. I suited their purposes, and that's about it. I was a proxy for their many needs."

"Were the other 'middleman' deals similar?" asked Jackie.

"To a great extent, but more and more it became Economics 101 and regular dealmaking. Plus I was usually referred to people by what you might call satisfied customers, so my compensation was just about always a given. I suppose I made some big contributions, and I hope I changed some lives for the better, but I would have been just as happy running our chain-store operation. I also thought it would be a good thing to go to my 'faraway land,' as the Thais called it. Besides, I even missed you two clowns a bit.

"Ultimately, the failed magician thing got to me and it had become time. But hey, it's like the press in the USA and their 'hero becomes bum' deal."

"You talking to me, pardner?" said Jackie, putting on his best tough-guy face.

"I'm talking to you, pal," said Richie as he rubbed Jackie's head vigorously. "And I'm damned glad to be back here to tell you personally."

*   *   *

I had spent the entire day in wide-awake daydreaming mode interrupted only by the trio of lovely—one lovelier than the other—women attending to me. There must be tiers of professionalism, and these ladies must be in the uppermost reaches. They just seem to know when I'm cruising along in recovery and when to supplement my meanderings with one therapy or another.

I had finished my prescribed workout and enjoyed a tasty salad for lunch. I was anxious to regroup with our returned tycoon, so I enabled my newfound abilities to expel tensions and relax. Soon the 101 and I were back in daydream central.

Over dinner, Richie filled us in on his plans, formative as they were. He'd be taking up residence in D.C., because he had promised to lend a hand to the State Department, the Department of Commerce, and the Ex-Im Bank on some global trade matters in developing countries. He also wanted to build a house in Florida.

We got around to our big reunion coming up and had a quick unanimous vote that we'd be in attendance. More than the reunion, we also wanted to visit with our folks. We didn't talk about it, but we wanted to thank them again for all they had given us, and each in our own way, wanted their validation.

Jackie remarked that for once, and only once, in the last eight years we didn't have to rush. We didn't have to risk leaving things unsaid until the next who-knows-when get-together might be. We would be practically living on top of each other.

A couple weeks later, it was showtime. The RAM IPO debuted. It was a kick for Jackie and me, because Richie invited us to the uptown headquarters of NASDAQ for a brief, but enjoyable celebration. *Who woulda thought it?* It was a wonderfully oversubscribed IPO and went to a handsome premium. As Richie's friends from the rim would have said, "Everybody very happy." Jackie and I just giggled.

Richie now routinely traveled in some pretty heavy-duty circles. As we had expected, he remained his steady, gregarious, relaxed, and confident self. Of all the many people impressed with Richie, Richie was not one of them. He was invited to many A-List type functions and attended a few. He coped very well at these gatherings, generally arriving early and leaving early. He also gracefully resisted the many and continuing efforts to push him to celebrity status. I attended a few of these affairs, but only because Richie asked. I generally find them annoying.

There is, to me, a particularly annoying bit of behavior at

cocktail parties or other gatherings of the famous and the would-be famous folks. It occurs when I am in a casual conversation with a new acquaintance and said new acquaintance is only partially attuned to me, because his or her real purpose is to identify and to be seen with "someone really important." I am not bothered by not being important; I've made a career of being anonymous and, if possible, avoiding the photo-op shots that people seem to treasure and display proudly. That's fine, but I find the over-the-shoulder neck cranings to be quite rude. And I don't like being treated as a temporizing intermediary either.

I'd been in a number of these affairs with Richie, and he was usually one of those sought-out by the affiliation-needy, especially as he was accorded "most eligible bachelor" status by the NY press. Some were more graciously grounded than others, but they'd bore in on my friend. He'd always greet the person but would, without fail, direct the person to me with "say hello to Nick Drizos, a great pal of mine." It had some stopping power, but then things would go on as before. Richie thought it all kind of silly.

Richie had reacclimated himself to the states, and we began to get ready for our visit back to Will's Grove. Richie had his own plane, which I regarded as a quiet asset; it was for convenience and privacy and not for show. Jackie and I were not surprised when he suggested we book ourselves on a commercial flight, and we were pleased. Above all, Richie was not given to ostentation.

It was a three-day weekend for us, the first day with our folks. We visited our own families separately and then had a group dinner at a surviving restaurant from our earliest remembrances. It couldn't have been much better. We'd been fortunate over the years to be able to provide a number of things for our folks—some needed stuff around their homes, a couple of vacations, and things of that sort.

This time it was little things, gestures that said "thank you" and "I love you." Photo collections, old letters, and things that went right down our treasured, happy memory lane. Recollections that brought tears and smiles.

Our three families were always pretty close, but had gotten

closer over the years when the three tadpoles had gone off to play in the bigger ponds. Our group dinner began with a nine way hug outside Papa Bouchee's, the place which had been a real treat to visit when we were kids. It was a happy night. We offered a number of toasts to our folks. In one form or another, they all centered on our gratitude for their generosity and how much they had done with so little in such difficult times. But my most pleasant recall was, and will always be that of heads nodding. Validation, as the modernists call it. They love us, and they are proud of us.

We attended the reunion most of the next day, and we did a good job of getting with the programs. A lot of our classmates had labored for months to get everything right for this bash, and we weren't going to deflate anything. But the fact remained that the trip was mostly about our parents.

On the way to the reunion, we happened by the wading pool where we became Vikings on that far away, long ago day. We'd been friends before, but that episode remained the glue of so many years. It was as I had remembered and we each stared at it for a few moments.

We had a farewell brunch at Jackie's house, and soon enough it was time to leave. We had rented a van and piled all nine of us into it for the ride to the airport. Our luck held, and it was a gorgeous day. We had our driver take a few snapshots of us, and we all said our good-byes again.

They watched our plane blend into the horizon, before heading home. The three of us sat in separate seats, each of us to attend to his own feelings in his own manner.

For my part I think our folks bore a kind of inconsolable grief for the way the world turned out. They had wished us better. This from a generation which had spent the most vital years of their lives in the most horrendous part of the twentieth century. Theirs was a generation that just never stopped giving. And they worried about us. We knew we'd never find the words, not even in Jackie's great unpublished book, with which to say you've done way more than you'll ever know. But we had done our best.

I strained looking back till they were rendered tiny dots, but

I'd connected these most important dots, and they would always be connected.

During the plane ride home, I recalled the opening overlay from "I Never Sang for My Father" in which the narrator says something like "Death ends a person, but it doesn't end a relationship." I was given once again to my wistful ways, but any sadness would always be wrapped in a greater enduring happiness.

I think the three of us each knew that there wouldn't be many, if any, more of these visits. It was sad, but it was good. It was right. We had left little unsaid.

Maybe I had come to a logical place to pause, because I sat up for no particular reason. I think I had been awake, but in any event the sun had hardly moved during my latest catch-up with myself.

I had recalled, and it seemed, relived, a period of several years in a matter of a few minutes. Given my difficulties with staying "on point," I began to wonder how recall works, anyway. What is memory? Is it a motion picture that's uniquely stored? When the near-death folks see their entire life flash, is that just the picture on extremely fast forward. Or is one just being emptied out and packing his inner being, as the soul departs with one's earthly experiences?

Or is memory a series of impressions or pictures, like key words or key phrases, which the brain can reassemble into a story when requested. Maybe it's like those little cards we used to play with where there would be a person in a slightly different position on each card. Then when you'd fan them by, it looked like a movie.

Or maybe I'm just nuts.

I was aware of a slight sound and was pleased to see Gail again.

"Just stopping by, Nick, I didn't mean to bother you.

"No bother at all. About how long ago did you leave me to myself?"

She consulted her watch and said, "Just about twenty minutes."

192

I did the Drizos slump in my chair, and Gail stepped forward.

"Are you feeling okay, Nick. Can I get you anything?"

"I don't think so, but can I bend your ear for a while?"

"Nick, as we've been saying around here, you're not job one, you're job only. Bend away."

"I think I'm doing a pretty good job of getting back to the here and now, but I've been bringing up a number of personal memories in the process. I have a tendency to get nostalgic, so I wonder if I'm really making any progress."

I told her at some length about my inabilities to control my disorderly thought process. She listened attentively and thoughtfully.

She said, "You've talked about this with just about everyone on the staff, and we've discussed it among ourselves. You've gotten pretty popular around here, and we're all of the opinion that you're progressing very well. I'm sure the mental side is tough enough, but you were also banged up quite extensively, you know. I'll be at the central station if you need me. . . . "

I was enjoying my solitude, but that was a simple matter in such a lovely and peaceful setting. I found myself moving into my Nick-is-a-blank-page mode again. Conscious or not, I was back in my self-styled dreamland.

We had returned from Will's Grove and were back to our chosen endeavors. One day I began thinking about the long-enduring organism which had become Jackie-Richie-Nick. To this day I don't believe I have a stitch of envy, but the contrasts among us are stark.

Generally, Jackie's the smartest, Richie is a natural, Nick's the digger.

Personally, Richie is admired, Jackie's respected, Nick is loveable.

Speaking, Jackie is eloquent, Richie is lucid, Nick sounds like he studied at Berlitz under Leo Gorcey.

Writing, Richie is economical, Jackie is powerful, Nick writes like he talks.

And so on. Big differences in most aspects for guys who had stayed so close over the years. Another puzzlement.

193

Jackie and Richie were blowing through town, so we had a quick impromptu dinner. Life was good, and most everything was going well, so I laid my personality inventory findings on them.

"We all left Will's Grove to hit the outside world. You two became princes, which pleases me no end, but I'm still a toad."

In an instant, my two pals drew back in their chairs and tossed their napkins at me, right in my face. This had become one of our many rituals when one of us said or did something that qualified as "goofy."

"Where the hell did you come up with this one, goofy?" asked Jackie.

"Listen, 'dipshit,'" another of our longtime fraternal designations for off-the-reservation words or deeds, "you've always been the soul and conscience of this union," Richie added. "You were the one that started the whole Viking deal. You were the one who pointed out that Leslie Howard, and not Bogie, was the hero of *The Petrified Forest*. You were always ahead of us. And mostly, you were the one that insisted on fair play everywhere, all the time. I can speak for Jackie when I tell you we've always wanted and needed your approval. We've all done well, we've treated others well, and we haven't missed any meals, especially you, so what's your beef?"

"Yeah, and I've also always been the most sentimental," I mumbled as I started to get a little teary.

I had given their napkins back to them, and they threw them at me again. It looked like something out of the Bowery Boys where they would smack Huntz Hall with their baseball caps or whatever else might be handy after one of his malaprops.

People at the other tables didn't know whether we were part of the entertainment or just a ménage-à-strangeness. I was somewhat embarrassed again, and the two of them grabbed me by the arms. I guess they had re-upped for some more years of being pals.

I continued to be busy with my trading and brokerage business. Richie's portfolio had gotten so large that I had to get him to start spreading his assets among several managers. He complied, unwillingly, but insisted I run the largest single portion. Jackie's account had also become substantial. In addition, the adherence to basic honest principles had served me and my clients well. I was also managing money for some very high-net-worth individuals and a number of high-profile endowments and institutions.

I had a total staff of twelve people, and I had been lucky in attracting the kinds of folks who would have fit in nicely with Les and the other old-timers.

Over the next year the staff would grow to twenty-five, and our business more than trebled. The first twelve joined me over a period of several years, so that we thought and spoke as almost one person. We got along well, because we liked and respected one another.

But, the world and with it the financial landscape, was changing at a hellacious rate. The seventies had been a lackluster period. The Dow Jones Industrial Average, as good a proxy for business levels as any index, was about 750 at the beginning of the decade and just about 750 almost twelve years later. Just about dead flat. Jackie used to say, "It looked like my brain activity on life support," meaning not a great deal of activity.

The seventies had been a wrenching period with no shortage of adverse events. The post-Vietnam years was a painful time by itself. Then came the world wide recession of 'seventy-four. Heap on a presidential impeachment, and it wasn't what one would like to call uplifting. But while the stock market and business in general weren't going much of anywhere, it was oddly enough a fairly good and stable time for bond trading. Bonds were a relatively safe haven, so our little shop did quite well.

Then came the 'eighties, and the proverbial roof blew off. The USA had not only learned to cope with the new globalism, it flourished. Or so it seemed. To meet this challenge, most of the once capital-starved Wall Street firms went public and were now capable of carrying large inventories of securities. The numbers of financings exploded as did the size of the financings. By the end of the 'eighties, the DJIA would be around three thousand. Large debt financings of, say, five hundred million dollars, which had previously taken up to three months and required a lengthy syndicate of investment banking firms, were now being done by

195

one firm in a couple of days. And the employment levels on the street followed suit. MBAs poured in, lured by the siren call of the old bitch-goddess named instant riches.

As happens in a number of situations, I awoke one day and noticed that the business had changed. This might seem a bit shocking to some, but when you spend most of your adult life doing what you think is the same thing, it is difficult to absorb and digest all the apparently small day-to-day changes as they occur. It's not a linear deal in which you adjust as you go along. What is probably more accurate, you get more and more displaced from your moorings but don't notice the widening gulf. It's a one-day kind of thing where more suddenly than you would like, you realize you're out of your depth and way too far from your own shore of safety and comfort. Worse, your old mooring dock may not exist anymore. That kind of change is a quantum change for a guy like me.

There were other difficulties. The old-timers who had been with me didn't mesh well with the newer folks, and vice versa. Les's preference for harmony was not to be. While I was a little late in assessing my new and changing surroundings, it was time to refit my talents into a smaller and more comfortable universe.

It was becoming pretty clear that this was not my game, and I'd have to find a more placid pond in which to splash about. I conferred with my two lifetime advisors, and they did as expected. They supported the decision and each asked what they could do to be helpful in the process.

My timing was good in some respects. The markets were very heady and it wouldn't be difficult for any of the staff to find a new home quickly. In fact, it was kind of a relief in some ways, as many of these newer guys would let me know from time to time that they could go elsewhere for more money. "A lot more money," some would say.

It was kind of fun that one such big-timer was in the process of reminding me of my good fortune to have him onboard and that he could do a lot better at another firm at just about the instant I had resolved my last lingering doubts.

I recall saying to Mr. Wonderful, "Well, my good man, that sounds like something you should do. It will be tough, but we'll try to survive your absence." Then I grasped his hand, shook it vigorously, and patted him on the back.

He gave me the "you're kidding" look, but I wasn't. I then walked him over to Alice who served the function now known as HR, and asked her to make sure that our friend was accorded every courtesy during his departure.

Space was also in high demand, and as I had been at a very attractive address, it was an easy matter to get new tenants; thus I had no squabble with the landlord, who wrote the new lease at much higher rates. The new occupant was also a trader and was very happy when I acceded to his desires to purchase a large part of my computer systems. I even made a few dollars on that trade.

Because the financial markets were so buoyant, it was one of those unusually happy times in which to make some major changes. All of the newer people opted to stay in NYC as did two of the old-timers. A couple of others decided to call it a day, and the remaining eight left with me for the smaller pond called Florida.

It was a good choice and we were up and running very quickly. We were also of a size where we could run our practice in the old-time way. Les, Scotty, and that crew would have been pleased. It also happened that there remained a fair number of investors who subscribe to one of Les's Laws, the one that says "Sometimes the best way to make fast money is the slow way." These are the folks I call real investors. They don't catch the euphoria in the wild bull markets and they don't get wiped out during the downs.

So, as between tunnels and blue skies, the three of us, now in sight of fifty, were enjoying the latter.

We continued to get together at fairly frequent intervals. We had been to a few funerals in Will's Grove, and we remained grateful for having said and done the important things while we were able. What might have been sad farewells were thus softened greatly. Our skies were decidedly blue.

Jackie had evolved to senior statesman status and stayed near Fort Bragg because of, and despite, his unwillingness to do the lapdog routine for the ever- politicized and politicizing D.C.

crew. Richie had been back in the states for several years, and had become a working, but anonymous, philanthropist. He avoided photo ops, unless, and only unless, it would do some tangible good for the effort at hand. He had become a bit of a mysterious celebrity.

In late 2000, we all converged in Florida and chartered a fishing boat, not of any desire to catch anything, but just to be in a low-decibel environment and out of sight of land for a few hours. It was just the three of us and the captain. There was no mate aboard, which I thought a bit unusual, but Richie had made the arrangements, and none of us were into the macho man Hemingway thing anyway. The fish were safe, unless they got impossibly careless.

Our conversations over the past few years retained our free-ranging style, but we were spending more time on world and national events, usually wondering if things had to be screwed up or whether homo sap just liked it that way. We also discussed politics fairly extensively, although more in terms of what would be good for the nation than what would suit us as individuals. We were pretty well aligned on most issues, but often differed on the best ways to achieve desired ends. We were taking a breather from our scholarly exchanges when Richie piped up.

"I've got some news for you two, and I wanted to be in a quiet and peaceful setting. To get to it, I'm getting pretty serious with a lady friend, and I don't want you to hear it anywhere else or after anyone else."

"Get out," I screamed.

"So is this for publication, off the record, or what?" Jackie asked.

"It is one-hundred-percent off the record, and you two are the only people I have told, so if there are any leaks, you're as good as dead."

So here we were, three bachelors in our forties. The usual pattern is that priests go over the wall heading out. We had wondered if we would ultimately seek admission to The Brotherhood of the Perpetual Celibate. Not that we didn't all like the company and pleasures of women; we'd just never experienced that biggest of moments. We'd even hung our monk names on each other.

We were Pater Slater, Alabaster McAlister, and Jesus Drizos. We intended nothing disrespectful, and we were confident that God had a sense of humor.

"And the victim?" I asked.

"Her name is Mary Lancer Blaine," said Richie.

Jackie and I gaped at each other and mouthed "Mary Lancer Blaine." Jackie joined me in the famed Drizos dumbfounded look. We did it again, "Mary Lancer Blaine?" It was a name like Mary Tyler Moore. Just as there could be no Mary Moore, there could be no Mary Blaine. It was Mary Lancer Blaine.

"I know, I know, the D.C. barracuda. But listen, fellas, we've been together for over a year now. People can be misunderstood. I want you to meet her and, as importantly I want her to meet my two best friends in the world."

I'm thinking, Here's another chapter for Jackie's great yet-to-be-published book; how to tell a pal that he's just signed on for a lifetime train wreck. I'm also thinking this babe has outslicked the slickest of the slick on Capitol Hill. She's known as Mary the Merciless; Richie's a dead man.

I'm elsewhere again when Richie's voice comes booming through my latest trip to somewhere over the horizon.

"Hey, pay attention, we're all having dinner tonight. I've got reservations at Alfredo's, and we'll be in our own private room. Cocktails at seven, and dinner sometime later. That's the deal. Who's coming?"

Two hands went into the air. What do we know, and who are we to argue with Marco Polo II?

Jackie, being the more urbane of us, says, "So, Richie, how did this come about?"

"Like most things, when you least expect it. As you two know, better than anyone on the planet, I've been lucky beyond belief as far as falling into things as far as money goes. I've also been lucky in that I neither deserve nor need most of it, so I've been trying to find some good homes for all this dough. By the way, it keeps coming, and won't stop for another several years, mostly because of the oil and natural resource deals."

"And don't forget your magic, O great one," added Jackie.

"As you can imagine, I've gone for a few nifty dekes along the way, and have been skinned a couple of times, but I've also been able to help a few very worthwhile and uplifting causes.

"There are a lot of LMs in the crowd where money congregates. 'LM' is my short hand for 'land monsta.' I used to use that expression for nasty and/or nasty-looking women, but now I use it to describe the bunch that will do anything for some dough.

"I'd gotten pretty good at being able to tell the a pickerel from a pike, thanks largely to my continuing devotion to your renditions of the priceless teachings of Les, Scotty, and the many other old-timers, but the hustlers keep hustling. Ya see, Nick, I really was paying attention all those years."

Jackie grabs Richie's arm and says, "We know you, Richie, and we know what you're trying to get done. We've been onboard for that for years, and we take your lead on all this stuff. What does any of this have to do with Mary Lancer Blaine?"

"Hey, Jackie," says Richie with a trace of gangsta toughness, "I read your dopey columns to the bottom before I say anything, so shut up for a while, or you'll hear two sounds. Bang and thud. Like you hitting the floor. You take my meaning?"

"Easy, big fella, I apologize. No offense."

"Well, I get dragged to a lot of these high-fashion functions where the big folks do their star turns for this cause or that. Some are particularly worthy in my estimation, and it's too bad that they need the support of the flash-and-dash celebrity set.

"Since you're in such a rush," said Richie, looking a tough look at Jackie, "I'll give you the short version."

Jackie picks up on Richie's shtick and says, "Okay, RAM, I'm in no hurry. I get your drift. Give me the whole story with all the details."

"That's my pal, Jackie. Does he speak for you too, Nick?"

"Absolutely, great one." I nodded with a trace of mock goofiness.

"You two know better than anyone that I fell into all this stuff I have, so I've been trying to put it to good uses. There's plenty of good homes for the dough, but I've come to be most drawn to those situations where I can help the disadvantaged or variations on that theme. Over time I've been focusing on kids and Vietnam vets.

"With the kids, the idea is to get to them early and to try to get some positive things going. Then to get other kids in with them and compound the effect. They need the basics and they need to know about the world they live in. When it works, it's like no other satisfaction; when it doesn't, it's heartbreaking. But without the effort, you get neither.

"The vets are different. The kids are getting a raw deal, and the vets already got a raw deal. And I appreciate the help you two have given me.

"Anyway, I'm in D.C. for a fundraiser about vouchers for school choice. We had a good turnout and the best possible speakers. No celebrities other than Jay Bancroft, who does a great job of getting the audience focused. He's not only the best warm-up guy around, he contributes his time and money to this effort. The speakers were all locals who made the case for the funds better than any big-name guest.

"I'm getting ready to leave and I get approached by a very attractive woman. She might have had a drink or two, but she gets pretty much in my face and says, 'so you're the great RAM?'

"I don't usually draw any attention at these functions, so I do my best well-mannered Will's Grove posture and say, 'My friends call me Richie. I'm pleased to meet you Ms. . . . '

" 'Blaine, Mary Blaine,' says she, giving me that but-you-already-know-that-look.

"I nodded, giving her my cocked head version of sorry-but-I-haven't-had-the-pleasure, and added, 'Ms. Blaine.'

"She then asked if I would care to join her at her table for a drink. I said that would be a pleasure, but that I had to leave. With that, we exchanged glances and I was off.

"A few days later, I stopped by a bank which has been doing some import/export financing with Thailand and was talking with the vice president who handles that area. We got through our business pretty quickly."

"He asked, 'Can you spare a few minutes?'

" 'Sure.'

" 'Good. Our CEO is in today, and he wanted to say hello to you.'

"So he leads me to another of the big offices that seem to go with CEOs, complete with a secretary on each side of the door."

" 'Go right on in, Mr. Trent,' said one of the two gatekeepers, 'Mr. Larson is expecting you.' "

"My traveling companion said, 'Mr. McAlister, say hello to Mr. Larson, our CEO.'

" 'John,' said my new friend.

" 'Richie,' says I.

" 'Would you excuse us, Trent?'

"In a moment, we were alone with that same old silence hanging between us. These guys are all pros at the situational stuff; I think they take a secret course in it. He motions me to a seat and I find myself on some very comfortable leather.

" 'Mr. McAlister,' he says, with his sincere look notched up to about a nine, 'I am pleased you could spend a few minutes with me. We are very appreciative of the assistance you have provided our little bank with business opportunities in the Pacific Rim. It has been very high-quality business and has been important to our financial performance.'

"I guessed he prefers Mr. McAlister, so I just said I was pleased to be of some help."

As the 101 and I are listening to Richie unfold this story, we recall that his inclination is invariably to be of help. Whether he knows folks or not, unless there is something palpably odious, he almost always says, "How can I be helpful?" We have come to believe it is part of his persona. It is like an interpersonal form of osmosis, because people, in turn, usually end up asking the same of him. I have concluded that he is one of those guys who convinces people nonverbally that they can really do some swell things together—things that they would never be able to do separately. Some refer to Richie as fatalistic, but I have found him to be somewhat of a mystic with a flux of positive energy surrounding him. More times than not people become agents of his benevolent will. And I'm not being melodramatic.

But we roused ourselves from our Jungian episode and returned forthwith to Richie's story. . . . I don't think we missed much as the bank guy was droning on . . .

" 'Well, we are very grateful indeed. I know you maintain a busy schedule and I don't want to presume, but would you be interested in expanding your presence with us as it relates to the Rim?"

Richie continued, "I think he was taking a breath, but that was of no interest, so I said, 'You're not presuming at all, but I've pretty much shut down that part of my life.'

"He had the look of a guy by the river whose big fish was getting away. He notched up his sincere look to its highest level and added the insider whisper, 'It could be very rewarding, Mr. McAlister.'

" 'It's very nice of you to consider me for something like that, but I'm pleased just to maintain my existing relationships as they relate to the Rim. When they run off, I'll be closing the book on those chapters.'

" 'It was nice meeting you, Mr. Larson, but I do have to get to a luncheon meeting.' *A make-believe luncheon.*

" 'Ah yes,' he said, while rising. 'Most importantly, please know how much we appreciate the introductions you have made for us.' We were two strides from his smartly decorated big door when he added, 'I heard you ran into my friend Mary Lancer Blaine the other night.'

" 'I take those do-you-know-so-and-so-because-I-do comments to be infantile and annoying, but I put on my best Will's Grove gee-you're-going-too-fast-for-me-puzzled-look and said, 'Mary Lancer Blaine? Mary Lancer Blaine? Oh yes, we exchanged hellos a few nights back.'

" 'You should get to know her, Mr. McAlister. She holds more keys to this town than the city greeter.' With something resembling a wink he added, 'She could be very helpful to you. And some think she's the prettiest woman in town. I'd be glad to reacquaint you if you'd wish.'

"It was time to do my very bad imitation of some of the dandified limpos I'd been running into from time to time. 'That's very kind of you, Mr. Larson, very kind indeed, but I must be off now.'

"We shook hands. He had taken that course as well, and I left as graciously as possible for my pretend luncheon.

"A few days later, I'm at the Joe Childress School, an inner-city privately funded K-twelve with about three hundred minority students. I'm not even sure what a minority is these days, but this school is doing extremely well. It's posted the best test scores and SATs of any public school in the city, and it's up there with better known, high-tuition private schools.

"It was started by a couple execs from big companies who made some dough, but weren't getting much satisfaction. To be more accurate, it was started by one guy; he later dragged his equally successful brother into the endeavor. He, Michael, visited this neighborhood and had some meetings with parents, which were arranged by a local minister. The deal was that this school would be tuition- free on a first-come, first-serve basis, so long as the parents would sign on to some heavy-duty volunteer work if they didn't have full time jobs. In that case, it would be lighter-duty volunteer work. But in either case, the parents, or parent, would agree to support the program at school and at home.

"It started out a few years back as a K-through-four school with about fifty kids. They offered comparable pay packages to teachers, and were quickly way oversubscribed. I won't bend your ears with the particulars, but this school operates at about fifty-five hundred dollars per student, so for one and a half million bucks, we're a long way toward a great school. By the way, that's about half the national average. And about a third of the D.C. average.

"We don't think we can keep it at the tuition-free level, and that's not the best idea, anyway. At the same time, I've made some friends who have similar net worths and similar outlooks, so getting a few million dollars together was not what Jackie would call heroic. We have proved, however, that involvement, motivation, effort, and management beat money every time.

"We were at a stage of trying to create a fund of several million bucks or so, such that the annual income would be maybe two and a half million. The school would then be solvent even if the parents had to come up with a few bucks. And there's plenty of dough out there for good causes. You paying attention, Nick?"

"Yes, Richie, I'm paying attention," I stated, as he caught me in one of my classical blank stare episodes.

Richie continued, "There's a dress code; the kids wear uniforms. Things that create some pride in the school and the individual. We have banking day where the kids get used to depositing some dough. We have guys and girls coming in to talk about hobbies—stamps, coins, model building, those things. We have folks from major magazines come in and talk about faraway places. We have business folks, mostly entrepreneurs, who talk with the kids. We don't have enough kids for major sports, but we do pretty good in basketball, tennis, debating, chess, and we have, I believe, the only inner-city golf team. We've got a lot going on, and the parents are wonderful. More than money, teachers, and facilities, when you have the parents, you're halfway home.

"You bozos didn't ask me what we do if the kid has no parents."

I piped up, "I would have if I'd thought of it, but I think you're doing a pretty great job as it is, so don't be a ball breaker. Okay, what if the kid has no parents?"

"Good question, Nick. In that situation, any blood relative can stand in so long as they continue to be contributors. In fact, we will even allow a non-blood relative stand in if we think he or she will stay the course. The whole deal runs on commitment. If either the kid or the parents fail to live up, they get a severe reprimand. A second default, and they're gone. We haven't had many defaults. We hold to our principle of the student's being here so long as they keep their end up. Maybe that's why we don't lose many. And it probably won't surprise you to know we have the highest SAT scores and the highest college acceptance rate in the District. More importantly, this school and its like are the only tickets out for these kids. Many of whom are—there is no other word—adorable."

So Jackie and I are gaping again at our pal. Who knew? I'm thinking. Richie never fails to surprise me, or should I say to gratify me with his spirit and style. One just has to love this man.

"So anyway," Richie continues, "I'm talking with a bunch of quiet money guys about what Michael and the parents have gotten done, and it's going really well. We're not going to have much trouble to put several million dollars together for the trust fund, so I'm feeling pretty good.

"The kids and the teachers are enthusiastic, and that's really the whole deal, so I'm feeling really good. We're about to leave when a van rolls up, and guys with camcorders on their shoulders start running around our little campus. I didn't know anything of the sort was planned, so I look around only to be greeted with shrugs from Michael, the staff, and the parents. I'm not a "happy chappy," as my Thai friends would say and neither are my quiet and camera-shy co-investors.

"Then I see some familiar faces. Mind you I'm not big on the D.C. scene, but I read the papers. Here comes Senator Varlow strolling along in his, to me, most disagreeable manner. And two steps behind is the queen of the A-List, Madam Mary Lancer Blaine. Trailing the pack is the somewhat charismatic and ebullient camera hound Senator LeFlore.

"When the cameras started rolling, my friends and I headed for the exit door as if somebody had yelled, 'Incoming, hit the deck.' Michael, the headmaster, tries to intercede, but the show moves on. Soon enough it turns out to be an election year photo-op for the good senators, and things calm down a bit. A few scenes with some of the kids are shot, and all but one of the camera guys take off.

"I figure it's over, but it's not. The Senators summon Michael and me to 'chat with them a bit,' so we do; we accommodate their eminences, only because we're not in the business of making enemies. We accommodate them, even though we know they are here first, and by far foremost, to count some more votes. Varlow tends to be against public programs, so he is generally neutral/favorable to our efforts. LaFlore is owned by the teachers' union, among others, but his flashing smile often gets folks to disregard his major allegiances. And he is the best vote counter this side of Jersey.

"They then do a bit of streetside politicking and ask some perfunctory questions to which they respond, 'Uh huh, uh huh, uh huh'. Next, some carefully orchestrated poses and a few dynamic scenes of handshaking. And they're off. Oddly enough, they were so totally repugnant, phony, and offputting that one of the investors said he'd raise his institution's commitment by a couple million dollars. So it wasn't all bad.

"All in all it's been a good day, we moved the ball a few yards, and we're all feeling pretty good. My associates and I say our good-byes, and I'm about to rally with Michael and head home. Then I hear a distantly familiar voice say, 'Hello again, Mr. McAlister.'

"I'm feeling a little feisty so I say, 'Hello to you, Ms. Blaine.'

" 'Mary,' says she.

" 'Richie,' says I.

" 'Looks like you had quite a day, Richie.'

" 'It was very gratifying, Mary.' And we more or less just stared at each other for a moment or two.

" 'Well, I've got be getting along, Richie. How about a drink some time?'

"I went back to the lame-o thesaurus and said that would be lovely."

"She smiled and was on her way.

"I took her kind-of invitation to be right up there with all the sincerity of the usual 'let's have lunch' deal. Maybe even with 'have your people, et cetera.'

"I can't say I didn't find her attractive, because accuracy would demand the word 'stunning.' I did find her repellent, however. She seemed to epitomize the D.C. scene at its worst. I was reminded of Jackie's comments on NYC vis-à-vis D.C. when he said NYC is a tough town, but not mean; D.C. is a mean town, but not tough. Lots of dandified guys and sissy boys. I guessed that she fit right in.

"That was almost as good as Nick's comparison of NYC to LA. He said, 'In NYC, you wake up and look out of your apartment window to see a squirrel looking in at you. In LA, you look out to see a guy dressed up as a squirrel looking in at you. There was clearly an approach-avoidance thing going on.

"I was spending a fair amount of time on three situations similar to the Childress School in D.C. and returned to my apartment a few days later. My fax machine had a few routine messages in it, and one which said 'How about a drink some time soon? MLB'

"Thinking I was being clever, I sent a fax back to MLB saying, 'I don't do drinks, but dinner some time would be OK. RAM.' And I thought that would be the end of our little verbal jousting. I had barely emptied my suitcase when I heard Mr. Fax rumbling along.

"The message said, 'Fine, see you at La Fontaine in twenty minutes.' I was bushed, but I've done crazier things, and La Fontaine was only five minutes away.

"So I spruced myself up and strode into La Fontaine just about twenty minutes later. I was met by the maitre d', who led me silently to the table of Mary Lancer Blaine.

"She remained one gorgeous woman, and people were eyeballing around to see who might be joining her.

" 'Good evening Ms. Blaine.'

" 'Good evening to you, Mr. McAlister.'

" 'May I join you?'

" 'Please do. I've gotten an early start. Would you care for a drink?'

" 'A drink would be very welcome, Ms. Blaine.'

In a veritable flash the maitre d', Marcel by name, appeared and took my order. As had become our habit, we just regarded each other.

"Reaching back into the lame-o book, I said, 'You look lovely this evening. Ms. Blaine.'

" 'Thank you, Mr. McAlister.'

"Being from a small town and lacking the sophistication of the lame-o crowd, I said, 'Is there something in particular I can help you with?'

"She said, 'As a matter of fact there is. What's your angle?'

" 'You mean what's my con? Is that what you want?'

" 'That would do.'

" 'Well, like anyone else, I'm just trying to rip off some inner-city school kids. There's a lot of dough in those mattresses.'

" 'Listen, friend,' she almost spat out, 'I know everyone in this burg and everyone has a deal going. There's no reason to come here otherwise.'

" 'Ms. Blaine, I should have said okay to a drink, because I'm not going to make it to dinner.'

"My drink arrived and I, probably inadvertently, said, 'Here's looking at you." I didn't say 'kid,' you'll be glad to know.

"I thought I saw the faint trace of a smile, but it didn't make no never-no-mind to me. It was one drink and adios.

"She was collecting herself, and life's too short for make-believe drama so I said, 'Listen yourself, friend, I'm just working on a few social causes, which I think deserve some merit and some dough. That's the deal, that's the only deal, so you might want to prance your cute little butt back to the A-List folks, because you'll die of boredom looking for any juice from me. I'm a plow horse, not a show horse. Your calendar would be better filled elsewhere.'

"I then reached over, clinked her glass and said, 'Happy days, MLB, gotta run.'

"I started to stand up, but she put a restraining hand on my arm.

"I sat again, but added, 'No joke, Ms. Blaine, I'm a little tired. I try to keep my good manners on, but your stuff is very tiring. Almost as tiring as your attitude.'

"She cocked her head a bit and gave me the look that Donna Reed gave Montgomery Clift in *From Here to Eternity*. The look she follows with 'You're a funny one.' I'm not equating Donna Reed to MLB, because Donna's character, Lurene (aka Alma), was what the GIs called a sidewalk hostess. I had no idea what MLB's real deal was. And, as a totally disconnected matter I wondered for the first time how she got my fax number. This was all getting pretty strange."

Richie paused a bit, and Jackie and I just looked at each other. We were also very big on Donna Reed and her academy award-winning role in *From Here to Eternity,* not to mention her great part in *They Were Expendable* with the Duke and Robert Montgomery. This was getting dramatic.

"Sounds like the date from Hell so far," said Jackie.

"It was," said Richie, "and I was starting to get steamed."

It took a lot to steam Richie, so Jackie and I found ourselves getting back in Will's Grove as our storyteller drew us in.

"So, long story short. I got up, thanked her for the drink and left. I could feel the eyes of the folks at the other tables, who had been wondering who Mr. Mystery was, hot upon me as I left. And that was that."

And where was I anyway. . . .

The slightest of noises got my attention. It was the elevator door opening. I awoke, or more probably, became aware of my surroundings again. I found myself looking at Jack. I noticed the sun was getting pretty close to vertical.

He said, before I could inquire, "you've been alone with your thoughts for about an hour and a half. That is, since I was last here. How are you coming along?"

"Oh hi, Jack, I'm fast forwarding pretty well, and I'm at a point where Richie has had his first encounters with Ms. Blaine as he calls her."

"You're really blasting along, Nick. Would you care for a bite of lunch or something?"

"That would be good, Jack. By the way, I apologize for my outlandish behavior of the past few days."

"No apology required, Nick. I think Ben mentioned that to you, and I second it. Honest."

We were just taking in the brilliance of the beautiful day when another very attractive woman appeared pushing a cart which I presumed carried our lunch.

"Say hello to Gail," said Jack. "She's been attending to you since you arrived here, but she has drawn many of the time slots while you were asleep."

I rose and said, "We've met, but hello, Gail. Thank you for all your attention." The Nick 101 and I gasped, I hoped inaudibly, at her loveliness. The woman thing again. There's pretty, and then there's Gail. What is she doing here?

"My pleasure, Nick, we're all pleased to be of assistance. I'm going to leave all this here and get back to my other duties. I'll be back in a while."

The setup included all manners of small sandwiches, one tastier than the next. And there was one bottle of Killian's, which was a fitting appointment.

We passed the next few minutes with small talk, including

Jack's telling me that the long treasury bond was trading at a four-fifty and that I would be back at my desk pretty quickly.

"Thanks again. I think I'm getting there."

"As you know Nick, we know how things have sorted out, and I can give you a boost here or there if you wish."

"Thanks, Jack, but I'm coming along okay, and I think your first advice about me making my own way is probably the best advice."

"As before, Nick, you can stay up here or you can go back to your room."

"I'm really enjoying the outside world, Jack, so I'd like to stay up here for the next episode or two."

"That would be fine. I'll clear this stuff away and we'll get together in a little while."

We nodded, and he disappeared into the elevator.

If anything good had come out of this ordeal, it was my new-found ability to relax and get peaceful with myself. So I turned once again to thoughts of floating along to nowhere in particular.

I was in a still shot picture with Jackie and Richie again. It was like a freeze frame, and we were still at dinner. I thought to tell the projectionist to roll 'em again, but instead I just plunged further into a blissful state of no energy. Soon enough Richie began to speak, or I picked up while he was speaking. Anyway, I was back into Richie's unrolling story . . .

"A couple nights later," says Richie, "I was taking one of my long strolls around the Lincoln Memorial and across the tidal basin to the Jefferson Memorial. The moon was waning in a starlit sky, which, along with the illuminating lights, made the memorials especially prominent. I usually stop at one memorial or the other and imagine talking with Tom or Abe.

"This evening I was sitting on the second tier of steps and looking up at Mr. Lincoln. I was aware of a presence and I heard a familiar voice say, 'With malice toward none.'

"I said, without turning, 'Hello Ms. Blaine.'

" 'Hello to you, Richie. That's one of my favorite Lincoln phrases.'

211

" 'And mine as well, Ms. Blaine. Now, if you'll excuse me, I'll be getting along.'

" 'May I join you?'

" 'Thanks for the offer, but the lovely evening is company enough for me.'

"Okay, Mr. McAlister, I was out of line the other night and would at least like to square things. A few minutes of me eating crow shouldn't be a hardship for you.'

" 'Let me make it easy for you, Ms. Blaine, you're tenacious and that's admirable. But you're also cynical, and that's not. You're like Oscar Wilde said, about knowing the price of everything and the value of nothing. We'd be best served if we just went about our own lives. So, once again, good evening.'

"Rough," said Jackie, "real rough, Richie."

"Yeah, Jackie, but I think the three of us are pretty much the same in some regards. We'll each go for a con one time, but that's it. You can have one—and only one—on me. That's it. I just had no patience left, so I started down the stairs again.

"She game bounding down after me and took a nasty spill, ending up with her legs over her head and her arms in the shrubbery. I went to help her up, but she waved me off and clambered to her feet. She was a mess, and I felt a twinge for her.

" 'Are you all right?' I asked.

"And she replied: 'Do you mean did I break any of my cynical bones? Yes, I'm all right. No, I'm not all right. I came here to apologize, and I don't see why you can't take a few minutes to talk with me while you finish your precious walk.'

" 'Okay, Ms. Blaine, I'll try one more time. Not that it's any of your business, even though everyone else's seems to be yours, I got lucky in the far-east and I'm now trying to do a few worthwhile things. I focus on trying to be helpful to two groups. The first is Vietnam vets, who were treated shamefully and who have every right to be cynical. The second is inner-city kids and trying to get to them before they become cynical. That's my angle, as you would put it, and neither you nor I would be served any better with more conversation. I hope you're all right, and good night.'

"She just stood there as I turned and went down the few remaining steps.

" 'Wait,' she said and started after me once more. This time she slipped again, and started to fall. I tried to keep her upright, but we both went sailing into the shrubbery. Several small groups of tourists and evening strollers had been witnessing this show. Some probably suspected a bit of domestic violence. Not wanting to compound this fiasco, I got her back to her feet, offered her a steadying arm and we headed toward the reflection pool.

"Once away from the curious glances of the onlookers, I stopped to brush myself off.

" 'You're not only tenacious, Ms. Blaine, you're dangerous. We're standing on level ground, so you ought to be able to get home without totaling yourself.' I'd said good night, and I started off once again.

"Tenacious was an understatement. I got a few steps into my retreat from herself when I heard something snap. This time it was a heel breaking. Down we went again.

" 'Jesus, Blaine, you're lethal!' I said as we sat on the chilly concrete tangled together again.

"She started to sob, and more people began to mill around us. It was time for damage control. I retrieved her heel, gathered her rumpledness to her feet, grabbed her arm firmly, and off we went with an icy silence as our mutual companion. I took one last look at the scene of the accidents and took in a view of people just shaking their heads and muttering to each other.

"We were well along the length of the reflection pool, on flat ground and quite by ourselves.

" 'Blaine, what is your problem?' I asked her.

" 'Mr. McAlister,' she replied, 'I said I sought you out to apologize and I think you could give me a few minutes. Now I'm sorry for being a klutz. That's my problem.'

" 'Okay, Blaine, everything's just fine . . . '

"She must like the look-you-in-the-eye deal, because she did it again. This time without taking a dive. She stood there, holding her heel, and said, 'how about spending some time with a third group?'

213

" 'A third group?'

" 'Yes, those who have become cynical, but don't want to be.'

" 'Such as?'

" 'Such as me, Mr. McAlister.'

"Now guys, have we been played and conned a few times?" Richie inquired.

"A couple maybe," I said, looking at Jackie for an affirming nod.

The three of us have made careers out of being straight to the point of being laughed at. The word on us is that we're "linear" thinkers and incapable of nuance. We're capable, but we just don't play that way. If some one asks us something, we answer. If we don't know, we don't know. The rope-a-dope just isn't our thing.

"So here I am with this strange person who has just served up a question. It was decision time again. For reasons I don't understand, I decided to engage her.

" 'What do you have in mind?' I asked.

" 'Just some talk, private talk away from everybody, and a two-way promise that everything said stays between us.'

" 'Blaine, I'm from a small town, but I'm really not as dumb as I look. Why would I ever think you could respect a confidence?'

" 'Because I'll look you in to the eye, woman to man, shake on it, and swear to it. That's why.'

"I got back to Nick's old story where sooner or later, and after all the intervening niceties and bullshit, things come down to yes or no.

" 'All right,' I said, 'why don't we try to start out as friends and see if things work out that way?'

"And she responded, 'That would be agreeable to me.'

" 'Okay, I'll take your handshake, and I'll be Richie. How would you like to be called?'

" 'Mary would be fine.'

" 'Well, we've had a hell of a start, Mary, so how about this? We'll walk over to the Jefferson Memorial and talk a while. If we'd both, and I mean both, would like to continue, then maybe we get together again sometime.'

" 'That's a fair deal,' she said, and we shook hands.

214

"It was almost as if some unseen power turned a switch. Conversation flowed effortlessly. We had parked ourselves on a park bench near TJ's memorial and noted with surprise that it become almost midnight.

" 'I'm sure we both have busy days coming up, so we'd better call it a night.'

"Before she could object, I whistled for a cab parked next to the old mint building, ushered her into it, gave the driver some dough, and told her to see her to her door. She smiled out the window and was gone.

"I walked around for a while and got nearly to Capitol Hill before I could find a cab. It had been one of my more interesting evenings in quite a while. I have always thought the antidote for cynicism is sincerity, and Mary Lancer Blaine was a case in point. My hunch machinery told me there could be a very nice person under that confused and confusing public personality.

"A couple days later I sent her a fax and inquired if she might be free for dinner on any of a number of dates. The fax was answered almost immediately, which I appreciated, and the closest date was selected, which I appreciated even more. She closed with 'Details to follow?' and signed it 'M.'

"I faxed back 'Pick you up at 7:30 tomorrow. Hope you like Italian.'

"Back came 'Italian is fine. Looking forward. M.'

"It was an out-of-the-way trattoria on the Virginia side. I'd been there a few times, but I wasn't a regular, so there was no fuss. Nor were there any A-Listers. Just two people at a quiet table in a quiet setting. We enjoyed each other's company and had no lulls in conversation. On that first night, we were all over the place from home to school to the present. It was a little frenetic. How's that Jackie, 'frenetic'? But enjoyable. I guess my guard was still up, but I found trust displacing and replacing apprehension just a bit.

"I dropped her at her apartment and walked her to her door. I didn't want to come in, and she didn't offer. She just looked at me and said, 'I'd like to do this again. If you call or fax, I'll say yes.' Before I could say anything, there was a door between her and me.

"For the next few days I found myself thinking about the third front in my small war against cynicism. Where would M fit? I wondered. The kids aren't so much cynical. They're really blank pages borne of indifference, so there are at least some obvious avenues to get to them. The vets are tougher. There are some real cons in there, who are perfectly okay, but are just playing the game and milking the system. The tough ones are the guys who want to reemerge, but are basically captives of past horrors trying to make their ways in a strange and hostile world. So where would M fit?

"We started having lunches and dinners frequently. They were always enjoyable, not least for her conversation and viewpoints, but also because she was a fashion model of understatement. I also attended a few of the big-name functions with her, but she always took care to limit those to events for which I had some affection and attraction.

"She'd also been out to the Childress School a couple of times while I was visiting. Each time she gave me advance notice; each time she brought a congressman or senator who was very much pro-voucher, and each time there followed some good press the next day. The trust fund was also coming along nicely. Soon the school would be self sufficient, and I would be able to stop by just to see friends.

"Even though I had stopped seeing other women, none of our time together was romance. Except that it was. For me, anyway. When she would take my arm, or give me a pat, it tingled with unspoken romance. All of our partings were memorialized with a kiss on the cheek.

"After about six months, we must have been on converging courses. At dinner in another homely, but perfectly fine little restaurant, she said, 'do you know what I would like?'

"I don't, but I'd like to know."

"You speak often of your friends. Friendship is important to you, isn't it?"

"It's probably number one. What else is there? But what would you like?"

216

"I want to be your friend, not a friend, but friend. Does that translate, does it make sense?"

"It does. Friend to me means that the number one question is always, 'How can I be helpful?' Does that square with your understanding?"

"It must, because all I know is that I'd like to spend more time together and just see where it goes."

"We spent the next six months together doing all manners of things. She joined me on a number of trips to inner-city schools and to vet organizations. We always took commercial flights and stayed in separate quarters, not that it's any of your business. Plus she was an absolute natural at these many meetings. She always added something and everyone liked the way she said and did things. If she said she'd follow up on something, it happened the next day.

"We were having lunch on a most pleasant spring day at one of the outdoor cafes on Connecticut Avenue. It happened to be the first anniversary of our less than cordial meeting. I made note of that and handed her a small package which contained a small necklace with a heart. Not that imaginative, just appropriate.

She started to speak but I pressed on and said, "This has been the happiest year of my life."

She said, "There is nothing I would rather have heard on this day." Then she handed me a small neatly wrapped package and a card. It was a three-panel picture frame. The center panel was a picture of us while the other two were taken at the Childress School and at one of the vet home sites.

"I half stood and, leaning across the table, kissed her. I had hoped to embarrass her and cause a scene, but she kissed me back. It wasn't big time, but we did get a sitting ovation from the small crowd in attendance.

"That night we were walking along the tidal basin and I proposed to her. I fully expected her to beat me up a bit the way I did during our epic session twelve months before, but she didn't. She just said, yes, yes and yes.

"I've had a few lady friends over the years, but I never lived

217

with any of them. Just liked my privacy too much. But since we've become engaged, Mary and I are now under the same roof.

"So there you have it. We're engaged and I want you two to stand up for me. More than that I want you to expand your friendship with me to include Mary. In particular, I want us all to get together next week in Florida. Can do?"

What were we going to say? "Absolutely," Jackie said for the two of us. "Give us the particulars, and we'll be there."

Richie and Jackie melted away and I found myself alone looking at the sun which was now low in the sky. I just sat there, taking it all in and wondering about the past several years. It was time for some human contact, so I tapped on my little buzzer.

My pseudo Greek chorus of murk and clarity were well ordered this time with no ambiguities to speak of. It seemed like a good time to join the conscious, so I did—with an ever increasing feeling that I was becoming Lord of the sedation drugs. Probably just a conceit, but as I challenged myself toward wakefulness, Jack appeared once again and said, "Beautiful day, Nick."

"Beautiful day indeed. I guess I've been enjoying my solitude for about four hours now."

"Just about, Nick. Anything you care to talk about?"

"Richie has just finished his story about the courtship of Mary Lancer Blaine. At the same time, and irrespective of all the weirdness of recent times, I'm most taken with my important friendships. I've been told along the way that if you've got your health, everything is pretty good. I think, for me, friends and friendships are the things that matter most.

"But tell me Jack, if you can, about my recall of things. It seems that some events are recalled in a flash. Others of comparable time proceed at slower paces. What can you tell me?"

"Short of wiring you up, not a great deal. It could be that some of the time you are just blank, or it could be that some of the time particular details captivate you. Or it could be that you play and replay certain things and just recall them once."

"In other words, you don't know."

"In specific words, I don't know."

I liked Jack and his no-bullshit ways. So, in the words of my friends, how can I be most helpful to whatever it is that we're trying to get done.

"I know this is getting a bit boring, but you've come along better than we had expected. I can tell you that you're in for some swell times and some tough sadness. I can tell you more, if you wish."

"Thanks, but I think I'll stay on this course. I assume that your offer to help is open ended, Jack."

"It is, Nick. Just call me."

"Could we grab a bite here this evening? I'd really like to enjoy a sunset, and I'd like your company if you are free."

"My pleasure."

We had an enjoyable dinner and Jack's company was very much to my liking.

"I know you'll let me know when I'm getting into 'can't tell you land,' but how'd you get into this business, Jack."

"Only in the strangest of ways, like many of the others among us. I was out of med school and on my way to a lifetime in pediatric surgery, when I was summoned to Vietnam. After a lengthy tour of enduring the horrors done to young men and women, I began to lose my resolve for pediatrics.

"After my discharge, I refocused my thinking toward wartime trauma. In the course of pursuing this new field, I was assigned to a number of VA hospitals. We were doing, and continue to do, fine work on the physical side, but we lost many fine young people due to mental collapse. They just gave up.

"I came to realize that the larger contribution might be putting minds and spirits back together, or at least making my best effort. I took off two years to study normal and paranormal psychology and some psychiatry, and then returned to the system.

"A particularly gruesome part of my work was with vets who had, in addition to all else, been interrogated and tortured savagely as POWs. The worst cases were those who had little or no will to live and no ability to confront and banish these very real and very terrifying demons. We've had some success, but not a great deal. What is most amazing to me is that most of us who made that trip have managed to return to normal, or nearly normal. The body really tries to eradicate painful memories, but in many cases, it is just overwhelmed. That's probably the real and intended meaning of the overused word 'trauma.'

"But you asked how I got here."

"I did, but what did work. In the successful cases, I mean."

"I don't think I really know for sure. The only course that yields any success is to supplant the horror memories with something pleasant; it's no more complicated than that. Sometimes a given person can be directed to particular events and effectively exorcise himself and move on. Sometimes. But that's what most of us have done in one fashion or another. The ones among us who are normal or nearly normal. Some can face those days down and be at peace with 'that's the way it was.' Others, of different constitutions, can live with 'it was them or us.'

"Like I say, I'm probably more amazed that most people get through such things as well as they do. I'd like to accept the axiom that the brain can't replicate pain, except that I've seen too many cases where the symptoms, at least, pretty well negate that argument.

"So the toughest cases, the heartbreakers, are where the guy is just frozen in time alternately enduring and evading the ceaseless replays. As near as I can tell they endure until they are fatigued. It sometimes bears strong resemblance to seizures with incredible energy focused until it ultimately dissipates. Sometimes fatally.

"There is also a school of thought which relies on drugs and psychotherapy, another name for more drugs, but I'm not a believer. First, the drugs are extremely potent and just knock the hell out of these guys. Second, as in more cases than not, no one knows what the side effects really are. If it came down to push and shove, I might go for tranquilizers, but only because it might bring some peace. So, I'm not much of a drug guy.

"Because of my work with the vets, I was consulted occasionally by some of the intelligence agencies with similar problems. But before you ask, the answer is no, I didn't then, and don't now invade people's minds. I'm a reconstruction guy, period. That's most of my story."

"So, tell me Jack, where do I fit in the spectrum of cases you've seen."

"You're way toward the easy end, Nick. The good news for you is the many friends you have and the reservoir of inner strength that has accrued from them. The bad side is your friendships and the hurt to you when one of them is driven off the fairway. Mostly, you're a strong and straight guy. You don't have a lot to hide, and thus your faculties would very likely pull you through. Do not discount, however, that you got roughed up quite badly. In all, you'll be okay. Your biggest problem will be to grapple with some grief, but you'll get through it."

"Am I mistaken, or did you just drop a big dot in front of me."

"I did, Nick, and you'll handle it. We've been yakking away here for quite a while. I don't know about you, but I'm getting a little weary. Not with you. I've just been running long hours, and it's catching up. How about you?"

"I was going to suggest that myself, but you know what I'd really like if you don't mind?"

"And that would be?"

"A bit of scotch on the rocks with a splash of water. I'd really like a shooter."

"I'll even join you if Ballantine's is okay with you."

"It's my favorite, but why am I not shocked?"

"It was easy. I don't know if you really prefer Killian's and Ballantine's, but we may be more kindred than we know."

Jack left while I wondered what the rest of this joint might be like. Before I could get too far into one of my fantasias, he re-appeared with a tray on which were a handsome bottle of Ballantine's, two glasses, some ice and a small pitcher of water.

"You can make yours to suit, Nick."

I did and he made one up for himself. I was heavier on ice, while he made up the difference in water. It'll all be water sooner or later I thought to myself.

"Here's to your return to bond trading, Nick."

"Thanks, Jack and here's to you and the folks for all the care."

"It's our pleasure would be the wrong phrase, but we're glad we could be of help."

"Do you suppose there will ever come a time where you'd be

able to tell me the real deal about this joint and some of the cases you've worked on?"

"In a word, Nick, no. That's not to say we might not run into each other some day, because I'll be packing it in soon and hoping to return to something just a bit more normal."

"Like?"

"Like I want to get back to pediatric surgery. I've been on this tour for several years now. It's a younger guy's game and it takes a great deal of energy. I hope to be of some use to these guys part of the time, but if I don't take a shot at normal, I think I'll go nuts. Plus I have two kids of my own, and I've been shortchanging them. I need to get into their lives before my absences cause some real grief."

"More than fair. I've talked to some guys who insist it sometimes takes more courage to leave these situations than to stay with them."

"That's a common thesis, Nick, kind of a way of avoiding one's own troubles by immersing oneself in other's. And I think there's something to that. My punch line is that I'm kind of exhausted and won't be very productive if I don't take a shot at the normal thing."

"Makes sense, I said. By the way, do you know Slater and McAlister?"

"You mean Richie and Jackie? Yes I do."

"Good guys aren't they."

"If you call devoted friends good guys, I guess that would be an OK way to put it."

"You've met them?"

"I've met them and met with them."

"But that's not something we're going to talk about is it, Jack."

"Nick, that would be a bit of a detour from your present course. Not to mention violating confidences, which you three seem to be sensitive about. But at another time, it would be my pleasure."

We enjoyed our shooters.

"I haven't done any heavy lifting, but I'm getting a bit

drowsy. I'm going to wash my face and brush my teeth. I'll be back in a couple minutes."

When I got back, Jack was gone. A note read, "Talk with you later."

I rarely sleep on my back, but I was comfortable, so I thought I'd just rest my eyes for a few minutes.

7
Richie and Mary and the Senators

October 26th

Drowsy was the right word. The Nick 101 was just about to inquire if my friend Jack had livened my cocktail a bit when I started floating again. I'm not a good sleeper; in fact I'm an awful sleeper, so I welcomed the oncoming respite.

This time the screen was white. No images whatsoever. Then a whirr and the projector restarted.

Richie had left us to rejoin his beloved, so Jackie and I sat there contemplating each other and, each in our own way, our vacant minds.

"Exciting day, eh, Nick?"

"So you say, pal, so you say."

We continued to just look at each other. Each of us, I'm sure, was wondering how to start what would be a long conversation

After what seemed a sufficiently awkward silence, I said, "Well, Jackie, what do we know about old MLB?"

"We, as in what do *I* know. That *we*?"

"Well, you spend more time in D.C. than I do, so what do we know?"

"First of all, Richie says it's Mary, so for us it's Mary. Okay so far?"

"Okay so far."

"Well, I've been at a number of those cloying social dos in D.C. I've seen her a number of times and I've met and chatted with her on a few occasions. For starters, she is all that Richie says. She is beyond gorgeous. I haven't spent any appreciable time taking her measure, but I always found her to be gracious with a bit of an edge. I don't know if it's caution, a protective shield, insecurity, or just part of a greater personal agenda."

"Well, Jackie, I don't want to be a total dick, but Richie is what you might call prime beef eligible bachelorhood on the hoof. True love and lots of dough seem to find themselves pretty easily."

"He's also no dope," replied the learned Mr. Slater.

"He is certainly no dope, but he has made a career out of letting the other guy have a free first shot. He's dodged most of the bullets along the way, but those were mostly just money deals. This is about our pal's life."

I found myself thinking about the book and the chapters of that book, which have never been written, and I was starting into one of my unproductive thought loops.

"Richie has gone through life largely on autopilot, but he's made a lot more good calls than bad. It was clear that his story was about change. Him changing toward her and vice versa. So why don't we go back to our own square one with a blank slate and let it unfold? And besides, what's the worst that can happen. Some bimbo walks with half of his dough and he ends up with a half vast fortune instead of a regular vast fortune—get it, 'half vast'?" I didn't really believe that, but I said it more or less to get a rise out of Jackie.

"No, the worst that happens is that his heart takes a hit, and he becomes a different Richie. So, Nick, it looks like we've been asked into the game, and we should play it Richie's way. We're either his friends or we're not. It's your 'yes or no' thing again, Greek."

"That's probably why you get all those awards for clear and concise thought. I'm on board; let's do it that way."

Richie and Mary had taken up residence in Avery Springs, Florida, and maintained a condo in the D.C. area. He continued with his work on some D.C.-based charities. Mary had greatly curtailed her activities and had shifted her time largely to Richie's endeavors. She had dropped for the most part from the party scene, although she did maintain relationships and acquaintances with the leadership of both houses and some very senior old-timers. She remained an A-List invitee, perhaps because of her increasing scarcity and her somewhat known life with a mystery man. A very charming and oh-so-eligible mystery man. The ladies still loved Richie, maybe even more so now with his handsomely graying maturity.

When not in D.C. or at one of Richie's many undertakings across the country, they tried to spend as much time as possible in Florida, especially from November through April.

April was still cherry blossom time in D.C., and despite T. S. Eliot's dim outlook, the month of April seemed to be one of the relatively happy periods there. Maybe the thawing of the mild winters thereabouts induced a bit of short-lived political goodwill.

Richie's mom had died a couple years back, and he and Mary visited Big Richie, as he was still known. They got on very well. Big Richie was delighted at the prospects of attending Richie's wedding. And that was fine, a righteous priority. Big Richie had met Mary before we did, and, you know what, that was fine.

The big day for Jackie and me came quickly enough when Richie asked us to spend a day with Mary and him in Avery Springs. It was a fine November day when I picked up Jackie at the airport. We motored on up to Chez McAlister-Blaine and approached the front door.

I had expected Richie to play official greeter and to seat us somewhere after which Queen Mary would descend the staircase. The Nick 101 had to flip to Plan B when Mary burst through the door and greeted us. Jackie and I were standing more or less shoulder to shoulder when she put an arm on each of us and smiled warmly.

A smiling barracuda, said the 101. Holy mackerel, said I to myself. Talk about gorgeous. I went right back to Jackie's observations about the three or four Academy Award shows he'd covered. I remember him saying that it was unworldly glitz and glamour, and that while some of the guys were prettier than the girls, everyone was just plain pretty. Then there were the outfits, which ranged from tastefully elegant to totally outlandish. And on and on he would go, describing the pageantry.

"In each of those three years, however," he noted with an uncharacteristic enthusiasm, "then there was Natalie Wood. She

226

wasn't a nominee in any of the years I attended that craziness. She was just the most understated beauty on the planet. She wore a minimum of jewelry, and her hair was simply done. Always in some fairly plain outfit. And always singular. She was so for real that you wouldn't recall any specific attribute, just the whole picture. The overly used word 'aura' was well applied to Natalie Wood."

And with Mary Lancer Blaine. She had a presence and she was a presence. She was a showstopper. What show I don't know. I trusted that would come later. I don't think I gaped and gawked, but that would have been okay. Moreover, to use one of my favored "elegant" words, it crossed my mind in a hustle that if any two human beings should have kids, these were they. Ava Gardner was so pretty, she used to make me sweat. But Ava was AAA ball; Mary was the big leagues.

"I'm so glad to finally meet you two in person." She did a snappy about-face and wedged herself between the two of us. *An obvious foreshadowing,* grumbled the 101. She then guided us through the front door and bid us official welcome to their place.

"Come with me," she said. "Richie is out on the patio."

Richie looked up and rose. "You're a bit early, I thought you wouldn't be along for a while. . . .

"Ooops," he continued, "I've been out here longer than I had imagined. I screwed up again. I'd hoped to introduce you and Mary to each other, but I see you've already met."

"We have," said three voices. The chorus of frogs had grown.

"Well great, how about some coffee or something?"

Mary directed us to sit and went off.

"So you've really gone and done it, eh, Richie?" said Jackie.

"I have and I'm very happy about it. My fondest desire is that you'll validate me once again with your blessings."

"You know we do," I said.

Richie had been fooling with something that looked like an eastern artifact, which had caught our attention.

"Oh this thing, it's a good fortune statue from Pang. You know, the oil king of southeast Asia. He's now Mr. Big in that part of the world. Funny how things turn out."

"Funny indeed," I said, "look at the three goobers from Will's Grove. We haven't done too badly, have we?"

"No, you haven't," said Mary as she wheeled back into our presence with a tray of good-looking stuff. "No you haven't at all. We can offer you some juice, pastry, and coffee or tea. I understand that you're now into the decaf thing, Nick."

"I am, thank you. I was in the early stages of the caffeine tremors and had to take some kind of action. I think I'm through the withdrawal phase."

Despite the 101, I was drawn to Mary. She was dressed very simply and had a take-me-as-you-find-me air about her. She was also just about the poster girl for my over-forty thesis. The sharp lines of her nubile years had given way to the fabled Nick Drizos glow. She had particularly attractive laugh lines, and I love those lines. The casually falling neck-length auburn hair also suited her. But then, for all my cosmopolitan flair, I'm an easy sell. Plus, call me what you will—bond trader, wealth manager, financial advisor—I've basically been a peddler all of my adult life. And no one is an easier sale than another peddler, as the 101 reminds me constantly. Jackie was his usual implacable journalistic self. This was one instance where my visceral approach to life left the ever-so-objective Jackie in the proverbial dust. When I say she was/is gorgeous, know that it is a Greek—lover of all things beautiful—who is speaking.

I have noticed over the years that many, maybe even most, women seem to regard husbands or impending husbands as turf to be defended, or at least not to be shared. The messages and signals to those ends start at various times, but more often than not, friendships of longstanding tend to unravel and dissipate pretty quickly. There has also been no shortage of evidence to that effect in music, literature, and personal experience. I had thus expected to see some initial evidence of a first veil setting some boundaries. My senses were telling me otherwise.

Mary said, "I'm really glad to see you two. Usually the lady of the house asks if you would like to tour our abode, so I'm not being rude. We can do that any time. If that's okay with you, I'd rather enjoy the day and your company. I know a great deal about the three of you, going back to the Beau Geste days. I wouldn't mind ending up as Susan Hayward. But what would you like to do?"

"I'm for that," said the laconic Jackie. "Both the company and the Susan Hayward deal."

"We have heard a little about you as well, especially since you've been dominating our pal's thoughts for some time now. But, tell me, was it really as auspicious a beginning as Richie would have us believe? It's especially important to us, whom you may ultimately judge to be country bumpkins, but we are classical romantics."

Mary smiled and began to answer but Jackie continued, "And, if so, how did things get resurrected?"

Mary smiled more broadly. "Mr. Slater," she said, "I see you have your investigative journalist hat on today. Will this be for attribution, off the record, or what?"

Jackie got it and said, "Off the record, strictly off the record. I apologize. I'll try to be a real human being, but I'm just totally curious to hear the real version."

Richie smiled along with Mary, but I can see Richie anytime, so I turned back to her.

"I know you two a bit, and as far as I'm concerned I'll be an open story. We did meet at a function in D.C. More accurately, I barged into him and was particularly off base. I can give you a short thumbnail as to how I got that way if you'd like."

Caught with a mouthful of pastry, Jackie just nodded.

"There are three punch lines that make up the short version. First, if I hadn't been ill-mannered, I might not have met our friend. Second, if I hadn't tracked him down at the Lincoln Memorial, I'd have felt like a total jerk. And third, if he hadn't answered my fax, I'd have been heartbroken. I would have gotten over it, but I'd never know what I know now. Which is, he's what my life is all about. Period."

Cool, I thought to myself, with the 101 saying things like *Naïve bastard.*

"Anyway I am the only daughter of Robert and Emily Blaine, who are both deceased, and the niece of Jesse Lancer, the former senate minority leader from Wyoming. Hence my middle name. I had a very happy childhood in Cheyenne and was a bit of

229

a tomboy. Riding and roping were still part of everyday life then, and I enjoyed being around robust, enthusiastic people.

"Jesse was one of the last frontier guys and wasn't just a good man, he was a very good man. He would have been the man that Joe Starrett and the folks from *Shane* would have wanted to represent them. It was filmed in the Tetons in Wyoming, you know."

"Shane," I repeated.

"Oh yeah." She grinned. "I'm an old movie freak, too. Maybe not as much as you guys, but there are some movie theaters in D.C. which feature the great old ones. We've gotten to like the Fred and Ginger oldies as well. Maybe you haven't seen Richie on the dance floor lately. A very dashing fellow, and we've found a few quiet places that feature the old big-band sounds, too. Mostly we like old movies because they advocate fair play. That sounds kind of fey these days, but we are very big on fair play."

"Dancing," I mumbled. "Richie?"

"I know, Nick, you were always the best dancer. Well, you've got some competition."

As I have noted, I love stories and I was liking this one. Just to salt it a bit, I said, "Okay, Mary, how about this line from what movie: 'Destiny has held its hand out to you, gentlemen. Do not reject it.' "

"That one's easy, Nick. That was our favorite snob James Mason in *Five Fingers*. I always liked his haughty ways and the manner in which he just about spat out his words."

How can you not like someone who likes old movies? Cool, I'm thinking. *Jerk,* said the 101. We then spent a few minutes playing what-movie-is-this-line-from? Great lines including: "Lions and tigers and bears, oh my" or "'Twas beauty killed the beast" or even "Tomorrow is another day."

"My dad died when I was fourteen and Jesse, he didn't like to be called uncle Jesse, just Jesse, became my surrogate father. After high school I went off to college in the east and would often visit Jesse on the hill. I had wanted to attend college locally, but mom just said no. She always said I could end up wherever I pleased, but not before seeing more of the world. She used to say that travel is even better than formal education. The more you

230

know about the world you live in, the better you'll be. So I traveled quite a bit, and it was good advice. It was particularly good, because I learned to look for similarities rather than differences in people. That may sound trivial, but most of my schoolwork up to that time focused on the bizarre differences from one culture to another. In short I found that I enjoyed people with differing points of views. After a while I became pretty good at engaging them. Most of the time I would find more similarities in folks than differences. Most of the time.

"I majored in history and political science, and I greatly preferred history. My mom became very ill soon after I started my junior year, so I dropped out and returned to Cheyenne. She was a young woman, not yet fifty, and she died just after Christmas. It was the second of my two great sadnesses, less than six years apart, and I lost interest in returning to college.

"I attended to my mom's estate, settled her worldly affairs and decided to stay in the Equality State. We're also known as the Cowboy State. One of the few states with two nicknames.

"Oil had been found in the eastern portion of our state, and I soon hired on with a surveying and seismology company doing a combination of mostly clerical and some fieldwork. It was one of those jobs that tire you out constructively, and was a good way to deal with grief.

"Jesse would stop by from time to time. He was not only a very good man, he was a very smart man. He knew when it was time to leave me alone and he knew when it was time to prod me along.

"He was very aware of my mother's advice about traveling and the world around me, probably because he had given her the same advice years before. She would enthrall me with stories of her travels. So much so that I thought actually packing up and going would be superfluous.

"Jesse would often preface his remarks with a reference to sails and ballast. While he remains a cowboy to his very essence, he had also served in the navy during World War II and often invoked nautical metaphors. Sails and ballast was his way of saying that you need both direction and balance.

"If he had one particular talent, and he had many, it was balance. What fits where? When does it fit? When can things be done effectively? He had it pretty well figured to leave me alone long enough to get over my losses, but not so long that I'd give in to inertia. Timing was often at the center of his thinking. He had determined it was time for me to put up my sails again.

"Among his other enviable traits was sincerity, especially where his niece was concerned. And he was protective of me to a fare-thee-well. At the same time, he had never been married and, of course, had no kids of his own, so he had a blind spot here or there as a result. I mention that because part of his advice wasn't what I would call flawed, but it was incomplete. Plus he knew me from my days as a pretty good cowhand, so he didn't worry much about some of the present-day perils for young girls. Nonetheless, one could not have had a better or more loving friend.

"So it was back east again. and school flew by. I was in a number of activities, but politics wasn't one of them. In fact, I went the other way. The so-called activists used to drive me to distraction. It always struck me as an enormous conceit to be running around at age twenty two, or so, and telling people what was right and how to run their lives. Unimpeded by their lack of practical experience, these people were propelled by their disdain for the generation before them.

"Being righteous and certain is often a deadly brew. Anyway, an irony is that I run into some of these folks now and again. Many are quite messed up—broken marriages, problem kids, drugs, booze, domestic violence, gambling, one affliction or another—but they're still pitching others on the way it should be.

"Sorry for the digression. At this rate we'll be here for week."

Cool, I thought again. *Moron,* came the predictable echo from my cynical alter ego.

"Not at all," said Jackie. "I'm with you on those folks. Being engaged and interested is laudable. Doing the Gestapo routine is not, so you'll get no beef from me. I got tired of those people in college pretty quickly."

With a really neat nod, she continued, "Nonetheless Jesse convinced me that I should at least do a turn in D.C. to see firsthand how things work, or don't work, in that important part of the world.

"His advice, and it made some sense in those days, was if you're going to be in the east, take advantage of it. There are three great eastern cities—Boston, New York, and Washington. Someday they may well make up the predicted megalopolis, but for now they are the Big Three: Boston for old-world culture and education, New York for the hurly-burly of business, and D.C. for politics. Take your choice. Do all three if you wish, but do at least one. Since Jesse was in D.C., the choice was easy.

"In those days the Senate had one counsel for both sides of the aisle, and Jesse put my resume in for a gofer slot in the senate counsel's office. I got the entry-level job and it turned out to be a great way to see 'the world's greatest deliberative body' at work.

"It was a vastly different world. The federal budget was less than one-eighth of its present size. My boss, Will Davis, was an absolute gentleman and a walking font of history. He had taken and passed the bar exam the very day that the market crashed in 'twenty-nine. There wouldn't be that many law school classes for a while, so he found himself thrust into a bewildering torrent of assignments. He could really tell stories, and he had no shortage of them. He had also become what was known then as a 'lawyer's lawyer.'

"When a bunch of lawyers were deadlocked, or when legislators were in a logjam, they would often call for Will Davis. More often than not, he would unjam the particular works. And, most importantly, never made it a 'you win, you lose' deal. He just about always managed to leave each side with a good feeling of dignity. A very talented guy."

Richie, definitely not the star of today's program, jammed himself into the conversation with, "And if Mary knows anything about us, she knows how we are with stories."

Before slipping back into his attentive listening mode, he gave Mary a small hug. They might as well have been two lightbulbs sharing and feeding from the same electricity—each other.

"Mr. Davis happened to be sitting next to President Roosevelt on December seventh when he got the news on Pearl Harbor. He told me the president went limp with horror and told him, 'I knew they'd grab the Philippines, Will, but I never thought they'd hit Pearl.' To this day I still read or hear something about how the president was complicit. No sense engaging them and no reason to violate a confidence either.

"He also told me about the lineup of judges during the big impeachment, and the way it could have been." She stopped and looked at Jackie and said, "I'll even give you the name of the judge who might have heard the case." Leaning over, she whispered into Jackie's ear.

"That's the way he told it to me. It would have made a great story, but I've never said anything about it except to these two. How about you?"

"Same here. No real point, because in the end it played out as it did. It was a confidence and the woulda, coulda, shouldas ought to stay among friends. Doncha think?"

Jackie said yes and I nodded.

"I've been gassing on here for quite a while. How about a beer of something?"

"I like stories, but I'll bet you've got a Killian's or two in the reefer," I said.

"How about you, Jackie, beer or a gin and tonic?"

"It's a little early for the hard stuff. I'll join Nick."

It was good. We were all very much at ease. Mary is a definite keeper, I thought. The 101 growled something like, *God, you're an easy sell.*

Mary disappeared from sight and earshot, so Jackie piped up, "Well, great one, you haven't asked us what we think."

"No and I won't. For two reasons. First, you just met and second, it's a done deal. This is the way it's gonna be."

"So," Jackie retorts, "why are we here?"

"Because, Jackie, there are things I know and things I don't know. One of the things I know is that Mary and I are right for each other and that she's right for you two bozos. And vice versa."

"Are you on autopilot, or is this one of your rare thought-out deals?"

"I've always been on autopilot, Jackie, I've had to be. I'm just not as smart as you two."

Mary returned, but this time the three of us were ready and we started to rise. She gave what would become her well-known palms out and down, which had become part of our silent lexicon.

Nonetheless I helped seat her and said, "You were talking about your days with the senate counsel."

"Oh yes, Will Davis was a most admirable man. He was one of the great lawyers in that he moderated excessive behavior. He was a very calming person and often defused things before they became senseless, irreversible or, as is too frequently the case in D.C., catastrophic. For example, one day a high-ranking and high-profile senator came racing into our little subterranean office. He wanted this file and that file on one of his colleagues from the other side. I'd have just signed a copy of whatever he wanted out to him.

" 'Instead,' Mr. Davis just said, 'you are certainly welcome to those files, but you know I'll then have to accede to the other side's requests for the files on Senator X and Senator Y.'

"Our visitor was quite agitated and snapped, 'Oh really, what do you have?'

"Davis directed him to a file cabinet, opened it very deliberately, paged through some hanging folders and produced a few documents. 'Feel free to browse through these. I'll be in the other office. Just call me if I can be of any assistance.' In about five minutes, we heard the door close. The files were piled neatly and our visitor was gone. Peace ruled for another day."

"He was very evenhanded and was one of those special lawyers who is called upon when a hopeless deadlock had moved from unproductive to overheating nastiness. He could usually find a way to offer each side an aspect of positive focus, thereby facilitating disengagement and a few more days of peace. He could find some way for everyone to leave with dignity intact, but I already mentioned that. I guess that ability sticks in my mind, because it seems to be a lost talent.

"He was called upon repeatedly to verify rulings and procedures. It was a great place from which to view the smooth sur-

235

faces of the theoretical and the jagged edges of the practical. They didn't teach the latter at college.

"Jesse was in his first term and would later serve as minority leader. Like Davis, he was a calming force. Those two words don't usually suit each other, but he was literally a calming force. In a bit of a surprise, his party regained control of the senate. In more of a surprise, he stepped down from his leadership position. It had been almost unanimously expected that he would become the majority leader.

"When I asked him why, he said, 'There's sails and there's ballast, I'm ballast. I'm better at keeping balance and staying on course than I am at setting the course. I have a hand in setting the direction, but I see myself as a very good first mate and a not-so-good captain. Besides, this may be my last term.'

"That was another surprise, but he was of the opinion that he was in danger of becoming more Washington than Wyoming. He also thought the seniority system employed in both houses was the single worst attribute of American government. He proposed legislation on several occasions that would eliminate the notion of seniority in the Senate after one term. Long story short, he thought very little of seniority. Between the seniority system and its first cousin, committee chairmanships, it gets kind of hopeless sometimes."

"I met with him several times," said Jackie, "and I concurred with him one hundred percent. The irony is that his bills never made it to the floor, because the seniority system of chairmanships thwarted his every attempt."

"He was fond of saying, 'The guys in the senate can do three things that most regular folks can't. They can get elected, and I'll grant that takes some talent. They can spend more money than they have. And they can count votes. Boy howdy, can they count votes.' And, in the end, Mary, he would say to me, 'It's all about votes.' As for me I love that expression 'Boy howdy', especially when coming from a real article like Jesse. Some expressions really suit the speaker and that's one.

"He'd remind me that the senate was concocted by the founders, whom he adored, with its six-year terms of office to be a counter to the quick changes of passions of the populace and of the lower house. We agreed that for decades they had done a masterful job of moderating willy-nilly social change. Whether for the good or otherwise we would leave to history. He also carried a dog-eared copy of the U.S. Constitution and Declaration of Independence with him at all times. I love the man. He is as straight as straight could be."

"So Mary, how many years did you spend in the Senate Counsel's office?"

"Just about four years, Nick. I had thought I'd do something else when Jesse stepped down, but I was approached by the new majority leader to join his staff. I had been in his presence a few times and thought he was an okay guy, but I wouldn't say yes or no without Jesse's viewpoints and advice. I was more surprised that Jesse agreed to do one more term after refusing the majority leader role.

"I was still quite unfocused and had little idea of what I wanted to do for the longer term. Jesse always advised to focus on things in which I have both talent and passion. I can't say I shared the passion of most of my young contemporaries on the hill, but I was pretty good at organizing and getting things done. In the end, it seemed like a good place to spend some time and it might be a good place to be from when I got more serious about my life's journey. So I signed on.

"It turned out to be a very interesting place to be. The majority leader's office is like the terminus of a great pilgrimage. There was no shortage of traffic. Senator Anderson was a quite decent human being, as much so as one can be in that environment, but he was a vote counter of the first order. Right and wrong were important on some level, but the odds of a visitor walking away happy were in direct ratio to the visitor's abilities to do something for the good senator. The books on favors due versus favors owed were kept with meticulous precision.

"If I may short-circuit my long windedness, it was very much the opposite of Richie who's pretty much made a career of doing things for people who have very little to offer. The practical thing to do versus the right thing to do. But our friend doesn't think that way."

"It's not so much that he doesn't think that way, Mary," I interjected, "it's just that he's wired differently from most folks. It may have been the water in our little town, but he's always been his own guy. What is an effort toward generosity in most people just comes naturally to our friend. It always cracks us up when he does something for somebody and just disappears, leaving the beneficiary with that what's-in-it-for-you look of puzzlement on his face. And it looks like you approve."

"I do approve, but more than that I consider myself lucky for the time we've spent and for whatever time we'll have together."

"As long as I'm doing a good job of interrupting, let me ask you a personal question." Without pausing for acknowledgement I plowed ahead. "I've known you for almost two hours now, and you're what I'd call stunning. Happily we're all at an age where the teenage tension thing is long gone—"

"Nick, she said as she patted the back of my hand good-naturedly, you're among friends, what's on your mind?"

"Well, Mary, if I may say again, you're what I'd call stunning, and D.C. is one of the great seats of predatorship, if I may coin a Drizoism. Didn't you get hit on just about every day?"

"There was some of that, Nick, but remember I was under the ever-watchful eye of Jesse Lancer. More than a senator, he was regarded as a bit of a frontiersman. Plus he was a tall guy and had a fair amount of old west weaponry displayed in his office.

"But you're quite right. D.C. is a funny place. Power and hanky-panky seem to seek each other out. And when hanky seeks panky, not too many places are more obliging and accommodating than your nation's capital. And, in the end, it's no more than what boys and girls have been doing since Caesar and Cleopatra had their little deal. Or what you see on the soaps most afternoons.

"But you asked me a direct question, so I'll give you a straight answer. I would get hit on a bit, but someone would usually advise the hitter that something terrible might happen if he persisted.

"There was also an episode which put a further halo of protection around me. Someone stole Jesse's car. Right out of the senate parking lot, and right out of his high-priority parking space. He was whizzed. And it was a big story in the otherwise sleepy hamlet called D.C.

"It must have been a slow news day, because the theft got a lot of coverage. Jesse was popular to begin with, so when his car was stolen, there was more than a little sympathy. Jesse is also a good-natured guy, but he has a no nonsense side. When interviewed on this slow day, he observed that where he came from, horse thievery was a hanging offense."

The reporter said, "And?"

Jesse obliged the reporter by saying, "So that was my horse, and I better not get my hands on that lowdown thief."

Now Jesse was no country rube, so he gathered the earnest young reporter to him around the shoulders and said, "I'm kidding, young man, I'm kidding. You get that, don't you?"

The earnest reporter looked classically deerlike into the camera and said, "He's kidding folks, he's kidding."

Nonetheless, car thefts dropped measurably for the next couple of weeks, probably out of homage to the greatly popular Jesse, before moving back to their rightful position as the number three business in the local economy. And Jesse received over one hundred faxes from guys who offered themselves as a posse to recover his car.

"No, Nick, I don't think anyone was going to mess with little Mary. There was some romance here and there, but no serious hitting."

"We have this thing, Mary, about engaging people. So how am I doing?"

"Nick, you're worth the price of admission, but you might have heard that expression a time or two."

Yes, I'd heard that a time or two from my friend of all these years. "Jesus, Richie, is there anything that our new friend doesn't know?"

"Probably not, Nick," said Richie, but I did promise Mary I'd be four square about all my baggage. Since you're a large part of it, I thought you'd be pleased that I've come clean with all my many burdens."

"Oh, so now I'm a burden?"

"Are you quite finished, Nick? I'd rather hear Mary's story," said Jackie.

"I am, I just wanted a little attention. And I got it, so back to you Mary."

"Life on the majority leader's staff was pretty good. It was one of those things where you are so perpetually tired that you don't have a great deal of time to reflect on much of anything. Jesse used to say that D.C. was at its best before air- conditioning became pervasive. Prior to that major creature comfort, the pols used to go home or elsewhere to escape the great dismal swamp in July and August. The country then got a respite from their ever-intrusive handiwork. Then came the cursed air-conditioning, and cool offices probably contributed as much as anything to keeping the blur constant.

"Anderson's staff was divided into two main parts, the political and the organizational. The former was for the more zealous and combative among us and was nasty more of the time than not. I gravitated to the organizational side, where I had some talent. After three years I was asked to assume the role of chief executive assistant for the senator. The political side scripted his remarks day by day and counted votes to assure the efficacy of the remarks. My task was to make sure things happened correctly and on time and in managing his logistics.

"As happens in D.C., there is this thing called power to which those seeking favors gravitate. There is also perception of power, which is not the same thing but is often assumed to be. I was seen with the senator several times a day at one function or another and soon became regarded as a gatekeeper. At some point along the way, I was told I had become an A-Lister. That meant being seen and being captured on film with just about every dignitary one can imagine.

"Because of my proximity to power central, many attempted to use me as the path to himself. I wasn't necessarily in the business of making friends, not with these folks anyway, but neither was I in the business of making enemies. I had become a pretty good mistress of maybe, which with hope doing its eternal thing, was usually received well by my assailants. From time to time I was able to be of some help to a constituent or a worthy under-

240

taking here or there, but I was mostly a high-profile gofer. Over time I began to acquire a little edge, and here's why.

"Today there are an increasingly greater proportion of women in government, but in those days, D.C. was still overwhelmingly a man's town. And I was a woman in a man's town, so I tried to balance a couple of old aphorisms. On the one hand: if a politician says yes, he means maybe; if he says maybe, he means no; if he says no, he's no politician. On the other hand; if a lady says no, she means maybe; if she says maybe, she means yes; if she says yes, she's no lady.

"It became obvious that while I preferred to be regarded as a lady, most of the folks I encountered where looking for an in or an angle of some sorts. The choice was to be a pushover or to be somewhat formidable. Over time I guess I became somewhat formidable. Much of that was like Richie's being on autopilot. I guess it was largely an unconscious survival thing, but I soon became no one to mess with.

"In the course of my tour with the majority leader, I was present at meetings with just about all the senior senators and congressmen. I don't say congresspersons either, Nick.

"After seven years, I'd seen and had enough. These elected folks are like any other crowd. There are some exceptionally talented guys, some real dummies, and the majority of mostly regular people. Just about all of them are for sale for one thing or another, however, and the first mission is to keep one's seat. Successful people in D.C. understand the game and thus play it well. I was merely affiliated with a center of power, but, as a natural consequence, I had become an untouchable. Had the senator ever slipped or taken a serious fall, I would have been in yesterday's fashion section.

"There were only a couple of folks who pushed their ego trips to the fullest levels of achievement. The clear winner in that regard was Senator Varlow. He was as senior as anyone in the whole city and did a masterful job of catering to his constituency. Even with his almost unequalled seniority, he was not the chairman of any committee. He was a ranking senior member on three committees, which I always found more than a bit strange, and he was the unquestioned master of pork barrel. He was so good that he was reelected several times, even with incredibly high negative ratings from his own state. But people will put up with a lot when the good times are rolling. By contrast LeFlore used to jerk his chain.

"He, Varlow, was also the most frequent visitor to the senate counsel's office and was always checking out personnel files. It didn't dawn on me till much later that he had probably put together the best single dirt file on his potential adversaries. Today it would have been called Snoop Gate or something like that. It was also rumored that he employed detective agents in this regard. He had something going for him, because he was a name caller of no small note, but not a name callee.

"I had given the position a good effort, and I was regarded as quite competent at running my portion of the senator's affairs. But Jesse's advice and assessments would assert themselves and resurface at increasingly regular intervals. I had some talent, but not much passion for the place.

"The other essential personage in this cavalcade of characters was the irrepressible Senator Charles LaFlore. His love of the Senate was exceeded only by his self-adoration and adulation. It had been said that the only job to which he would be more suited would be the CEO of a mirror company. He was right off the covers of *GQ* and unerringly resplendent in his very expensive suits. He was photogenic, telegenic, and just about every-genic. He was beyond charismatic, he was a walking spectacle.

"To his credit he was regarded as a skilled parliamentarian and a most effective legislator. He was also somewhat unique in that he could call attention to himself as no other, but he could also enjoy a joke at his expense. One time during one of his impromptu chats on the senate steps, a disgruntled person yelled, 'Hey LaFlore, you're not conceited, you're convinced.' And he'd answer, 'I know, I know. Isn't it great?'

"Our hero then took a step toward his detractor and said, 'What a lovely day. How about a beer at my favorite saloon.' Within several seconds, the newly conjoined Damon and Pythias were headed arm in arm to a well-known thirst parlor. What happened next, one can only imagine. These two and Jesse made for an interesting trio as they were among those most frequently interviewed and thus appeared together quite often. Jesse from Wyoming, Varlow from the far west, and LaFlore from the Southeast.

"Anyway, Senator Anderson was reelected in a breeze. The next day, following his victory lap, I turned in my ticket. I hadn't wanted to create any problems during the campaign, so it came somewhat out of the blue. His immediate response was to offer more of everything, but I wasn't running for reemployment, so I just said no thank you. Most of my colleagues were surprised. It was like the old joke about leaving show biz, the cleaning up after the elephant deal, but if anything I had probably stayed too long. It was definitely time to go.

"A couple of weeks in the Caribbean was very welcome, and I returned to D.C. to find a literal avalanche of employment offers. It was flattering, but I was smart enough to know that most accrued from my employment with Mr. Powerful. The relentless perception thing was at work again.

"I went back to Wyoming for a visit and saw Jesse, among the old-timers that I knew. Most of the folks that were my age were all over hell and gone. Industry had moved in to a fair extent, and it just was a changing place.

"For his part, Jesse thought I had two major options. First I could teach government at the university. He thought I'd be especially good at that, and wake a few kids from their intellectual slumber. According to Jesse, half the kids thought Martin Sheen was the president. Or Geena Davis. Otherwise, he thought I should do a roundtrip to D.C. and do something 'elevating'. His last words to me were of caution. He said, 'I probably won't be in D.C. to look after you, and not that you need it, but be careful. There are three especially bad varmints in D.C., and they're all named Senator Varlow. He's the worst of the worst.'

"I wasn't really ready for the college-level show-and-tell time, and I thought there might be some opportunities for the elevating thing, so I held my nose and went back to D.C. And I filed away his last piece of advice about Varlow.

"After trying to follow Jesse's advice, I decided to reinvent myself in the world of PR. It wasn't based on heavy-duty logic, just that there were a number of elevating causes and I knew my way around D.C. pretty well. In time I signed on with Purcell-Adams, which was the second or third largest such outfit in the area and was a highly regarded one. Purcell-Adams had several sides to their practice, and I was slotted in on the nonpolitical fundraising side. It turned out that nonpolitical and fundraising don't really go together all that well. There are some congressmen who will lend themselves to fundraisers just because they believe in them or because they have a soft spot for the particular subject. Others will make a token appearance for the photo ops. The majority, however, are mostly very good vote counters and favor exchangers. Turns out that very little is done in D.C. without the intersection of quids and quos. What's in it for me may not have been invented in D.C., but it was certainly perfected there. I came to call it the town of itchy backs, because of all the mutual scratching going on. Nonetheless, we managed to get some much-needed funding for several of the more downtrodden and deserving associations in the country.

"A given fund raiser is not unlike a Hollywood production, except that it plays one time in one place. It may or may not be televised, but it will be in a prominent ballroom. The event is preceded by months of PR, which focuses primarily on the organization, its mission, its success to date, and its urgent need for continuing funding. Some are enhanced by celebrities in attendance and others benefit from a popular and engaging emcee. It has to be 'the place to be' on that particular evening, so a glittering dais of important people is the sine qua non. The media has to be a co-conspirator. It's not the Oscars, but there is a similar pomp to a successful event.

"For the first couple of years I was so busy with these events that I lost track of time and of myself. I was going sideways again. While there had been some real satisfaction from the first few successful events, it was largely show biz, and there was little, if any, connection with the ultimate recipients.

"I pushed ahead for another two years, but by that time there were more things bothering me than were pleasing or gratifying. First we were paid way too much money. I really hadn't noticed, because most of what I made went into the bank and I lived very modestly. Second the slice paid to people like us seemed overly large. I hadn't paid any attention to that either, because I spent no time with the financial people. I had assumed that the overwhelming majority of the funds went to the advertised recipients. Not the case. Finally, I began to believe there were more than a few cases of fraud and thievery.

"I had succeeded mostly in tiring myself out in doing something that fanned no passion whatsoever. One day while at home with the flu I was watching a show about the triumphs of dirt-poor people who had been given not a handout, but a hand up as the latter-day cliché goes. They were all over the country. Nobody had ever heard of them, because they were not news and because they couldn't deliver a lot of votes. I just decided in a flash I would try to get involved directly.

"I did some research in D.C. and became acquainted with a Catholic priest by the name of Father Darnell. We visited on several occasions and I told him I wanted to go where I could do some good.

"One night we were having dinner in a particularly bombed-out part of the District, and he said, 'Mary, we have no shortage of places which would welcome you. I can tell you about some of them if you'd like, and what we have been trying to do.'

" 'I'm not Catholic, Father. Is that a requirement?'

" 'No, it isn't. Just a good heart and a strong stomach. And, if I may anticipate your next question, we aren't driven by the conversion business either. We run missions, and we do our best. If people want to join us, that's fine but it's not a condition. Our focuses are poverty and ignorance.'

"Long story short, I turned in my ticket again and drove myself to a small dusty town in the Texas panhandle, some miles east of Lubbock and Amarillo. It was the worst part of the inner city of your choice, just without the big buildings. The work was obvious, it was indeed poverty and ignorance. One worse than the other, but the ignorance was the more manageable of the two.

"Poverty, it turns out, is the nicer word for no sanitation, healthcare of the most rudimentary sort, and filth. It's a rough combination and it feeds on itself. It also means no money.

245

"You may recall my hierarchy of donators. The only ones who would be of help here were the goodhearted. The photo-opers and the vote counters would go elsewhere. There were also opportunities if someone were willing to scream and yell a bit. Nobody knew me in these parts, so nobody knew I wasn't much of a screamer. Without much effort, I became Mary the Screamer.

"Anything within reason was fair game. If it meant shaming people into doing something decent, then so be it. So, I'd scream.

"The screaming was directed at the local, county, and state government. And sometimes at nationally known merchants and healthcare providers. After a short while, I learned that screaming and yelling only works with the government folks if you're on the short end of the stick, as we were. I also learned that no screaming and yelling worked better with just about everyone else. If you tried hard enough, you could find something good in most, I say most, non-governmental outfits. Governments have little shame and less conscience. So screaming is the ticket for results with those guys."

So we're listening to Mary's story, which, to put it succinctly, was not what I thought a Mary Lancer Blaine was all about.

Jackie pipes up, "So how can we help? We're not without some talent, you know."

"I know," replied Mary. "Who do you think old RAM talks about most of the time. There's an occasional reference to Pang and some of his Thai pals, but he's been wanting to get us all together for quite a while now. There's plenty to do. And, you Jackie, you could do another Edward R. Morrow Harvest of Shame- type documentary anytime you wished. And we could use the help."

"Just say when," my friend the great writer responded.

"I had met all kinds of goodhearted people along the way. One was a fellow from New York by the name of Tom Pulling, one of the good guys from the New York crowd. He has pals all over the place and he put me in touch with Jim Coriston. Jim was an old Pittsburgh guy who became a big deal with one of the big national auditing firms, but he was constant in wanting to be of help. Among other things he became the financial advisor to the

San Francisco Archdiocese where he did a lot of good work gratis. Among other uplifting deeds, he made a few trips to Bolivia and followed up with a fundraiser to bring clean water to an inland community. That struck us as an idea worth stealing, so we stole it. I should add I never felt the slightest twinge of guilt when stealing an idea that might benefit the most miserable among us. Never.

"So, for our part we would steal any good idea, so one of our projects was clean water for our panhandle town. I will say we always asked permission to steal the ideas first.

"We were able to raise some money in Dallas from some folks I knew. I'll say this for the Texans; they've probably done as good a job as any state, and better than most, in the matter of assimilating Mexicans. They may call themselves Hispanics, and they may be called Hispanics, but they are Mexicans. And mostly they are nice people as well as proud and very hard working. They're gritty, too.

"In the course of about eighteen months, we made some major progress. I'm not here to tell you that it was Israel sprouting orange trees out of the desert, but it was progress. It was also like shoveling stuff against the tide, but we made progress.

"We had a semblance of a local economy including an HMO of sorts, some stores and a movie theater, which doubled as entertainment and as the audio-visual center of the local school system and the emergency ward of our nonexistent hospital.

"We made our money and resources really stretch, but money was an issue. There was just a limit to what we could do in our version of a cashless society.

"So there I was again at one extreme or the other. In D.C., I had some talent and access to money but no passion. In Texas, I found great purpose and happiness. I had plenty of passion but limited access to money. There had to be something in between. I felt like the friend of Senator Anderson who bought a castle in Ireland and converted it to a luxury hotel. When asked how he was doing, he'd say, 'The only way to make any money in the small luxury hotel business is through the bar, but that's a problem. Our customers are Irish and American. The Irish love to drink, but have no money; the Americans have plenty of money, but don't drink.' He should have hung on; Ireland is now the land of the prosperous.

"Pardon the tangent, but I was trying to dramatize my passion/accomplishment quandary. Every once in a while I tried to take a step back and see if I could discern any real progress. I had taken a lot of mental pictures and notes when I first arrived, so successive pictures were of great value when they showed some clear achievement.

"I was tired, I was happy tired, but I needed a break. I had been speaking with Jesse on and off, and I had been thinking more and more frequently to visit with him. It was one of those things where intention gets buried by each day's emergency.

"I absolutely hate it when someone whom I had been honest-to-God been meaning to call, calls me and the best I can do is a lame 'I've been meaning to call you.' I hate it, but that's exactly what happened when I got a call from Jesse's next-door neighbor. And the news was worse, Jesse was slipping.

"Wake-up call, or call it what you will, I was back in Cheyenne the next day. Jesse looked surprisingly strong and alert, compared to what I had braced for. He was up and around and enjoying the big sky. Montana claims the big sky, but Wyoming is pretty spectacular in its own right.

"Some retired politicians look like caricatures, in fact many presently serving look like caricatures, but Jesse was still the tall and straight frontiersman. His long silvery white Buffalo Bill mane would have been laughable on others, but it just fit him perfectly. Webster must have had Jesse in mind when he catalogued 'ingenuous.' He just looked like the lion he was, an old lion, but a lion nevertheless. And a huggable lion.

"His steely blue eyes were still vibrant, and while he walked about with pained effort, it was clear he was still a young man but with a worn and aged body of sinew. He had been waiting for me with one of his usual lunches. This time it was sandwiches and iced tea. Sometimes it's just not possible to know how much you miss someone till you see them near the end of the trail or as Jesse referred to it: 'curtain time.'

"Jesse was economical with his words. No wasted motion in word or deed, and no ambiguity. He drove folks crazy in D.C. on the talk-show circuit with his 'yes' and 'no' answers. Those folks were used to campaign speech answers from the other great pretenders. Maybe that's why he enjoyed celebrity status in both Wyoming and in D.C. For whatever reasons, he was as real as they come. When he told me he was glad to see me, I took his full import. He knew, and I knew, he didn't have much time.

"In a further economy of words, he told me I was a personal treasure to him, and I started to cry. I've got a fairly vivid imagination, or so I've been told, but I never imagined a world without Uncle Jesse. It's maybe one of the great things about being human, the ability to suppress things and thereby avoid great pain until the day comes.

"He told me how proud he was of me, and that just brought more of the same. He was one of the few people in the world who could say 'Hey darlin'' without conjuring up the notion of some sleazy guy trying to get into my pants.

"Oops," I said.

"Sorry, Nick, just trying to make a point about a truly great man."

"I take your point, Mary." And Richie just chuckled.

"And say it he did. He asked me how things were going in the panhandle. I told him that D.C. had plenty of money and power but no heart and soul and that my panhandle friends had the opposite. As I would expect, he told me I better find a way to get the best of both. And, of course, he was dead right. Economically and financially, dead right.

"The thing I probably loved most about him was that he was an honest-to-God tough guy. He always told me that every day on this earth was a gift and that he would try to make the most of each gift. And if things didn't work out one day, he's just try harder the next.

"As far as I know, he only ever had one mortal enemy in all his days and that was Senator Varlow. While we were together he said, 'Darlin, that Varlow is the worst human being I've ever met. I've seen 'em all, and he's the worst. Don't think I've been out on the range too long, but I wouldn't be surprised if he had something to do with my failing health. He's just no good and low-down. I don't think I hate anybody, but he sure comes close.

249

If you can do me a favor after I cash in, I wouldn't mind if you took his wheels off.

"As more than an aside, I'm happy to tell you that Jesse is still with us. And he's still as sharp as ever. It may be the regenerative power of his beloved Wyoming. He's also still called upon with some frequency by former colleagues, as well as some earnest newcomers. Especially by those who appreciate his sails and ballast precepts.

"As a result of talking with Jesse, I decided to hold my nose and do one more tour in D.C. to connect big money with big and deserving projects. I was about six months into my second incarnation in D.C. when I concluded that my big plan just wasn't going to work out. It came down to doing bite-sized projects in Texas and getting some good things done or playing the old game in D.C. I just wasn't smart enough or tough enough or something enough to get big money for far-away projects. The "who cares/no publicity" projects.

"Worse, I could no longer play the Mary the Barracuda game. It turned out the D.C. crowd put up with my shrillness and bitchiness only because they thought I lived in power central. I never thought of my many tasks that way, so maybe the joke was on me.

"By far the worst, however, was the fact, becoming ever clearer, that D.C. is all about D.C. and that good works are all about the folks in front of the camera. I had come to the end of the trail and was convinced that Mary Lancer Blaine was a fraud. A well-intentioned fraud, but a fraud nonetheless.

"The capper was to follow when I was doing a relatively low-level audit of the several campaigns I had worked on in this interregnum. I discovered not only disingenuity, but also excessive fee structures and some downright larceny.

"I had a few choices, and only a few. I could stay in D.C. and try to blow the lid off some of these scams, or I could retreat to Texas or Wyoming and apply my skills and energy to small but meaningful projects. Needless to add, I was in a distracted, dysfunctional, and combative state. Hostile might be a better word. I had gotten to a stage where I truly believed most of the honest folks had taken their leave. At least from this place called D.C.

250

"It was that very night when I met your pal. I had promised a friend to attend one of the few functions that I thought was really straight. As Jesse always said, a promise is a promise. So, dutifully, I went. I tried to get with the program, but I was done. I made the effort to be pleasant when I happened to observe Richie. I was still part of the connected crowd, and I had heard of Mr. McAlister. He struck me, as you can both appreciate, the most relaxed man I had ever seen, truly comfortable with himself. At the same time, however, I had seen some of the best cons invented and I hearkened to Jesse's longtime advice that if it appears to be too good to be true it probably is too good to be true.

"So there I was, registering about nine-point-eight on the hostility scale and there was my target for catharsis. I was in my most uncharitable state and I was about to make the single worst bad judgment call of my life. As you probably know, I was rude in the extreme. I was also totally disarmed by his demeanor, as well as his dismissal of me, and in a moment, became convinced that he was a guy who had nothing to prove. And that I had made an incredibly bad mistake.

"At that very moment, I vowed to set things straight. If nothing else, I would set things straight with this stranger to whom I had been abusive. Then, and only then, I would get on with being the best Mary Lancer Blaine that I could. In Texas, Wyoming, or wherever.

"After a few days of playing Lieutenant Columbo, I tracked him down at the Lincoln Memorial. The rest you more or less know. That's the most mercifully short version of McAlister-Blaine."

Jackie and I were okay with this. I knew it and Jackie knew it, the way we know a lot of things. It was okay.

Just to be a jerk, I winked and said—doing my best Richie impression—"Okay, so how can we be helpful? Like what could you want from us guys?"

She smiled. We melted, and she went on, "I want several things. One is your friendship, your lifetime friendship. Another is for you three to keep whatever you have and to grow it over the next God-knows-how-many years. The last is perpetual free and open access to each other."

251

"I couldn't bear to have less of Richie than he has become, and you two are a large part of what and who he is. I will be offended and greatly hurt if you two don't continue on with him—and me—as you have before.

"I've told you how it is we came to meet, and I'll add one more item. You have paid me a compliment or two already, Nick. Being called stunning is a quite nice thing. I'm aware that I am not unattractive, but neither am I very experienced with men. I haven't had many romances and nothing that resembled an affair or a liaison. It seems as if I've always had a compass or a governor of some sort that designed me for one man. I don't know where that came from, but that's the way it is. Along the way in D.C., it often got back to me that I was either a lesbian or a world-class cock teaser. Maybe that's what got me the Mary the Bitch handle.

"Jesus, Mary," roared Richie as he almost went over backwards in his chair.

"You said honest, Richie, and honest means honest. Plus we are all well out of our teens. And anyway, and in addition I'm good and tired of the mincing politically correct bullshit that has imprisoned and poisoned our natural way of speaking. While I'm about it, I'm particularly weary of hearing about the N-word or the F-word. What happens if there are two N-Words. Will someone then refer to N-Word number two? Who thought up this total nonsense? What a royal pain in the ass."

The three of us looked like an ad for a can of Harvard Beets or the inside of the control room at Three Mile Island during the near meltdown. Except that she made total sense.

The ensuing quiet was very quiet, if you don't count my up-and-down shoulders-moving laugh but no sound emitting piece of theatrics, and the only one who could restart things was Mary, which she did.

"In more specific answer to your question, I want Richie body, mind, and soul. I'll get more graphic as you wish."

"So, Mary," I said, wondering why people begin sentences with "so," "are you telling us that you love our pal?"

"Nick, you're smarter than you look."

She was well into our lexicon, so I just giggled.

252

Hard-bitten Jackie chimed in with, "Sounds like an okay deal to me."

I knew what he was thinking. This was no ordinary relationship. This was Tristan and Isolde. This was the real deal. I agreed, and the Nick 101 didn't even murmur.

"That's all?" I asked.

"Well, there are some other things, but I'll let the RAM man put those to you."

"We plan on getting married twice," said Richie, "once in Will's Grove and once in Wyoming. Mary's parents are gone, but my dad will give her away in Will's Grove, and Jesse will perform the service out west."

"That's pretty swell," I added, "but you don't need us for any of that."

"Sometimes I think the two of you sleepwalk through life," Richie said. "I'm going to need two best men. Are you two available?"

Before I could pipe up, Jackie advised that the two of us would walk through the Fires of Gehenna for him, and that put a bit of closure on that item.

Jackie's glance at me was less than perfunctory, so I muted out with a nod, a big nod.

"There is one other thing," Richie added. "You know I have a lot of dough and a lot of big money interests."

"Yes, great one, we know, we know," I said. "So?"

"So," he responded, "Mary has signed a pre-nup."

I was deflated. Totally deflated. "A pre-nup," I repeated. "Are you nuts? Where's the romance?"

"Don't yell at me, Nick. Talk to her."

"That's the deal," said Mary, "that's the only way it works. I love your pal, but that's the only way I'll take him. No baggage and no stuff. There's nothing in this for me except for him. And you two without a visiting-hours poster. I think that's a pretty good deal all around."

It's a funny thing when expectations and reality collide—especially when the collision results in an unconsidered outcome. It was even funnier to see Jackie and me almost total Richie in the process of trying to be the first to hug Mary.

So there was Richie, feigning annoyance with Jackie and me at our crude outburst. But he composed himself and inquired, "So do I have a deal, and do I have two best men?"

The frogs answered as one that he did indeed.

We four spent the rest of the day and early evening having a grand time. We were a happy lot. I think Jackie and I deemed Mary to be the realest of deals, and we rejoiced that two people like these could find each other. We were a happy lot indeed.

I awoke again and glanced at my bedside clock. It was early in the morning. I don't think I made a sound, but when I next looked about, there was Gail. She was beautiful, as I may have noted before. Especially beautiful.

The particular beauty may have been a residual of my happiness for Mary and Richie, but I don't think so. At that particular instant, I was just thinking about Nick—about Nick and Gail. There was something very different and very special in the air.

"Are you okay, Nick?" she inquired. "Is there anything I can get for you?"

"No thank you, Gail. I'm pretty good. In fact, I've just had a major up. Richie and Mary are getting married."

Gail looked a bit puzzled. She seemed to want to let things drop unsaid, so I did.

She then said, "It's coming up on breakfast time. Will you be joining the rest of us, or would you rather nod off again?"

I'm not usually very forward with women, but even the Nick 101 failed to act as my usual inhibitor, so I piped up with "Would it be possible for you to have breakfast with me—on the terrace?"

Professional as always, she smiled and then said, "Nick, you know everything is done here right down the line by the numbers. But you are getting under everyone's skin, so I'll ask the boss. Okay?"

Okay indeed, I thought. After my recent past, a maybe is like a major award.

I don't know if I even closed my eyes, but once again I was back where I left off. The two weddings took place a few days apart. Each was a beautiful but understated affair. In the first, at Richie's home, his dad gave Mary away, and I was the best man.

254

We were down to four surviving parents—Richie's dad, Jackie's mom, and both of the elder Drizoses. They were overjoyed, especially Richie's dad, who smiled and cried his way through the ceremony.

Father Shea, motoring past eighty in his rickety but upbeat manner, presided over the affair and noted most touchingly that Mary and Richie had, in reality, been married to each other long before this particular ceremony. The thought being that these two souls were destined to seek each other out. He may have taken a bit of romantic license, but this was just a part of his usual and beautiful homilies we had come to expect over the years. He was one of those gifted folks, who could plop heavy thoughts right into one's lap with a feathery touch. At that specific reference, Jackie and I smiled at each other in affirmation of Father Shea's observation.

For Richie, especially Richie at home, this ceremony was Irish Catholic all the way. It didn't matter much, though, because Mary and Richie were well into their own very unique spirituality.

It was all very ecumenical. Richie the Catholic, Jackie the Jew, and Nick the Greek Orthodox. Maybe that's the long-term glue which had held us three together so tightly. Catholics and Jews are fairly definitive, but we Greek Orthos show much greater flexibility. We're at home just about anywhere. And why should that not be the case I suggested to myself, with a seconding vote from the 101.

For her part, Mary the Protestant was happy to cast her lot with Richie and company. She said, on more than a few occasions, that she found the variety very broadening, very settling and peaceful. I had always found that an interesting observation and could only wonder if Raj might be melded into this amalgam of spirits, but that would be for another day.

We enjoyed a swell dinner at The Eagle's Nest, a small local restaurant overlooking the Chained Horse River. And we had a grand time. There were plenty of toasts and no shortage of funny stories and remembrances. I'm sure I could recall just about all that was said that evening, but it was the pervading atmosphere that persists with me.

It was just one of those times when everything was right. Where talk just wasn't required. Not superfluous, just not required. It was welcome, it was warm, but it wasn't required. The only imperfection was our missing folks, but even that was okay. We toasted them, and we were all aware of their spirits among us. As to my time worn model of life being alternatively blue skies and tunnels, the sun shone brightly—all day and into the evening.

The older folks began to tire at about nine, which, as it occurred, was a fine time to end the festivities. At about that time, the thought of a honeymoon struck me. If there was a master plan, I was not aware of it. I think Jackie was in the same state of ignorance. We had signed on and needed only the receipt of our marching orders. Nonetheless, it seemed to me that Mary and Richie would want some privacy, so I asked him for some enlightenment of his unfolding grand scheme.

"That's thoughtful of you, Nick, but Mary and I have been married for quite a while. In fact, we were married in a civil ceremony in Arlington the day before we started living together. It's the old-fashioned thing; living together means marriage to me. We, I'll speak for me, I have been on a honeymoon ever since."

Most weddings may be about man and wife, but these two are about friends and friendship, I quickly surmised.

"I heard that Mr. McAlister," said the soft voice which had become familiar. Mary cocked her head a bit and looked first at Richie and then at me. "It hadn't mattered to me. I had been argued out of the piece of paper thesis long ago, but Richie was insistent. And you know, as well or better than I, Richie is rarely insistent. It wasn't an option or a condition; it was the way things would be. And it's been the best time of my life."

Richie took the floor, thanked everyone for their presence on his happiest of all days, and pronounced the evening at an end. On cue a photographer appeared and took a few of our signature pictures, including the group hug.

256

We'd scarcely reassembled on the sidewalk when old faithful Harry Lester pulled alongside the curb and ushered the seniors into his new van. In a few moments they were headed home.

I was to learn later that Harry's new van was courtesy of Richie. As part of the deal Harry promised to chauffer the folks as they might require as well as to visit them at regular intervals. As usual, no mention would be made of Richie's involvement.

I also learned later that Freddie Nesson, the owner of Eagle's Nest, received a new multistation range for his kitchen which was accompanied with a homely little note wishing him "many years from his friends in Wills Grove." The "many years" reference was a tip of the hat to me, and I picked up on it. "Many years" in Greek ("Hournia polia") is a big-deal toast, reserved for only your closest of friends. In any event, I am sure that our folks would be Freddie's guests from time to time. As they say in New York, it was just so Richie, meaning understated.

It was an evening for which to pause in appreciation. In addition to the enveloping happiness for Mary and Richie, it was an unusually lovely evening. One forgets how brilliant the sky is overhead small-town USA away from the urban clutter. And the celestial brilliance only worked to amplify the happiness of our little earthbound quartet.

Commander Richie jolted me from my suspension in serenity and advised that we would head forthwith to the Aviator Motel, receive a wakeup call at eight a.m. and be airborne in his jet at nine. Breakfast would be onboard. And so it was. I'm one of those guys who has gotten really tired of flying. It was fun and novel at first, but became work after only a relatively short time. I don't blame the airlines, because they do their best, but they are in one very tough industry.

I'd been fortunate in most of my air traveling to sit in the front of the bus. For the most part, the service has been good and mostly the folks were pleasant. If I had any beefs, it was usually with passengers who left their good manners elsewhere or didn't think them required while flying. Airports and airplanes seem to have moron magnets, but I usually got from Point A to Point B pretty much on time and without incidents of any consequence.

Nonetheless I still harbor a mystery that not even the Nick 101 can address satisfactorily. I would take a routine five- or six-hour flight from one coast to the other, usually in first class. I don't recall any particular stress or heavy lifting, but I would invariably be bushed upon arrival. I've heard the thesis about recirculated air, but that just doesn't seem to explain my fatigue. When the post-September 11 security was notched up, flying and I became just about incompatible. I still love being different places, but the getting there is a major deterrent. My motivation to travel has thus taken a major nose dive in recent times. So, on this particular day, it was a treat to be on a private jet and to be with my best friends on the planet. It was a fine day for flying in every respect.

A little less than three-and-a-half hours after liftoff, I found myself gaping silently at the majestic Tetons under a cloudless blue sky. I'd been in the Rockies and the Cascades, but I'd never seen anything quite like the Tetons. It would likely remain the singularly most breathtaking panorama I would ever gaze upon.

I was jostled from my near dreamlike state by the familiar whirring of the 101, apparently today's travel section editor: *It's not the rocks and the terrain, Greek, it's the company and the circumstances. You're with your lifelong friends with a bit part cameo in a fantasy romance. That's the deal.*

And he was right, of course. The same way in which some backyard burnt beef and beer becomes a five-star affair when you're with your friends in a happy—make that joyful—setting. Is friendship the universal amplifier, or what?

The landing followed a long and shallow nose-up glide, in bump-free air, and we taxied quietly to the gate. While I've never made what most folks would refer to as the truly big bucks, I can't say I lack for much. Had I hit the definitive big time, however, I would definitely have bought a jet. Not for the show-off thing, but the ability to pick up and blast off somewhere at a time of your choosing has to be among the greatest of privileges. And deplaning in a crowd of four or five people is easy to accept as well. As we were all traveling light, we were out the door, through the reception area and in front of the grand terminal in no time.

My gaping resumed. I'm told that Montana, another state I have not visited, lives up to its Big Sky nickname. Judging by the almost delirious blue of Wyoming, Montana must be something unto itself. Nonetheless, even irrespective of the gala atmosphere dancing in my psyche, Wyoming is a monument to natural beauty.

So I just stood and gaped about. In the course of doing my best rotating three-sixty tourist gaze of wonderment, I came eye to eye with Jesse Lancer. I'd never met the man, but I'd seen enough pictures of him to connect the name with the face.

He strode right toward me and extended a hand. "You must be Nick, and this other fella must be Jackie." He shook hands with us vigorously, as we would have expected." *Take a bow, chubby,* grumbled the 101.

"Howdy, Richie," he continued.

"Howdy" anywhere else and from anyone else would have come across as celluloid syrup, but from Jesse Lancer it was as right as could be.

"I don't want to be rude, and I look forward to spending a lot of time with you fellas, but first things first." That, of course, was to hug his darling Mary.

Both I and the Nick 101 commended Jesse in respectful silence for his good judgment. They made a great pair. Jesse was still a bear of a man and thus a world class hugger. And Mary would make it to the top ten list of huggables any time, anywhere. And God and Richie forgive me—not necessarily in that order either—but, in addition to my descriptor of "stunning," Mary has the nicest ass ever bequeathed to a woman. It was the kind of picture, which would have frenzied the paparazzi. Happily for us, they don't make the march to Wyoming that often.

I can't say who was happier, but I can say it didn't matter. Once again, as was becoming the norm, the atmosphere obviated the need for words. It was just another happy time.

After a few more moments of hellos and polite dalliances,

Jesse squired us to the nearby parking lot and ushered us into his four-wheel SUV. I'm not a big fan of SUVs. I'm not an antagonist either, but they do seem to make a great deal of sense in Wyoming.

Nobody objected when Jesse asked permission for Mary to sit right alongside him, and the three of us piled obediently into the second and third rows of seating where we sprawled out comfortably and took in the singularly beautiful scenery.

I had been given to believe, from casual conversations with Mary, that Jesse had been subpar and maybe even failing. It crossed my mind that perhaps Mary's presence was one of those great tonics, but he maintained a high level of enthusiasm and all the appearances of a man in fine humor and health.

It was about a one hour ride to Jesse's "spread" through truly breathtaking picture-postcard scenery. Snowcapped mountains and gently roiling rivers and streams framed our ride; first over an interstate and then a most pleasant state highway. The last several miles were on a county road along which were, one after another, small ranches, probably of a few thousand acres each.

At about two thirty, we arrived at Jesse's place. It was situated on a plateau with a sweeping panoramic view of the plains and of the Tetons. During the drive, Jesse had informed us that it was about four thousand acres, small to medium-sized for this area, and was a working ranch on which he raised both cattle and sheep.

I'd seen enough westerns in my time in which the range wasn't big enough for cattle and sheep, and violence usually ensued, so I piped up.

"Senator," I began.

"It's Jesse, Nick, now and forever. I appreciate the courtesy, but Senator Lancer is long gone. My name is Jesse. To you and everyone else. Youngsters can call me Mr. Lancer if they wish, but I prefer Jesse."

"Jesse it is," I complied. "Maybe I've seen too many movies, Jesse, but just about every time cattle and sheep got into the same story, guns blazed and people died. Was that just poetry and stories, or was it for real?"

"Oh, it was real enough, Nick, but it was also from a different time. I got the idea of cattle and sheep coexisting just as one of my many country boy 'why-not?' ideas. I was probably trying to make a point that had less to do with animals and really more to do with people. With a little care and management, there was room enough for both. It was a useful analogy when I was in local and state politics. Later on it was replaced by the Rodney King theme, but it worked for me from time to time.

"I even used it a time or two on the senate floor in both partisan and international situations. I was pretty careful about using my down-home stuff sparingly lest I become a cartoon. Like anything else, it would have become tiresome with overuse, but every once in a while it was a productive reference, so I kept its use to a minimum. My continuing battle in that so-called 'world's greatest deliberative body' was to support the thesis that over the longer term a little amity, cooperation, and some expansive thinking would be more productive than the steady diet of wrangling, backbiting, and toxic nastiness which seemed to flower so naturally in D.C. I wasn't kidding, so I still maintain cattle and sheep.

"But today is not about anyone but Mary and Richie. They have paid me the greatest of honors by coming here today, and I intend to enjoy it. If anyone had ever told me I'd be presiding over my favorite niece's wedding, I'd make them swear it would be so. Except for Mary and Richie, I'm the happiest critter around these parts. My only instructions were to preside over a simple ceremony, so simple it will be. Plus, I've never gotten to utter the words, 'By the powers vested in me,' so this is an additional truly crowning moment for an old-timer like me."

By a coin toss, the only fair method possible, I had been designated as best man in Will's Grove, so it was now Jackie's time to shine. Jesse had asked everyone to take their places, but the melodrama in me surfaced in a rush. "Hold it, Jesse," I implored. "I'd like to walk Mary down the aisle. With her permission, of course."

Mary beamed, laid her elegant arm on mine and we strode the five or six paces toward Jesse's altar where I joined Mary's and Richie's hands. Quite satisfied with myself, I withdrew respectfully.

Jesse took full advantage of his moment. We all knew him well enough, even we two new guys, knew that he cherished this moment infinitely more than addressing his celebrity colleagues in D.C.

It was an unpretentious, bare-bones civil ceremony as requested, but Jesse has sought and received permission for the inclusion of two readings. He read softly but passionately from Ecclesiastes 8, 1-22 and offered his own, and very unique, heartfelt interpretations. Most noteworthy among them was that of humility at all times being the best clothing for those who would be true to themselves and to do good in God's world. The theme was, in a word, fitting—most fitting.

As he prepared for his second reading, none of us failed to note the condition of the old bible. It had obviously been in the Lancer households for generations and was equally obviously read with great frequency by this quietly devout man.

After his first reading he paused and noted that there were many readings from the New Testament which would apply handsomely to Mary and Richie. He referenced a few including the Beatitudes, True Riches, and others. Upon reflection he settled upon The Comparison to Salt and Light. In his own wondrously understated way he referred to Mary and Richie as the salt and light of the earth and went on to commend them for their many ongoing good works.

He had obviously given great thought to his role, and his great love for his niece was inescapably evident. Then again, this was Jesse Lancer. Tough, and even fearsome from time to time, but without question a considerate and caring man.

The Jesse touch was applied beautifully, but all of us giggled as Jesse got to his pre-advertised line "by the powers vested in me, I now pronounce you man and wife." And perhaps for his own sense of approval and emphasis, he added "again." Having become accustomed to this ritual with each other, Mary and Richie were already locked together while Jesse could only mumble, "You may kiss the bride."

Our Jackie is very well known for his abilities to fluoresce

262

thoughts and events through the written word. Had it been sought, there is no doubt he would have recounted the two ceremonies in touching and lasting terms. Jesse had an obvious complementary talent, specifically that of adding to a surrounding or occasion just the right amount of heartfelt memorialization.

And in clear demonstration that he would not be remiss with respect to his many duties and privileges on this happiest of days, he "ahemmed" forcefully a couple of times. "Gentlemen," he intoned, regarding Jackie and me directly, "please welcome Mr. And Mrs. Richie McAlister." Thus prompted, we joined him in a cheerful round of applause. This time Richie beamed while Mary blushed noticeably, mostly I gathered, in respect of her beloved Jesse. So we might have total representation, I thought I overheard the 101 saying something to the effect that *you done good, Jesse.* In sum that was accurate, Jesse had done good.

"And now for the reception," Jesse continued. At his lead we followed him from his den to the dining room, which had been rearranged into a wedding reception area complete with a few simple but strikingly beautiful floral displays. Also on display were Jesse's thoughtfulness and his own old-fashioned frontier sense of romance. It was a nice touch.

A popping champagne cork restarted the affair. After filling five flutes and passing them around, Jesse resumed his combined roles of justice of the peace, uncle of the bride, and host.

"Please allow me," he started while raising his glass, "to thank God for this most beautiful of days and for the privilege of sharing in Mary's and Richie's joy. I know Nick and Jackie join me in wishing for you all the best life has to offer. This we especially wish for you two, as you have already made life so much better for so many. And a long, happy and healthy life together."

It was short and elegant and summed things up so very nicely on a particularly beautiful day. We were obviously in the presence of a natural leader, so we obediently awaited our next set of directions.

With his arms around Mary and Richie, Jesse led our little procession out onto the veranda for the post-wedding repast of sandwiches and iced tea. We quickly discovered Annie, his neighbor and good friend, who had loaned her touch to the festivities, and bade her to join our group. We were all pretty sure that Annie was Jesse's girlfriend, but this was Mary's day, so no other romances would be recognized. Annie joined in and was a welcome addition. When in Wyoming, do as the Wyomingites. And so we did.

After our luncheon, I had the good fortune to spend some time with Jesse walking around his ranch.

"I truly respect the friendship you fellas have retained over the years. It takes a lot of effort to stay friends, especially in these frenzied times. I really admire the three of you, because in the end, what else is there aside from real friendships and a bit of happiness? There isn't much of that in D.C. Even Harry Truman used to say that if you want friendship in D.C, go buy a dog."

"I don't disagree one bit, Jesse. The three of us have been pals, as we're fond of saying back east, for over forty years. A 'fella' couldn't have better friends, not to say that your niece isn't something special. And not to say that Richie isn't a lucky guy, either."

"She really is, Nick, she really is. I honestly believe anyone who doesn't like Mary probably wouldn't like anyone. By the same token, the same goes for Richie. I'm just happy that they got together. And I'm delighted that they allowed me to commemorate their happiness in some small way. It was very thoughtful of them. And you and Jackie as well for trooping out here."

"Our pleasure, Jesse. You don't get that many opportunities to do something spectacular in life, and, for three guys from a little town in western Pennsylvania, this has been pretty spectacular. Besides, door-to-door service in a private jet isn't exactly a hardship tour.

"It's also a pleasure to be in your company, Jesse. May I ask you, and I promise to retain all confidentiality, why did you really leave D.C.? I ask, because you are really and sorely missed."

"I'll be glad to talk with you about anything on the condition of confidentiality, Nick. It's not the content, because my opinions may have matured and may have been fine-tuned a bit over the years, but the basics have been pretty enduring and are quite well known. It's just that I had my turn in the spotlight and I'd much prefer to leave things to my successors. I don't want to upstage them anymore than I ever want to look down the muzzle of one of those TV microphones again. Anonymity is even better than I had imagined."

"Fair enough, Jesse. So how come you called it a day and stepped down from the senate?"

"It's pretty much as I have said publicly, Nick. First, I would have voted for term limits anytime, so three terms was more than enough. Second, the seniority system just about defeats what the Founding Fathers had in mind for representative government. The same is true for committee appointments. Third, and maybe a little bit strangely, I think I was able to make a greater contribution while my party was in the minority. Sometimes it's more important to have a solid foot on the brake and some sense of direction than an overly enthusiastic hand on the throttle. Fourth, if you're serious about trying to improve things as you go, the job is a killer and just wears you down. So, for those and a bunch of related reasons, it was time to step aside."

"Speaking of being a killer, you look pretty solid to me. And, I don't mean to be nosy, but I had gotten the impression from Mary a while back that you were having some problems."

"I was, Nick, but a funny thing happened. I was on hand several months ago at the opening of a new regional healthcare center. It's just down the road a few miles. In fact, we passed it on the way here from the airport.

"A few years ago, my heart went out of rhythm. The particular term is atrial fibrillation. It's not necessarily life-threatening, but it does slow you down a bit. It's a fairly common thing. There are several million of us walking around with this condition, and it is eminently treatable with fairly low-level drugs. Oddly, however, I seemed to be struggling more than the diagnosis had suggested.

"In any case, I happened to be talking with the young doctor who had been chiefly responsible for the new center. He found my energy level to be unusually low for someone of my general health, and he asked me to stop by to see him.

"He isolated my low-energy situation very quickly and associated it with the particular anticoagulant which had been prescribed for me. In a matter of days, he prescribed a different, lower dosage anticoagulant and advised me that I should expect a sharp increase in my overall energy level in just a few weeks.

"I had been receiving my medicine via a mail program funded by my Senate healthcare insurance. Dr. Axton, the new fella I mentioned, enrolled me in a new mail-order program, but advised me to continue receiving the old medicine and to forward it to him at monthly intervals so that he might perform important analysis and perhaps avert other instances similar to my experience. He also asked me to comply with his request in strictest confidence, which I did.

"His diagnosis and prognosis were quite accurate. In just a few weeks I felt enormously better, and I've been in an improved state ever since. I'll never be one hundred percent, but seventy-five to eighty is one whole lot better than fifty percent and heading south, which is where I had been prior to my happy coincidence. Needless to add, I am very grateful to Dr. Axton."

We spent the balance of the day talking about all manners of things. I'd be asking about things of the past and Jesse would keep nudging me to look forward. "The past is okay for reference or to restate an object point, but most everything else is yet to be, and that's where your head and thoughts should be."

Smart guys come in all shapes and ages, I thought. The 101 did not dissent.

No one had been paying much attention to the time, and it was a minor shock when Jesse announced it was approaching seven p.m. and time for the sunset cocktail hour. We closed the day with a simple dinner, once again courtesy of Annie, and called it a day at about ten as the group mainspring had wound us all down, largely due to the freshest of fresh Wyoming air, pretty much en masse.

Did I sleep well that evening? I guess so. Again the purest of clean air, to which I was not accustomed, has a way of knocking you into a peaceful slumber without your cognition. Which is to say, I slept marvelously.

We rallied with Jesse and Annie for a simple breakfast of coffee and rolls at around eight-thirty or so. Everyone was well rested, and each of us commented about the narcotic, sleep-inducing qualities of the Wyoming air. And it would be another fine day for flying.

It had been a most pleasant interlude, being with people we enjoyed amid the virtual absence of anything resembling agendas or timetables.

In keeping with the pace and style of our surroundings, we absorbed the surrounding grandeur and filled ourselves with pictured moments in this most beautiful of surroundings. We then dallied over second and third cups of coffee all the while storing these wonderful memories for the months and years to come.

This time around, it was Mary who became group commander and snapped us back into reality. Jesse seconded Mary's directives and was joined by Annie, who instructed us to leave everything as is and pile into Jesse's SUV. Ever responsive to legitimate authority, we all complied.

This time Annie rode shotgun, with Mary and Richie in the second row, and Jackie and me in steerage. The ride back to the airport was as pleasantly scenic as the day before. We had put the additional requested touches on the Blaine-McAlister union, and had welcomed two new friends into our little circle of amity. Separately I wondered to myself if we might be recalled in a while to witness another frontier wedding. I found myself hoping that when and as Jesse might tie the knot with Annie that he would invite Jackie and me as well. Richie and Mary would be indispensable, but I hoped that Jesse would regard things as incomplete without Richie's and Mary's pals. After a bit of my usual daydreaming, we found ourselves at the airport.

We exchanged our good-byes and best wishes, Mary and Jesse most prominently, and proceeded onboard. With only a few regional jets and a manageable number of private planes in the traffic pattern, we were airborne and headed east in a matter of minutes. Being together had been the main attraction, but the convenience of Richie's plane had made travel a nonissue and heightened the enjoyment.

In a bit more than three hours, we dropped Jackie off in Raleigh Durham and continued on to our homes, via Tampa, where we would resume our happily changed lives.

267

8
Jackie and Fran

October 27th

The next several months were the bluest of blue skies as measured by my longtime barometer of life. One is either enjoying blue skies or working through problematic tunnels of one sort or another. This was blue-sky time.

The four of us got together a fair amount, sometimes just for dinner and sometimes for a couple days, but always in great joy. Mary was the essential constant and more than brightened things and lives wherever she went. Some people can just do that. Second only to Richie, Jackie and I considered ourselves fortunate to have Mary as the centerpiece of our new quartet. And my abiding friendship with Raj continued as before.

Jackie was very on top of his game and, in a surprise—to me, anyway—had become a more than frequent companion of the columnist and very well known TV personality Fran Monfort. This liaison had begun with some back-and-forth between the two of them in their respective columns. I don't recall which one of them opened the dialogue, but rather quickly the ongoing repartee acquired a sizeable following. It started as a kind of cult thing. At first, some folks would buy the respective newspapers to see if Jackie and Fran were conversing on that particular day. Later, they were accorded space in a number of op-ed columns from time to time where they took various positions on worldly, and sometimes not-so-worldly, events. It was a quite good deal for the many flagging newspapers. They would often bill Fran and Jackie on the front page with a preview of the subject at hand.

Their inter- and intra-columnar conversations were reminiscent of the 1940s and '50s when news giant Walter Winchell—the guy who would begin his Sunday evening news broadcast with "Good evening, Mr. and Mrs. America and all the ships at sea"—was the big man of the media. Of course nobody knew what that all meant, but we listened eagerly nonetheless. This guy, this Walter Winchell, was one of the last honest-to-God kingmakers of American journalism. Sometimes one of his columns would end with something like "DR [presumably Damon Runyon, a literary giant in those days], see you for lunch at Jack Dempsey's at twelve-fifteen." So we had seen this type of chatter before, but now there was the hint—and better yet—the promise of some romance. And we all loved romance in those days. It may be a lost art today, but nothing beat things when some smitten guy would say something like, "Gee, Doris, you're swell." Today that would get you laughed onto the bus back to Steubenville, but in those days that was hot stuff. And, you know what, you could do a helluva lot worse.

Anyway . . .

Sometimes they agreed; often they sparred vigorously, but never—and this seemed to be key—disagreeably. It was always mannerly and sophisticated. And elegant. Maybe it wasn't Winston Churchill and Lady Astor. Or Dorothy Parker and Robert Benchley. More like William Powell and Myrna Loy, those timeless sophisticates. But, for our time and place, it was a nicely served touch of class. Maybe Fred Astaire and Ginger Rogers without the music.

What seemed to manifest from these public and highly literate billet-doux, was, at least on the part of their audience, a bit of new found appreciation for civility in general and between a man and a woman in particular. For my part, I was well on my way to dubbing Ms. Fran Monfort "a knowing woman." That was and remains a rave from Nick Drizos. The 101 would caution me to wait and see, but I was headed down "Knowing Woman Lane" with my latest protégée, Ms. Monfort.

Their popularity was the more surprising, as newspaper circulations were generally collapsing, accelerated by the often cited dumbing down, which was very much in evidence and in full flower on the one hand, and TV, which required no brains at

269

all, on the other. Viewers had given in to the easy ways of TV and to the seductive beckonings of colorful check-out counter magazines with large print and accommodatingly low literary demands.

Nonetheless, Fran and Jackie grew steadily in popularity. I think part of it accrued from an unmet, unserved and, a larger than one might have suspected, thirst for erudite civility. As a more than routinely interested observer—Jackie is my friend—I gathered that a number of people had wearied of the constant and totally inflexible hammerings and yammerings of talking heads engaged in what had been billed and presented as debate, but bore more resemblance to so much compost.

For the most part Fran and Jackie hewed to their convictions, but, from time to time, one or the other would concede, ever graciously, that a fine point had been made by the other. On more than a few occasions they either found middle ground or, in rare instances, one would become converted to the other's viewpoint. None of this was ever gimmickry or gadgetry. It was earnest, honest, and it showed through. As much as anything, it was a welcome respite from the media pit bulls masquerading as humans. I personally think and believe that some part of the audience became persuaded that the object of debate, or any social intercourse for that matter, is to find something upon which to agree. The pit-bull thing would remain the preferred diet of the faithful, if mentally undernourished, ideologues, but many readers found Fran and Friend, as they were sometimes called, to be a major antidote for much of the modern-day angst. They served it tastefully and with a good humor, somewhat evocative of days long past. Even after several months of their increasing popularity, they had never met. This may have added to the show biz or mystique, but that's just the way it was. Literate pen pals with a growing audience. What would they do next?

Over time, it became obvious that these two people enjoyed each other, as, at unexpected intervals, they would digress into the land of the personal. About eight months into this engaging affair, Fran closed with a postscript that she was free on Friday and that he should order her martini—on the rocks with olives. To my knowledge that was the first overture. An unanswered overture, as I expect Jackie, for all his Cagney shtick, was somewhat shy. Nonetheless, the 101 and I saw this as a portent of what might follow.

Scarcely later, they were discussing and debating the merits of a commercial investment in Brooklyn, which had profound implications for both the state and the borough. Fran closed her remarks with the many world-class contributions to humanity made by the well-known avalanche of folks from Brooklyn in a summation showcasing her support for the mammoth project.

Jackie started his next column with an answer which went something like: "Amen, Sister Fran, amen. You needn't remind your humble colleague, and obedient servant, as to the many wonders of Brooklyn and all that has been done by its sons and daughters in so many areas over so long a time. Ye are truly preaching to the converted. Did you know, however, beloved, [here Jackie borrowed shamelessly from the new testament to make his point] that Brooklyn in the nineteen fifties was the only place, yea the only place in the world, with five radio stations, four newspapers, and no left fielder?"

This response, about baseball in the 1950s was totally unresponsive, totally un-Jackie Slater and, if parsed, made no sense. Nonetheless it was of good humor and just registered with the readership. For reasons best understood by the folks who constituted this avid readership, it was a watershed event. It may have been the essential good humor, which characterized these two pen pals. Whatever the ultimate reasons—it soon became water-cooler talk in hundreds of offices   their following expanded dramatically. Some have speculated that we were watching a courtship, a most literary and elegant courtship. And maybe that was the right take. In any event, an increasing number of folks seemed to look forward to the next exchanges.

Fran, for her part, started her next column with something like: "Beloved indeed, it is time—it is time for you to ask me to dinner." She then went on with her thoughts for the day, but closed with: "P.S. I will accept anytime, anywhere."

For the next several days, op-ed columns were filled with commentary on this prospective meeting. To that point, the incoming ran 98+ percent in favor, although a couple of writers complained about the loss of mystery and intrigue if these two should get together.

And, if we had any doubt about whether we are a nation of voyeurs, that query was rapidly resolved. The advice, overwhelmingly to Fran, came in torrents; what to wear, opening remarks, the indispensability of coyness, her position and responsibilities as an emancipated woman and, well, you name it. Most guys just thought Jackie should get it on. But we are the far simpler of the species.

While hardly a major media event, as we have come to regard that term, this was big stuff for print journalism and attention to this impending event was a well received tonic. Neither Fran nor Jackie was interested in the hype game, and each was content to proceed more or less according to Emily Post.

As I have observed many times, it's great to have a pal and it's great to be a pal. I'd probably extend that to: what is better? Enduring as we have for these many years, there is no question—none whatsoever—that Slater and I are pals. Because we are.

At the same time, only a pal can embarrass you beyond redemption. So it was that I received a call from the estimable Mr. Slater.

"Nick."

"Hiya, pal."

"Have you been following the Fran and Jackie show?"

"Why would you even ask me?"

"Well, I'm going to have dinner with Ms. Monfort in New York, and you have to come with me."

"I have to come with you? I, an unknown bond trader, have to escort, chaperone or otherwise appear at the elbow of Mr. Literacy? I don't think so. Or, to put it another way, are you nuts? As in NFW, taking care to maintain high literary conduct with my pal."

"What are you talking about, you're my pal. You've got to come with me."

On this particular occasion I took the old banker's advice and got down to the yes or no conclusion quickly and with appropriate, suitable force.

"Here's the way it's gonna be, Jackie. You are going to have dinner with her in a quiet joint in Manhattan. This is all about romance, friend. R-O-M-A-N-C-E. There are only two things worth a whit in this world, Jackie—truth and romance. If romance blossoms into L-O-V-E, then there are three, but until that time, it's truth and romance. It's like our pal Mary doped out, 'Destiny has held out its hand to you. Do not reject it.'

"You will be, Jackie. You'll enjoy it or you won't. If you don't, all the pals in the world won't help. If you do, you'll bring me along the next time. That's probably not quite right. If you do enjoy it, you'll do a few more go-rounds before giving me a thought. That's how it's gonna be. And that's how it should be. Over and out."

"But . . ."

"But *nothing*. Let me know how it works out."

I'm not too sure of all that many things, but I am confident that I was 100 percent correct in that particular instance.

I can't say that show biz didn't creep into this affair to any extent, because it took a couple of unforeseen turns. Unlike Jackie, Fran was a regular on a number of cable news programs. Her views, and I'm sure, her very attractive face and shape were sought out by a number of broadcasters. She was fairly well known in that capacity. She'd be disappointed if she knew I said so (or even thought so), but she was/is a babe and had become a bit of a talking head herself. At least she was on the air enough to be regarded as such by some. Plus she had very nice cleavage. But, and this is a critical "but," she was so charming and so "with it" (right out of the 'thirties/'forties, maybe 'fifties) she could draw your eyes to hers. She had staked out the beginnings of rising to a Nick Drizos "knowing woman." They're something. They know it, but they don't rub your snoot in it. They are just so smart and so cool. But, I'm just like you—talking about what I see and knowing little else. In the end, some are regular Joes and Janes and some would be starters on the Interplanetary All Know-Not Team. La Monfort was a cut above, a very substantial cut above.

I'll admit, I was beginning to think there might be a pretty special woman in this sophisticated and lovely package. This from one who has gone for more than his share of misdirections, so I'm happy to just play it out. Nonetheless that was my message for Jackie. It was delivered well and taken well.

Jackie said, "Okay," and we ended that particular phone call with absolutely no ambiguity. I felt very good, because it was good advice. Jackie knew it and I knew it. In the end, you may call me a bond trader, but I'm in the advice business; that's what I do. This time I had done good, as the 101 quickly confirmed.

As the impending get-together neared, the interest of their now expanding following increased, and the news guys and gals would needle her. This wasn't all bad, but Jackie had little tolerance for most TV guys, so he decided the time had come to meet the lady behind the keyboard and to be done with the folderol. He picked up on that word, "folderol," years ago, and it had become one of his life's companions, especially when he became a bit piqued or, as I suspect in this case, anxious. We all have traveling verbal expressions with which we associate. I have always enjoyed, as I probably mentioned, the semi-regal sense of the word "moreover." Richie, by very stark contrast, he being so at total ease with himself would often offer, "I was just wondering." So we are all prisoners to some form of rhetoric or, as a shrink friend of mine would say, "frozen locution." As it occurs, Jackie liked "folderol."

Mind you, it wasn't a total mystery hour. La Monfort was without question a most attractive lady, somewhere in the Drizos power alley of late thirties or early forties, more probably the latter. And Slater was noted by many for his Montgomery Clift brooding good looks. It wasn't a blind date, as both were pretty well known. The appeal was obvious.

The dinner took place at a quiet place in Manhattan and was a major event for the two of them. It was warm, it was cordial, it was everything that they, in reality, had suspected or had known it would be. It wasn't that they connected; the greater truth was that they had been connected for quite a while. This was more accurately a reaffirmation of what they both had expected. At dinner's end, while neither knew how the particulars would play out, each knew they were important to each other and would likely be ever thus.

274

Without doing the cheesy show biz thing, word got out that our two celebrity friends had gotten together. Ever the gentleman, Jackie deferred to Fran in the matter of making things public. She merely closed their next tête-à-tête with "Greatly enjoyed our dinner. Would say yes again, should you be so inclined."

And so it went. The columns continued as they had, and, in the process, they became an item. Their audience continued to grow, most likely because it was just an unusual deal, a classy deal. An unusually classy deal.

They did do a couple of TV shows together, but mostly soft human interest stuff as opposed to Jackie's main venue of hard news and big issues. Certainly not the sound-bite pseudo-news shows, as Jackie had labeled them. He always offered precedence to Fran in these situations, only because he thought it naturally right and proper. Under the heading of unintended consequences, this only increased their individual and collective popularity, since most of the audiences were largely women. They admired Fran tremendously and marveled at how Jackie was so solicitous and unthreatened. It was just Jackie in Richie's auto-pilot mode, just being Jackie. No pretense whatsoever. It was a good deal all around. They liked each other, and the public seemed to like them. And nobody was happier than I.

Per my prediction and advice to Jackie, I did get summoned somewhere after date six or seven. I wasn't offended, and by this time they were well on their way to being committed to each other anyway.

Since I had already met Stunner 1, as I had come to regard Mary, I was ready for Fran. I was at my cosmopolitan best and enjoyed our first of a few dinners together. This dinner was mostly about Fran and me, since she and Jackie had already become pretty well acquainted. It was a fun time, and she was more forthcoming than I had any reason to expect. Except for one item; Jackie had probably bent her ear mercilessly about our notion of pals and all of the loving baggage that we'd been toting around over the years. That's probably at the heart of things, but I liked her and I think she liked me. But you know what? It doesn't matter about me; this is about Jackie and Fran. Well, that's not quite true; it is somewhat about me, because I'd rather gain a new friend than lose an old one. The 101 rumbled a bravo of sorts.

So I hope it goes the way of Mary and Richie. It takes too long to make good friends and it hurts too much to lose one, but I'll swap out my happiness for Jackie's any day. Fran and Jackie are a little more complicated than Mary and Richie, so I don't know how it's going to work out. My gut tells me that it's a good thing and will go well. I feel that way particularly because Jackie has gotten so at peace with himself, and, at the same time I just get a good feeling about her.

Richie and Mary were as delighted as I when Jackie sprung the news on them. As much as we are all pals, however, I have to concede that I felt especially good to be the first of Jackie's confidantes vis-à-vis Ms. Monfort.

The five of us got together a few months back, and it was a fine time. It was a bit peculiar in that there were two couples and the stag me known as "Nick." On the one hand I was becoming more removed and marginalized. More importantly I retained my two lifetime pals, had gained one new friend and, from all appearances, was in the process of adding another. So, after a few minutes, it became obvious that everyone was comfortable with this starting lineup. It was a very nice time.

It was a very nice time largely because all pretensions were left by the wayside many years ago. We probably all have scars and stuff of one sort or another, but being oneself was not only sufficient and mandatory, it was naturally easy. It was a setting for people with no interest in impressing anyone. It was like a lot of well-run companies where there is no need for a policy and procedures manual, because everyone is of one mind and spirit.

To me, Fran is somewhat akin to Mary in that she is keen on expanding her number of real friends. Like Mary, she had a very good grasp on the Richie-Jackie-Nick thing and has no interest in monopolizing Jackie. That's another thing about knowing women, they are very secure. They know themselves, they like themselves, and they have much going on in their own right. They are the antithesis of cloying; they need no validation. They welcome it, but it is not a requirement. They are expansively confident. For me, it's unavoidably attractive.

It thus dawned on me, on this particular day, that people who are confident and comfortable with themselves tend to be generous and expansive. By generous, I am not referring to money. I mean a generosity of spirit, which tends to become one with selflessness. I became convinced then and there that that was probably as good an explanation for the bonds between and among my two pals and me. And Mary, too, of course. I also had my first inklings of a similar sense of Fran as well. During one of my frequent Drizos fades, I was taken back to Les Horvath's story about the destructiveness of envy. For us, there had never been any; only admiration and friendship. I was especially happy about the exceptional two women who were now part of our ménage à whatever-it-was. For my part, I have had a number of lady friends whose company I enjoyed greatly, but none evolved to the Richie-Mary level or even to the level to which Jackie and Fran seemed to be progressing. They were not affairs or even dalliances, just nice times spent with nice ladies.

Richie and Jackie were a couple of princes—one with great wealth in a naturally appealing persona, the other a brilliant earnest mind who always commanded attention and respect. So, I would wonder to myself what are the odds of three pals coming out of the woods of western Pennsylvania and making our way so well.

It was a pleasing notion, but the fact remained that I would just have to become my own unique kind of prince. Then the Nick 101 then elbowed a thought into my otherwise thoughtful reverie. *Okay,* he began, *Richie and Jackie both stared death in the face while you served out your time in the relatively peaceful Fort Gordon, Georgia. But then, you must be something special in your own right, because you have been the intended recipient of two very specific and very personal hits. Richie and Jackie may have seen the horrors firsthand, but it wasn't personal. Yours was.*

I'm not sure what that musing was ultimately all about, especially since neither Richie nor Jackie had any sense of my personal excitement. It had been known only to Ben, probably Raj and me. Aside from the triggermen.

I sat up with a bit of a start, feeling neither anxious nor calm. It was time to regroup again. My sterile room was as before, but I was beginning to anticipate leaving this less-than-hallowed setting very shortly.

Nonetheless I settled back into one of my cosmic queries and wondered how, in the context of six billion souls on the planet, Richie and Mary and Jackie and Fran could collide with each other so wonderfully. Okay, I recalibrated down to only three hundred million in the USA, after another nudge from the 101. Either way, they are both gigantic numbers and, while I am sure there are such things as soul mates, or special people who can enlarge each other in so many ways, how does this happen? Neither the 101 nor I had a ready answer, so we cheerfully retreated to the notion that what was good for Richie and Jackie was good enough for us. The anti-envy thing. And so it became time to regain full consciousness again.

I was in one of my neo-classic Drizos vacant stares when the lovely Gail intruded, in a most welcomed manner, into my field of partial focus.

"And how is our friend Nick this morning?" she almost chirped.

"We're pretty good, thank you," I answered, using the editorial "we" for no particular reason, and thinking simultaneously about Mark Twain who abhorred that construct. Twain had observed that the use of "we" should be confined to royalty, pregnant women, and people with a tapeworm. I still don't know why I have these Drizos flashes, except that I'm just wired that way. A thought about some wiseass remark by Noel Coward also vied for attention, but was shooed away by both me and the Nick 101.

I'd like to think this latest flash was over in a nanosecond, as the last thing I wanted to be was rude to Gail. Or to embarrass either of us. Somewhat recovered, I brought myself to a smart upright position in my functional, but antiseptic, and otherwise uninviting, bed.

Before I could even attempt to become my engaging and dashing self, terry-cloth pajamas notwithstanding, Gail took charge.

"How about lunch today on the patio?"

"I beg your pardon?" I managed.

"You're too old, or I should say too mature, to be playing coy,

Nick. You asked me to lunch just a short while ago, and now I'm accepting. It's probably one of your better options, soldier."

"Absolutely" was all I could manage. Destiny extending its hand again?

"Okay, it's ten-thirty. I'll be back at twelve-fifteen. Spruce yourself up, and I'll see you then."

Holy mackerel, I mused to myself and the 101, *I have become a prince.* Out of happiness and elation, generally difficult to find in these surroundings anyway, I decided to rest my eyes for a couple of minutes.

In a moment or two I was back in float mode and continuing to fill in lapses and voids with uncommon celerity, buoyed no doubt by the prospects of romance in a strange hospital. I thought of Louis Hayward, the unquestioned king of B movies, and of the envy he must be now enduring in that silver screen in the great beyond. He was the best of that genre, the unquestionable best; *The Man in the Iron Mask* or maybe *The Count of Monte Cristo* in particular, with no less than Joan Bennett in both. But he'd probably trade in his harp and some other heavenly amenities to step into my sanitized slippers right about now. This was hot stuff. Lunch with Gail. Holy mackerel, indeed. Even if it is a mercy lunch, which it most likely is.

I had come a far piece, as they say in Will's Grove. I'd done better than a lot of folks would have imagined. I was making my way, all things considered, pretty well. I had two world-class pals, I'd met the former senate minority leader, not to mention his niece, and I'd been singled out for extermination by some force of evil. Is that important, or what? What a hot shit I've become. Some want me dead, but some pretty outstanding folks want me otherwise. I'm actually starring in my own B movie. No one will ever get to see it, but so what. Like getting a hole-in-one while playing solo. Or whizzing down your leg with a dark suit on as the old Madison Avenue bromide goes. *Yeah,* piped up the 101 as if on cue, *nobody notices, but it gives you a warm feeling.*

Plus, better to reign in hell than serve in heaven, muttered the 101 doing his best turn at Eddie G. Robinson as Wolf Larsen in *The Sea Wolf.*

It's an unkind mirror that won't let you look like Cary Grant

279

just once in a bit, but I did my all to accommodate it. I also did my very best post-shower toilette and outfitted myself in the dashing elegance of sparse but thoughtful wardrobe, provided. In an apparent touching fit of whimsy, some someone had brought in one of my Izod shirts with Mickey Mouse displayed prominently where the alligator was usually posted. The one I usually reserved for important intramural sessions in my trading business. I donned it with the macho pride of El Cordobes, Manolete, Domenguin, or the matador of your preference. We probably have a word for macho in Greek, but for now I was its personification.

It was close to straight up noon, so I cranked up the CD player I had been given. A TV or radio was totally out of the question, as even a pea brain like me could have, and would have, determined my approximate location from the broadcasts. I was clearly in with a clever lot.

It was good that I would be departing soon, though, because being conscious but otherwise removed from that which had been normal ambient noise—the ubiquitous news or talk shows—was probably deleterious to one's mental hygiene. I think I got that particular phrase from a prescription of some sort, but it seemed to stick with me. I liked the deleterious reference. I also liked the notion that I was to be released shortly, because I had had quite enough of the local hospitality care and generosity, outstanding though it might be. It was time to be Nick 1 again.

They were good sorts at my R&R center and offered me a wide variety of CDs—music, narrated books, whatever might occupy a soul in recovery.

I have two favorite female singers. They are Jo Stafford and Vera Lynn. Jo, because more than most, she could lock onto a note and hold it till I was breathless. She also sang many ballads in minor keys in such a haunting way that the words would pierce the most reluctant heart. Vera, on the other hand, probably won WW II as much as Winston, Ike, or the other bravest of the brave. Maybe you have to be from our generation, but her rendition of "We'll Meet Again" may have kept the spirits of more millions alive than will ever be known, as we went on to crush Adolf and his band of psychopaths.

That wonderful song is also the last we hear from anybody, meaning a real person, in *Dr. Strangelove* as Slim Pickens rides the big one earthward. To this day I find that conclusion both enraging and heartwarming. In the end, the real end as suggested by Stanley Kubrick, I'd probably be okay with Vera and her hopeful song. And what a voice.

On this particular day and at this particular time, I opted for the greatest love ballad ever, namely Jo Stafford's rendition of "I'll Be Seeing You." I had skipped it back to its track for a third time when Gail appeared. She was out of her whites, which was no small culture shock for me, and was just a vision in a plain skirt and simple blouse outfit. In all manners of places and circumstances it occurs, and someone usually observes, that simple is elegant. It was simple, and she was elegant.

Something prompted me to cast aside my bumpkin tendencies and to rise to this swell occasion. It all came surprisingly easy, and I mustered a cheery "Good afternoon, Ms. Gail, you look lovely today. I'd address you properly, but, what with all the excitement and incidental confusions of the past many days, I don't recall your last name."

"Gail or your Ms. Gail will do just fine, Nick. We just don't use last names here for the more obvious of reasons. That aside, how about some lunch?"

"Best deal I've had so far today." *Clever,* snarled the 101.

In a couple of minutes we had negotiated the secret elevator and were on the equally secret patio in what was another glorious day. I had been gaining confidence at an increasing rate in the past few days, perhaps owing to my sense of acquired seniority in this mystical place. I was close to being in a 'what-the-hell' state, given the prior attempts on my bond-trading life. And given that I appeared to be a survivor.

While I can still be a wreck around "knowing women," and I was clearly in the presence of one, I nonetheless inquired, "So what is a Gail?"

"You mean how did someone like me end up in a place like this?"

"Yeah, that's about it."

"I'll be happy to give you the short version, but first let's make sure you're okay with our luncheon menu. We aren't able to get broccolini in this part of the country, but I was able to snag some stone crabs with a couple of different sauces. That, along with a couple new potatoes and a blue cheese salad, is the best I could pull together on short notice. As a consolation, there are also a couple of Killian Reds, so I hope that will be all right with you."

What I was thinking had little to do with lunch, but I managed to indicate that the impromptu menu was just fine. I was just happy to be in the presence of a real human being and especially happy that the presence belonged to this particular human being. Lovely, just lovely.

"Well, Nick, you'll be leaving us shortly, and I must say you have become quite popular with the staff hereabouts. Everybody likes you. I would take that to mean that we guess you're a pretty decent guy in your regular environs. The kind of guy we'd be pleased to have a beer and shoot the shit with. You might want to know that we minister to a fair number of bozos and hammerheads, so you should take that as a major compliment."

"I do, Gail, I do, even though—pardon me for saying—this is a more than somewhat weird place in its own right. No comment about your flowery metaphor."

With an arched eyebrow, she managed a "no comment" of her own. "That is, there would be no comment if you weren't such a colorful storyteller while you sleep. And entertaining as well."

I was aware that I was starting to redden, but I also felt good about the present company, so I made a major effort to get back with the program. That is, to the extent I could stop gawking at the lovely one. Did I mention she is gorgeous?

And also at the smart one. I've been onto something with my "knowing woman" thesis for a few years now, and here I was having lunch with Exhibit A.

With a generally uncommon ease, and following a little flick of her head, which sent a couple of errant hairs to their intended settings, she said, "So, Nick, you'd like to know how I got to a place like this."

282

Before I could nod or get assenting words out, she had added, "Especially since I'm what a lot of guys might call attractive or maybe even glamorous. Guys like you. Right, Nick?"

Every once in a while the fabled invisible hand—or providence or whatever you might care to call that rarest bit of inspiration—bursts onto center stage and does something memorable as it relates to the course of one's life.

Before I was aware of any conscious thought, I had said, "The glamour is obvious to all, but there is something within you I already hold in high esteem. All for reasons for which I have no understanding. I just know I'd like to get to know you. Not get to know you better, just get to know you."

I can't say she flushed or was taken aback in any major way, but I did note an almost imperceptible sidewise tilt of her head, which only old movie aficionados like me would be smart enough to take as encouragement. I'd also like to think she silently and quickly mouthed the words, "That's good, Nick, that's good." Maybe she did, and maybe she didn't.

A very strange feeling overcame me. I had made an important connection. It could never be taken away. Maybe it would increase or maybe we'd part at this level of make-believe intimacy. It didn't matter; I was just very happy.

"I'm here, Nick, the reason I'm here, in briefest form, is to honor my mom and dad. They're both long dead. My father is a marine. He's dead, but—"

"I know," I continued for her, "once a marine, always a marine." I wasn't being a smartass, and she took it as intended.

"Did he die in combat?" I asked.

"Kind of. He died in Vietnam, but basically after it was all over."

"I'm sorry, Gail, I'm truly sorry."

"I know you are, Nick, but, as we've come to understand, life goes on. And rather than make you play investigative reporter, I'll give you the summary version.

"I also know how you are with movies, Nick, especially old movies, so this will be really easy for you to pick up on. You know the scene at the soda fountain in *It's a Wonderful Life* where Donna Reed says, into Jimmy Stewart's bad ear—the one that

283

Mr. Gower had beaten—"George Bailey, I'll love you till the day I die."

"My mom and dad saw that movie on TV together when they were about twelve and she repeated that—except into one of his two perfectly good ears—'Terry Williams, I'll love you till the day I die.' And he said the same. And there was no doubt.

"They were grade-school sweethearts to many, but lifetime sweethearts to each other. They went off to separate colleges, but were close enough to be together most weekends. They got married right after graduating from college, except that they had eloped during their senior year of high school. Only a couple of their closest friends ever knew that, and they were pledged to silence under penalties of unspeakable unction.

"Mom was fine with living together or whatever would allow them to be with each other. And, besides, women were burning their bras in celebration of the wonderful feminist epoch to unfold. Marriage was déclassé, and all the hip women were decrying the piece of paper symbolizing a male-dominated societal ritual as extraneous and certainly not needed by all these earth mothers.

"And to be truthful, she was fine with just being together. She had been sold on the piece of paper being worthless and the commitment being all-important.

"But not her Terry. His attitude and conclusion was simplicity at its best. He would say 'If it's the commitment that matters, then you should have no trouble being a signatory on a piece of paper. Or let me say it another way. If I'm not good enough for your signature, then maybe you should find one of those guys who is willing to sign on to that feminist bullshit. I'm looking for a real woman and a real partner for the rest of my life.'

"And no, Nick, before you ask, I never found my Terry Williams. Some romance, but nothing like my mom's Terry. Maybe another day, anyway . . .

"There was nothing Neanderthal or Cro-Magnon about it, and it didn't take Mom long to see she was blessed with a different kind of guy. Most of his contemporaries were setting records for getting laid in those days because free milk was a poor incentive to buy the cow, as they used to say. But that's where her hip

284

lady friends were headed back then. Of course, being mostly wiseasses themselves, the ladies would inquire, 'Why buy a pig just to get a little pork?' Clever, weren't they? And don't ask me what Sigmund Freud really meant when he asked, 'What does a woman want?' She just knew that she wanted Terry, and that one person on the planet thought her totally special. That clarity occurred in an instant and was to endure for their lifetimes. Short though they were.

"Terry was also duty-honor-country all the way, so was Mom and so am I. Either you are or you are not, and I do not care to argue it.

"He went off to Vietnam in time for the Tet Offensive and was elated with the hard-won and costly victory. The North Vietnam regulars had been smashed and, as General Giap would later write, it was all over. But the Washington folks managed to insert defeat where victory should have been. Terry had thought Vietnam would emerge as another South Korea, but our leaders had other priorities.

"He had done a fourteen-month tour and came home to a most grateful wife and daughter. Disgusted with Washington's politics, he set about reentering the civilian world. He had foreseen outsourcing and other mega-trends and started a supply-chain management company, which was successful from day one. He was the realest of real men. He was quiet, but no jive; he was no one to jack around. And he was the best dad a young girl could have."

I had known Gail forever in my dreams, but probably for less than several hours in actual human time. Nonetheless, the way she spoke just went into my receivers as they were meant. I nodded, as I suspect she knew I would, and she continued.

"Mom would later say she was reconciled to her loss and was just so lucky to have had him while he was here. Even as a pre-teen I knew better and knew such comments were to console me and to help me through my grief. She did her best to put her brave face over her broken heart. Not a day went by when Poe's poem *Annabel Lee* didn't flash through my mind—especially the phrase which included 'but we loved with a love that was more than a love'—because that was my mom and dad.

"The excursion, as he used to call it, into Vietnam went totally south. At first, he would brood darkly over it. Later, which became archetypal Terry, he would develop plans and schemes to alleviate the suffering of that fiasco's victims. So, while he was running his own successful business, he also raised millions for wives and children of 'the excursion.' Probably more than the government he came to loathe and despise.

"At length, the Washington intelligentsia had screwed things up beyond repair. The USA was in a full-fledged retreat. They had bitched things up beyond their usual limits. As you might surmise, we have come to expect little from the government and have rarely been disappointed. And, it's not that they are dumb; it's more that they are just bad people.

"Dad was resigned to the failure, but several of his pals—do you recognize that word, Nick—were assigned to airlift the last of the folks out."

"Pals" had registered—and resonated—with me. I can only assume that I had been quite chatty in my many semi-conscious states during the past few days. Yes, pals is a serious deal and is not to be used lightly. I further suppose that Gail knew I would be most receptive to the word and what it implied for her dad.

"It was the worst and most humiliating assignment there could be. Putting your tail between your legs and beating it—especially when you were most likely on the right side of things. Not clearly, but most likely.

"So, the next thing we know, dad is headed back to 'Nam to assist in what he called 'The Great Humiliation.'

"It was over, but the slopes couldn't even let us leave peacefully in disgrace. They fired on everything, including the unarmed helicopter into which Dad was loading the most fearful and grief-stricken of folks. And one round from some minor player in our great drama rendered him dead."

I sat motionless in what has become my time-honored "I-don't-know-what-to-say stare." Jackie wouldn't have done much better either, even if he will one day compose that most elusive book, essay, or whatever he will end up calling it.

"Mom was devastated but never wavered in being the best mom she could. She and I became more than mother and daughter. We were best friends and were the best supporters two women could be. She invested herself in me totally as both my mom and my dad. She got me through college and then just expired. She was a young woman, but got to a point where she just had no more to give. I could embellish and amplify, Nick, but I think you have a sense of things.

"I know you're speechless, Nick, but don't trouble yourself. They're both gone, and I'm reconciled. I choose to look at the joy we had over anything else."

I could only manage a heartfelt but clumsy, "I'm sorry. I'm so sorry. I can go back to my room if you wish."

"It's okay, Nick and believe it or don't, it gets a bit easier—more tolerable anyway—with each telling. Especially when you are with warm human beings.

"Before you ask, I'll tell you. I made friends with most of the providers of booze you can think of. Not unlike your pal Slater, I was with some vets and was taken by their courage and resolve. It also became clear over time just what Mom and Dad would have expected of me.

"There being no better place to honor their memory and to be in their presence, I went back to school and dedicated myself to putting the living, but broken, back together. After several years, I had occasion to meet some of the folks who have had an impact on you, Nick. In particular, the one known to you as Adams in addition to other names.

"I am now near the end of my three-year tour, that being regarded as the outer limit for this fairly stressful vocation. But I've been around some exceptional people . . ."

"So, all in all?"

"So all in all, it has been a fatiguing but uplifting experience. And, while our mission is totally straightforward, the place has its own strange and demanding ethos."

"For example?"

"For one thing, self-expression and discourse have to be pushed to new heights of candor. It is as they say in Vegas: 'Everything that happens here, stays here,' except that it's all jive there and it's a one hundred percent for true SOP in this place. And it has to be, it just has to be.

"We can't allow or permit anyone, burdened by his or her many experiences here, to have a meltdown outside these premises that could compromise the joint. No uncertainties, ambiguities or conflicts can go unresolved. All have to be addressed right on the spot. Thus, if someone is being a dick or a cunt, you have to jump on it right away. We can't have some sensitive underachiever go on to any of those sob sister shows on the outside and spill their guts. That would put us, from 'Adams' on down, right out of business. Part of the staff's responsibilities is to query us continually to assure that everything has been aired. We can't guarantee that the results will be totally satisfactory, but the process is straightforward. It's always final exam week here. It's an unremitting and deadly game, so you get it right or you're out. Sometimes it seems unbearably barbaric, but that's the way it has to be. To my knowledge it has worked pretty well."

I picked up that nothing she said was for shock effect. The joint, as she called it, has its own norms and lexicon, which are suited to getting their stuff done. Little else matters in the joint. She didn't speak for shock effect. I was beginning to understand the ethos of this joint. It was hardly a wellspring of happiness and, in fact, was closer to being a precipice above a pit of despair.

"This was and is dark stuff, truly dark stuff, and there was no room for ambiguity. Everything has to be dealt with as it arises and, more times than not, brutally. Thus the clear and unambiguous language. Things are addressed and dealt with swiftly. Burning embers of ambiguity or torment were simply not tolerated. The nuanced thinkers and roundabout rope-a-dopers would not, could not, gain access here.

"If the load got to be unbearable, the broken party would be treated, debriefed, deflated, and offloaded into a more civil and civilized environment. I have gotten the sense that those departing this institution and others bearing similarity thereto, invariably affected relatively smooth reentries to the greater outside world. Not unlike most, I say most, combat vets who are generally able to set the many horrors aside and resume essentially normal lives. Chalk it up to human recuperative power.

"This ability to forget, or to compartmentalize, horrors and instances of great pain may be a more telling human trait than

288

the opposable thumb. Perhaps not unlike women's abilities to sublimate the pains of pregnancy and delivery; else the global population problem might have been addressed and laid to rest centuries ago with a negative growth rate. When two have one kid—and only one—they aren't replacing themselves, are they? So it's probably a good thing that women manage that pain so effectively; else some of us might not be around."

I found myself staring at Gail while these many background thoughts raced around my inner self. A strong jab from the 101, and I snapped to a straight-up position of attention.

"With all that goes with the job, and you've seen a fair bit of the joint, you'd probably agree that three years is most likely the outer limit . . .

I nodded as she continued.

"A few have stayed longer and others have done multiple shifts here. And some have begged off with less than the three years done, but the statistics tend to support the three-year term as just about right."

I had managed to take a few bites of my lunch when she added, "That's the short, but fairly complete, story of how I came to be here and how I will be leaving in the next few days. The way things are going, you and I could be discharged on the same day, each being processed out—separately as is our custom, of course.

"So, Nick, what will you be doing after your days with us?"

"Back to work, I would suppose, although I've been told there will be some fanfare for a few days. But hopefully, or God willing and the creek don't rise—as we used to say in Will's Grove—something else will come along and sweep me off the front pages. I hope so, because mine is a small town, and I am not big on the celebrity thing in any event. With the exception of my clientele and a few friends, nobody's ever heard of me, and I like it that way. Or, in the words of one of my tiresome clichés, 'I'll leave that to the folks in *Who's Who* so I can stay in *Who's He*?

"Maybe I can connect with some pals and duck out for a while. . . ."

"You mean Richie and Jackie?"

"I do indeed. Did I talk about them much?"

"You did, but tell me something. How come you are, Nick, as

I am guessing that at one time you were Nickie, but Richie and Jackie have managed to keep their adolescent tags?"

"I've wondered that as well. It may have come about from our high school hockey days. We were pretty good in most sports, but hockey was our best. Richie and Jackie were forwards, and they were both very good skaters. I was the goalie and received a few honors here and there and became known as Nick the Brick during my sophomore season. Nick seemed to suit me, so it hung on, and I'm just as glad. There's a time to be Nickie, but for me that was long ago. On the other hand, Jackie and Richie seem to fit. Richie has no rough edges and no need to be anything other than Richie. And with all his wealth, Rich would be a bit much. And Jackie keeps Slater from his compulsion to be way too serious. It lightens him. I've given your question a fair amount of thought and I keep coming back to something like that."

"You guys are pretty tight, aren't you? That's rhetoric. I know the answer and I'm not being nosy, but tell me about the word 'pals.' It seems to conjure up something special for you three."

"Well, actually it's probably more accurately four, counting Mary, and it may be on its way to five with Jackie's new friendship now blossoming."

I then did a bit of a monologue on the critical building blocks of friendship and the exalted status of the word "pals." She seemed to get it, and I sensed she took it as a good thing. She commented on our maturity over the years as opposed to some guys who get together as motivation for all manners of sophomoric behavior. I got the idea that being stiffs or squares or whatever nametags are included in the current lingo wasn't all bad. That there was probably a place for sincerity and friendship without a big light show.

We both got quiet at the same time and took a few bites of our simple, but tasty, fare.

I was starting to get a bit confused and displaced from our little oasis in time and space when Gail inquired, "So, where are you with the ladies, Nick? Someone special somewhere?"

Given her comments on my being a Chatty Cathy, I knew she was aware of my oh-so-available status. But there was nothing mean or nasty about her or her tone, so I answered straight up. "No one at the present time, but it would suit me fine if there were. . . ."

"I surmised as much, Nick, although I'm a bit surprised. You've got a ton of stuff to offer. . . ."

"A ton?" I asked, taking the obvious reference to my corpulence, diminished though it might be.

"I didn't mean that, Nick. You're a good guy and fun to be around. From your semi-conscious renditions, it's clear that you like and respect women a great deal. You're not one of the find 'em, feel 'em, et cetera guys."

My impending reddening retreated as she spared me the 'fuck 'em, forget 'em' part, and that was just as well.

"It's nice of you to say. As we get along in years, there are few things as welcome as kind words."

"Well, Nick, maybe you have to get a bit more into the flow of traffic and assert yourself a bit more. Though I wouldn't necessarily go to the level of one of your drug-induced proposals to me. . . ."

Oh, no, I thought. What might this be? Even the 101 began to tremble.

" . . . the one where you mused about going facedown between my legs. . . ."

In a most uncharacteristic rush, my self-confidence hit an all-time high. I even made it clear that I would override the 101 until further notice.

What the fuck, I thought to myself. The old Nick would have gone holly berry red and shrunk to diminutive status in his womb-like chair. But we're talking about two-time hit target Nick Drizos who, among other things by his own proclamation, is past the teenage tension which seems to dog most of us longer than we would like. Besides, as the lovely one says, it all stays here. Thus, no problem. Just do a Jimmy Cagney: Get your lines straight, stand on your marks, look 'em in the eye, deliver your stuff, and, most importantly, be sincere.

I liked this woman, and here I was at a major crossroad. I could either stand up for all I believe or take a dive. I chose the former.

"You know as well as I what was meant by any such . . ."

"I do indeed know, Nick. I know well the vast differences between lust and true passion. I know very well what you meant and intended. And I'm totally okay with it all. In another time and place, it might have been something special. As it is, I'm glad we have met. You're an okay guy, and there aren't that many of you around."

No, there aren't, I thought to myself. There really are not.

"We'll be headed our separate ways shortly, but you never can tell what might be around the next bend. The six degrees of separation might well be an overstatement."

"It might very well be."

Our little luncheon had gotten quite a bit more intense than I would have foretold, but it was a marvelous time. We spent the next hour or so, our allotted time, on decidedly more inconsequential matters. Before very long, as it seemed, Gail was escorting me back to my quarters.

We got back to sterile city, as I had become fond of so designating it, and even though I was largely past the dreaded teenage tension of bygone years, I could feel a case of the shakes coming on.

And, either bless her heart or damn her, Gail picked up on it, which only reaffirmed that she was exceptional.

"Here's the real deal, Nick. I'll be processing out for the next few days and will be going through debriefing. Hereabouts when we say debriefing, we mean getting it all out. My replacement is already here, so I most likely will not be seeing you again. You're an okay guy, and you'll be just fine. It's been a pleasure to be part of your 'put-together,' so give me a hug, soldier."

I did, and it was the most arousing few seconds of my entire life. It may well have been the most pleasant few seconds of my life. It was like being weightless and omnipotent at once. Mostly it was just for me, and it was a wonderful thing.

She then patted me on the head, kissed me on the cheek, and was gone. There was no doubt; it was an almost mystical connection with another human spirit. It had been worth it to be almost blown away. Maybe I should get car-bombed more often.

I had changed out of my civvies and back into my government issue PJs and was ready to make myself available for a nap when I beheld a new face.

"Hello, Nick, I'm Suzette, but my friends call me Susie. I'm going to be with you for the next day or so, and I've been told you don't wish to be called Mr. Drizos."

"Hello, Susie, nice to meet you. Are you new here?"

"I am, Nick, and I understand you'll be leaving us very shortly. Maybe, as an experienced hand, you can help break me in. I couldn't be much newer. I'd appreciate anything you might suggest, which would help me get accustomed and to do the job well."

My thoughts roamed back to the HR person who must be some piece of stuff. Where do they get these folks? And, I should mention she was right out of the same physical mold as Gail, JoAnn, and Jeanette.

"I would be pleased to help start off your tour here as smoothly as possible."

"Well, from your schedule, it's time for your rub, but given your anticipated release schedule, it's totally discretionary, so just let me know. . . ."

"I'd love one, Susie."

"Okay, Nick, here's your big towel. Just cover your fanny, and I'll be right back."

Cover your fanny. She must have been making the rounds with the other ladies. In other situations, I'd think I was in with the Stepford wives, but these women were as living and breathing as the Connecticut ladies were robotic. Too much, I thought, too much. And little Nick the 101 echoed the same thought.

As before, the rub was a real treat and, as before, she managed to get to most of my "fanny" without creating any embarrassment.

"Okay, Nick, you're in great shape. Your skin looks like it should be in a poster for Oil of Olay."

Yeah, Industrial Strength Oil of Olay, I mused once again. *Harty-har,* came the inner rumbling.

"What else can I do for you?"

"Susie, I just had a swell lunch, and I'd really like to go off to dream land for a little while. Do you think you could give me one of those great booster shots to put me out?"

"I'm sure the answer will be a crisp yes or no, and I'll be right back, Nick."

She was totally with the program and reappeared only moments later.

"You'll be glad to hear, Nick, that your ability to nod off is just about totally under your control. I was told to inform you that the strength of our sedatives has been decreased steadily and continually as your release date draws nearer. Thus, you'll not be having any dependency problems. Just thought you'd like to know."

"Thank you, Susie, I do appreciate it." One can not fail to be impressed with the thoroughness of these folks. I should say patriots, for that is truly what they are. There is no way they can be adequately compensated for the great things they do, and by this time I had become totally convinced that I was a very minor case. And they do it all anonymously. If that isn't a definition of patriot, I don't know what is.

I had just "rested my eyes" for a moment, as we used to say, when I saw Susie with an alcohol swab and a friendly-looking needle.

"Here we go, Nick."

A little scrub-a-dub and a "pinch," and the 101 and I resumed a free fall into pleasant valley. I knew enough to know I would be missing these little trips to faraway places when graduation day came.

Falling is usually not a pleasant activity, but here it seemed to be more than a bit of all right. I can't recall ever being as happy, nor as much at peace. I was indeed both weightless and omnipotent. All that which might have bothered me in another life, now seemed totally irrelevant and vastly trivial. I felt like that colonial flag, which warned, "Don't tread on me." I was in deepest REM territory, like out cold.

I was off in dreamland again, courtesy of happy chemicals. It was yoga times ten and Zen times some other large number. Maybe this is what Jesus really meant when he said: "Peace to you, I offer you my peace."

To many, if not most, of the Faithful, the highlight of the mass is Communion. I understand that and I respect that, but to me it's the offering of Peace. And the older I get, it seems that Peace is the real thing, but the aim of this particular dive into slumber was to check in with my chosen profession as a philistine bond trader. Down, down, ever so nicely down . . .

The other world into which I was descending was once again wonderful. Chemically induced, but wonderful.

I was getting good at picking up where I left off in my nocturnal meanderings, and this was no exception. Things were generally okay, neither blue skies nor tunnels, but some foreboding was clearly afoot. I decided to check back into the world of business, because, if I believed my many hosts and hostesses, I'd be back there in jig time. Ah yes, the wonderful world of financial services. The familiar landscape was unfolding before me once again.

The financial services business, the large sector in which I participate, continued to be good, but I was sensing that the easy days—the days where just about all participants could make some significant dough were moving to the end phase, the phase more or less induced by the pedigreed morons who sit atop the larger financial institutions. This was important to me, because I'm still all about doing well by my clients. That's paramount. The words of Les Horvath and the old timers still resonate like Douglas MacArthur's "Duty, Honor, Country" speech. You have to do well by your clients; you just have to. But there are land mines along the way.

Our industry—banks, insurance companies, brokerage firms, leasing companies, and all manners of financial service boutiques—enjoys wonderful fundamentals. We can grow at ten to twelve percent or more in most years, even when the Gross Domestic Product is moving along at two or three percent per year. It usually takes more than one dollar of capital to get one dollar of growth, so we enjoy a built-in multiplier. Plus our industry not only finances all the new stuff but also refinances existing assets and businesses. We are thus greatly advantaged structurally and fantastically privileged.

Predictably, however, the big timers get episodic urges to ac-

celerate the growth in their businesses. If we've learned anything, however, we should know that there are sustainable rates
of growth for the mega-large companies, and there are dangerous rates of growth. In the same manner that motors and car engines have red lines on them, so too do these companies. But
when entering the hubris phase—which is boringly predictable—the business plans are revved up and these giants shift to
flank speed. The captains of industries so demand.

And one should bend over and get ready for the worst.

If that's correct—and it is with history as the best
no-bullshit arbiter—the financial service companies can grow
nicely and retain smart equilibrium at rates up to maybe even 15
percent per year. But not much good happens above these levels,
partly because at a steady 15 percent, everything has to double
in five years and that's tough to do. Having twice as many smart
people, twice as many buildings, twice as many everything, et
cetera. It's just hard to do. Not many big companies can sustain
such high rates of growth. So a 15 percent per year compounded
growth rate for big companies is a very big deal. And a very big
and flashing warning sign.

A couple of particularly noteworthy things usually occur.
First, at such higher rates of growth, a given company is "pulling
in" business from the future. Thus when the future arrives—and
it will—that business will not be there and revenues will take a
nose dive. Second, it is the responsibility of the financial services
industry—and here is meant specifically the banks—to lend the
last safe dollar. That is their obligation to society—the social
contract if you will. That last safe dollar for these purposes is
usually around that same 15 percent growth level. What then
transpires is that the lower quality, and perforce riskier, deals
are prosecuted. They just come out of the woodwork at this late
stage in the business cycle.

And here's the other rub. When greed overtakes good sense,
lower quality deals always generate higher fees and income for
the banks, since higher risk means higher fees, so profits actually increase for a while. Profits actually go through the roof just
before judgment day. Then, as it must, judgment day
comes—again. The laughable part is that we get treated to a cho-

rus of "Who knew?" Well nobody, except for those who were paying attention. The captains were in the saloons. Whooping it up.

It's a cycle that has less to do with finance than with human behavior, by which is meant greed. Rather than toot along at a safe cruising speed, the captains of finance push the handle to all engines full. The conclusions are predictable, but the cycle seems irresistible.

Part of the pathology is that the biggies in these mega institutions cheerfully confuse stewardship with ownership. And that is saying it more charitably than is merited. These guys are de facto custodians and are supposed to look out for their customers (who pay all the bills), the shareholders (the owners), the staff, and employees (the real stars), and their suppliers and vendors, but they behave very differently—almost regally—as befits them. The money damage is one thing, but is often exceeded in human misery. The greater truth is that some of these guys—many of these guys—simply cannot say, "Enough is enough." Maybe because they just don't know enough to know when to say it. These guys—the biggies, the grandly pedigreed biggies—are regarded as something like celebrities when the cycle gets going.

Their big parties and other excesses will be found—predictably—on the society and gossip pages, as if there might be a difference. It wasn't always like that, however, and in any event they are not celebrities. Celebrities can sing, dance, tell stories, play an instrument, make motion pictures, take off their clothes and look good doing so—stuff like that. These guys can make some money, so their celebrity is all about the garish ways they spend said money. Otherwise, these guys don't have a great deal going for them.

And, as an aside—and a quite important aside—well-run small and medium-sized companies are the best. Those companies don't get so big that the bosses can't know most, if not all, of their employees and their customers as well as their shareholders. People count.

And the CEOs of these kinds of companies have every opportunity to identify themselves with their respective company's products and services. Plus, these companies produce most of the innovation and real growth for the benefit of all. Not to mention create most jobs.

It's not that the CEOs of the mega companies are inhuman, but they tend to regard themselves as some sort of minor deities and they generally don't relate especially well to working folks. And that's reflected in hiring and firing practices where they deal mostly in numbers. When business is good, they call down to the HR boiler room, "Get me five hundred bodies." When things go south, they then call in the division heads and tell them to get rid of five hundred bodies. As I have come to see it, they're not inhuman, they're just disconnected. Numbers on pages and money in their pockets just require bodies. It's a simple, if not nasty, calculus. In so-called up markets, they lay on people with a fury. When things turn down, bodies go out of windows. These CEOs just aren't very well connected to the folks. Especially the CEOs of the mega financial service entities. Just about everybody who can steam up a mirror held under his nose can figure that.

But the big companies are vital and necessary because they do the large- scale things. It's just that we would be much better served if they would err on the side of stodginess rather than chasing growth. The fact is they just aren't very good at growth. The growth they do manifest comes largely from squashing little guys who have pioneered and developed good ideas and new markets and from acquisitions. They may not be villains and bad guys, but neither are they admirable in that many respects, either. But they do get paid a lot of dough to act out their grandiose phantasms.

As I manage a great deal of wealth, I have to form viewpoints on the investment environment, and over the years I have developed many viewpoints. In getting to my investment conclusions I often rhapsodize along the previous lines. I may not be correct, and the things I take to be cause and effect elements may likewise be incorrect or maybe even just flat wrong. Something is correct, however, as my investment history of performance is always near the top within the category of those seeking moderate to significant returns with relatively low risk. I'm just not part of the Wild West. I'm the right choice for certain folks with well-thought-out goals and objectives who are willing to be smart and patient. Those craving excitement should go to the track or Vegas or enlist a hedge fund. Meaning, go elsewhere.

My current attitude, based on very clear and observable patterns, is that we're due for a pretty serious "correction," which means going into defensive mode for my many clients. I may not make much, or any, money for them, but I'll do my best not to lose any. As I've observed and noted countless times, these folks are getting along in years, the dough was hard to make, and this is no time to go to the races with their capital. And the advice from the old-timers continues to ring in my ears: "There's a time to buy, a time to sell, and a time to do nothing." The smartest among us are those who adhere to these basic and homely maxims.

This particular time around, this particular time out on the great dance floor of high finance, the boys at the Fed kept interest rates extremely low for entirely too long. According to Finance by Nick (with a preface by the 101), interest rates are ultimately the most determinative factors of prices, price levels, and values. The effect this time, per always, has been to increase the prices/values of all real and financial assets. While nobody can ever call timing with precision, we do know that the higher one goes, the farther one will ultimately fall. It looks especially adventurous and nasty this time around. We're pretty high up, and some have noted that we're working without a net. And with lots of fancy new "securities"—derivatives, credit swaps and the like—which had never been seen or tested in large numbers or in mass financings before. Bombs away; look out below!

So we try to assume the best defensive postures we can, but there are limits to how much one can safeguard one's clients. If the "correction" is big enough, everyone gets hit to some extent. It's like the man said: "When they raid the whore house, the piano player goes to jail right along with the girls."

I was in this process of completing my latest mental edition of Finance Strategies by Nick when I got a call from Richie. Could I come to his place and give him an update on their available investable assets and some help on certain of his many trust accounts for his donee beneficiaries.

Could I? I was on my way in minutes. It would be difficult for the uninitiated to sense the uplift afforded me from a call from Richie or Mary. Here they are doing incredible things for the unfortunate and for the disadvantaged and they call upon me for some help. Like I said, "right away."

9
Murder

October 28th

It was about a ninety-minute ride to Richie's place, and a beautiful day on which to be up and about. It was just after Labor Day, and we had all gotten together only a couple of weeks earlier. That time Fran came along and, I must say, acquitted herself beautifully. It looked to me and my caring senses that she was as big on Jackie as Mary was on Richie. We had a swell time. There's that word again "swell" but that's what it was. When you have a small group of friends who can make their own entertainment—however they do it; lively conversations, stories and the like—you have something special. And something special it was. I think Fran became a keeper—a term of endearment for our little ragtag bunch of crusaders—that day. Not that she would care, because at bottom if she and Jackie were simpatico, the rest was icing, dessert, or what you will. And that pleased me no end.

With my many forebodings set aside I was enjoying my leisurely drive on a relatively uncrowded interstate. I even put *Come a Little Bit Closer* into my CD player and made it about forty seconds before other thoughts invaded.

In very short order I was in front of Richie's tastefully unobtrusive home. Set back from the country lane–type road with about a hundred yards of a poplar- adorned driveway, it was a very handsome and welcoming tudor. Kind of a smaller, pocket-sized but tasteful stately Wayne Manor.

There was a service van of some sort, with the letters "L" and "M" displayed prominently, parked in front of the house. I was startled somewhat as it accelerated swiftly past me and sped off throwing great amounts of gravel as it went. I thought that strange, but chalked it up to twenty-first-century behavior.

I had expected to be greeted with an open door by Mary, Richie, or both as was always the case when I visited. Instead I rang the pleasant doorbell and waited a few moments. I rang again but still no answer. As it was a lovely day, they must be outside, so I walked around the house to the elegant but tastefully appointed patio they had just completed. Nobody there.

Next I peeked through the lead glass windows of the study. Then it was all replaced by a clanging disorder. Broken glass and confusion. And noise and sweat, profuse sweat. And the color red. Except it wasn't the color red. It was blood.

"Jesus, they're dead. Richie and Mary are dead. Christ's sake, what have I done? They're dead. They're all dead. And I did it. I caused it!"

Of a sudden, I sat up as though my spine had turned into a piece of coiled spring steel and gazed through my wide open but unseeing eyes at the carnage I had caused. "Richie and Mary are dead. For Christ's sake, I killed them. What have I done? For Christ's sake, what have I done?"

The continuing slaps and smacks to my jaw made my teeth rattle and my toes tingle. I felt like Faye Dunaway getting slapped around by Jack Nicholson in *Chinatown*. With no small amount of pulsating pain, my now focusing eyes gave way to something resembling normalcy, and I found myself with upstretched arms to avoid more smacks from Jack. Or one of the other guys made up to look like Jack. They can't fool me. I'll take my secrets with me.

"You're okay, you're okay, and Richie and Mary are alive," the voice kept saying.

It appeared to be coming from the body owned by Jack, but I had become aware and attuned to treachery. I was in their interrogation facility, but I'd withstand anything they can throw at me.

They think they can trick me into polite conversation and all manners of revelation, but I'm on to the whole schmazz. Duty, honor, country. That's all that matters. Make the guys proud.

"Go ahead and beat the bejeesus out of me, you cretins, I won't tell you squat."

The room then went to a deadly quiet. This is clearly where they ice me, but I just don't care. I'll take it all down with me.

"Smack him again, Jack," said a voice I knew I recognized. It was Richie.

Then another voice reiterated the same directive. It was Mary. And then Jackie.

A considerable weight seemed to loft itself away from me, and I found myself gazing and gaping at Richie, Mary, Jackie, Fran, Gail, Raj, and Ben.

They seemed to say in a chorus—a Greek Chorus of sorts; how's that for an irony?—that "we're all alive."

The ensuing smacks on my jaw seemed to propel me into a new, if not strange state, and I continued to gape and gaze about.

I expected to hear Cher yell, "Snap out of it," as I began to understand my new circumstances. Instead I got Ben, who inquired, "Are you with us, or shall I have Jack smack you around some more?"

The cloud of versed residue lingered but the sextet of friendlies was taking on greater definition with each passing second.

"I think I'm back, but stop smacking me around if you are truly friendlies.'

"We are friendlies," said a voice resembling that of Jackie Slater. "Yes, it's me, Jackie, so please sit up, and I'll have Ben tell you what and where you are. Okay?"

My traveling companions—muck and clarity—took the occasion to square themselves away most quickly. I had the feeling of being vaulted into a lucid present day setting.

Anyway, nobody was here. Not Richie, not Jackie, not Raj . . . nobody. It was all about me and how I wanted things to be, so I had them assembled somewhere in my mind as a Greek Chorus. A big imaginary Greek Chorus. *Funny, real funny,* groaned the 101. I had opted to trust Ben and his merry bunch of degenerates once again, but this time I was going to get to something bearing at least faint resemblance to the truth. I was exhausted and tired of the byzantine crap these folks had been laying on me.

Even a dumb trader like me can figure—at great length—when he has been a piece of bait. No more, no less, just bait. I'm not sure what I was supposed to attract or catch, but I'd finally seen the "Cast of Characters," and right across from where it said: STARRING NICK DRIZOS, it said: BAIT. Right, my character was "Bait."

"Okay, yes I'm okay, so tell me . . . what happened."

Then the voice attributed to the guy I have come to know as Ben took over.

"First, and most important, Richie, Mary, Jackie, Fran, and Raj are all alive. Richie has been shot in the shoulder, but he is alive and okay. All of the others are well in every respect. Do you read me? I say again, Nick, do you read me?"

"I read you. Just hold a razor over your right wrist and swear to me in blood that the five you cited are alive and well. And you should know, I'm just about ready to send you to your final flaming hell."

"I don't have a razor, but I do have a thirty-two-caliber snub-nosed revolver. I'll put that to my head and swear that what you have just heard is true. Will that do?"

By this time, I had tired of the histrionics and my vision was pretty damn good. I concluded—for good, ill, true, or otherwise—that Richie, Mary, Jackie, Fran, and Raj were all alive. That became my principal premise as I decided to sit in for another turn of the wheel, which was becoming a decidedly heavy-bread, all-in game.

"Like I said, I'm okay. So what now?"

Then Shane took over and said, "I'm aware of your primary social group—the folks about whom you care deeply. They are all under heavy watch. We are now getting to what we spooks call the end game, and you and I are the two featured end-gamers. Do you read me?"

I had kind of sensed that I might make it to a final scene shoot-'em-up one day, so I said, "Roger and okay. Just take a minute and give me the plan, because if I didn't get Richie and Mary almost killed, who did?"

"I can only tell you, Nick, that we call them the other side, and that's all you should know and all you have to know."

"You've almost gotten me killed a time or two, and now you want me to sign off on your pledge to safeguard the most important people in my life. Is that the deal?"

"That's the deal, Nick."

I looked about, and friend Shane had remorphed back once more into the real Ben. I sensed I was in some new environs, and so I asked Ben if I had been relocated from my mysterious surroundings of the past several—what was it? Days, weeks?

"Yeah, Nick, we checked you out of the Alabama Arms a few days ago. You had guessed where you were. Maybe from the types of trees and flora, but you were correct. We're now back in the Sunshine State where we can strike at our adversaries quickly and effectively. Just don't ask where. As we say, you don't need to know.

"We've got big work to do, so I'm going to give you the fast version, okay?"

I just looked at Ben and said, "Okay, let's get to it. No jive for a change, right?"

"No jive, here's the way it was. It's October eighth. Things have been peaceful. You had your car accident, but because you'd had a couple heaters, you thought you just had one too many and nodded off. You regard yourself as fortunate and get back to thinking everything is pretty normal. Later in the week, you get a call from Richie to meet him at his house at four p.m. for drinks, because he has a special treat for you and wants you to help him out with some funding situations.

"You blast over to his house and arrive at a few minutes before four p.m. No answer when you knock on that gigantic front door, but his car is parked prominently in the driveway. So you knock again with the same results.

"It's not like Richie one bit to invite you somewhere and then not show up. Like it's never happened. So you go around to the side of the house and look in the den window. There to your shock you see Richie and Mary entwined and face down in an increasingly large pool of seeping, oozing blood.

"You rip down a substantial tree limb and break a den window. You crawl in and roll the bodies over. To your great surprise, it's not Mary but Lily Sanford. And she is dead. Then you roll Richie over. Yes, it's Richie and he is breathing, but only in shallow breaths. You dial nine-one-one and set about stopping Richie's bleeding.

"In very short order, the EMT folks arrive followed within minutes by the local cops.

"The cops called for the coroner for Ms. Sanford, but only after the EMTs removed Richie to the local hospital. They then take your statement, thank you for cooperation and send you on your way.

"As soon as you reached your home, you went to work looking for my alpha number and found it in your cable TV bill under 'Customer Service.' You were more than greatly upset and suggested in strongest terms that we meet by the waterside at a designated marina slip pronto.

"We did and that brings us pretty much to the present," says Mr. Ben, "with the following pertinent addendum.

"To give you the shortest possible explanation, the other side had glommed onto your affiliation with Raj and believed one of you was the handler. Later they assumed that Richie's great wealth and charitable works were fronts. He was, they concluded, the nexus of some important anti-terrorist financing, therefore . . ."

"Okay, Ben, enough, I get it. I am now back to the early part of October when we got together on Schooner Pier per my alpha call. I recall it like this . . ."

" 'Hello Nick, how are you?'

" 'Hello, Ben you are a real prick. I visit with you guys in your spook facilities and tell you in all good faith, just like the Boy Scout I probably am, about storing data on managed beams in the radio-electric spectrum. You guys for your part are having a great time jerking me around while I'm totally out of it.

" 'But the joke's on you, Mr. Head Spook, because during one of my chemically induced naps, I finally doped out your National Resource jive. You guys, or your techie supporters, had been working on beam bending (what I call 'beamology') for several years for just about the opposite application I had discussed.

While I was storing data, you were looking for new data—more specifically 'targets.' Probably your major application being that of directing an electro-photography beam around corners or into caves and maybe find some of those troublesome guys like Osama Bin Laden. Right?

"I'm talking to you, Ben, right?"

But he just looks at me with that 'what else is new' look that he and his cadre have developed to an art form.

"Finally it hits me. Why would these guys care about what some whackadoodle bond trader thinks about bending electronic beams. And why transport me to Weird-O central to rally with Mr. Spook and his minions?

"It doesn't make any sense at all unless they can use me for some important purpose. What purpose? And then all the bells go off. Mr. Spook has a mole, and he needs some bait to get the spook and his handlers to expose themselves.

"Then I come along with my screwy ideas about a related technology but for totally different applications, so you figure this might be a good way to entrap your mole. That's what this whole exercise was all about, wasn't it? Your mole.

"At first I thought the mole was Hunter, but that made no sense. So Berkeley is your mole, isn't he? When I saw Hunter at Bayside Bluffs, he was there to protect me, wasn't he?"

"The deal is that you set me and my loved ones up just to catch a mole, didn't you?

"Didn't you?"

I had expected Ben to be red-faced, since I had caught him in one of his spook games, but he was quite relaxed.

"You're right as far as you go, Nick, but you just don't go far enough. Yes, we had a mole. Yes, we had it figured that the mole was Berkeley, and yes, we used you to maybe scare him into revealing his cell mates, or as importantly, his handlers. We had Berkeley pegged for quite a while, but we needed to get to his handlers. We would have taken it from there, but it became obvious that his colleagues included some important U.S. public figures. We had Berkeley pegged some time ago. It was like Cagney in *Thirteen Rue Madeleine* when he fingers Richard Conte as the Nazi infiltrator, because, 'He was just too good.' That was Berkeley's fatal flaw; he was 'just too good.' The deal was to get him to lead us to the other players—the other far more important players. We just took a page out of Don Corleone's playbook. We kept our enemies closer.

"This wasn't some dipshit spook deal as you would put it, Nick. We had intercepted some big nasty transmissions, and we didn't have the luxury of constructing a more elaborate operation.

"I've been mostly straight with you, Nick. We like you and respect you, but we had uncovered a world-class plot and we were at max urgency. So did I dangle you out there as bait to get to our necessary end? Yes, I did. If it gives you any comfort, I'd have dangled my wife and kids out there. This is the dirty degenerate game I have signed onto. Sometimes you can traffic in what we call structured half measures, and sometimes not. This time we had uncovered what could well be the biggest terrorist attack of all time.

"This wasn't a bunch of spooks playing some stupid field game. This time we had intercepted what was coded in as 'Operation Triple Crown.' There were going to be big time blasts in three U.S. cities. With standard practices, it was clear that the cities would be New York, Chicago, and Los Angeles. But our intel has gotten a great deal better and we, us guys in our little dipshit spook organization, intercepted some cell-phone traffic in which the other side carelessly used horse- racing lingo.

"I'm not going to take you inside our code breaking, but very cleverly and pretty quickly, we determined the three cities in the Triple Crown would be Seattle (as in Seattle Slew), Omaha—those two having been Triple Crown Winners—and Louisville. Why Louisville? We don't know, but since the Derby is run on the first Saturday in May, it stood to be great symbolism. Not great cities, but big enough to show that the other side could hit wherever and whenever they chose. If they could prevail, it would show they could hit anywhere; that was what was so important about Seattle, Omaha, and Louisville. And anyway you cut it, May is perfect symbolism, as May Day represents power to the oppressed and all that bullshit. Get it?"

I knew better by now than to even try to answer, so I just nodded.

"So we were ready for them, but it remained to break down their plants and cells.

"You happened along, and we knew that Raj had been compromised earlier. So bringing you to Invictus was the natural move. The other side could be made to believe a handler relationship existed between you and Raj. The objective was to provoke Berkeley into a state of panic and for him to contact his handler. We were talking about millions of lives and tens or hundreds of billions of dollars, so anything and anyone was of interest to us if we were to prevail . . . and that's our job . . . to prevail.

"The Invictus facility you visited was not operational at that time. In recent months, a number of our better considered operations came up short. Disastrous events were avoided, but we failed to grab the operatives. It was then that we started to go after the mole. We had moved Invictus to a new location, but kept the older facility in apparent working order with a full, but inactive staff. None of the personnel from Invictus I were transferred to Invictus II. Our principal focus was on surveilling Operation Triple Crown and to hone to faultless perfection a plan to immobilize it without incident. The corollary plan was to surface and to deal with the mole. Thus Berkeley remained at the old facility. We kept Hunter there as well so as not to alarm Berkeley.

"So, yes, we dangled you out there to see if we could get Berkeley to panic. Did we use you? Yes, we did. Did I lie to you? Yes, I did. That's what we do when someone—a bad guy—is placed highly in our government and is fully capable of compromising us further and of causing widespread damage. Would I do it again? Yes, I would. That's what we do.

"I hope you understand the whys and hows, but it's just good guys and bad guys. We also thought we had you protected all the way, but that wasn't the case. The higher-level mole compromised us but good. And, to underscore the acumen and tenacity of our rivals, they planted the car bomb in your vehicle many months earlier. And there it sat. Small, practically undetectable and, needless to add, extremely powerful. Detonation could wait till it pleased the other side. And that's why we believed our security on you was totally adequate. As I hope you will appreciate we can't surveil what occurred before we commence surveilling.

"As I said, Raj had been compromised but good. His friendship with you was well known. To us, it was worth the shot to see if Berkeley would get unnerved.

"That was the short version—sum and substance—of our alpha conversation on October third, immediately after the attempt on Richie and Mary, even though it wasn't Mary as things turned out. Lily, happily married for many years, had been assisting Richie in an important fund-raiser. She, and her presence there, were totally innocent.

"Thus it was, Nick, that you deduced our using you as bait to catch Berkeley and his higher-ups. The problem was, and remains, that we underestimated their capabilities. And that is something we try mightily never to do. Our underestimation was not from our cockiness but rather from their finely adjusted talents and 'sleeper' resources here in D.C. and other areas. We failed to grasp the scope of their many penetrations. This is not the amateur hour we are facing. And I should add we can thank some of our Boy Scout congressmen for denuding our capabilities so well.

"But that's the good part—perhaps the best part—of our particular franchise. When we screw up like this, there is no public dustup because we are, for practical purposes, unknown. We may get our asses chewed privately, but we are also able to redouble and or redirect our efforts with no outside complications.

"Moreover, as there are no headlines, the other side knows neither the full extent of the damage their actions have wrought nor our reactions. So we truly make the most of bad situations.

"So there you are, Nick. I confessed totally to our goals and how we employed you to those ends. Like it or not, you have become a part of the posse, haven't you? Do you now recall your actions after you caused me to come clean as to our aims and objectives?"

I felt like someone smacked me a few more times, and the "tilt" sign went on and off a few dozen times. Then came a tidal wave of intense clarity banishing murk, and in an instant I was in Fatima's Garden, except this time all would be known to me.

"I'm totally with it, Ben, and here's the way it's gonna be. I know to a certainty that you had the satellite camera rolling, so, first thing, you're going to take me back to Invictus—and that would have been my second visit—to see the films of this latest episode, aren't you? Because you have those films. From deflected 'beamology,' don't you, Ben? Don't you? You know who shot Richie and killed Lily, don't you? And you're going to tell me, aren't you?"

"I guess I do and I guess I am, Nick. There's no denying your membership at this point. I will tell you that we may both get killed in this final chapter. You do understand that, right? This is no bullshit. We're dealing with folks who place small value on life. We'll do the same. Are you all right with that?

"And I should tell you we won't be going back to the Invictus facility. It would be time expended unnecessarily on travel, and we have all of the required assets within a few miles of us right now. You can think of it as your second visit to Invictus."

"Yes, Ben I get all that happy stuff, so let's get back on the case. I'm ready for some final resolutions—mine or theirs—so let's move out. And this time I won't be taking the versed.

"Then, Ben, the second order of business will be to serve up Lily's murderer and bring the rest of that nonsense to a close. I want to see some miserable bastard swing, get it?"

"If we can, we will, Nick, get it? Understand a few ground rules, Nick, our mission is to prevent losses of life and destruction of assets. It's not that Lily is inconsequential, but there is no way we'll compromise our objectives for any individual. If we can bring the murderer to justice, we will but that's not our franchise right now. Get it?"

I guess I got part of it. I wanted justice for Lily Sanford, but maybe we were in the national security game and maybe facts, truth and justice would all be stood on their collective ears. This is one weird world in which we live with no shortage of degenerates running around.

"Okay, Ben, let's do it."

I was about to throw myself in with Ben when the 101 reminded me there was an impending trial. All else, no matter how important, would have to wait.

Richie was being arraigned for the murder of a Lily Sanford by one T. J. Hill. Mr. Hill, had been accorded the title of "dumbest white man on the planet" by a local journalist of some prominence who took great pains to communicate to blacks, Hispanics, and whoever else might have an interest, that the reference to "white man" was out of consideration for other ethnic groups and not meant to convey anything—anything—which others might find racist, offensive, or insulting. No, this was meant to be a singular accolade for our Mr. Hill. Plus he was and is a real jerk.

Hill was a political hack of the first magnitude in a county that took note of such practiced sycophancy. As he had neither pride nor self-esteem, he had carried water for the bigger time political hacks and was owed a considerable debt. As remuneration for his many services, he was placed on the county court as a justice. Much to the surprise of just about no one, he was a total—no exaggeration—total disaster. He was an embarrassment to the very notions of law and justice. That he didn't know the law was a considerable, but very small impediment. And he was also unimpaired by humility or any of the more gracious qualities humans sometimes exhibit.

He was so inept that more than a few observers noted that, like some of the jurists in Jersey, that was the first time he had ever sat on a bench which wasn't in a park.

He set records for unexcused absences, disturbingly inept trials, and abominable courtroom demeanor. His verdicts were also reversed more than anyone else's in the history of Florida jurisprudence. Needless to add, that took some serious effort. In a word, he was a disgrace. Many called for his immediate removal.

One of the more gifted politicos in his county rode effectively to his rescue—more from concerns of self-preservation than anything else—and pronounced that he, Hill, was exactly who and what was required as county prosecutor, and would he please consider such a career change. Other heavies in this drama made it clear that so long as he enjoyed breathing, he would be well served to play the statesman and to accept this important offer.

Some people are born disasters, and so it is with T. J. Hill. He would have managed to become a laughing stock of equal measure as prosecutor as he had been as a justice with one exception. That exception was Thomas H. Hughes, known as "Hog-Nose" for reasons appreciated by many but understood by few.

Hughes was an incredible public servant and he was, for all practical purposes, the principal bulwark of justice here in Marabella County. Hill was fortunate to have Hughes in the county government and was saved from self-destruction on many occasions by old Hognose.

Hughes was another of those people known by three names, such as James Earl Jones or William Howard Taft. Not many would identify with Jimmy Jones or William Taft. That's as it was with Thomas H. Hughes. Why he diddled with Marabella County when he could have been a big force in state or national politics, nobody quite knows.

He was, among other things, a 'Nam vet and an important leader in a wide variety of civic programs. Folks just looked to him for approval and validation. When something would come up in the county, it was very common to hear, or even to see in editorials, "What does Hognose think?" When he spoke, the audience was usually doing a collective nod. The man had a real presence and a great deal of stature. He was totally approachable and clearly loved the folks and his surroundings. His many gracious qualities combined to assure his status as the local favorite.

It seems that he was one of those guys who understood his "celebrity" and who elected to use it for the greatest local social good. There was no question he could have acquired far greater fame or wealth here or elsewhere, but here he was and here he would stay, or so it seemed.

In the local scheme of things, he was the yin to T. J. Hill's yang. They sort of canceled each other out. On several occasions, Hill attempted to prosecute innocent folks, as that was Hill's ticket to the fame he so zealously—and not surprisingly or unscrupulously—sought. Invariably those cases would be dismissed as a result of Hughes's efforts and intervention. Hughes rarely, if ever, took credit or bathed in the limelight of publicity in such circumstances. The more typical pattern would be a sprinkling of facts and constructive evidence placed strategically before an investigative reporter or maybe an alert but rookie public defender. Of course there is no such thing as an investigative reporter; most such folks just hang about till somebody tips them to something. Then they are christened as "investigative reporters." They are otherwise quite useless. A few were smart enough to say prayers of thanks for THH.

Hughes made several such reporters "great," again by laying out a bread crumb trail of facts for the gents and ladies of the fourth estate to prove a putatively guilty guy innocent. He was always expansive in his praise of the press, as his only concern was justice. If some newsperson got a bunch of credit and basked in the sunshine of celebrity, that was okay with THH. Privately, he thought very little of journalists; much as Ted Williams always rated pitchers the dumbest folks on the planet. Nonetheless, he was happy to lift their careers if justice were served. An unusual guy. An unusual, and very selfless, guy.

Similarly, he often laid out a comparable trail of evidentiary bread crumbs for Hill or one of his severely limited sycophantic assistant D.A.s when a definitively guilty party was about to escape through the Swiss cheese screen operated by this seriously impaired and incompetent prosecutor.

As it occurred, most folks seemed to sense that Thomas H. Hughes was a wonderful American and were aware of their good fortune. Rhetoric may abound, but, in truth, there are really very few dedicated public servants. And old Hughes was one. His talents certainly did not go unnoticed.

As great a man as THH was, as fine a man, and he is, there was still a reality of idiocy and self-absorption in the mix by the name of T. J. Hill. Hognose often wondered if Hill had been consigned to Florida as a sort of purgatory for him. Or maybe, as a variation on *It's a Wonderful Life,* the Hills of the world would ultimately get THH his wings.

And Hill would not disappoint. He had already charged Richie with Murder One and had him in the county jail in an orange jumpsuit with no bail. If there were an all-time all-star misguided team of malicious folks, Hill could have laid considerable claim to the captaincy.

Mary heard the terrifying news while doing some truly mag-

314

nificent things in her beloved Texas panhandle. She said she'd be back there, and indeed she did go back. This was particularly uplifting and wonderful, because the long-suffering folks in that area had heard one empty, unmet promise after another. Mary was a different breed, however. Among other things, she had gotten some MIT and Texas A&M undergrads to execute a number of public-utility functions including bringing clean well water to the town. She had also created a local economy based upon export of the town's distinctive Hispanic ceramic dishware and other related products. A once totally depressed area was on its way to becoming a small but impressive Renaissance City, USA. But once she was informed of Richie's situation, she was on a chartered Gulfstream with irresistible speed.

By the time she landed in Orange Vista, the seat of Marabella County, Hill had already violated just about every one of Richie's constitutional rights. There are guys who would cash in on a train wreck—or even cause a train wreck—if that suited his purposes. T. J. Hill was one such.

In particular, he had leaked all manners of scurrilous rumors about Richie and Lily Sanford. In addition, he invaded Mary's safe deposit box, quite illegally, at the local bank. Therein he found an aging copy of the pre-nuptial agreement between Mary and Richie. He then planted the most vile story that Richie would have offloaded old Mary for Lily, except for the pre-nup. This, of course, made no sense, as the pre-nup provided that Mary would get nothing in any situation. But Hill counted on the well-known fact that most folks don't get past the headlines, often including the press.

This time, specifically including the press, the frenzy was on.

To this point, and to everybody's satisfaction—albeit in total ignorance of the facts—everybody, but everybody, just knew that there had been a burglary gone wrong and that poor Lily Sanford, a bystander, had been shot and killed in the process.

But old malicious Hill did his best to paint a most hideous picture. He quickly contended that Richie had been "tomcatting" around with Lily for some time and would have offloaded the tiresome and shrewish Mary had it not been for the troublesome

315

prenuptial agreement still safely guarded by the villainous Mary Lancer Blaine McAlister.

He went on to suggest that Richie had therefore engaged a professional hitman to kill Mary and to wound Richie, thereby creating a favorable illusion for the dastardly Mr. McAlister.

Nobody who knew the couple would have believed that Richie was in love with anyone on the planet except Mary, but the play on the prenuptial agreement did have some impact. It was probably the case that most of the populace in Marabella County believed Richie to be 100 percent innocent, but again old Hill managed to poison the waters of good sense with his detestable actions. Because this was big stuff for Hill, he would bend every effort to assure that trial would be forthcoming quickly.

Although partially sedated from the effects of a large caliber hole in his shoulder, Richie was eager to join the battle. I and others advised him to engage legal counsel ASAP. Richie's inclination, knowing he was not guilty of anything, was probably not to engage any lawyers. When we insisted, however, he relented and told us to get Eddie Muns and John Riordan on the case.

Muns and Riordan were vets—Muns being army artillery and Riordan being navy. Neither had served in combat, but Richie had come to know them as he had come to know so many people. And he liked them. He deemed them both honest and honorable.

When I pointed out that neither was a criminal lawyer—Muns was a corporate attorney, and John specialized in real estate closings—Richie answered that he wasn't a criminal and didn't want a criminal lawyer. He trusted these guys, and that was the end of that. Mary had just asked him quietly if he was sure that's what he wanted.

When he said yes, Mary said, quietly but almost fearsomely firm, "You heard him. Get to it." And we did.

Ed arrived first, and Hill was waiting with his salivation totally unchecked and undisguised. He maliciously leaked—blared was more accurate—that Mr. McAlister had engaged a couple of incompetents. At the same time he was relieved that Richie hadn't engaged one of the NY or LA "dream team" criminal-law out-

316

fits. It couldn't bode better for old T.J. He had tilted the field most cleverly.

A substantial crowd greeted Ed Muns when his understated cab pulled up at the Vining Stables Hotel. The press was well represented with all of the "nationals" assembled for the impending drama.

At first Ed played the happenstance visitor with a big "who me?" expression, but he was quickly recognized. The ill-mannered and inconsiderate members of the news corps then did a fine collective job of impeding his entrance into the hotel.

Despite the national attention, this was a local show. Thus it would allow one of the more energetic Orange Vista newshounds to draw the spotlight unto himself. Seizing upon what might well be his Warholian fifteen minutes of fame, Mr. Local all but barged into Ed and thrust a mike into his face. Probably knowing he had a shot at one question—and one question only—he made it a beauty.

"Mr. Muns, just what do you expect to accomplish in what is so clearly an open-and-shut case of homicide? You clearly can't know the facts and you have no competency [some of us expected to hear other words like "gravitas"] in criminal law, since you're just a flack for corporations." Having strutted his stuff, the reporter took a half step back, looked about nodding to his peers, flashed a self-congratulatory smile and awaited a response.

In the next few moments, Richie's always solid judgment was once again made evident. Abundantly evident.

Ed Muns was known in his circles in southern California as being judicious and, for the most part, noncombative. He had been very successful for a host of reasons. One such was that he never engaged a provoker to no avail. Another was he only spoke—and then he spoke with great authority—on subjects and matters he knew he could defend and support indefinitely. This was a seasoned pro. He didn't make a practice of playing straight man for the amateur hour, as would be seen.

After assuming a relaxed posture, Muns addressed the eager journalist. "Well," said Ed, "and what is your name again?"

Muns had fired a subtle, but effective first shot. This casual rejoinder was devastatingly unsettling to the news guy. Muns was supposed to wither. Who was interviewing/questioning whom here? We were about to see a real pro at work.

"My name is Nelson Carter," came the weak, almost stuttering response. The accompanying body language was a sight to behold and enjoy. Mr. Carter started to extend a hand and then reconsidered. Knowing the cameras were on the reporter, Ed let him squirm and squiggle for an effective moment.

Ed then smiled and turned perceptibly away from Carter and toward the assembled crowd—another well done, subtle dismissal of an overly eager news guy.

Turning back to Carter, Ed said, "Well, I can't disagree with your comprehensive evaluation, aside from your reference to open and shut. That was your expression, wasn't it? 'Open and shut.' "

The attendant cameras then caught our news hero displaying yet more decidedly unconfident body language followed by a weak nod and a weaker half smile.

"I will say that I don't know the facts any more than you do." There came a low level groan from the bystanders. "And I'm certainly not any more of a criminal lawyer than you might be." The dramatic pause for laughs by Muns was fulfilled quite neatly. "But I can tell you this. There is literally no way that Richie McAlister killed Lily Sanford or anyone else. I'll ride this year's Derby winner before Richie McAlister would harm another human being. That's what I do know.

"Now, Mr. Carter. It is Carter, isn't it?" said Muns, laying a theatrical hand on our newshound's shoulder and locking eyes with the now-deflating younger man. "I'm sure that a seasoned and professional journalist such as yourself would never breach our most cherished presumption of innocence and use the expression 'open-and-shut' before all the facts are in, would you?"

Muns turned to leave and then concluded with, "We can count on that, can't we?"

With a friendly pat on the young man's shoulder and with a jaunty spring to his step, Muns then disengaged masterfully. It was brief, but it was devastating.

And there it was. Game, set, and match. Deftly and subtly, in his chosen style and demeanor, the old pro had set the tone.

The gathering carnival atmosphere had been diffused and defused. There would be no L.A. celebrity circus this time. Florida would be denied, and the assembled pool of piranhas would have to look elsewhere to fill their tabloid tastes.

Ben had watched the ambush as he called it and was quickly convinced that Muns was indeed a very smart and savvy guy. He did cringe at Ed's reference to the Derby, but assumed, as he had to, it was just coincidence and would not register with anyone.

Ed then disappeared into the lobby where, to his good fortune, the reporters had been barred.

He strode past the registration desk and into the waiting arms and tearstained face of Mary, who had been hiding behind ultra-dark sunglasses. He kissed her cheek and hugged her; they had been friends for many years. It had been she who introduced Ed and Richie to each other a few years back.

Without a word, they left through the rear exit and into a waiting car. They sped away to the home of a friend who had moved out and offered it to Mary as a safe house.

"I'm so glad to see you, Ed. I . . ." And she started to sob again.

"I wouldn't be anywhere else. I'm not going to tell you not to worry. Go right ahead and worry, but we are going to get this silliness dispensed with. You can count on that. So go ahead and worry, but be confident."

The comfort that Mary took in Ed's presence was immeasurable. She thought how lucky she was in this disconnected era featuring warped sensibilities and misplaced priorities to have such wonderful friends. Not just people of great smarts and stature but people of such innate goodness and generosity of spirit. While terrified, she felt truly blessed. Thoughts of the valley of the shadow of death entered her psyche with a new and totally personalized meaning. Ed was beside her. . . .

Retrieving and recalling the horrendous impressions of the shooting must have been a bit of a tonic—maybe more like a bromide—for me and the 101. Maybe it was more like shock theater, but it seemed to serve as the busting of my psychological logjam. Murk and clarity remained in a virtual death struggle with each other, but before long clarity would banish the other fellow.

It was October 9th, and I met Ben in a parking lot after having done a serpentine arabesque through one building after another to assure I was not followed and compromised. I was to learn later that my course was being followed closely by a couple of deep-cover agents. In the case I had been followed, my "shadow" would have been dealt with harshly. The stakes had been notched up significantly, and while I was aware of a general heightening, I had no reason—or background from which to establish any reason—to believe that the tactics would rise in nastiness in a similar proportion.

I met Ben, dressed masterfully in stylish but drab garb that rendered him eminently forgettable. I started to marvel at his abilities to literally blend in with the woodwork, but that was his job, wasn't it?

He spirited me into the backseat of a car while he jumped into the passenger seat and we were off.

There was an initial silence, so I inquired, "Where are we going?"

Ben piped up quickly and crisply. "We're going to a safe house a few miles away. I'm not going to have to sedate you, but I will ask you to put on this blindfold and lie on the seat. This is one hundred percent for your own protection. The whereabouts of this, or any safe house, is information you don't want to be carrying."

It made sense, so I complied.

There followed a number of maneuvers—accelerations to highway speeds, turnoffs onto various access roads, and several variations of turns, presumably all part of the evasion manual.

At length we came to a stop and proceeded slowly to another stop. It didn't take a Columbo to discern the sound of a closing garage door and the engine being turned off.

Ben gave me the okay, and I was once again fully sighted. I paid very little attention to my surroundings. It was just another building or home somewhere. I had concurred with Ben that I didn't need to know anything about this particular geography. Surprisingly, the usually contra-disposed 101 grumbled assent. We were only interested in the content and the actions that would accrue.

I was ushered into a room, which looked like an upscale media center in an equally upscale home, and directed to a seat. There before me was coffee, ice water, and a variety of small pastries along with pads of paper and ball point pens, which I knew would be confiscated at the end of our session.

We were joined by Tom Hunter and two younger, very average-looking guys who occupied seats some distance behind.

Ben began, "Nick, you know Tom."

"I do, Good to see you again, Tom."

"Nick, may I call you Nick?"

I nodded.

"I'm sorry, really sorry, about the episode at Bay Bluffs. I missed that one. I had the right tail on the right guy, but he just outmaneuvered me. I'm sure glad you made it through that one."

I was taken by his sincerity, so I just mumbled something about being new in this racket and presumably paying my dues.

Ben broke in and said, "Okay, we've got lots to cover and lots to get done, so let's get started. I'm not going to introduce you to my two colleagues. It's not out of rudeness, but we've managed to do enough violence to your life with the guys you have already met."

He'd do stuff like that. Just when I would start down the thought path that he and his "colleagues" were a bunch of deranged degenerates, he would flash his all too human side. I was getting closer to a final resolution on Ben. Christ, I was getting closer to a final resolution on everything. Specifically, he is a patriot of the highest ranks and echelons, and has been called upon to do the worst to accomplish the best. He was indeed George C. Scott in *Hospital*. It's taken an obvious terrible toll on him, and I know I couldn't do it. He had done heroic stuff; he would do more heroic stuff, and he'd get jack-shit credit for it while he was alive. And he would be called upon again. Like he said, it's a nasty business.

"The rest of us here have been through this stuff many times. This is decidedly not SOP, but given what you've been through—and truthfully maybe what we've helped put you through—you deserve no less, so this is a go-through for you,

321

Nick, and it represents just about everything we know that has transpired on your watch."

"My watch? Like I'm now a blood brother?"

"What would you like me to call it, Nick, or how would you like me to phrase it? As you will, I'm talking about the events that involved you or that we got you involved in, okay?"

"Okay."

"You had a secret clearance when you were in the army, so we're inclined to trust you. We're dealing with stuff here that goes way beyond Top Secret and is referenced in colors with black being the ultimate. For your purposes, the operative color here is quite dark, but we think we know you pretty well, so here's what we have surmised and concluded.

"I've told you we picked up on the data traffic we intercepted which the other side foolishly labeled Operation Triple Crown and that we had discovered a mole at the highest level of Invictus. At this time, we still don't know whether the two items are related and/or connected, or whether 'yes or no' will have profound impact.

"We did know that the mole, no name is necessary, has a handler and/or cooperative agents in the states. I will tell you that we think we have fingered him, the handler/colleague, but you do not have a need to know anything more than that. If it became public knowledge it would be a shocker, so you really don't want the burden of that particular item. Because I, I should say we, meaning the country, owe you so much I will close this loop if it is all possible. I say this because his identity came in part from your presence and from certain miscalculations his colleagues made concerning you. I don't mean to turn this into a mystery hour, so I will say again that I will reveal all—or as much as I can—when and as it is possible. Okay?"

I was getting a severe case of dry mouth and reached for the water, but managed a weak "Okay."

"As to Triple Crown, it is now October and the actual event is scheduled for May—Derby Day in fact. As I told you during your visit to Invictus, we monitor movements of money, stuff, and people. In this instance we picked up on movements of people, many of whom blast through our porous borders, and of certain chemi-

322

cals being moved to what we would call important staging areas. Those data and some significant, but inconclusive transfers of money, reaffirmed Seattle, Omaha, and Louisville as the targets. Since some of our adversaries regard themselves as poets, the three cities loomed as extremely likely. I can also tell you the explosive material is non-nuke and is greatly similar to that employed by Timothy McVey in Oklahoma City. Relatively massive amounts would each do more destruction and violence than was the case in Oklahoma City.

"Let me say, also, that we are used to plants and diversions, and it is possible that Triple Crown is a decoy for other actions. We will continue to press for other similar data and circumstances, but for right now, we are taking Triple Crown as a for real exercise. We have a plan to neuter it well before Derby Day, but, as with other data, you would not benefit from such knowledge.

"You should appreciate that we are quite accomplished and terribly vigilant in the execution of our several missions. I will also tell you, however, that luck or unforeseen occurrences play mightily in this game. Sometimes folks get careless; sometimes they overreach or sometimes galvanizing events just occur.

"As quick examples, our U-2 overflights of the Soviets back in the 'fifties, were supposed to take place at eighty thousand feet or higher. Maybe detectable by radar, but out of missile range. Powers was at something like fifty thousand feet—for reasons still unknown to many—and got shot down. Or Nixon's fiasco. Bad judgment. Should have come clean and apologized, but the cover up will always get you. Or having a judge who looked at the Nixon situation like a great shark in a school of delectables. Or Reagan when he wanted to put missiles in Europe. Thatcher—bless her—agreed wholeheartedly, but the continentals did not want to provoke the red bear. Then—for reasons nobody understands—a Russian pilot shoots down Korean Airline Flight 007. The attitude toward Ivan changed—spun on a dime—and the next thing anybody knows, Reagan plants his missiles on a very welcoming continental Europe. And the Evil Empire falls. Hard work, yes. Some luck, you bet.

"My point being the other side blinked. It may well bear relation to your visit to Invictus and may have caused a bit of a panic followed by a dangerous contact between mole and handler. I tell you this because we almost got you killed and we owe you. As before, when and as I can flesh this messy business out I will, okay?

What was I to say? "Okay."

"I should also tell you that you must—and I mean *must*—place all your blame and anger for the unspeakable things which have happened to you squarely upon me. Here is what, as a decent human being, you should know. Raj remains your greatest friend. He is heartsick over the violence which occurred to you. Truly heartsick. If you ever had a true friend, it is Raj.

"In what was a most regrettable interval, Raj was compromised and rendered useless in the matter of establishing the linkages to our Mr. Mole. It was I who suggested that Raj bring you here and that we might induce our mole to take the bait. It was a crazy long shot, but we had little else going for us then. It was like third and long late in the game. We needed a Hail Mary, and you were it.

"Raj, whom you and I both know to be very nonviolent and nonvehement, was especially vehement in his opposition to such a move. For good or ill, I prevailed but only after assuring Raj that no harm whatsoever would befall you. With greatest reluctance, Raj agreed. But only after extracting from me my pledge that all efforts would be made to keep you safe. Your friend Raj is indeed a friend, a great friend. It was I. I was under great urgencies, and I browbeat Raj into serving you up. To catch our mole and maybe to protect the nation. It was I.

"It was thus that we dangled you in front of our mole, and it was thus that we have a shot at averting a number of national disasters. I am not going to ask for your understanding or for your condoning our actions, but that is the way it all formed. Later, not uncommonly, it began to run with a mind somewhat of its own as the scope of our mole's relationships exceeded our imaginings. No apologies, but I do hope you get a sense of what we're all about. And before you say bullshit, Ben, let me tell you that you are indeed a national resource. Maybe unwitting, but . . .

"You know as much right now about Mr. Mole as we are go-

324

ing to tell you. The rest of our drill today bears on Richie and Lily Sanford.

"The van you saw with the prominently displayed "L" and "M" was Richie's cable guy. Like you, he tried the front door and then ambled around to the side where he saw the grisly scene with Richie and Lily. He took off abruptly and that's what you saw.

"What you should know is that he did call 911 as soon as he cleared Richie's property and described the scene he had witnessed. Old Hognose was on the scene, monitoring the nine-one-one calls, and promptly snagged Mr. Ronnie Caruso. His story checked out right away. He, Ronnie, had had a couple scrapes with the law. It was thus understandable that he would be willing to call in the homicide but that he wanted to remain otherwise Ronnie Anonymous. We rallied with Hognose and came to the same conclusion. We then brought Hognose into our confidence and made him part of the posse. This was of little or no risk. We had both served in 'Nam. I was well aware of what kind of guy he was, totally high-grade.

"In the interim, old Hill was at his vitriolic and nasty best and was rebutting Richie's brief statement. That Hill was, and is, a prick was obvious to most fair-minded folks pretty quickly.

"First, he had browbeaten a seriously wounded and greatly distracted Richie into making a statement before several members of the press with klieg lights on and focused sharply. Moreover, Richie stood there with his bleeding stanched, but obviously weakened considerably and unaccompanied by legal counsel. In his bullying best, Hill proceeded with his brutal onslaught. And the gutless, perhaps lazy being the better descriptor, press was—as usual—every bit the collective abettor.

"Richie, nearly unconscious and clearly weakened from loss of blood, stated that the door had been busted in and a guy appeared brandishing a pistol and a blunt instrument of some sort. As Richie was sitting near his gun collection, he reached for his Smith & Wesson thirty-eight. In response to two shots from the intruder, one of which hit and killed Lily while the other tore into Richie's left shoulder, Richie got off three rounds and insisted he hit the intruder at least once.

"Hill closed this pretrial kangaroo session by saying that while Richie's weapon may have been fired, it was clearly a diversion and was probably fired outdoors well after the fact as there were no bullet holes in the walls.

"Happily for all, a young lawyer—with no vested interest, with "no dog in this fight"—stepped in and insisted that this savage assembly be disbanded and that Richie be afforded some first-rate medical attention. And so it was, but Hill had succeeded in poisoning the atmosphere very effectively per his usual style.

"But, as we get back to the matters at hand, Les Horvath would have been proud of you, Nick. You have correctly doped out our deal with deflected beam photography. We had low-altitude satellites, complete with our new technology cameras, beamed on you and some other folks. One such was the guy who operated the van which had been at Richie's home just before the cable guy.

"You might be interested to know that he was the guy who owns the tow service which was standing by—coincidentally—the night you almost went over the cliff at Bayside Bluffs.

"He is what we call a high-value player, because he will likely provide us with the links we need between and among our mole's colleagues and handlers and maybe the authors or collaborators on Triple Crown.

"But I don't have to bend your ear. Let's take a look at what we've got."

With a nod from Ben, the lights dimmed and a screen dropped from the ceiling. A projection beam materialized from some apparatus behind me and washed a somewhat granular moving mosaic onto the screen.

Ben then offered an explanation. "As you would expect, Nick, resolution of this device depends on the size of the subject. We can organize billions upon billions of pixels and can thus show relatively small objects in great detail. Bigger stuff gets a bit hazier and at some stage of enlargement, detail gets lost in larger shapes to the point of not being useful.

"We're very new with this technology, so we tend to apply the settings for things about the size of a car. In that modality, we can make out some details in people. If we happen to be in a real-time application, we can functionally zoom in for discernment of smaller targets or other items of interest.

"We commissioned 'Rufus' to active duty several months ago. Since you had coined the term "beamology" and since we were keeping you highly surveilled, you were one of our first subjects. Long story short, Rufus was on duty the night you were at Bayside Bluffs. It was happenstance that we telefilmed—our term for this new technology—the truck that towed your car away. We were able to pick up a few markings and some clear shots of the license plate. In short order, we tracked the vehicle to a garage building in Laidlaw, a small town a few miles from here. Understand that we are working very diligently on resolution. It's not great at present, but it was good enough to get us some otherwise not attainable data and information.

"Laidlaw is accurately described as a blue-collar/no-collar town of several hundred folks. Trailers and fifth wheels were very much in evidence with most front lawns strewn with all manners of once functioning but now rusting machinery. It was decidedly not a tourist magnet, and thus a particularly good place for conducting activities away from milling crowds and prying eyes. In addition, the little town is only partially electrified, with much of it being in total darkness at night. Another attractive feature for the other side.

"The building in which the tow truck was housed was a single-story affair of about ten thousand square feet. There was a minimum of comings and goings and no traces of any significant commerce. While we were less than proficient in safeguarding you, we had stumbled on a potentially high-value asset thanks to Rufus being in service at the Bluffs.

"Given the low levels of traffic and the manner in which this building was effectively tucked away, it did not take much brain power to imagine old Tucker's Way as a combination safe house, storage facility, and staging area. Subsequent events and data collections made that premise ever more reasonable, but as you can probably surmise, there is usually little benefit to acting on less than compelling data unless in desperate or extreme circumstances. Thus the waiting game.

"The big validation occurred on the day Lily was killed. We had been refining Rufus, and were continuing to use you as one of our principal training vehicles. We set Rufus to scan Richie's driveway for no particular reason other than to test the ability to scan a given amount of land. We had expected to see you drive up. And we did, but we got a far richer picture than we had anticipated. Please don't ask me if I would reverse things if I could to save Lily. You know the answer; you know the totally unacceptable answer.

"Set as it was there was no way we could have foreseen or reacted to Lily's murder. Instead we got shots of the two vans leaving and of your arrival. As we mentioned, we were able to dismiss the cable company's van and concentrated on the other vehicle. I can't say we were surprised when the license plate tracked to two-nineteen Tucker's Way.

"The building is the functional headquarters of one Judson Vorhees. To call him an assassin or terrorist would be to diminish his stature unfairly. He is an extremely accomplished and multitalented agent for hire. His skills embrace max-proficiency in the highest and latest technology as well as penchants for remorseless killing. He has been diagnosed repeatedly as a merciless sociopath and has been tied to revolutions, coups, weapons sales, and a variety of large-scale terrorist operations.

"He has a cadre of colleagues and technicians—many of whom are illegals—who are domiciled within a few miles of the Tucker's Way facility. As a result of our surveillance, we have been able to develop some important patterns. The building offers signs of little activity by day but houses meetings of sorts at fairly discernible intervals, usually involving from four to six individuals who arrive and depart on foot under cover of darkness.

"We believe that they will be having an important—for our purposes, maybe critically important—meeting tomorrow evening. They are one step removed from panic having failed to kill both you and Richie, whom they believe to be one of our supporting financial operatives. Our principal thesis is that they will be meeting to regroup and maybe to change their headquarters, as they have not been particularly successful in recent times.

"It's a bit of a gamble, as a positive outcome for us is not assured, but we have played this fish out as far as we can. We will be raiding them tomorrow evening with a view toward catching a couple of biggies and sweating them for linkage and other critical information."

I was tending toward the openmouthed stare again, and the Nick 101 was without his usual wise-crackery and was one hundred percent compliant.

Before I could ask why I had been included, Ben resumed. "Nick, as I've said before, you've done all that was asked of you and more. You deserve a medal and the nation's thanks not to mention the president's, but you know that's not a possibility. This particular operation is about as well thought out and as well contingencied as we know how to do, but it could all turn to shit in a nanosecond. We'll either clean out this nest of vipers or we'll end up on the short end of the nasty stick. That being the case, you'll be joining us tomorrow. Not in the actual operation. That will be me, Tom, and a dozen fully trained assault troopers.

"You'll be here with a couple of our folks who will be in constant commo with us guys. I'll be taking you home now. Tomorrow you'll go to work as usual and stay till the market's closing bell. Then you'll have a drink, one drink, and dinner on Schooner Pier at Gracie's. You'll take a walk and generally dilly-dally until about quarter after eight.

"At that time you'll go to the train station and get into the drivers seat of a 'ninety-eight Accord. Keys and directions will be under the seat. You'll drive into at least two parking lots and will change cars per the directions in the Accord. In the other cars there will be hats, sunglasses, moustaches, stuff like that. You'll either feel like a dink, or you'll get what we're all about. You'll have directions to do some easy evasive maneuvers such that when you get back here you'll be confident you did so without being followed. There will be a coded knock and passwords, which you will find along the way. As we used to say on Madison Avenue, a child of three can do it. Got it?"

Before I could even gesticulate, he said—and why was I not the least bit surprised?—"good."

Thus we departed in another nondescript car with me doing the blindfolded deal prostrate in the backseat. About twenty minutes later, we were at my house and I departed the car wordlessly.

I'll see you tomorrow, I thought to myself.

But tomorrow was October 10th and tomorrow never came. At least for some of us.

10
Good-bye to Some Swell Folks . . .

October 29th

"Well, good morning, Mr. Drizos. You'll be leaving us now. Speaking for all of us folks at St. Luke's, we'll really be missing you."

It was Susie, radiant and just as pleasant as could be, but what the hell was she talking about. St Luke's? St Luke's is in my hometown and I'm still in . . . Oh yeah, it all came to me in a rush that I'd be released in my hometown, maybe even as a hero of sorts. I managed to sublimate my desire to hear Gail just one more time and managed, "Thank you Susie. I'll miss you, too."

They, those crafty folks, had transported me home. They must have given me one fine Versed cocktail, because I didn't feel a thing. But here I was, ready for release back into the stream with the other fishes.

I glanced at Susie, and she gave me a naughty wink. I don't know where these women come from, but I had just spent God knows how long with three of the greatest, now four, that God ever fashioned from a rib. Yeah, they are known as women, but more than that they are just wonderful human beings. I don't recommend getting blown up, but I'm not sure I wouldn't do it again just to be around them. Like I said they are not only incredible women, but just so much more.

And then comes Susie. She's going to wheel me out of here as though I'd been in her care for the past several whatever it was. Is there anything these women can't do? Incredible.

"Well, Nick," said Susie, "it's the breakfast of your choice, and then it's back to being everybody's favorite bond trader and wealth manager."

"Roger and amen, Susie, just feed me and stand aside."

A little table awaited me on which there had just been delivered two beautifully poached eggs on whole wheat toast, a glass of orange juice, and a cup of joe. Very nice indeed.

It was difficult to believe I was going to stop being a patient. It was not in the least enjoyable being a functional captive, but the folks were so extraordinary. And it was more than a fringe benefit to get to view my life from earliest remembrances to the present. There were several punchlines as the old timers would have said, or "takeaways," as the present generation seems to prefer about my stay. Without doubt, however, it was the selflessness of the folks I met here. These folks don't make a difference; they are a difference. Maybe I'll find a way to do some good stuff down the road. That, I think would be my best tribute to these folks.

"Get ready to say good-bye, Nick," said the lyrical Susie. "Would you like your last rub-a-dub, or have you had enough of us?"

"Susie, I'd take it as a personal kindness if you would shake up my faltering circulation one more time."

"Okay," said my newest friend. "Just roll over and . . ."

"Cover up my 'fanny' and you'll be right back."

Good soul that she was/is, she stifled a guffaw down to a very ladylike giggle. Even the 101 applauded.

"Be right back, Nick."

And back she was in the proverbial flash. The rub was wonderful. The funny thing was I don't even know if I wanted it. I know I just wanted to retain contact with these folks. I was starting to get a bad case of separation anxiety, and that was 100 percent weird. Maybe it's just the way things are when some folks steer and manage you through some tough times. I think that might be it. There would be bonds, however invisible and however unrequited or unfulfilled, that would endure. I could only hope I registered with them to some degree. Am I redundant, repetitive, or what?

The rub ended, and I felt part of my life coming to a finish. That was silly, of course, but I am nothing if not a sentimental slob. And, you know what? I know they liked me. No group of people could be that kind absent some real feeling. That would be my ultimate "takeaway." Even though we would probably never meet again, I had made some lifetime friends. It also struck me that prior to my falling in with these folks I had, maybe, aside from Richie and Jackie, two or three friends in my other noninstitutionalized life. I had made more friends in a few weeks than I had in a lifetime. Weird. Maybe not.

Susie showed me to my dressing area, where a small assortment of outfits were laid out. I chose a polo shirt with a horse emblem and a pair of chinos to go with my sockless loafers. As I glanced at myself in the full-length mirror, it was easy, and welcome, to see that I had lost quite a few pounds. I can't say that I had become a dashing caballero, but I was slimmer by measures. I was thinking of a snappy commercial. "Want to lose weight? Try a car bomb."

I turned to Susie, and both of us knew that only a hug made any sense. And so it was. I have come to enjoy hugs and find them quite sensual. With Susie, it was suitably sensual, but I'll never forget those couple of seconds with Gail, and I found myself imagining her in Michigan or Colorado or Idaho or wherever she might be.

Susie and I just nodded to each other, but then it crossed my mind that while I had been able to spend some real time with Gail, I hadn't been able to say my good-byes or thank-yous to JoAnn and Jeanette.

I started to say something about that when Susie handed me three envelopes. I was going to open them when Susie piped up. "They are from Jeanette, JoAnn, and Jack. They said to read them at your leisure. If you wish to respond, you will figure out how to do so. I can tell you that they, each in their own way, love you and wish you the best. So take them along with you. I'll be leaving you now, Nick. You know where I'm going, so wish me well. Love to you from all of us."

And she was gone.

Then a guy who looked like an extra from a Bela Lugosi film appears with a wheel chair and says, "Climb aboard, Mac."

He had scrubs on and walked with a decided limp. His hair would have let him double for the Scarecrow in *The Wizard of Oz,* and he had a complexion that seemed more suited to a corpse. This was topped off with the cheapest pair of sunglasses I have ever seen. I felt good to be in his care.

He blasted me around a corner and into a room and closed the door with a flourish of certainty.

"Hiya Nick, long time no see. Whaddaya hear, whaddya say?"

Well, I have gotten to the point in this drama where little, if anything, surprises me.

"We'll whaddaya hear, whaddaya say, yourself. It's either James Cagney as Rocky Sullivan in *Angels with Dirty Faces,* or it's that great American, Ben Adams."

"Hiya, Nick."

"Hello, Ben. What's today's deal?"

"Well, Nick, it's all over. You can go back to being a real person."

"No stuff?"

"No stuff!"

"Well, fill me in Ben, since I wasn't around for the last few rounds. And by the way, thanks for the great protection on ten/ten. It was really a hoot to be blown into space and to land in one of your convalescent homes. I was supposed to monitor the Great Raid. And I didn't have any worries, because Ben the Great was protecting me. Remember? What happened?"

"Okay, Nick, and I should say I'm about thirty seconds from taking this clown outfit off and beating the shit out of you. You want to know what happened? I'll tell you what happened.

"You had been doing your serial dinners with Raj for months before I ever heard of you. Then Raj got compromised. How? I don't know how, but he got compromised totally. As you'd been seen with him on many occasions, the other side thought you might be on his team. So they planted the car bomb about a year ago—long before you ever heard of us or vice versa. Brilliant. All they had to do was to leave it inactive or to activate it if they had reason. Thanks to our mole and some other stuff, they figured you were on our team, and they pulled the trigger. Our surveillance and protection was very good, but, as I've told you before, we can't defend against things which were already in place.

"It's now October twenty-ninth, so let me fill in the big blanks for you. We did raid the Tucker's Way facility very successfully. A firefight ensued, and several of the other guys were killed. Others, including Judson Vorhees, were taken into custody and are becoming what we call useful citizens in a faroff sanctuary.

"Your pal, Mr. Berkelely, who as a mole never existed, continues in that mode if you take my drift."

"You mean he's dead."

The 101 piped up: *Christ almighty. Yes, he's dead.*

"And now, Mr. Nick Drizos, I'm going to load you with a burden because, as I've told you before, you were invaluable in the many situations we have successfully addressed. We used you as we had to, but use you we did. So here's a big piece of it which you can carry to your grave, and, because I've come to know you, I know you will. Senator LeFlore was Berkeley's colleague. Probably not his handler, but definitely his colleague. The other side had gotten into him in spades. I don't know whether was drugs, money, women or what, but they co-opted him to the max. We had some pretty good evidence, and the records we recovered from Vorhees, complete with some nasty pictures, pretty much iced that situation.

"By the way, LeFlore was killed in a freak accident on the San Diego Freeway a couple days ago. Bad luck. The president spoke at his services. I guess being a senator is a high-risk profession.

"You should also know that it was LeFlore who intercepted Jesse Lancer's meds and almost put him down for the count.

"As to Richie, Hill did his best to cock up a love triangle story and get Richie fried, but happily for all who love justice, Hognose was on the scene. He dug up the slugs that Richie had fired, including the one that hit the guy who killed Lily. Unfortunately, Hognose had to gun that guy down in a firefight near Tuckers Way, by coincidence. There was a lot more to the story, but between Ed Muns—a hell of a good lawyer—and Hognose, Hill's case evaporated. And so did Hill. Lily's family was very supportive of Richie and Mary. They remain convinced it was a burglary gone bad, and I hope they always retain that belief. Together

335

they funded a foundation in Lily's name. It was a senseless killing and a tragic loss of life, but they did their collective best to keep alive the memory of a lovely woman.

"That's about all you have to know, with a couple of other defining details.

"I had told you that wherever possible, cover stories should be as truthful as possible, and I stand by that. Except that this story has so many bizarre aspects, the truth would never survive. So brace yourself for some real beauties.

"Taking things one at a time, I'm now going to wheel you out in front of a bunch of camera-laden newshounds. You can practice your smile, because you're a hero. A field rep from the bureau, FBI to you, is going to present you with a Certificate of Merit and a medal for your work in bringing down a major money- laundering operation, which in turn funded a number of large-scale drug operations. The Bureau guy will thank you for your service and will thank God that you survived that horrendous attack. He will go on to point out that people like Nick Drizos who are willing to put their lives on the line are the greatest of heroes in our country."

And he did, and the crowd just outdid itself. Every once in a while I would manage a wave and a smile, and the crowd would erupt. It was heartwarming, if totally undeserved. All I did was get in the way of a bomb, because I had a friend in the wrong business. The wrong guy in the wrong place at the wrong time. Plus, being a single guy with no particular affiliation, it was a crowd of strangers. I had a few friends—business colleagues—out there, but it would have been really swell, yes swell, if someone I really cared for had been in that crowd. So there it was, and there I was. A piece of modern drama with me, Nick D., playing the hero who wasn't. But it made sense in some cockeyed way. I'd be accorded some free drinks for a while in some of the saloons, and then things would be forgotten. And that wouldn't be all that bad, either.

Before too long, my assistant was wheeling me to a jitney bus, which I supposed would take me home.

There was no one around us so I stood and regarded old Ben. When I say old, I wasn't being flippant. He just looked spent.

"So is it really over, Ben, or should I expect to meet more of the crazy folks in your milieu?"

"Yes, Nick, it's really over. As I said, you did stuff that acclaimed patriots could only wish they had done. It's a very weird and dangerous world in which we live, and you have made it safer for a spell."

I had been standing quite close to Ben and the distinctive essence of booze—scotch in particular—made itself very evident.

"You're not reupping with old John Barleycorn, are you, Ben?"

"Well, Nick, I did have a double for breakfast this morning. I used to call scotch the 'Breakfast of Champions' and I may again. Maybe I'll fall off the wagon and maybe not. I just don't know. You've seen some of the horrors facing the so-called civilized world, and it's pretty awful, isn't it? I've seen a bit more and my friends in the bottle sometimes make it easier to face. So, we'll see.

"I'll be moving along now, Nick. I can't tell you too many times that you have done great service. You also know what we will be addressing in May or thereabouts. To that end, I have asked to be relieved. The president accepted my resignation, and Tom Hunter is the new boss. He is terrific and has the respect and admiration of everyone in the organization. Succession should always be so easy. Plus we're going to get a new president, and I've broken in enough of them. This new one could be a real beauty, and Tom is the right guy.

"I'll also tell you that, for the good of all of you, I suggested that Richie, Mary, Jackie, and Fran all stay away from our little town here and let all the potential lingering radiation die down for a little while. They are all looking forward to getting together with you. Mary and Fran want to comfort you, and Richie and Jackie just want their pal back. You know what you can tell them and what you can't. Right?"

I just nodded.

"Like I said, I have talked with Richie and Mary and I told them as much as I could. They understand that you were a totally unwitting party to some extremely bizarre stuff. Each of them told me that nothing would break the bonds of pals. They

337

repeated that expression 'bonds of pals' a few times and said you would know what it meant. They're looking forward to seeing you, but they understand that you should probably reinsinuate yourself into your life here before venturing forth again.

"I would also feel awful if I didn't tell you that Raj will be in touch, and I know you two will pick up what is a wonderful and enduring friendship. He was just placed in an untenable situation and has had bouts of great torment and aguish. He is relieved and delighted that you are safe and well, effendi.

"And you and I may yet cross paths again. If so it would be my pleasure," he stated, extending his hand.

There being not much else to say, we shook hands and he ambled off. What should have been relief in me was instead an emptiness. The things that Ben did were categorically insane, but they had come to seem natural. And I had come to like and admire him a great deal. It was under the heading of someone's gotta do it and that someone was Ben and the others like him. I got to thinking maybe this is like women and pregnancy in that I'll forget the painful stuff and get on with living.

I spent the balance of the afternoon going through my accumulation of mail and set things into piles for action later on. That seemed reassuring, so I made some coffee and dialed into the evening news knowing that it would never be quite the same for me. And it wasn't. The so-called big events just didn't register as before.

Soon enough, it was dusk, so I decided to stroll over to Schooner Pier and admire God's work. I hadn't seen a sunset in several days, so this was a particular treat. It was magnificent—the big orange ball just dipping below the horizon. I always enjoy the last couple seconds when there it is and then there it isn't. Someone's in his heaven and all's right with the world, I thought to myself.

I was stretching out on my chosen bench which seemed unusually comfortable and was wondering to myself whether I would fall asleep before I knew it was time to return home. I don't think I much cared either way. I was that relaxed. Or was it relieved. Either way I was not especially motivated to do much of anything physical. I was happy for my pals, especially in the truth and romance departments. I felt no sense of envy, although I would like to be there one day.

I think I was nodding off, wondering if I could control and direct my dreams as before, when I felt a soft hand on my shoulder. Even before I heard the voice, I knew it was Gail, and my heart began to race.

"Hello, soldier. I said we might meet again. Want to take a walk with an old friend?"

"Absolutlely, then we can . . ."

"Slow down, soldier," she said while taking my hand in hers. "Slow down, we have plenty of time. Let's just enjoy the moment; we have plenty of time."

"Yes, we do; we have plenty of time."

Epilogue

The three of us—Jackie, Richie and I—had come a far piece as Les Horvath might have put it. We had no knowledge of the surging tides and crosscurrents of fortune we would witness, confront, and endure along the way. But, in a grander sense, we were quite well prepared for just about any eventuality because of the unconstrained investments which had been made in us by our folks and by a host of other selfless old-timers. Because of them, we had, all things considered, pretty good basic values and judgments. And those would serve us well. We had spent most of our lives in a golden era, and we would continue to reap and enjoy that which those before us had so selflessly planted, cultivated, and nurtured. It is unlikely that the ensuing generations will be as fortunate, but we three will do our best to repay the many kindnesses bestowed upon us.

Gail and I have become an item, if I may employ understatement. I enjoy her very presence as I never knew a body could. She is just a wonderful person in every respect. She is so special in the extreme that just about everything I do these days is done with the thought of being worthy of her respect and admiration.

Our original trio, which had grown to four when Mary arrived and later to five with Fran, was now six. We are a happy lot and know enough to live for today and to be excited for tomorrow. We spend little time looking backward, except for an occasional object lesson or some pleasant nostalgia or to reaffirm certain timeless principles. I think we are all taken with the temporal aspects of this special journey called life, and we are very much into wishing peace and happiness for all. And I should say that, as each of us has done very well in the material world, we are quite happy to be of service to those among us who haven't.

The essential glue that bound Richie, Jackie, and me was no more than a desire by each of us to see the other two do well. It

341

seems to have rubbed off on the girls as well. We've gotten to the other end of Les Horvath's advice about blowing out someone else's candle not making yours burn any brighter. It's back to that thing about kindness; the one quantity that doesn't observe the rules of arithmetic. With most things, the more you give away, the less you have—but not with kindness and generosity of spirit. It just seems the more you give, the more comes back to you.

Richie keeps doing his many projects. He really has little choice, because he has so much capital to put to good purposes. And he doesn't want much of anything for himself aside from Mary, who remains an all-time stunner. Jackie and I were often called upon and ultimately became full-time members of his Board of Advisors. This was and remains especially fortuitous, because it not only allows us to make a contribution here or there, it is also allows the six of us to get together at very happy and welcomed intervals.

Mary continues to be—there is no suitable alternative word—stunning. Despite the effects of time and the energy with which she addresses her many charitable activities—not to mention her total devotion to Richie—she remains so, and I may even have an explanation.

There is no shortage of beautiful women in today's world and they, including Mary, not uncommonly have oceans of compliments heaped upon them. Many actually develop a need—an almost discernible urgency—to be showered with such praise, which then becomes internalized and absorbed. In Mary's case, however, it seems that such praise is met with a smile and quickly reflected back on others. Thus, while some striking women feed on such accolades, Mary seems to be on automatic pilot and radiates that which she receives. She just doesn't need it, as others might. I have mentioned this to Richie and Jackie, and they seem to get it. If I had Richie's natural ease or Jackie's observative and expository talents, I would complete the thought more elegantly. However it works, Mary is just a mirror of kindness and friendship. And that may explain her glowing being.

As you might imagine, Jackie, among many other things, heads up several programs oriented toward reading and, especially, writing. He has turned on more than a few young folks, many severely disdvantaged in one way or another, to the power of the written word and has probably pushed quite a few into productive lives that simply would not have occurred without his influence. And he has convinced countless other kids that writing a letter to someone just beats the holy bejeesus out of calling them on the phone. Christ, said Jackie, any moron can do that. And, mostly the kids agreed. Who knows? There may be a Fitzgerald or a Faulkner under Jackie's widespread wings. But you'll never know if you don't make the effort, and Jackie's in there with his great energy and in all his literary elegance. He's making the effort. And, not incidentally he remains very widely read and much admired. Greatly admired. He may yet write that book. I needle him all the time.

Fran has been like a blossoming flower with more facets emerging continually. She and Jackie are like a motor-generator set with each charging and invigorating the other. She remains a TV commentator but has shortened her schedule to spend more time with Jackie and their twin boys. She has taken up the written word and gives Jackie a good tussle now and then. While Jackie still maintains his column *In Other Words,* Fran authors a supplementary column called *On the Other Hand.* As before, they continue with their good-natured and elegant back-and-forth sparring. I continue to think of them as a latter-day sophisticated and elegant Myrna Loy and William Powell. They are very popular. More importantly, they adore each other.

Gail and I spend a lot of time with impaired kids. One such program we support is called SMART, which introduces these kids to horses. Sometimes we do no more than walk the kids around a ring on horses. Psychologists and other folks who have been trained in special education and related studies tell me of this practice's profound positive effects. I take their word, but the smiles of these kids is enough proof for me.

We also support a couple associations that focus on kids with

Down's Syndrome. These kids are something special. For one thing, I've never met a kid with Down's who didn't have a totally sunny disposition. I always gently pat them on the head, and they seem to like that. What I'm really trying to do is to see if I can get some of their good nature to rub off on me. We get no end of satisfaction in being with these kids. I don't know if we are making a difference, but it seems like a good thing to do. And if giving something makes one feel good, well . . .

In all, we three princely adolescents from Smalltown USA have done pretty good, or do I mean to say 'well'? While I can't speak for Richie and Jackie, I harbor no doubts they'd agree that we did the best with what we were given, and prime among those gifts were the unwavering love of our parents and the incredible generosity of the old-timers who preceded us. All kids should be so fortunate.

We all carry some bruises and a number of remembrances from those things which didn't go all that well, but we managed our way through them and haven't—I'm pleased to say—yielded to the sinister forces of cynicism and negativity. The world was not without its many asymmetries and dislocations, as Jackie would frequently remind us, but we stayed on the dance floor in the big ballroom and we even cut a nifty step or two here and there. Life is good; especially if you determine to make it so. Maybe only if you determine to make it so.

Our favorite almost in-law, Jesse was summoned to the White House in December, where he was debriefed by the outgoing president himself. He was shocked to learn that LeFlore had turned, but he was even more shocked to find that Senator Varlow was a total patriot. Varlow had been willing to be perceived in the most negative light to be of maximum value to the country he loves. He glided under the radar and made contributions that few will ever appreciate. Moreover, it was Varlow who discovered the plot to degrade Jesse's medications, and it was Varlow who tipped off Dr. Axton. This apparently caused LeFlore great difficulty with his cohorts when Jesse didn't die. Even though Jesse had retired to Wyoming, he stood as a symbol of everything the other side hates and detests. That must have been an intolerable irritant.

Mary says she had rarely, if ever heard Jesse swear, but he turned the air blue for quite a while, mostly pounding himself for being "one dumb son of a bitch."

I was to learn, through Jesse who swore me to secrecy under penalty of extreme unction and unspeakable violence, that Varlow was a totally manufactured name and personna. He was in fact a Czech who, as a boy, witnessed and endured the Nazi madness. Later he became a well-known freedom fighter and led revolts against the Soviets in Hungary and Czechoslavakia. As his colleagues were being ground into submission, U.S. Army intelligence cocked up an elaborate plan whereby his "dead body" was produced and identified to the satisfaction of the Russians. He was then smuggled into the U.S., where he quietly and purposefully emerged as Janos Imre Varlow.

With the very important help of a couple of patriotic and sensible right-wing, cold warrior organizations, he insinuated himself into politics, at first locally and then nationally as the much reviled but constantly reelected and powerful Senator Varlow. In fact, for practical purposes, he was one hell of a double agent.

He became one of the "princes of pork," as he had vowed to do whatever might be required to be in the position of the most powerful anti-totalitarianist he could be. In such position he would willingly face and endure all manners of jeerings or criticism. Jesse came to admire this man greatly and to appreciate his three most important tenets of life: freedom, freedom, and freedom.

Jesse must have apologized at least a dozen times, but Varlow would only say that if he could mislead so good a man as Jesse, he was pleased with the effort. The two have the greatest respect for each other, and when Varlow quit the senate, he moved to Montana. He, Janos Imre Varlow, and Jesse visit often and have become extremely close friends.

The new president was very savvy politically—as in he could count votes with extreme precision—but he was otherwise a

345

considerable lightweight. He insisted on acknowledging Jesse and Janos for saving the nation. Jesse and Janos clung tenaciously to their anonymity and both went ballistic along with Tom Hunter at such a stupid suggestion. They began referring to the new president as "DB," standing for dumb bastard. At length they convinced the CINC of the need for absolute secrecy, but he still insisted on hanging big medals on Jesse and Janos.

As a compromise, Tom Hunter dusted off a couple of big historical, but still classified, U.S. intelligence successes, and suggested that Jesse and Janos be commended for them. This worked well, considering the goofiness of the new principal resident at 1600 Pennsylvania, who thought the idea just wonderful. It was thus that Jesse and Janos were recognized by a national audience at the Kennedy Center.

Even though they—Jesse and Janos—wished for solitude to just enjoy the natural beauty of Montana and Wyoming, they had become permanent heroes. Accordingly, they were sometimes asked to appear on the important Sunday-morning news programs. From time to time, they would relent and subject themselves to that most intrusive medium. Once there, they always did a one-two for their side of the argument with such great vigor that viewers could only wonder if the likes of these two guys would ever pass this way again. Real men? I guess so!

Jesse did indeed marry Annie. We six attended, and Senator Janos Imre Varlow was the best man. This time, Jackie and I did the readings. I think we acquitted ourselves as thoughtfully as Jesse had at the Mary-Richie wedding. If not, it wasn't for lack of trying.

As May approached, Tom Hunter and his staff continued to manage the supersecret op Triple Crown with incredibly great aplomb and skill. Ben had advised there would probably be diversions and a variety of misdirections and deceptive ploys along the way. I have no way of knowing, but the sinister plot was destroyed with scalpel precision.

The only reason I know for certain is that the new president, already a poll watcher of the first order, wanted a big headline. Hunter was furious, as public disclosure would put an end to

346

what might have been a devastating penetration of the other side's network. And, after years of incredible effort and heartache, Invictus could be thoroughly compromised and rendered useless.

Apparently the new chief was even going to commend Hunter and his outfit publicly. I have no way of knowing for sure, but I think it a good bet that the former president and Ben, sober for the occasion, came to town and convinced him otherwise.

The new president would have his way, however, and would ultimately take political credit for intercepting and dismembering the dastardly plot. Hunter, being a quanta or two smarter than the Man created a nifty cover. As the president thankfully knew only the sparest of details, Hunter had some significant elbow room in which to maneuver.

There thus followed another elaborate spreading of the "bread crumbs" so that the FBI and the CIA were directed to various separate aspects of the overall Triple Crown plot. They, of course, took credit gleefully. Hunter and his bunch were ingenious in creating trails such that the two goliath entities had to share data and cooperate; something, that despite years of coercion and cajoling, had rarely occurred. The particularly skillful part of Operation Hunter was the inclusion of the New York cops. Hunter had always been of the opinion that the NYPD, when on their game, was by far the best intel organization in the states. He had hoped for example that when the Homeland Security agency was established, the D.C. guys would instead just increase NYPD's budget to allow them to create an anti-terrorist function. And I agree.

In any event, Hunter took a couple of his longtime NYPD colleagues into his confidence and together they masterminded this most vital exercise. The NYPD had control of the critical coordinating data and was thus able to bring the two lumbering institutions to heel. It was masterful choreography. Some things don't change. Hunter and the NYPD guys literally dodged some potentially horrendous outcomes, and the D.C. crowd got its show biz for the year. But the NYPD was, without question, "the star of the show."

I have no idea now what the other side is up to these days, but I sleep pretty damned well, all things considered, knowing that guys like Tom Hunter remain on duty on a no bullshit basis. And before him, Ben and Raj and Jesse and Janos. And old Hognose. It remains that there are some incredibly dedicated folks out there. While most of the broad populace will never know them or will never appreciate firsthand the results of their unceasing dedication, it doesn't diminish one bit the great work they do. God bless them.

I did get to speak to Raj a few times and those were among the most bittersweet exchanges that two straight guys can have. After being compromised, he was offered non–field agent positions at a number of security agencies. He elected the polar extreme alternative, however, to decompress and remove himself from the game until he could become just an ordinary joe. This is one of the funny perversions in the spy biz. A guy can actually retire and basically make his new status known publicly. And he won't be bothered. He was a few months away from that position when I talked to him last. We would be getting together again.

Ben did, in fact, turn to booze again. He bought a case of scotch and lit out for an undisclosed island. Prior to shoving off, he informed Raj that he would either finish that case and take the pledge or buy another case. Apparently he bought a few more cases and was in pretty much of a death spiral when Raj tracked him down.

Raj offered to go down the same slope to self-destruction with Ben if that's what he wanted or to do the rehab thing. Raj was just totally devoted to Ben and he was fully prepared to go lights out if that's what Ben wanted.

For reasons, none of us will ever totally understand, Ben opted to join Raj. Together they climbed out of Ben's self-made abyss of total destruction and became actual persons again.

I'm told that Ben and Raj are both in the company of women they adore. Some might be surprised that such affiliations can happen so quickly. I'm not. First, Ben and Raj are incredibly wonderful human beings. At the same time, men and women

348

seem to be able to find greater appreciation in each other as the time clock ticks on. Why? I'm sure I don't know the causes, but I do know that that's the way it is. I wish it had been otherwise, because I can only lament those lost years of post-adolescence when the many voids might have been filled with caring and tenderness, but better late than never at all.

For me, I'm just in a wonderful relationship where honesty is the coin of the realm. Honesty is truth's brother, and I've been told all my life that the truth will set you free. I don't doubt that, but love is pretty good, too.